HE WOULDN'T GIVE UP TIL SHE GAVE IN.

Catlin was disturbed by the predatory stare she was receiving. "If you have come to discuss the contract . . ." she began, holding her dress against her nakedness.

"I never discuss business in bedrooms." Lucas's voice was low, like the muffled purr of a panther. His dark eyes raked her with a mixture of irritation and unappeased desire.

Catlin detected the hunger in his eyes as she wormed her arms back into her gown. "Then what is it you want from me?"

"I want you," he told her simply and directly. "You make me mad as hell sometimes, but I still want you in my arms. I want to feel you responding . . ." His voice dropped to a deep . . . overworked heart leaped . . . you and me, violet eyes . . . well as you fight."

His mouth took possess . . . . . . he knew she was flirting with disast . . . . . . way to counter the onrush of sensations th . . . through her blood.

"You provided the fire," Lucas breathed raggedly as his lips grazed her eyelids and cheeks. "Now feed the flame, Cat. I can't be satisfied until this blaze burns itself out."

TEXAS TEMPTATION

GINA ROBINS

ZEBRA BOOKS
KENSINGTON PUBLISHING CORP.

*This book is dedicated
to my husband Ed
for all his assistance and support. Love you . . .*

GOODNIGHT LOVING TRAIL

KANSAS

DENVER

PUEBLO

NEW MEXICO

RATON PASS

INDIAN TERRITORY

RED RIVER

FORT SUMNER

TEXAS

HORSEHEAD CROSSING

FORT CONCHO

FORT McKAVETT

FORT TERRETT

RIO GRANDE

PECOS RIVER

SAN ANTONIO

Part 1

*Those who play with Cats
must expect to be scratched.
Cervantes*

Chapter 1

San Antonio, Texas

Catlin Quinn knotted her fists in the folds of her blue satin gown as guns barked in the late afternoon air. She wasn't surprised that the stagecoach in which she was riding with three male passengers was being chased by one of the numerous gangs of outlaws that ran rampant in Texas. This was yet another disaster on the long list of catastrophes that had plagued her the past two years.

Catlin was hurled sideways into the stocky man who was wedged into the seat beside her as the coach raced over bumpy roads that were nothing more than ruts left by preceding traffic. Another volley of bullets zinged past the windows. The wobbling stage skidded around the sharp bend in the road, flinging passengers from side to side.

"Get down!" one of the men growled as he tried to shove Catlin facedown on the floor.

Catlin glared at the chestnut-haired man who had been flashing her suggestive leers and remarks since she climbed onto the stage. Being stubborn to the core, Catlin refused to plaster herself at his feet like some simpering coward. She was certain the scalawag intended to take advantage of her, under the pretense of protecting her from a stray bullet.

"I prefer to die sitting up, thank you very much," Catlin snapped as she readjusted her cockeyed bonnet.

With a muted growl, the man grabbed her by the shoulder and rammed her down between the three pair of feet that were braced on the narrow floor of the coach.

It was at that moment that the jostling coach hit a deep rut in the road. Bodies were catapulted into the air and Catlin found herself at the bottom of the pile of men who tumbled from their seats. She wailed in agony when her right leg became the landing pad for three large bodies.

In the passengers' attempts to untangle themselves and regain their seats, Catlin's injured leg suffered even more damage. As she levered up on her elbow to inspect her throbbing leg, the coach came to a screeching halt, causing the men to tumble on her all over again.

Catlin let out a howl that testified to the full extent of her discomfort. Her leg had been broken at least twice, she was sure of it. She would be permanently crippled . . . if she lived that long. And judging by the appearance of the four masked men who yanked open the doors, she wouldn't last the hour. Catlin's wide violet eyes focused on the barrel of the Colt that was aimed at the occupants of the stage. She had assumed she was going to die with a broken leg and be buried under a pile of rugged-looking men who had been her constant companions during her journey from Louisiana to Texas. But from all indication she suspected she would be blown to smithereens and no one would know what to do with her unrecognizable body. The tombstone on her grave would bear no more than a question mark and the date of her untimely death.

"Get out," the redheaded desperado demanded gruffly.

The gleaming barrel of his pistol flashed in front of Catlin's face and she grimaced as knees and elbows gouged her as if she were a pincushion. When the three male passengers finally managed to pry their tangled limbs apart and step outside, Catlin's injured leg was so stiff and swollen it refused to bend.

"Come on lady, we ain't got all day," the bandito grunted impatiently.

A gloved hand clamped around her forearm to roughly yank her from the floor of the coach. The instant her throbbing leg was forced to hold her weight, Catlin yelped in pain. But there was no sympathy forthcoming. The redheaded buscadero snatched her purse from her hand to relieve her of all the money she had left in the world (which wasn't much to begin with).

Something inside Catlin snapped. She had lost everything she had to lose—her family, her fiancé and the plantation home that had been ransacked by Yankees. And to make matters even worse, she had lost the land that had been in her family for generations to wily carpetbaggers and a devious, scheming lawyer. Having lost all she held dear made Catlin daring and indifferent to whether she lived or died. Fighting back against all the atrocities she had suffered the last two years had become a habit with her—even when she faced impossible odds.

With a wordless growl, Catlin launched herself at the bandit—injured leg and all. Muffled curses gushed from her lips as she bared her claws and scratched the blue bandana that covered the red-haired bandito's face. Before Catlin could rip him to shreds, his compadres converged to pry the enraged firebrand loose from their leader.

"Christ! Are you nuts, lady?" the desperado snorted, pulling his mask back in place. "I've killed men for less than that!"

Catlin was too furious to be frightened. Her outrage numbed the pain in her leg. She was lashing out at life's injustices, once and for all. And if she were to die, she was going out in a blaze of glory, not in sniveling tears! Damn men everywhere. The bastards! They had stolen her blind, killed all those she had cherished. Damn the Yankee soldiers who had mocked her as they demolished her elegant plantation home. Damn the thieving outlaws who sought to rob her of the last few dollars she had to her name. Damn them all!

"She's a raving lunatic," one of the banditos hooted as he tried to restrain the wriggling bundle of frustrated fury who was still spewing inarticulate curses that consigned every man on the planet to the fiery dungeons of hell.

"Tie her up," the leader demanded before striding over to relieve the other passengers of their valuables.

"Tie her up? Hell, we can barely hold her!" the bushy-headed thief scowled as he wrestled with the wiggling spitfire in blue satin.

Catlin had been knocked down and pushed around one too many times in the past. She had sworn the day she left Louisiana she would never be antagonized again without putting up one helluva fight. And clinging to that valiant vow, Catlin fought the restraining arms like a wild creature resisting captivity.

Cursing a blue streak, the redheaded hombre stamped over to clank the butt of his pistol against the sandy-blond head that was snapping forward and back like a proud mustang battling the bridle and bit. Catlin wilted to the ground in a mangled heap. Her injured leg twisted into a most unnatural position beneath her, but this time there was no pain—only dark uninterrupted silence.

"If you can't handle a mere wisp of a woman, you better find yourselves another profession," the leader growled at his men.

Casting the unconscious hellcat a fleeting glance, the buscaderos stepped over her crumpled form to drag the strongbox from the back of the stagecoach. Once the banditos had collected their booty, they bounded onto the horses and thundered off in a cloud of dust, taking Catlin's last possessions with them.

The stage driver stared at the rumpled heap of femininity who was sprawled in the dirt. Never in all his

14

life had he witnessed such reckless daring by one of his female passengers during a holdup. When confronted by desperados, most women fainted dead away or stood frozen to their spots. But not this feisty chit. She had carried a chip on her shoulder the size of the Rock of Gibraltar since she set foot on his stage. At each station where they paused to change mounts and take meals, Catlin refused the helping hands of men who were eager to assist her in and out of the coach. She was determined to make her own way without a man's assistance. Pretty though she was with her shapely figure, long silky hair and wide violet yes, she was the most unapproachable female he had ever met. Her stiff, polite manners shouted things to men: don't look, don't touch, don't speak and don't get any closer than absolutely necessary.

Chomping on the wad of tobacco he had very nearly swallowed during his frantic attempt to outrun the banditos, the driver strode over and scooped Catlin into his arms. Her sandy-blond hair and her crushed bonnet dangled over his arm as he toted her back to the coach and propped her against the window.

Silently, the driver retrieved the pistol he had been ordered to toss aside and then hopped back onto his perch beside the guard. When the other passengers had clambered back into the coach beside the unconscious spitfire, the stage rumbled down the last eight mile stretch to San Antonio.

It was three miles later that Catlin roused from unconsciousness to be greeted by a throbbing headache and a pulsating leg.

A pin could have dropped inside the coach and it would have sounded like a ton of lead. The three men peered sympathetically at her, but Catlin didn't want their consolation. She merely glared at them for refusing to make a stand as she had done. She hurt all over and she was just as furious as she had been when the redheaded buscadero snatched away her purse.

Silently fuming, Catlin glared out the window, hating the world and everyone in it—especially men. Then she did something she hadn't done since she was a child. The tears that had been bottled up inside her for years came pouring out, washing away the exasperated emotions that had been simmering just beneath the surface. In the past she had been forced to be strong, but now everything she had was gone and she cried for all the times she had wanted to cry her eyes out and hadn't.

When her mother Cathleen had withered away and died of a broken heart after news arrived that Olin Quinn had perished in battle, Catlin was left to hold the crumbling plantation together. And then came another devastating blow—the news of her fiancé's death. There had been times when Catlin had wanted to shed buckets of tears, to roll over and die, just as her mother had done when the world she had known came tumbling down around her. But Catlin was too much like her father: fiery, tenacious, and determined. Olin Quinn had fought with his last dying breath to save the South and Catlin had battled to save her home. She had lost everything and now her only crusade was to survive, no matter what the odds. And even surviving took tremendous effort these days.

Now, all she had left was gone and Catlin gave way to the tears because of the pain that split her skull, the throb in her broken leg, and the anguish of watching all she had known for twenty-two years evaporate into a cloud of dust. It was all gone, like leaves swirling in a cyclone. The South had fallen and nothing would bring it back. Catlin had fought to the bitter end and then she had run from the memories and the torment.

Muffling a sniff, Catlin wiped away the residue of tears that mingled with the dirt that stained her cheeks. Her first score and two years were behind her. She had closed the door on yesterday and boarded the stage bound for Texas

16

to beg sanctuary with her mother's older sister. Aunt Martha would take her in, Catlin assured herself as she struggled for hard-won composure. Martha Lewis had lost her husband the previous year and she was left alone to manage the sprawling ranch southwest of San Antonio. Together they would build a new life that was reminiscent of the glorious South and its traditions.

By God, she would not only survive she would prosper! She had already been through hell and there was nowhere to go but up, she reasoned. Catlin had consoled herself with the comforting platitudes that things could have been worse . . . until she reached the point of realizing things were as bad as they could possibly get.

Inhaling a steadying breath, Catlin continued to stare out the window, allowing the breeze to dry the last of her tears. She had made a fool of herself by bursting into sobs, but she had had her cry and she now was going to take command of her life. Tomorrow would be a better day, she encouraged herself. It had to be. But her first order of business was to get through this one!

When the coach skidded to a halt near the adobe Market Plaza, Catlin brushed the dust from her soiled gown. Before she sought out Aunt Martha she had to consult a doctor and have a splint strapped to her broken leg. And the leg was definitely broken, she diagnosed as she eased onto her hip to slide from the coach. She just had to resign herself to the disappointing fact that she would have to suffer the inconvenience of hobbling around on a crutch for the next few weeks. Another of life's unanticipated pitfalls, Catlin reminded herself sullenly.

Ignoring the helping hand the driver extended, Catlin levered herself to the ground, grimacing as she propped herself against the wheel.

Sensing the question Catlin was too proud to ask, the

17

driver gestured toward the wood-framed building that sat adjacent to the Plaza. "There's a doctor's office right across the street," he informed the rigid beauty who looked as though she had been trampled by a herd of stampeding buffalo and resented every moment of it.

"Thank you, sir." Catlin hobbled around to the back of the coach and paused to glance at the stubbled-face driver who incessantly chomped on his oversized wad of tobacco. "If I can impose on you to set my luggage beside the physician's office, I will never bother you again."

The driver broke into a grin. He couldn't help himself. This curvaceous blond was the proudest, most independent, stubbornest female he had ever run across. In comparison, Catlin Quinn could make a mule seem a most agreeable creature. She expected very little from men and demanded nothing more than their distant but polite respect. If Catlin hadn't been in so much pain and barely capable of standing on her injured leg, she would have undoubtedly collected her luggage all by herself.

"No bother," the driver mumbled as he pulled her satchels off the coach. "I'll notify the sheriff of the robbery while you tend to your leg."

Catlin offered him a token smile and a stiff but grateful nod before she limped toward the office. The wolfish whistles she received along the way added fuel to her already smoldering temper. The good cry she had allowed herself on the stage permitted her to blow off steam. But that didn't mean she wasn't still simmering with frustration. She most certainly was! The fact that a scraggly pack of wolves were leering at her put her in a worse snit than she was in already. Men! How she destested these pestering creatures. They killed, they raped, they robbed, they ravaged. They were lusty animals without souls or consciences. Only her father and her fiancé (God rest their souls) were worth their salt and now they were gone. The good men had died and the wicked flourished. There was

18

no justice in this world.

Clamping a hand around the supporting beam of the covered boardwalk, Catlin towed herself toward the doctor's office, but not before scowling at the surly group of men. Catlin growled at the audacity of the male of the species when one of the cursed *hombres* propositioned her, despite her go-straight-to-hell-and-don't-come-back glower. In a burst of fury, Catlin slammed the office door behind her. Dust dribbled from the cracks in the woodwork. Her fuming gaze landed on the magnificent physique of the man who was leisurely leaning a hip on the edge of a desk, scrutinizing her with faint amusement.

Catlin, however, found nothing amusing about being whistled at and propositioned while she was hobbling along on a broken leg and enduring an excruciating headache. She took one look at the handsome doctor and hated him on sight. He was a man, after all, and most worthy of her contempt.

"My leg is broken and my skull was split open by the desperado who stole my money during a stage robbery." Catlin rapped out the words in staccato. "Splint my leg and I will pay you for services rendered the moment I procure funds."

Lucas Murdock struggled to contain the makings of another amused smile, but it rose to put a twinkle in his eyes. Although the young lady had obviously been through hell, she had the heart of a lioness. This minx didn't get scared, she got mad, Lucas speculated. And although he couldn't say for certain, he wagered this virago slept standing up. She was that rigid and defensive!

The saucy blond was taller than average height, standing rigidly at five feet five inches. Lucas could see for himself what provoked the congregation of men to whistle and fling lurid innuendos at this sassy hellion. Even in her crumpled bonnet and the tattered, dusty gown that had been ripped loose at the shoulder seam, she was the stuff

19

masculine dreams were made of.

She had it all—the dazzling good looks, elegant features, a gorgeous body with alluring curves and swells that naturally aroused a man's baser instincts. Her vitality and fiery spirit enhanced her stunning appearance, making her a most desirable package of femininity. And those eyes. . . . Lucas sighed appreciatively. They reminded him of the colorful columbine flowers that graced the mountain meadows of Colorado with their vivid lavender and white petals.

In a way, she reminded him of Elise—the strong, willful beauty he had loved and would probably go on loving until the day he died . . .

"Well, are you just going to stand there?" Catlin snapped in pain and exasperation. "As luck would have it, I have stumbled onto a physician who doesn't give a whit about the Hippocratic oath. My leg hurts like hell, if you want to know. It must be broken in at least two places." Catlin ran her hand along the swollen knee that lay beneath yards of dusty blue satin. "Three places," she corrected herself. "I have a bump on my head the size of a gold brick and I can barely see straight. Do something, dammit!"

Lucas unfolded his swarthy frame from the edge of the desk and moved across the room with pantherlike grace. Catlin, who had developed a strong aversion to men, handsome or otherwise, instinctively stiffened in defense when he approached her.

"What in heaven's name are you doing?" she shrieked when the physician whisked her into his sinewy arms and strode into the adjoining room to plunk her down on the examination table.

"I could have walked in here," she spluttered, violet eyes flashing.

"On a broken leg?" Lucas questioned in mock concern.

"I walked to this office on my own accord," she

reminded him crankily.

When Lucas lifted the grimy hem of her skirt, his dark eyes traveled interestedly over her shapely appendage, taking note of the creamy flesh of her thigh. "Mmmm . . . nice legs," he complimented with a roguish grin.

The physician's outrageous bedside manner got Catlin's hackles up higher than they already were (if that were possible). Spewing muffled curses, she grasped her hiked hem and shoved it down to her ankle where it belonged. "My leg is none of your concern," she reprimanded him huffily.

"It is if it's broken," he chuckled, undaunted by her lightning tongue and thunderous glower. "But actually, I'm not—"

"Just splint the cussed leg without looking at it," Catlin demanded grouchily. Lord, she would give anything for a female physician!

Lucas had intended to tell this saucy she-dragon that he wasn't the resident physician she thought he was. Doctor Emmet Blake was presently delivering a baby and Lucas, who was a part-time veterinarian, physician and dentist when necessity demanded, had only stopped by the office to fetch supplies and medication for his employer. But this feisty spitfire whose blond hair sprayed about her like a tangled bird's nest and whose squished bonnet dangled off the side of her head, wouldn't allow him to squeeze a word in edgewise while she was having a conniption fit.

The quick peek Lucas had taken before Catlin snapped her dress back into place assured him there were no broken bones, only a twisted knee. But this amethyst-eyed harridan could never be convinced of that. She had diagnosed her injury before she hobbled into the office. And if she wanted to think she had a broken leg, Lucas was ornery enough to accommodate her. Splinting a sprain wouldn't hurt, he assured himself mischievously. The technique would immobilize the swollen joint. And

21

considering this rambunctious sprite's disposition, chances were she would be storming about, broken leg or no.

"Are you always this persnickety, even when you aren't in pain?" Lucas inquired nonchalantly, as he ambled over to the cabinet to fetch wooden splints and bandages.

"Are you always this casual and unconcerned about your patients?" she sniped.

Having retrieved the necessary supplies, Lucas pivoted to flash Catlin a wry grin that made his eyes glisten like polished ebony. "A doctor should always remain calm and collected," he declared. "If I get excited, you might too." His voice dropped to a low seductive tone that would have knocked the props out from under a lesser woman. "And if we both got excited, there's no telling what might happen. . . ." He broke into a rakish leer.

Catlin's gaze narrowed suspiciously. This handsome doctor didn't look or sound as if he were discussing the sort of excitement that went hand in hand with shock and bodily injury. His rich baritone voice resembled the purr of a lion that was out tomcatting around. Catlin, however, had no intention of being wooed or courted.

"Just splint my leg," Catlin ordered, tearing her eyes away from the doctor's swarthy physique and his flirtatious smile.

Dammit, she didn't want to notice how attractive he was. But there was a hint of savage civility about him—an intriguing paradox that piqued her curiosity. The cap of raven hair that surrounded his face glowed blue-black in the late afternoon sunlight that splattered through the sheer curtain. The cream-colored linen shirt strained sensuously across the broad expanse of his chest. Muscles rippled beneath the thin fabric, assuring Catlin that this particular physician needed no artificial model when he studied anatomy. He was the shining example of what the human body should be. All of his parts were in just the right places and he was extremely well-sculptured. And honest to goodness, she shouldn't have noticed such things!

Against her will, her gaze drifted over his square face. Strong commanding features were not plastered there, but rather etched with masterful skill. The Divine Artist had patiently labored over His masterpiece, giving this man unforgettable features. He possessed a rugged, earthy quality that appealed to a woman's basic instincts. He wasn't a dandy garbed in the fancy trappings of a gentleman. He was a man's man and a woman's dream—except for Catlin's of course. She wasn't in the market for a man.

Dark, entrancing eyes were embedded beneath thick black brows and long velvety lashes fanned out from those sparkling chocolate brown pools. Full sensuous lips were pursed in a smile—the devastating kind that involuntarily drew a woman's gaze and held it steadfastly. The physician had a small half-moon-shaped scar on the left side of his jaw, but other than that he was pretty nearly perfect and all too easy on the eye.

Her inquisitive perusal dipped to shoulders that were as wide as a bull moose's. The trim-fitting shirt tapered to his narrow waist and Catlin doubted there was an inch of flab on his virile body. If there was, she couldn't imagine where it might be! Long, extremely muscled legs were clad in bright blue trousers and extended into his polished black boots. Before Catlin stood six feet three inches of the most arresting mass of male pulchritude she had ever seen.

Even her fiancé couldn't hold a candle to this powerful monument to masculinity. Benjamin Saunders had been a fine figure of a man. Although Catlin hadn't been in love with Benjamin she had respected and admired him and she mourned his death. He would have made a good husband. He had cared for her, even if their marriage had been arranged by their families. Catlin would have been content with her lot, knowing she couldn't have done better if she had made the match herself.

But now Benjamin was gone, and so was her entire way of life. And the only men left on earth couldn't meet her high expectations. And as strikingly attractive as this doctor was, he could never overcome the unforgivable sin of being born a man. His gender was plagued with innumerable peccadilloes and Catlin had no use for any of the men who had been spared during the war—Yankee and Confederate alike. The Lord had obviously needed a few good men surrounding Him and He left the rejects on earth. The women who endured the War between the States were forced to tolerate the less desirable males until their time came to be removed to a higher sphere. Just her luck that the desperados who robbed her hadn't had enough compassion to put her out of her misery permanently. . . .

Catlin shook off the dreadful incident and her wandering thoughts. Even though it was the last thing she had intended to do, she found herself ogling this ruggedly handsome physician again. This raven-haired doctor oozed with sensuality and devilish charm and he easily aroused a woman's secret desires. Fortunately, hating all men in general prevented Catlin from falling head over heels for this one man in particular. He was a magnificent specimen but Catlin wanted nothing to do with him.

"I thought *I* was the one who was supposed to be examining *you*," Lucas taunted as he watched those lively jewel-like eyes run the full length of him, not missing one minute detail.

A deep skirl of laughter rumbled in his chest when he noticed the profuse color that rose from the base of this nymph's swanlike neck to consume her exquisite but smudged features. She blushed when she was embarrassed or angry. The increase in color that flooded upward was like a rising thermometer.

"I wasn't gawking," Catlin lied to save face and then

tilted a haughty chin. "I was only sitting here wondering how long it was going to take you to tend my broken leg. Honest to goodness! Your patients could die on the examination table long before you finished dawdling and finally got around to treating them." Her violet eyes narrowed warily. "And by the way, what is the percentage of recovery for your *victims?*"

A deliciously ornery grin cut slashes in his tanned cheeks, making the half-moon scar wrinkle like an accordion. "Actually, my percentage is quite high," he boasted as he set his supplies aside. "I usually manage to dispose of the patients who need killing and save the ones who deserve to live."

"And just where do I fit in?" Catlin challenged, elevating a delicately arched brow.

"That all depends on whether or not you permit me to examine your gorgeous set of legs," Lucas told her frankly. "If you persist with your modesty, gangrene might set in and I'll be forced to chop off the injured appendage."

Catlin gnashed her teeth and begrudgingly lifted the hem of her soiled gown. When Lucas placed his lean fingers on her thigh she jumped as if she were sitting on a scorpion. "Don't waste time with examination," she muttered awkwardly. "It's broken. I'm sure of it. Splint it and be quick about it. I'm in a hurry."

"Very well then, grit your teeth," Lucas instructed.

She braced herself when Lucas grabbed hold of her ankle with his right hand and clamped his left hand around her thigh.

"Ready?"

Catlin nodded grimly and closed her eyes. When Lucas gave a quick but forceful yank to place her jammed knee back in its socket, Catlin let out a yelp. Lord, that hurt!

While Lucas scooped up the wooden splints and positioned them on either side of her swollen leg, Catlin half-collapsed on the table. His keen eyes swam over the shapely thigh, noting the clover-shaped birthmark that set above her inflamed knee. Very nice legs, he mused admiringly. Very nice indeed. In fact they were every bit as tantalizing as Elise's.

Only a scant few women had come along the past five years who measured up to Elise's captivating beauty and untamed spirit. But this blond-haired firecracker was her equal.

As memories enshrouded him, Lucas contemplated the sultry brunette who had stolen his heart. Even if the war hadn't demanded his time and his talents, Lucas would have been forced to leave his family's plantation in Georgia. A man couldn't live under the same roof with his older brother's wife—loving her, wanting her, knowing he would make life difficult if he stayed. Elise had been open and honest in her feelings, just as Lucas had been when he fell in love for the first time in his life. He was a man who was in the habit of stating what was on his mind and he didn't mince words. If he liked what he saw he said so. And if he didn't, he said that, too.

When Elise demanded to know why he felt inclined to leave home, he had told Elise that he loved her. And with wide, shimmering eyes, Elise had admitted there were two men in her life—the one she intended to marry because she loved him and the one she cherished, despite her affection and respect for his older brother.

Andrew Murdock had assured Lucas there would still be a place for him at the plantation after they returned from battle. But it wouldn't have worked, not when Lucas coveted Andrew's fiancée. Lucas had told his brother so, in his customary forthright manner. With head bowed, Andrew confessed that he knew how Lucas felt and he would have given Elise her freedom if he hadn't loved her with every beat of his heart.

And Lucas had quietly replied, "If it were anyone but

Elise, there would be no conflict between us. She can't have both of us and I, like you, care far too much to ever be content to share her without possessing her—mind, body and spirit."

Andrew hadn't taken offense to his younger brother's candor. He too was a man who believed in being straightforward. He couldn't condemn Lucas's affection for Elise. Andrew knew how it felt to be hopelessly in love with her.

Regretfully, Lucas and Andrew had waved good-bye and galloped off to fight. Lucas, however, vowed not to put down roots anywhere until he could look upon Elise without desiring her in his bed and in his life. That had been five years ago and Lucas was no closer to forgetting the one woman who held the key to his heart than he had been the day he left.

As a scout for the Confederates, Lucas had thrust himself into danger with devil-may-care panache, earning one medal of bravery after another. Because of his reckless daring, he had been discovered by a ruthless group of Yankee guerrillas. Although he had been severely beaten and tortured Lucas refused to give out information about the Confederates. Even under penalty of death he had defied the vicious marauders and they had cut him to pieces before kicking him into the river and leaving him to die of his wounds.

When the war ended, Lucas and Andrew both returned to the plantation that had been spared the ravages of battle. Lucas gathered his belongings and bid farewell to Elise and Andrew, then traveled through the Southwest like a restless spirit. He used his experience to scout for the Army in the West and battled the elements as well as renegade Indians. He had driven cattle north for ranchers who had a surplus of stock but found their market for beef to be a far piece from their doorstep. He had taken a supply train to Fort Douglas in Utah and had been caught in a blizzard on the Laramie Plains and forced to winter in a makeshift camp. He had been starved and beaten by desperados and renegades, but he had gained valuable knowledge. Lucas had finally wound up in Texas, employing his doctoring skills and his broad knowledge of animals and men to make his living.

To forget his obsession with Elise he had bedded his fair share of women along the way, but nothing had erased Elise's bewitching image. The sultry brunette who teemed with spirit and inexhaustible energy was a part of him that time and distance couldn't erase. Lucas had become a dedicated bachelor who was chained to his past, certain he would never fall in love but once in his life. Although he hoped some female would come along to distract him, he believed that the Lord had made only one woman who could have satisfied him.

"Ouch! Dammit all! This is not supposed to be a tourniquet," Catlin squawked when Lucas absently bound up her leg like a mummy, cutting off circulation. "What are you? Some kind of quack? How much intelligence does it take to splint a broken leg?"

Lucas shrugged off the insult like a duck flicking rain from its back. "How did you injure your leg?" he inquired, concentrating on his task.

"Three men fell on me," she ground out bitterly.

"The poor men. Will they be coming in to be stitched back together? Surely a woman like you wouldn't allow such an atrocity to go unanswered," he taunted unmercifully.

"I strongly dislike you," Catlin blustered.

If the insult pierced his pride, it didn't show. Lucas accepted her opinion of him in stride. He never had put much stock in what people thought.

"And I have the irrational urge to make love to you," he had the nerve to admit without batting an eyelash. "I'm attracted to you, but I'm not quite sure why. Maybe it's

28

these gorgeous legs. . . ."

The remark served its purpose. It shut her up like a clam. Catlin clamped her lips together so quickly she nearly bit her tongue in two. Crimson rushed into her cheeks like a tidal wave.

"Now, let's have a look at the knot on your head," Lucas suggested as he twisted his flustered patient around to inspect the back of her skull. "Is your vision blurred?"

"Only because of blinding fury," Catlin muttered venomously.

Grinning, Lucas swaggered over to the medicine cabinet to retrieve the antiseptic and then dabbed it into her scalp. She yelped in agony.

"You could have prepared me for the pain," Catlin growled irritably.

"You knew it was going to hurt," he countered blandly.

"Honest to goodness! I never met a doctor whose compassion couldn't fill a thimble," Catlin fumed.

"That takes care of your leg and head," Lucas announced as he stashed away the leftover supplies. "But it will require surgery to remove that chip from your shoulder. Shall I schedule another appointment?"

Catlin looked as if she wanted to hit him. "I'll learn to live with my chip, just as you have learned to live with your monstrous apathy and stupendous arrogance," she hurled at him as she wiggled off the examination table. "I will pay you as soon as I find a job."

A roguish grin caused crinkles to fan out from the corners of his dark eyes. "For a few dozen kisses we'll call it even."

In all her twenty-two years, Catlin had never confronted such an audacious rakehell. Most men tried to seduce her with sly innuendoes and subtle passes. But not this quack doctor! He was blunt and to the point—a little too direct to suit her, in fact.

"I'd rather kiss a snake," she hissed venomously.

29

A bright peal of laughter resounded in his massive chest. "Which would you prefer, poisonous or nonpoisonous?"

"You are impossible!" Catlin spewed in outrage.

"And you are incorrigible," Lucas declared between chuckles.

For the life of him he didn't know why he was needling this proud, defiant beauty. It just came naturally. Their contrasting personalities demanded that he counter her insults and goad her until she ground her teeth in irritation. The truth was he delighted in getting her goat. Her inborn defensiveness invited his taunts.

"By the way, what is your name?" he questioned out of the blue. When she frowned dubiously, his broad shoulder lifted in a careless shrug. "I'll need your name to offer the sheriff if you never get around to paying me for my services."

"You will be paid in full, even though it will be more than you deserve," she sniffed, tilting her chin. "The name if Catlin Quinn."

"Catlin?" Lucas's penetrating brown eyes roamed over her appetizing figure, visualizing what lay beneath the form-fitting gown. Nice body, the kind a man could enjoy cuddling up to for a night of passion. Too bad the personality attached to this luscious figure worked as effectively as insect repellant.

Lucas shook off the thought. "I've never heard that name before. But it seems to fit the most unusual woman who bears it."

"It was given to me by my mother Cathleen and my father Olin. *Cat-lin,*" she emphasized in case this dunce of a doctor didn't make the connection. "And what is your name, sir? I should like to know so I can refer my future friends in San Antonio *away* from your office."

Lucas eased a hip onto the examination table and leaned over to light his cheroot. "My friends just call me Doc," he informed her.

"Do you have any?" she purred so sweetly that it took a moment for the biting words to soak through her syrupy tone.

"One or two," he replied, unoffended. "Far more than you probably have, considering your mean disposition." Before Catlin could hurl a suitably nasty rejoinder, Lucas retrieved a cane and thrust it at her. "This is for walking, not for doing bodily harm. I will probably get myself arrested for offering a weapon to a maniac."

Catlin put a stranglehold on the cane, spitefully wishing it was this man's muscular neck. While she was contemplating clubbing the ornery quack over the head, the door creaked open and the blacksmith poked his head inside to flash Lucas a smile.

"Your wagon is ready, Doc. The wheel is as good as new."

With a nod of thanks, Lucas snatched up the medication he had come to fetch and ambled toward the door. There he paused to toss Catlin a backward glance. "Unless you have your heart set on exercising your injured leg, I'll give you a ride," he graciously offered.

"No, thank you. I'm sure my destination would be out of your way and the company barely tolerable," she declared with a condescending glare.

"Which direction are you headed?"

"Southwest."

"Unfortunately, so am I," Lucas replied, bursting into a mischievous smile. "Come along, Cat. We'll make each other miserable for a few more minutes. I rather enjoy watching your face turn red with outrage and embarrassment."

"The name is *Miss Quinn* to you," she snapped as she hobbled on her splinted leg and cane. If walking wasn't so painful she would have marched off down the road to Aunt Martha's ranch. Putting up with this insulting excuse for a doctor was the lesser of two evils, she reckoned.

She had no funds to hire a driver and the doctor's charity was better than limping four miles on a broken leg. "I accept your offer, sir—"

No sooner were the words out of her mouth than Lucas closed the space between them and whisked her up into his sinewy arms. Despite her protest, he carried her outside to plunk her down on the wagon seat. She could smell the subtle fragrance of his cologne, feel the whipcord muscles that were mashed against her flesh. Catlin was astounded by the unexpected waves that rippled through her naive body when she came into physical contact with this arrogant rake.

Catlin couldn't quite figure the doctor out. She had the feeling everything he said and did was a deliberate attempt to get her dander up, that he derived wicked pleasure from aggravating her. From the instant they met, Catlin had been defensive because she was suspicious by nature and cautious by habit. She was a woman alone and she had to keep men at arm's length, lest she become vulnerable prey to lusty scoundrels. She had been squashed flat, broken her leg, been whacked on the head, and stripped of all her money. What did the good doctor expect her to do? Come prancing into his office as merry as the month of May, for crying out loud? Let him get robbed, beaten and squished a couple of times and see how it affected his disposition! Catlin would bet her right arm the doctor wouldn't be the picture of pleasantry either!

Chapter 2

"I could have climbed up here all by myself," Catlin muttered as she squirmed to position her stiff leg atop the wagon.

"You could have," Lucas agreed, setting her luggage in the wagon bed. "But I would have been deprived of holding your curvaceous body next to mine." Flashing her a sideways glance, Lucas watched another becoming blush stain her smudged cheeks.

"You needn't be so honest in your intentions," she grumbled acrimoniously. "I really don't care what you're thinking."

With the most masculine grace imaginable, Lucas swung onto the seat and took the reins in hand. "Would you rather I lie and say I picked you up so you wouldn't have to put excessive pressure on your leg?" he questioned.

Catlin knew, then and there, that sex was second nature to this physician. It left her wondering how many female patients he had seduced along the way. Her speculations were staggering. The man was an outrageous flirt who made no bones about what he wanted from a woman. He had probably entered the medical profession as an excuse to take a gander at as many female bodies as possible during his lifetime.

"You've got a helluva lot of spunk. I like you, Cat," Lucas announced as he popped the reins, sending the horses clattering off at a fast clip.

"I still don't like you," she countered and she meant it. "You are a man and I wouldn't bed you even if it meant terminating the human race, so don't ask me to, unless you thrive on rejection."

"I'll bet you're a virgin," he had the gall to speculate.

"That is none of your business!" she sputtered indignantly. Honest to goodness, how had he arrived at that conclusion? She certainly didn't have that information embroidered on her sleeve.

Lucas couldn't contain the bubble of laughter when the color washed up her face. "I prefer experienced women," he assured her before taking a puff on his cheroot. "In fact, I've never slept with a virgin."

In times of excessive frustration and anger Catlin was known to emit a spasm of furious, unintelligible hisses. This was one of those times. A rapid succession of muted, tangled curses spewed from her lips as the wagon whizzed past the Plaza, cantina, and dry goods store. And all the while Lucas had a good laugh at her expense. Catlin would have thrown herself off the wagon if she could have guaranteed she wouldn't break her other leg.

"I don't care how many women, innocent or otherwise, you have seduced," she snapped when she regained minimal control of her vocal apparatus. "In fact, I couldn't care less if you keeled over in a dead heap this very moment."

"Virgins must feel some innate need to protect themselves from men," Lucas surmised. "The ones I know spend most of their time building walls to prolong chastity. Sex happens to be one of the most wondrous pleasures in life. It's a pity you are missing out." Ah, he thrived on getting her goat.

"Will you stop?!" Catlin howled in frustration.

Lucas stopped alright—on the outskirts of town. He pulled the horses to a skidding halt, even though that wasn't what Catlin meant and she was nowhere near prepared for the abrupt stop. A surprised shriek erupted from her lips when she felt herself flying off the seat. If Lucas hadn't shackled her arm she would have tumbled from her perch.

"Shall we get this over with?" Lucas inquired, peering into her snapping violet eyes.

To her utter astonishment, he towed her toward him to plant a kiss on her lips. His mouth moved expertly over hers, his tongue probing to seek out the moist recesses.

His kiss was warm and inquisitive, testing her response, tempting her to kiss him back. Catlin's innocent body winced when a sinewy arm stole around her waist, mashing her into his hard, muscular contours. She felt his thighs meshing against her hip. Uncontrollable shock waves hit Catlin and her overworked heart leapfrogged around her ribs like a migrating toad. She swore this brash doctor had forgotten more about kissing than she could hope to learn in a lifetime. There were kisses and there were *kisses*. This handsome rogue gave new meaning to the word!

If this was an example of the kind of reaction other women experienced when the skillful doctor practiced mouth-to-mouth resuscitation it was a wonder the female population of San Antonio had survived! Honest to goodness, Catlin had never been so thoroughly kissed in all her life! There wasn't an ounce of gentlemanly reserve in his embrace. It was like being dragged into the vortex of a thunderstorm and suspended in motionless flight. Lightning bolts zapped her, setting fire to her nerves. A strange, undefinable ache nagged at her, burgeoning up from places Catlin didn't even know she had.

At first Catlin had been too startled by the kiss to protest. And later she was still too startled to complain. When

Lucas finally had the decency to come up for air, Cat gaped at him as if he had sprouted another head—one boasting devil's horns. As if he were satisfied with his experiment, Lucas took up the reins and refocused on the road. Catlin, however, sat there like a marble statue. An expression of stupefied disbelief was frozen on her elegant features.

"I enjoyed kissing you," Lucas admitted with his usual amount of candor. "You could use some practice, but you have strong possibilities, Cat. We would be good together in bed."

Her jaw hung open and her eyes popped. This raven-haired rake beat anything she had ever seen! He insulted her and then he kissed her speechless. He speculated on their reaction to each other in the midst of passion as if he were predicting the blessed weather!

How was a woman supposed to handle such a man as this? She couldn't, Catlin realized bleakly. It was like trying to tame a cyclone. None of her previous rules about men applied to this devastating rake. He was not the least inhibited or intimidated by her put-downs. His forthright honesty was a mite unnerving. Catlin had learned to counter subtle techniques and crafty schemes to strip her of her innocence, but this doctor's frankness knocked her completely off balance. She wondered if she were totally honest with him, just where this peculiar relationship might lead. As if she didn't know. . . .

Banish the thought! Catlin gave herself a mental slap for visualizing herself in this man's powerful arms, enjoying a few dozen more mind-boggling kisses. What was the matter with her? This demon could single-handedly wipe virginity from the face of the earth and populate the world all by himself! No doubt it was his greatest aspiration in life.

"You are considering the possibility, I see," Lucas taunted his blushing companion.

36

Was she so transparent? Or could this devilish wizard read her mind like an open book? Well, if he wanted honesty, she would give it to him and she would hold nothing back!

"I considered it," she admitted, fighting down another profuse blush. Catlin had never ever discussed sex with a man and it was a hurdle she found herself struggling over with great difficulty. "But I have too much respect for myself to buckle to the powers of passion for passion's sake. I have no desire to become a notch on your bedpost. I have set my aspirations in life much higher than becoming no more than the object of a man's pleasure. I'm sure you haven't far to look to find sexual satisfaction. So you won't be too disappointed if I decline joining you in bed to do whatever it is people do when animal lust overcomes them."

Lucas stared at the saucy blond for a long pensive moment. He couldn't say for certain what prompted the tender affection he suddenly felt for this rumpled beauty. Heaven knew, this fiery minx hadn't invited his compassion and seemed to want no part of it, being the stubborn independent female she was. Perhaps it was her remark about wanting something better for herself, he mused thoughtfully. Lucas had felt that same strong sense of self-pride when he turned his back on the one and only love of his life. He hadn't been satisfied to watch Andrew dote over Elise. He had refused to pine for a love that could never be or to wallow in self-pity. And so he had gone in search of rainbows, roaming from one place to another like a windblown tumbleweed. Now he had found what he wanted in Texas and had set about making plans to acquire it. He could have wired his brother for his inheritance and Andrew would have sent him the money posthaste. But Lucas wanted to establish a new life for himself, making his own way without his inheritance. He had wanted to forget his obsession for Elise in his own way, substituting new goals and new dreams for a future.

When Elise's delicate features rose to torment him, Lucas focused on Catlin's peaches and cream complexion, the wild mass of sandy blond hair and those incredible violet eyes that danced with living fire. For some reason, his heart reached through the haze of memories of the past to touch this fiery angel who sat beside him.

An utterly charming smile spread across his sensuous lips as he observed Cat's enchanting features. "If sex is out of the question, perhaps we could be friends. You look as if you could use one."

The comment made Catlin automatically put her guard down. She never had a male friend before. It would be nice to gain some insight into what made men tick.

Odd, how she reacted so spontaneously to this man. He had managed to crumble her protective barriers with a variety of unique tactics. Catlin couldn't imagine what prompted her to be so personal with the doctor, but the question tumbled off her lips before she could bite it back.

"What's it like . . . sleeping with a man?" she blurted out unexpectedly.

Lucas chortled in amusement when Cat blushed up to her perfectly arched brows. "I wouldn't know, violet eyes. I never slept with one."

"You know what I mean," she mumbled self-consciously. "My mother never got around to explaining the facts of life and my father would never think of broaching the subject with his daughter. And my fiancé and I were never intimate before he was killed in battle. I had speculated on the possibility of a wedding night, but being inexperienced, I—"

Lucas gaped at her. "Do you mean to tell me with this curvaceous body of yours and your extraordinary good looks that you've never even been touched?" His voice was incredulous.

Cat bristled. "You needn't looked so shocked. I'm not the last of a species that is near extinction. I have several

38

friends who share my ignorance of men. And the whispering of young wives offered very little praise for passion. I have heard it said that it was a man's privilege and a wife's duty. I have also heard that it is most painful and even . . ." She leaned closer to convey her confidential remark, even though there wasn't a soul around to overhear her. "sordid and disgusting. . . ."

Lucas took one look at her solemn expression and burst out laughing. In all his thirty-one years he had never met such a naive nymph. She definitely needed a friend of the male persuasion and a few lessons on the facts of life.

"You need not be so rude as to laugh at me," Cat pouted, her face flushing beet red. "How would I know what lovemaking is all about? I may go to my grave as an untouched spinster, but I would at least like to know what I purposely bypassed."

Lucas pulled the wagon to a halt again and stared down into those entrancing amethyst eyes that dominated her lovely but smeared face. "Passion exceeds the wildest imagination. At its worst it is pleasurable. And at its best, I expect it would defy description."

"Has it in your vast and varied experiences?" she found herself wanting to know.

A wistful smile hovered on his full mouth. Absently, he reached up to smooth the renegade strands from this bewitching elf's face. "No, but I imagine it would have been if I could have slept with the woman I loved. She would have made passion an even more wondrous experience."

Catlin peered into his rugged face, watching his eyes take on a faraway expression. "And so, to compensate for the woman you truly wanted, you have taken one female after another, settling for less than perfection," she guessed.

Lucas nodded affirmatively, unoffended by her perceptive speculation. "Elise married my brother. And whether you believe it or not, I respect the institution of wedlock. I do have a sense of integrity," he added. "I can't betray my own brother when he loves Elise as much as I do. She gave me back my pride and self-respect when I was certain no woman would have me after I was beaten, slashed and left for dead. She made me look past the scars and the bitterness, but she couldn't help me get over loving her." Lucas jerked upright and frowned. "Why the hell am I telling you this?"

"Beats me," Catlin responded, breaking into a grin. "I suppose it's because we are friends and confidants."

Lucas sat paralyzed, astonished by the sudden transformation. This dazzling blond was a sight to behold, even when she was in a fit of temper. But when she graced him with a radiant smile, he swore he was viewing a glorious sunrise.

"You are even more lovely when you smile," he murmured in masculine appreciation.

The unexpected compliment provoked her to grin again and Lucas was magnetically drawn to her. He hadn't meant to kiss her a second time, although this innocent maid needed to be kissed and kissed often. It had been a long time since he had been so impulsively attracted to a woman—five years to be exact.

Catlin knew she shouldn't be experimenting with Pandora's box of forbidden desire. But Lucas was the devil's own temptation. He had a unique way about him and she found herself wanting to develop the same technique of kissing the opposite sex deaf, dumb and blind. Not that she would ever need that knowledge. She only intended to broaden her horizons with men—for curiosity's sake, of course. There was something in the way his warm lips rolled over hers that made her want to explore the strange physical phenomena that was splintering through her naive body.

"Open your mouth for me, Cat," he instructed when she hesitated in returning his embrace. "Now kiss me back. . . ."

40

Catlin took the doctor's advice, concentrating on the tantalizing technique that had sent a fleet of goose bumps cruising across her flesh. She heard him groan deep in his throat when her darting tongue investigated the inner softness of his lips. His arms folded around her, mashing her throbbing breasts against the hard wall of his chest, allowing her to feel his arousal. Catlin jerked away. Her wide, questioning gaze locked with those dark, chocolate brown ones.

"You excite me," he assured her huskily, tracking his forefinger over lips that were as soft and tempting as rose petals. "It's a perfectly normal reaction when a man holds a beautiful woman in his arms. And you are that, Cat, plus so much more." A roguish grin dangled from the corner of his mouth. "And I'm the one who is going to be in agony, believe you me. Your throbbing head and leg are mere child's play compared to aching for you and not having you."

"I wanted to know more about the birds and bees, but you needn't go into such explicit detail," Catlin blustered, face flaming.

Lucas had never carried on such intimate conversations with another woman, not even Elise. And his affairs had been brief—spanning the length of time required to hop in and out of bed before going his own way. But this innocent child-woman, who was a walking contradiction, intrigued and fascinated him.

The thunder of hooves interrupted their intimate conversation. With extreme effort, he tore his gaze away from the bewitching blond whose moods were like an ever-changing kaleidoscope. When Lucas recognized Bo Huxley, he knew serious trouble was brewing; otherwise, Bo would have seen to the matter himself. Damn, Lucas had intended to get around to telling Catlin she didn't really need her splints and that she was only suffering a sprain. But there wasn't time to explain in a manner that wouldn't rile this fiery-tempered hellion. Yet, there was one thing Lucas did need to make clear before Cat became too relaxed, too secure with this new-found friendship.

"I was wrong, Cat," he whispered as his lips grazed her petal-soft mouth. "You arouse me far too much to settle for nothing more intimate than friendship. I'm back to wanting you in my bed. You start fires in my blood and I prefer to be not only your friend but also your lover. . . ."

Catlin blinked like an owl adjusting to sunlight when the candid doctor, having said his piece, swung down from the wagon with the grace of a cougar. In long light strides he swaggered toward the approaching rider.

"But what about your wagon?" she chirped, her voice one octave higher than normal.

"I'll catch up with it later." A seductive smile quirked his lips as his eyelid dropped into a suggestive wink. "And with you, violet eyes, if you aren't careful. . . ."

"I meant what I said," Catlin assured him, her chin tilting to that defiant angle Lucas had come to recognize at a glance.

"So did I," he assured her, his tone thick with unappeased desire.

His melting brown eyes swept possessively over her luscious figure and Cat trembled as if he had reached out a bronzed hand to caress her. Honest to goodness, even at a distance this dark-eyed devil was devastating!

"We've got trouble, Doc," Bo grumbled as he reined his laboring steed to a halt. "Young Jesse got thrown off one of those wild mustangs we've been gathering for the trail drive. He was dragged through the brush before he managed to worm his foot from the stirrup."

"Hell's bells," Lucas muttered sourly. "He shouldn't have been breaking broncs with so little experience." Stepping into the stirrup, Lucas swung up behind the bandylegged cowboy.

"He was trying to prove himself to the snappers who were razzing him," Bo explained, wheeling his horse

42

around to charge off to only God knew where.

Snappers? What the blazes was a snapper? Catlin wondered curiously. Was it some sort of Texas turtle? She didn't have a clue that men who made their living taming wild broncs had earned the name of snappers. In fact, she didn't know beans about such things.

Shrugging bemusedly, Catlin took up the reins and urged the horses southwest. It had been almost eight years since Catlin had visited her aunt, but the familiar surroundings allowed her to locate the ranch without difficulty.

A faint smile hovered on her lips, remembering her confrontation with the darkly handsome doctor. He was brash and bold and intriguingly reckless and Cat was far more aware of him as a man than as a doctor. He possessed a most powerful medicine—the kind that had absolutely nothing to do with healing wounds and everything to do with making her vividly aware of her slumbering passions. The doctor was dangerous, Catlin cautioned herself. He threatened her willpower as it had never been threatened before.

Wearily, Catlin slumped in her seat, staring straight ahead, seeing nothing. My, what a day this had been. Her emotions had been run through a meat grinder! And the dashing doctor had ground them worst of all! His parting words echoed in her ears, leaving her to curse herself for speculating on what it would be like to lie in his powerful arms, to discover what went on between a man and a woman when passion overwhelmed them. . . .

Catlin jerked straight up in her seat. She wasn't going to think about such things! she told herself fiercely. Indeed, she wasn't going to spare that handsome physician another thought . . . ever.

She left the wagon with a young ranchhand beside the barn and hobbled toward the house to begin her new life with Aunt Martha.

Chapter 3

Martha Lewis peered at the bruised and battered young woman who was standing on the stoop, propped on a cane. Surely it couldn't be . . . Martha adjusted the thick spectacles that sat on the bridge of her nose.

"Catlin? Is that you?" she squeaked. "What the blazes happened to you? Are you alright? What are you doing in Texas?"

Mustering a tired smile, Catlin hobbled inside. "Aside from the fact that I have endured a stage robbery, broken my leg and had a pistol clanked against my skull I'm in superb shape and I have come to visit you."

Martha clutched her heart before it popped out of her chest. "Sweet mercy, child, sit down before you fall down. I'll fetch you some brandy to calm your nerves."

Even at age fifty and slightly overweight, Martha could move like a streak of lightning when necessity dictated. As Catlin plunked down in a chair, Martha scuttled off to the kitchen to fetch the peach brandy, of which she was prone to take a few nips when her nerves were jittery. Snatching two glasses from the cabinet, Martha poured herself a quick drink and downed it in one swallow. Doing an about-face, she whizzed back to the parlor to thrust a glass at Catlin.

Her wide hazel eyes focused on Catlin's weary features. "Tell me everything and don't leave out even one insignificant detail," she demanded as she slopped brandy into their glasses.

Catlin began by explaining how she had lost the family plantation to the carpetbaggers who swindled her out of her land and the scheming lawyer who had bled her dry. By the time Catlin dredged up all the unhealed wounds she was in tears and so was Martha. Catlin then proceeded to describe the tedious journey from Louisiana to Texas by stagecoach and ended with the holdup that had caused her to lose the last cent she had. She did not, however, mention the rakish doctor or their intimate discussion during the ride to the ranch. By the time Catlin finished her monologue Martha had soaked her second handkerchief.

"You mustn't worry about your future," Martha consoled her niece, muffling a sniff. "You will remain here with me. I have sold the ranch and within two weeks we will move to town and you can begin a new life in Texas."

"Sold the land?" Catlin blinked in astonishment. She had scratched and clawed to hold the Quinn plantation together for two years and Aunt Martha had sold her land of her own free will. How could she?

"I am to receive three dollars an acre for it," Martha proudly proclaimed. "Lucas Murdock, the nice young man who had been managing the ranch since your Uncle Matthew's health deteriorated, has offered to buy the place. He has been taking care of everything for me since Matthew passed away."

I'll just bet he has, Catlin mused cynically. Lucas something-or-other had probably taken advantage of this kind-hearted, bereaved widow, cutting his share of the profits and convincing Martha that a huge ranch was no place for a woman alone.

"But the land is everlasting," Catlin declared, clutching

her aunt's hands in her own. "Everything else in this world comes and goes, but the land is here forever. If you give it up . . ."

Martha cut her short to verbalize her own opinion. "Land is for the young and ambitious men like Lucas who can make it work for them." Her hazel eyes locked with those vivid violet pools that were so full of life. "I think you want me to hold onto the ranch because you lost the plantation that was so dear to you, Catlin. That has made all land seem even more precious to you."

She gave her salt-and-pepper head a shake. "No, child, I have outgrown all this. Your Uncle Matt worked himself to death establishing this ranch. Though it has sentimental value to me, my dreams died with Matt. I'm too old and tired to cling to the memories and I have no children to offer an inheritance. The wealth I have acquired will one day be yours, Catlin. But this land is for strong, imaginative men who know no master. They defy the brutal weather, failing crops and unseen setbacks in the cattle market. Lucas is that kind of man. He has been good to me and he will make this ranch prosper. You and I will have a quaint home in San Antonio and we will live comfortably together. Lucas himself saw to the construction of my new house and has arranged a house-warming party for the day after he moves me in."

Lucas this, Lucas that. Catlin was already sick of hearing about the swindling cowboy who had sweet-talked Martha out of her vast holdings. No doubt he was willing to say and do most anything to shuffle Martha into a tiny little shack on the edge of San Antonio.

"For over two years Lucas has been organizing trail drives for us as well as other nearby ranchers and has taken cattle to northern and western markets. He arranged contracts with his acquaintances at Fort Sumner, Fort Stanton, and other military posts to supply beef for the Navajo, Apaches, and soldiers. He has taken several herds up the Goodnight-Loving Trail that was established a couple of years ago and several more through Indian Territory to Kansas. Lucas intends to drive the next herd all the way to Colorado to receive high prices from the gold miners. Thanks to him, I have a tidy nest egg to support us," she announced. "Or at least I will by the time Lucas returns from the spring drive."

"Do you mean to tell me you sold the ranch on a promise, even though he has yet to produce the cash?" Wide violet eyes riveted on her aunt who obviously didn't have a head for business if she could be so taken in by a no-account cowboy! Honest to goodness, what could Martha be thinking of?

"Now don't you fret," Martha murmured, patting Catlin's clenched fists. "Lucas will take care of everything. He always does. I'm anxious for you to meet him. Once you do, you will adore him as much as I do."

Catlin seriously doubted that!

"But at the moment, Lucas is overseeing the roundup of mustangs that will have to be broken to ride on the trail. An efficient drover like Lucas insists on taking a remuda of at least a hundred horses with him on the drive. And once he has trained the mounts he will be busy gathering and branding the other ranchers' herds," Martha went on to say.

Catlin felt as if she had arrived in a foreign country. Driving cattle to far away markets was new to her. The fact that crafty Lucas what's-his-name was in charge rankled her pride. The more Martha boasted Lucas's talents the less Catlin liked him.

"Since Lucas is anxious to start his own herd, he plans to gather some wild *cimarrones* from the brush country to sell with the other ranchers' herds. The profit he makes on the strays that have been roaming around Texas for the last decade will enable him to purchase prize stock and pay for the land," Martha explained.

"Texas cattlemen have been struggling since the war. Those who ventured through Indian Territory to Kansas have met with more difficulty of late. Jayhawkers have banned Texas cattle from their lands, claiming they are infected with ticks and that the herds should be quarantined. And Indian tribes have placed taxes on beeves that cross their reserved lands. But Lucas has been very successful driving cattle northwest, despite the hazards and difficulties of marauding Comanches and stretches of waterless desert." Martha nodded affirmatively. "Yes, Lucas will make this ranch what it once was before that blasted war."

At Martha's expense, Catlin grumbled to herself. That wily scoundrel was probably feeding Martha a crock of lies. But when it came time to pay for the ranch he planned to buy out from under her, he would probably dream up some flimsy excuse as to why he couldn't hand over the full amount. And being the generous, trusting woman Martha was, she would offer to extend the loan until only God knew when. Honest to goodness, this scheme of his could go on forever and Martha could wind up penniless!

"I think it best to insist on a written contract and demand cash in hand," Catlin advised. "If your foreman cannot make his payment, he certainly won't be able to afford to pay his taxes. And you, like myself, will find your land snatched away from you by some devious scoundrel who can pay the taxes. This vast ranch will belong to someone you don't even know for the mere price of taxes."

"You mustn't worry your pretty head about such things," Martha clucked, unconcerned. "Lucas will take care of everything."

Lucas—the leech—was going to take care of everything alright, Catlin silently fumed. He would take Martha for all she was worth and she would be walking the streets of San Antonio, begging for handouts.

"If my father taught me one thing, it was that business is

business," Cat insisted with great conviction. "It cannot and should not be mixed up with friendship because you may very well lose your investment and your so-called friend. Fool that I was, I assumed the lawyer I hired to handle my family's estate had my best interests at heart. But he caused me to lose the plantation and he reaped the profits from breaking up the acreages and complying with the Freedman Act."

"It isn't wise for you to work your emotions into a tizzy," Martha murmured with a compassionate smile. "After all you have been through lately, you need to clear your troubled mind of your woes." She poured her niece another drink. "Now you just sit back and give your broken leg a rest. While you are convalescing you can help me pack my belongings for the move to town. Before long we will be living in the lap of luxury in the brand spanking new home Lucas built for us in San Antonio."

"I did not come here to live off you like a parasite, Aunt Martha," Catlin insisted earnestly. "I fully intend to obtain a job to support myself."

"But that won't be necessary, my dear," Martha tittered. Her hands swept out in a gesture that magically cast all problems aside. "Lucas will see to it that we both live quite comfortably in town."

If Catlin heard that man's name one more time she was going to scream! "I intend to make my own way, Aunt Martha. And had I the funds, I would purchase this ranch myself."

Martha's hazel eyes twinkled with amusement. Catlin had always been full of undaunted spirit, even as a small child. She had never been afraid to take on the world and she was self-confident enough to believe she was as good as any man. Olin Quinn had taught his daughter to manage the affairs that were usually left to men and Cat was too lively and energetic to be satisfied within the restrictions of womanhood. But there was a limit to what even Catlin

49

would undertake.

"To command a ranch this size, you would need a husband and a bunkhouse full of cowboys," Martha declared with a sly smile. "Perhaps you should set your sights on Lucas. He could use a good woman by his side. Both of you together could make this ranch prosper as it once did before the bottom dropped out of the economy and plunged Texas into depression."

The mention of the man's name and all the glowing accolades from Martha set fuse to Catlin's notorious tongue. "I wouldn't marry Lucas whoever-he-is for all the cattle in Texas," she spumed, her face flushing apple red. "He is obviously a swindler and a cheat and you are too tender-hearted to see beneath his wily scheme."

The remark touched off a thought that Martha turned over once or twice in her mind. Lucas and Catlin would be exceptionally good for each other, she assured herself. He had wandered through women like a man thumbing through his wardrobe of shirts and Catlin was well past marrying age. She needed a dynamic, vital man to look after her. . . . To control her rambunctious spirit, Martha quickly amended. Cat was a handful of limitless energy who was chasing rainbows to compensate for the loss of her home, family, and fiancé.

Ah, to be so young and alive again, to possess such an aggressive zest for life! It would be the perfect match, Martha decided as she peered at Catlin's animated features through thick spectacles. Lucas wanted to make a name and place for himself in Texas and Catlin, Martha's only living heir, was chagrined to think the ranch was going to fall into someone else's hands. Catlin considered the land precious and dear. Her father had ingrained that philosophy into her head. And because Olin perished in the war, Catlin saw herself as the extension of his dreams.

What Catlin and Lucas needed was to join forces. Martha smiled wryly to herself as a scheme hatched in her

50

mind. "I'll tell you what, Catlin," she said with a melodramatic sigh that produced just the effect she wanted. "Since you have a better head for business and more experience in these matters, I will place you in charge of making the final stipulations on this financial transaction. Lucas can do business with you. I cannot be objective with him because he has been like the son I never had. Since you don't know Lucas, you can deal with him and I won't risk spoiling my friendship with him."

"I would be happy to assume the task," Catlin enthused.

Now she could save her generous aunt from that land-hungry weasel. Lucas something-or-other would pay exactly what the land was worth or he could rent the vast holdings. But Cat was determined to spare her aunt the agony she had endured when her family plantation was cut in pieces like a juicy steak and fed to the freed slaves contacted by her back-stabbing lawyer.

"That settles that," Martha announced before she gulped down the last swig of brandy. Contemplatively, she stared at the empty bottle. "I must remember to ask Lucas to purchase me another snifter of brandy. I have no desire to allow the good citizens of San Antonio to know their soon-to-be neighbor enjoys a nip of peach brandy before she retires for the night."

Catlin tittered at her jolly, rotund aunt. Martha was a most likable character who craved a nightly sip of the spirits. Yet, Martha intended to protect her reputation. As for herself, Catlin didn't give a hoot if someone saw her purchasing a bottle of brandy.

"I will replenish your supply of peach brandy," Catlin volunteered. "I'll see to the matter when I venture to town to find a job."

Martha's jaw dropped off its hinges. "You don't need to work and I doubt you will be permitted to hobble into the cantina. Decent ladies aren't allowed!"

"We will see about that," Catlin sniffed indignantly.

"The slaves have been granted their freedom and the right to vote. A woman can most certainly march into a saloon to purchase brandy. Women are not second-class citizens either. That was what this war was all about. All men and women were created equal!"

Oddly enough, Martha could envision this sassy blond on her crusade for equality. "Whatever you think best, my dear," Martha snickered good-naturedly. "But if you meet with difficulty from narrow-minded men, I'll fetch Lucas for your reinforcements."

"Lucas will not become my champion," Catlin spumed, unable to control her irritation with the man she didn't know she had already met. "I have long been fighting my own battles and I see no reason to change my policy now."

"Of course, you don't," Martha patronized as she levered her round body from her chair. "But just in case, you just give Lucas a holler and he'll make things right, just as he always does."

While Martha waddled off to prepare the evening meal, Catlin stared at her splinted leg and sulked. Men! What a plague they were to women. Well, maybe Aunt Martha had resigned herself to the fact that she had to depend on those of the male persuasion. But Catlin didn't have to. In fact, she would have been perfectly satisfied if the good Lord could see His way clear to transplant the male of the species on another planet in star worlds far far away. . . .

The vision of glistening black eyes and a roguish grin invaded Catlin's contemplations while she was in the process of consigning all men everywhere to another galaxy. A slow blush worked its way up from the base of her throat and into her cheeks when she recalled the intimate conversation she had with the doctor, when she remembered the warm, explosive kisses they had shared. It wasn't at all like her to take a stranger into her confidence and then allow him to kiss her senseless. Honest to goodness, that blow to her skull must have scrambled her brain!

Doctor or no doctor, Catlin vowed never to let that brown-eyed devil get that close again. He had made it clear that he wouldn't be content with a platonic relationship before he hopped down from the wagon and swaggered away. He had assured Catlin that he couldn't control his ungovernable passions and that he considered her fair game for his misplaced hunting instincts. It would be entirely up to her to ensure that she didn't wind up being another of the numerous notches on his bedpost!

Chapter 4

It was long after dark before Lucas returned from the improvised corral which lay a few miles southwest of the ranch. He was dead tired and his body ached from being jarred by the bucking mustangs that had an aversion to saddles and bridles. Young Jesse Lane had taken a frightful spill just to prove his manhood to the seasoned cowboys who worked on Lewis Ranch. *The soon-to-be Flying Spur Ranch that would be owned and operated by Lucas Murdock*, he amended.

When Lucas had reached Jesse earlier that afternoon, the men had poured a pint of liquor down his throat to ease his pain. After being dragged behind a horse, the boy resembled a skinned jackrabbit. His shirt was in shreds and his ankle had been twisted.

Lucas had set Jesse beneath a shade tree after administering first aid, and climbed on the wild-eyed colt that had torn Jesse to pieces. If Lucas hadn't tackled four more unbroken mounts before calling it a day he might not have had so many kinks in his back and strained muscles in his shoulders and thighs. But he wanted the broncs tamed for the trail and he had a zillion other chores to attend to in the next two weeks. The more snappers he put on the backs of the wild mustangs the sooner this phase of the operation would be completed.

It was rugged work and Lucas never expected more of a man than he was willing to do himself. After straining every muscle in his body he wondered if he was already too old for such rigorous work. Well, he simply would have to adjust to sitting down and getting up more slowly than he had the past few weeks, that's all.

Lucas had half his men breaking broncs and the other half gathering unbranded *cimarrones* from the brush country to add a surplus to his margin of profit. When Lucas returned from the cattle drive to New Mexico and Colorado Territory, he would be able to pay Martha for the ranch and offer Dr. Emmet Blake the full amount of the loan he had been granted to purchase necessary supplies for the trail.

A satisfied sigh escaped Lucas's lips as he eased his aching body into the only chair in his crudely furnished home. Tiredly, he sloshed whiskey into a glass. Lord, he was a far cry from the Southern gentleman who had once lounged in the elaborate dining hall in a spacious Georgia plantation. But Luke had been forced to walk away from the luxury of the past. And although his family plantation remained intact, he couldn't go back, not as long as he still felt this obsessive craving for Elise. Lucas had slammed the door on yesterday for his sake as well as Andrew's. He had acquired a taste for this wild, wide open state of Texas. It fit the man he had become in the past five years. This was where Lucas belonged—away from the sultry brunette who had been his first and only love.

A grimace tightened Lucas's mouth as he shifted uncomfortably on his hard wooden throne. Sure as hell, he would rise from bed the following morning, feeling all of one-hundred-twenty-five years old. When a man chose the profession of riding flighty broncs and herding longhorns, some parts of his body were bound to wake up slower than others. Lucas had learned to doctor wounds and broken bones out of necessity on the trail. Lord knew, he had been forced to administer first aid to himself and his men a hundred times the past few years. He had landed in enough tangled heaps, thanks to skittish horses and rangy cattle. But he always managed to scrape himself off the ground and bind his wounds before pulling onto another half-crazed mustang that had to learn that a man was the master of the horse. Some animals learned slower than others and Lucas had endured his fair share of bone-shattering crashes before the contrary mustangs realized who was boss.

One of these days, when he could sit back and enjoy his prosperity, Lucas vowed to hire a young competent foreman to take these beatings while he soaked his aching muscles and counted his cattle from a distance. But until then, Lucas knew he was destined to match his strength and will against horses and cattle. . . .

A muffled groan tumbled from his lips when he remembered the medication Martha had asked him to pick up while he was meeting himself coming and going from town. Hoisting himself up, Lucas tested the strained muscle in his thigh. Unfortunately, it had become stiff after he had finally had time to sit down. Hobbling onto the stoop, Lucas peered at the golden shaft of light that sprayed from Martha's parlor window. Martha was still puttering about, even at this late hour, Lucas predicted. Clutching the bottle of rheumatism medicine, Lucas ambled up the hill to the ranch house.

When Martha didn't immediately answer the knock, Luke eased open the door to sit the bottle in plain sight. She was probably napping in her rocking chair, he imagined. Martha would never admit it to a living soul, but she was prone to settle back and doze on and off in the evening while she read.

Tonight, however, the good-natured widow was scurrying around upstairs, putting her niece to bed. And if Luke had the faintest idea that Catlin was the "sweet little niece" Martha had mentioned once or twice the past two years, he might have known how the wagon found its way back to the barn. It wasn't one of his men who had rounded up the wagon from the neighbors as Lucas had presumed. In actuality, Albert the stable boy had taken it to the barn, thinking Lucas himself had left it at the house.

A vision of flashing violet eyes and windblown blond hair whizzed through Lucas's mind, putting a faint smile on his lips. That sassy termagant had made quite an impression on him, much to his surprise. Women were women, or at least they had been after he compared them to Elise. But every once in a while, a female came along to pique his interest. It never lasted long when he measured the chits against the tantalizing memories of Elise. But for a time, Luke could shove the tormenting thoughts back into their shallow graves and preoccupy himself with a soft, willing female.

Lucas missed a step on his way up to his own porch when he was assaulted by the sensations evoked by Catlin's inexperienced kisses. That saucy sprite had definite possibilities, he mused with a roguish smile. She had a lot to learn about men—other than hating them on general principle. And Lucas had no qualms about teaching her a thing . . . or three . . . about the sweet hypnotic pleasures of passion.

A slow burn worked its way through his loins. Lord, this was one night he would like to lie down beside something warm and shapely. He was tired, but he wasn't tired enough to deprive himself of the pleasures a woman could give. . . .

The indignant bellow of a calf dragged Lucas from his titillating contemplations. Veering around the side of his modest cottage, Lucas spied the thirteen hundred pound orphan steer that he had saved from certain death three years earlier. The calf's mother had never been able to rise

57

to her feet after birthing. The spindly-legged calf would have perished beside the heifer if Lucas hadn't found the vulnerable creature when he did. Lucas had named the bony calf Spur and had placed him with a milk cow on the ranch where he had worked for a time. For a while, Spur hadn't known if he was a dog, sheep, or calf and he followed Lucas around while he tended his chores, playfully nudging his adopted "mother" and constantly demanding to be fed.

Since Spur had become as tame as a dog and did not possess the herding instinct of most cattle, Lucas had strapped a bell around his neck and Spur had led thousands of cattle up the Goodnight-Loving and the Chisholm Trails. During the drives, when the other cattle bedded down to sleep, Spur ambled into camp to beg handouts from Lucas and the other vaqueros. Since Spur was even-dispositioned and rarely prone to stampede, he was invaluable as the lead steer for the trail drives. At the crack of dawn Spur was on his feet, following Lucas as they trudged the long miles, leading the other cattle to market. And when they reached their destination, the cattle and part of the remuda horses were sold, but Spur and the cowboys came home together.

Some folks might have scoffed at the fact that Lucas's closest friend was a broad, stout longhorn steer with a spread of horns that spanned six feet from tip to tip, but that was about the size of it!

Another annoyed bawl rattled in the darkness and Lucas hurriedly scooped up a bucket of grain. "I'm coming, for God's sake. Give me a minute," he grumbled as Spur stamped around like an impatient customer awaiting the attention of his dawdling waitress who was depriving him of his supper.

Holding true to form, Spur rubbed up against Lucas and eagerly awaited the sound of feed being dumped into his private trough. The moonlight gleamed in Spur's black eyes as he lowered his broad head and flicked out his long sandpaper-like tongue to crunch on his treat.

Affectionately, Lucas scratched the sensitive place behind Spur's ear. "I've been gone from dawn until dark," Lucas explained as if he were conversing with a human. "I'm surprised you didn't stamp up to Martha's porch and beg for a treat from her before I returned."

Spur snorted and then munched loudly on the grain. His wide head elevated to nudge Lucas, prompting him to pour the remainder of the grain in the trough. When Luke complied, Spur switched his tail and lowered his head. Allowing the steer to polish off his treat, Lucas strode over to dip up a pail of water to quench Spur's thirst. Satisfied, Spur went back to grazing the patches of grass that surrounded Lucas's cottage. There was never any need for Lucas to fuss about keeping the vegetation clipped around his doorstep. Spur kept the lawn mowed—except for a few weeds that didn't tantalize his taste buds.

"I met a woman today," Lucas told the grazing steer. "Not the usual kind. This one is made of fire and spirit." Plunking down on the step, Lucas chewed on a twig of grass that Spur had overlooked. "Hell's bells, how can you eat this stuff?" he snorted, tossing the stem of grass aside. "God, what I wouldn't give for a thick juicy steak . . . and a warm, willing woman. . . ."

Spur's wide head lifted to study the silhouette of the man who had folded himself onto the step.

"I wasn't eyeing you as a steak," Lucas chuckled. "Flapjack Barnett served us Pecos Strawberries for supper tonight. But if you ask me, a bean is still a bean, no matter what fancy name you give it."

Spur bellowed as he often did during these one-sided conversations and then casually chewed his cud.

After reaching up to light his cigarillo from the lantern that hung on the porch, Lucas eased back on one elbow. "Her name is Catlin," he rambled on from one topic to another. "I know, it's a strange name but Cat is a strange woman." He stared Spur squarely in the eye. "She hates men. Just my luck I have a craving for a blessed virgin who despises me, not to mention my obsession for another woman who is married to my own brother. And hell's bells, I don't even know where Cat is staying. She could be anywhere within a fifteen mile radius!"

With another grimace, Lucas dragged his feet beneath him and trudged into the cottage. He was too tired to think about that bewitching blond, especially since she wasn't around to satisfy the hunger that still gnawed at him. And Luke resolved not to go searching for that feisty nymph. Wherever she was staying was anybody's guess. But she was definitely off limits. Lucas didn't have the time to get involved just now. And even if he did, he knew his amorous attentions wouldn't be well-received. He had made it a point to inform Cat that he couldn't be content just talking about sex with a woman as desirable as Catlin was. Sooner or later his hunger for her would drive him over the edge and he would yearn to show her what lovemaking was all about. Then Cat would hate him but good!

Of course, she would be cursing him soon enough as it was, he reckoned, breaking into an ornery grin. The instant she returned to Dr. Blake's office for a checkup she would discover that her leg wasn't broken in three places as she had diagnosed. She would know he had played a mischievous prank on her and she would be fit to be tied. Lucas could just hear those tangled curses erupting from her kissable lips like an exploding geyser. No doubt that human keg of blasting powder would come gunning for him if she knew where to find him. Lucas was banking on the fact that Cat probably didn't know the first thing about handling a pistol. If she did, he could expect her to blow him to kingdom come for making a fool of her.

On that thought Lucas peeled off his clothes and

plopped down on his bed. If he didn't get some sleep he would never endure the following day, one that promised to be as exhausting and hectic as all the ones before.

But even as he shoved the thought of snapping amethyst eyes from his mind he found himself envisioning the fiery she-cat who had limped into Dr. Blake's office, looking slightly trampled and completely bent out of shape. His encounter with that firebrand had been the one bright spot in an otherwise tedious day.

The light tap at the door caused Lucas to bolt straight up in bed. Ordinarily he was a light sleeper, but lately it took a bell clanging directly above his head to rouse him from the depths of drowsiness. He was pushing hard, trying to tie up all loose ends before the cattle drive to Colorado.

Rising from bed was an effort. As he predicted, some parts of his body were slower to wake than others. Fumbling, Luke stuffed his sore leg in his breeches and limped across the room to see Martha's cherubic face amid the first scant rays of dawn.

"I knew you would be up and gone for the entire day, so I prepared you a hearty breakfast," Martha declared as she waddled inside to set her offering on the crudely constructed table. Her eyes darted to the unsightly scars that marred Lucas's massive chest. She never meant to stare at them when Lucas was without a shirt, but inevitably her eyes were drawn to the crisscrossed scars left by butchering Yankees. She couldn't begin to imagine the pain Luke must have suffered when he was tortured within an inch of his life.

Seeing where Martha's eyes had strayed, Lucas ambled back to his bedroom to don a shirt. Even though Elise had given him back his pride and self-respect after he had been cut to bits, he was still a mite self-conscious of his scars.

61

Elise assured him that he was still every bit the man he had always been and that women would still be attracted to him. But after the incident, it had been almost two years before he had dared to make love to a woman in broad daylight, afraid she would be offended by the marks on his chest and back. Time had diminished those self-conscious feelings, but Lucas was always careful not to display his marred flesh in front of women unless absolutely necessary.

The smell of coffee, eggs, bacon, and biscuits lured Lucas back to the kitchen. He sighed contentedly at the heaping plate Martha had uncovered. "You're a saint," he complimented, easing his sore body into the chair. "You always seem to know what I need before I think of it myself."

A sly twinkle flickered in her hazel eyes. "It's a gift," she teased as she peered fondly at the ruffle-haired giant who had folded himself into his one and only chair with more caution than usual.

Martha knew exactly what a bachelor like Lucas Murdock needed and she was scheming to see that he got it. Of course, she wouldn't be so obvious as to alert Lucas's preservation instincts by blurting out that her sweet little niece had come to Texas. Lucas would find that out at just the right moment—over dinner.

"How about if I prepare you a nice supper tonight. You've been working much too hard lately," she baited.

Lucas swallowed a mouthful of eggs and gave his raven head a negative shake. "As much as I appreciate the invitation, I've got two days' work to squeeze into today. You'd have to serve me supper at midnight, maybe even later."

"Tomorrow then?" Martha questioned expectantly.

"We'll be gathering another bunch of *cimarrones* tomorrow. After riding the brush all day, I doubt I can crawl to a table, much less show up at a reasonable hour,"

Lucas said with a tired yawn.

"Then the day after tomorrow," she suggested enthusiastically. "Flapjack Barnett may fill your belly with food while you're on roundup and trail drives, but he can't hold a fork to my cooking, even if I do say so myself. He attaches fancy names to his bland food, but it doesn't make it taste any better. 'Overland Trout,'" Martha's face skewed up distastefully. "It's nothing but glorified bacon fried in its rancid grease and if you didn't have an iron-lined stomach he would have killed you with his cooking by now."

"Angus Barnett does the best he can, considering the inconvenience of camp cooking," Lucas replied with an easy smile. "He still makes a mean pot of Sonofabitch stew. And it tastes much better if you don't ask what he throws in it."

"An appropriate name it is, too!" Martha smirked. "If you knew what was in that stew it would definitely make you sick." Her gaze shifted to those chocolate brown pools that could stir a woman, even at Martha's age. "I will expect you for supper at six o'clock, day after tomorrow. We'll have juicy steak, mashed potatoes and apple pie."

Lucas licked his lips in anticipation. "I'll be there."

"Good. We need to finalize the arrangements for the sale of the ranch. And I wouldn't think of moving to town until I treated you to one last homecooked meal. You've been a Godsend to me, Lucas."

Lucas folded his hand around hers, giving it an affectionate squeeze. "I have one favor to ask of you. Will you feed Spur tonight? I may stay in camp with the rest of the vaqueros."

"Done," Martha promised as she waddled toward the door. "And thank you for fetching my rheumatism medicine and . . ." Sheepishly she glanced over her shoulder. "The next time you're in town, would you mind replenishing my stock of brandy? It seems to have run dry again."

A teasing smile dangled from his lips as he laid a brawny arm over the back of his chair and shot forth a glance. "We've been tipping the bottle a wee bit more often lately, have we?"

Martha wasn't about to let the "Cat" out of the bag by confessing her sweet little niece had helped polish off the last dribble of peach brandy the previous night. "Rheumatism medicine," she declared, massaging her elbow. "Since I was out of the regular medication, the brandy had to suffice."

"I'll ensure that Albert supplies you with brandy and medication while I'm on the drive," he promised.

With a nod of gratitude, she hustled out the door and scuttled back up the hill to the ranch house to prepare Catlin's breakfast. Her merry chuckle drifted off in the breeze as she plotted the first meeting between the handsome Lucas Murdock and her sweet little niece.

After Lucas gobbled down the last bite of breakfast he pried himself out of his chair and ambled outside to wash his face in the rain barrel. But his brain was still full of cobwebs and some parts of his body still hadn't awakened properly. Scooping up the pail of water, Lucas dumped it over his head and then shivered as streams trickled inside his shirt. That should rouse the slow moving parts of his body, he reckoned.

While Lucas was shrugging on his leather vest and chaps, Catlin was being greeted by breakfast in bed. Unaware the sassy blond was right under his nose, Lucas strode to the barn to saddle his favorite cutting horse. The buckskin gelding knew his way around the brush country as well as Lucas did. Old Bill could turn and twist and out-guess the flighty *cimarrones* because of his years of experience. It took a special caliber of horse to ride the brush without leaving himself and his rider in a broken heap. Old Bill could tear holes in the thickets, drag a lassoed steer behind him and bring along enough broken mesquite limbs in his saddle to build a campfire. And when Bill shied away from a dense thicket, Lucas didn't push the steed to barrel into it. Bill was notorious for smelling trouble before a man could see it. The last time Bill had wheeled away from the gnarled underbrush, a seven-foot long rattlesnake had slithered out in front of a furious *cimarrone* bull and Lucas had kindly thanked Old Bill for sparing them both from disaster.

If all went well, Lucas would have a sizable herd of *cimarrones* gathered by the end of the following day. And if things didn't go well, Old Bill would have to see to bringing Lucas home and dumping him on the front step. That was, if Lucas was still in one piece. There had been times, when riding the brush, that he had been left to nurse his many scratches and bruises. Lucas had limped home with bandages plastered to his broken ribs and sprained ankles. But most generally, Old Bill paused at the porch after an exhausting day and Lucas managed to hobble inside on his own accord.

Resigning himself to a hard day's work, Lucas trotted Old Bill down the path, sparing the shapely blond he had met the previous day only a quick thought. But before the week was out Catlin was destined to be foremost in his mind. . . .

Chapter 5

Although Catlin was nursing a vague headache and a throbbing leg, she wormed into her clothes, determined to find a job to support herself. Under protest, Catlin hobbled downstairs while Martha summoned Albert to fetch the buggy. While Martha went back to packing the extra bed linen and dishes she could do without in the next two weeks, Catlin struggled out onto the porch.

A curious frown knitted her brow when she noticed the wagon she had employed the previous day was nowhere in sight. Apparently the seductive doctor had returned late in the night to fetch his mode of transportation. It was just as well that he hadn't made his presence known, Catlin thought as she struggled into the carriage. The encounter with the raven-haired rake had been unsettling. Try as she may, Cat couldn't squelch the vision of laughing brown eyes and a lopsided smile set in a craggy face. For a woman who had sworn to hate all men forever, Catlin was certainly entertaining one too many thoughts of that charismatic doctor!

Determined to dismiss the tantalizing memories, Catlin reflected on her conversation with Aunt Martha and her incessant references to Lucas—God Almighty—Murdock. Now there was a man Cat could sink her teeth into and hate, sight unseen! That sneaky sidewinder. How dare he try to swindle a tender-hearted widow out of her fortune. If Lucas wanted the Lewis Ranch he was going to pay its full value. Cat resolved, then and there, to draw up a contract for negotiation. A simple handshake and verbal contract would not suffice, even if Aunt Martha was sure it would. Lucas Murdock could scrawl his signature on the written contract and Cat would ensure that he upheld his end of the bargain. He wasn't going to weasel out of paying Martha every penny he owed her. Lucas Murdock, indeed! He would not and could not walk all over Catlin Stewart Quinn.

By the time Catlin reached San Antonio, she was quite comfortable hating Lucas Murdock. In her estimation, he was deserving of her disdain. Any man who would prey on a dear sweet woman like Martha Lewis was beneath contempt.

Concentrating on her purpose, Catlin tabled all thoughts of Lucas and halted the buggy in front of the newspaper office. Although she felt qualified to apply as a teacher in the community, she didn't relish the idea of hobbling around a classroom with a bum leg. Her talent with the written word might earn her a position with the newspaper, or at least she hoped it would. And Catlin could certainly give a first-hand account of the Reconstruction Era in the South!

Pasting on her most charming smile, Catlin limped inside the office to confront the bald-headed man who vigorously chewed on his unlit cigarillo. After rattling off a resumé of her education, qualifications, and her dire need to support herself, Catlin was asked to produce a sample of her news reporting ability. After reading the information about the stagecoach holdup the editor had acquired the previous afternoon, Catlin gathered her thoughts and jotted down her report of the incident on paper. When she was wielding a pen she was confident of her abilities and Jacob Ross's eyebrows shot up to an astonished angle when he read the precise, gripping account of the robbery.

"This is quite good, Miss Quinn," Jacob complimented her.

"It should be," she insisted with an elfish smile. "I was the woman on board that particular stage who lost all the money she had in the world. That is yet another reason why I'm anxious to have this job. And being a part of this newspaper would be a rewarding challenge."

Jacob thought for a moment then nodded. "And you shall have your finger on the pulse of this community. Perhaps new blood is just what this newspaper needs."

After Jacob introduced Catlin to his assistant, he acquainted her with the workings of the newspaper and showed her how to set the press. Catlin was the epitome of rapt attention, asking questions and listening carefully to the answers. She was one of those individuals who wasn't satisfied with doing anything halfway. Catlin put her heart and soul into each endeavor and she was determined to do more than simply fulfill Jacob's expectations. With her interest in the struggling economy and the upheaval in politics, Catlin vowed to keep the citizens of San Antonio abreast of what was transpiring in all parts of the nation.

Clinging to that noble thought, Catlin maneuvered into her chair to write the second article Jacob requested. When the report was completed, Jacob walked away with a broad smile on his face. The young lady had a knack for colorful yet succinct reporting; he had himself one hell of an assistant!

While Catlin was organizing another article for the upcoming issue of the paper, Lucas was whipping his lariat around his head. His intense gaze was focused on the heifer that was zigzagging through the sharp spines of brasada, chapparal, and mesquite. Lucas found the challenge of the hunt and capture stronger than any serum ever invented. With his senses tuned to his task, Lucas clutched the pommel of the saddle when Old Bill grabbed the bit between his teeth and cut a ninety-degree angle to get the drop on the calf that thundered ahead of him.

The trick of riding hellbent in the bush country was to shift from side to side on the horse's shoulder, moving as one with him as he cut through the dense thicket. Lucas was good at working efficiently with his mount. As Bill gobbled up the distance between him and the calf, Lucas leaned down, casting his loop from under the low-hanging branches of mesquite.

The creak of leather and the thud of hooves were the only sounds to penetrate Lucas's single-minded thoughts. When the moment was ripe, Lucas swung his lasso and ducked beneath another snaring branch. When the loop tightened around the heifer's neck, she let out a bellow to alert the other *cimarrones* of danger. Kicking and bawling, the wild-eyed heifer was dragged from the brush to find Bo Huxley waiting to hobble her hind legs.

"I always did say the two things that made a good brush roper was a reckless fool and a race horse," Bo commented as he knotted the tie rope.

Lucas chuckled at the teasing jibe as he and Bo towered over the floundering heifer, forcing her to tolerate a human's presence.

Wiping the blood from the numerous scratches on his face, Lucas expelled a deep breath and scanned the clearing where scores of cattle lay tied and resting on their sides. By the time the *cimarrones* were allowed to stand on their feet they would be too sluggish to stampede back to the thickets.

Bo spit an arc of tobacco juice and then mopped his perspiring brow. His gaze pensively worked its way over the lean muscular cowboy he had come to call friend the past four years. Bo had taught Lucas about survival in the Southwest and offered valuable information about its inhabitants—both the two-legged and four-legged kind. He and Lucas had lived among the elements, battled storms, cattle stampedes, and had warded off raiding Comanches at least a dozen times. Bo had allowed Luke to learn the hard way to ride like a bonafide "snapper." The procedure had been a lesson Luke had never forgotten—getting thrown from a crazed bronc, chasing the contrary animal down and climbing back on again.

In the beginning, Bo had singled out the toughest, most ill-tempered horses in the *caviada*, just to see if this green horn could stay on or give up. Lucas had given out long before he gave up. Once, he had been bucked from a mean bronc and his foot hung in the stirrup. Instinctively, Lucas had turned onto his belly, bounced his chin on the ground a couple of times, and his foot finally slipped free. He had wound up with that moon-shaped scar on his chin that had bled all over his shirt, but he had scraped himself off the ground and taught that contrary mustang who was master. It was that fierce determination in Lucas that had earned him Bo's respect. Nowadays, Bo would do most anything for Lucas because of his admiration for the younger man.

A fond smile grazed Bo's lips as he shrugged off the sentimental thoughts and focused on the floundering calf that was bawling her head off. "By this time tomorrow you'll have a huge herd to put on the trail." Absently, Bo massaged his aching back. "Damn, I'm getting too old for this nonsense."

The cowboy had been saying that for years.

"And if you retire I'm in serious trouble," Lucas commented with a smile. "You've taught me practically everything I know but I still have a lot to learn. You can't quit yet."

Bo chuckled at the compliment. "You passed me by two years ago," he drawled. "That's why you're doing the roping and I'm doing the hog-tying." Silver gray eyes swung to Lucas's scratched face. "Who was that little lady you were courting yesterday when I interrupted you? Anybody I should know?"

Lucas cast Bo a fleeting glance and then stared off into the distance, unsure he wanted to discuss Cat with anyone but Spur. Finally his gaze drifted back to study the stout cowboy who was anxiously awaiting a reply.

Bo was fortyish and looked a decade older. His face was leathery and weather-beaten by the relentless sun and wind that hammered across West Texas. There was a wide gap between his two front teeth and his nose had been broken so many times it had a permanent crook in it. Wrinkles cut across his forehead like wagon wheel ruts in the virgin prairie. Reddish brown hair and whiskers hugged his ruddy face. Bo was stooped, but he was strong as an ox. He had been shot up, shot down, thrown from one too many unruly horses and trampled on. But he was still as agile as a cat in the saddle and dependable in tense situations.

This tough cowboy was the product of years of hard living and death-defying challenges. He had endured his share of sinful flings with women, horses, whiskey and cards. But he was also the most seasoned, trailwise cowboy Lucas had ever known. He was a hell-busting, independent man who was too stubborn and set in his ways to think about leaving the lonesome cattle country and this grueling profession, even if he did threaten to retire once or twice every day. Bo was irreplaceable and Lucas counted on his expertise, knowledge, and friendship. In Lucas's estimation, Bo had only one flaw: the old buzzard was an incredible snoop when it came to Lucas's love life. He was forever trying to instruct Lucas on how to handle women, even though he wasn't too good at it himself.

"The lady is as pure as a mountain stream and she intends to stay that way," Luke declared as he plucked the thorns from his leather vest. "You're far too experienced for a full-fledged lady, spirited and feisty though she is."

"Look who's talking," Bo hooted, flashing Luke an ornery grin. "If she's so innocent, how come I saw you kissing the breath out of her? Looked serious to me."

"Your vision is better than I thought," Lucas muttered as he ambled over to mount the buckskin gelding.

"Do I hear wedding bells, Doc?" he teased unmercifully.

"If you do, it's because the sun fried your brain and you're hallucinating."

"I think it's about time you settled down with one woman," Bo advised. "From what I saw yesterday, you couldn't do better than that pretty little filly."

"Mind your own business," Lucas grumbled before he thundered off to locate another *cimarrone* to add to his private herd.

"What's so blasted funny?" Jesse Lane wanted to know as he limped up beside the seasoned cowboy who was still snickering to himself.

"What the hell are you doing on your feet, boy?" Bo demanded, casting Jesse the evil eye. "You will be no help at all on the drive if you don't give that ankle a rest. Doc gave you the day off."

"I can't sit around like a useless old woman," Jesse mumbled. "I can't run or ride very well, but I can still tie a calf in knots."

"I thought you learned your lesson yesterday, junior," Bo growled. "You don't have to prove anything to the rest of us. You'll be worth your salt when you get some experience under your belt. And you won't get it if you're limping around all the damned time." His muscled arm indicated the shade cast by the chuckwagon. "Go park yourself on a soft spot and let Flapjack Barnett bend your ear. He cooks better while he's jabbering."

Sulking, Jesse limped off to do as he was told and Bo chomped on his tobacco until Lucas came dragging another bawling *cimarrone* from the underbrush. To Lucas's chagrin, Bo was ready and waiting to offer more advice on women. It proved to be an even longer day than Luke had anticipated!

A tired sigh escaped Catlin's lips as she drove the buggy past Market Plaza after another full day at the newspaper office. It had been four days since she had seen the handsome doctor who had annoyed her to no end and kissed her blind twice. Catlin wasn't sure what prompted her to halt the carriage outside the doctor's office. She rationalized by assuring herself she needed to check on her broken leg, but that was only an excuse and she knew it. Perhaps she just wanted to retest her reaction to the man whose memory kept popping into her mind at the most unexpected moments.

Struggling from the buggy, Catlin hobbled into the wood-framed building to find a young woman rearranging the supplies in the medicine cabinet that sat in the corner of the outer office. Ginger Hanley offered a faint smile as her sad green eyes drifted to Catlin's stiff leg. A curious frown clouded Catlin's brow, wondering at the hint of unhappiness she detected in the woman's wide expressive eyes.

"Is there something we can do for you?" Ginger questioned politely.

"My name is Catlin Quinn and I would like for the doctor to take another look at my leg to ensure that it is mending properly," she announced.

Ginger blinked. "You're the woman who defied the desperados during the holdup, aren't you? I read your article in the paper."

After Catlin nodded affirmatively, Ginger excused

herself to enter the examination room. When she returned to usher the patient inside, Cat very nearly tripped over her stiff leg. Before Catlin stood a tall, thin man whose light blue eyes flooded over her from behind wire-rimmed glasses. He looked to be a few inches shorter than the handsome physician she had met four days earlier and at least ten years older.

With Ginger's assistance, Catlin eased onto the table. In a way, she was thankful the other doctor who rattled her so wasn't around. Catlin felt like a fool for seeking him out under the pretense of checking on her leg in the first place.

"You have certainly made a name for yourself, Catlin," Dr. Blake declared as he lifted her skirt to examine her leg. "Who set this for you?"

"The other physician who works in your office," she replied as practiced hands gently glided over her leg, removing the bandages.

Emmet's thick brows formed a single line over his forehead. "There is no other physician working with me, only Ginger—my receptionist and assistant. Doc Winston has an office on the other side of the Plaza. Perhaps he was the one you saw."

Catlin felt as if she had been hit in the midsection. She was so startled by the announcement that she merely sat there, stunned, while Emmet removed her splint. For several humiliating moments, Catlin tried to make sense of her encounter with the handsome rake. True, she had been clobbered on the head, but this was the office she had limped into when she climbed from the stage. She would swear to it!

Emmet Blake frowned bemusedly as he examined Catlin's leg and inflamed knee. "There is no fracture here," he informed her. "You had a severe sprain which immobility has probably aided these past few days. But the swelling has gone down and there is no need for a splint. A supporting bandage would suffice just as well."

Catlin silently fumed. That mischievous quack! The varmit she had encountered her first day in San Antonio had played a prank on her, damn his ornery soul! For four days she had maneuvered her stiff leg, enduring one inconvenience after another and all for nothing!

Dr. Blake carefully wrapped her knee, assuring her that she could remove the supporting bandage in a few days. Catlin sat quietly on the table, conjuring up a dozen methods of torture to practice on that wily devil when she finally got her hands on him. After the physician completed his task, Ginger assisted Catlin to her feet and followed her to the outer office.

"I'm afraid I have yet to receive my first paycheck from the newspaper office," Catlin explained.

Ginger offered a sympathetic smile. "Dr. Blake will wait until you can pay him. In fact, he is gracious about such things. He gave me this job as his assistant to help me pay for the medication my father needs to survive. If not for his generosity, my father wouldn't be alive today."

Again Catlin detected that sadness in Ginger's eyes, but she had no clue what caused it. Perhaps it was the torment of living with her ailing father.

Once outside, Catlin heaved an exasperated sigh. She had wanted to give a description of the quack who had splinted her leg, but she had been too embarrassed to admit she had been played for a fool. It infuriated her to think that ornery devil was wandering around somewhere, having a hearty laugh at her expense. Catlin had never been so humiliated in all her life. That rascal made her look like a ninny and Dr. Blake probably thought she was an idiot because she didn't know who had treated her for a broken leg.

Although Catlin was furious when she clambered into the buggy, she was trembling with outrage by the time she reached the ranch. She was baffled by the fact that two men had referred to that handsome varmit as "Doc." What the blazes was he anyway? A horse doctor? And if he was, why hadn't he said so in the first place? And what was he doing in Dr. Blake's office? Honest to goodness, this made no sense at all!

Catlin expelled a harsh growl as she eased from her carriage. She didn't have the foggiest notion who or where that charlatan was, but when she caught up with him . . .

"You're late," Martha grumbled as she buzzed around the dining room, setting plates and silverware as if she were dealing cards. "Lucas is coming for supper and he should be here any minute." She spared Cat a hasty glance, unaware that her niece was harboring a spiteful vengeance. "You had best freshen up and change before our guest arrives. And bring along that contract you drew up for the sale of the ranch. And don't forget . . ."

Martha rattled off several other commands, but Catlin wasn't listening. She was too rankled by her encounter with the certified physician to pay attention. Lucas something-or-other had chosen a poor time to invite himself to dinner, Catlin mused as she stamped up the steps, favoring her tender knee. Every step she took reminded her of her humiliation caused by that ornery quack. Catlin was spoiling for a fight and Lucas what's-his-name would soon be in the direct line of fire. She had a few bones to pick with that man, too!

Damn men everywhere, she fumed. That raven-haired rascal had confirmed her suspicions about the male of the species and Lucas whoever-he-was was probably another shining example of the worthless male gender!

Hurriedly, Catlin shucked her clothes and her bandage and sank down into the bath Martha had drawn for her. It was the first relaxing bath she had enjoyed since she had arrived. The others had been spoiled by the inconvenience of leaving her right leg stretched over the rim of the tub. And that was that wily scoundrel's fault, too!

Catlin scrubbed herself with such vigor she nearly

rubbed off her hide. The bath helped to ease her frustration, but not a lot. She was still muttering spiteful curses while she dried herself and squirmed into a fresh set of clothes.

Blast it, that devil deserved to be stabbed, poisoned and hanged for impersonating a doctor and for mortifying her the way he had. No doubt she would be writing her newspaper articles from jail after she murdered that ornery varmint. Catlin paused to consider how many women had been hanged for their crimes in Texas. With her luck, she would be the first. But it didn't matter. She would be doing the world a favor when she disposed of that brown-eyed viper who had passed himself off as a doctor in order to make a laughingstock of her!

The moment Martha heard the quiet rap at the door, she whizzed into the hall. Running a quick hand through her gray hair, she opened the portal to see Lucas towering above her, looking freshly scrubbed and as handsome as ever—despite the telltale scratches caused from high-speed chases through the chapparal and mesquite.

"If I were thirty years younger . . ." Martha sighed wistfully.

Lucas flashed the jolly older woman a roguish grin. "If you were thirty years younger I'd find myself at a banquet with a dozen other men," he speculated. "Matthew probably had to defend you like a dragon to prevent other beaux from stealing you away from him."

"I was pleasing to the eye in my day," Martha said proudly.

"You still are," Lucas declared as he bent to press an affectionate kiss to her rosy cheek.

"Flatterer," Martha smirked. "One look in the mirror assures me that I'm as plump as a baking hen."

Her arm slid around Lucas's waist to usher him inside.

77

"How is the roundup coming along?" she questioned curiously. "If the scratches on your cheeks are any indication, you've delivered a good sized herd from the brush country."

Lucas set his hat aside and extracted a bottle of peach brandy from his coat pocket. "We've gathered eight hundred head," he informed her as he offered Martha her brandy.

"How in heaven's name did you find time to fetch this?" she chirped, staring at the bottle.

"One of my men sprained his ankle during the roundup. He wasn't much help in gathering *cimarrones* so I sent him into town," he explained. A puzzled frown creased his brow when he glanced around the corner to see the extra place setting in the dining room. "Are you expecting another guest? I thought I was going to get you all to myself tonight."

Martha cursed Lucas's keen gaze. The man was always aware of everything that went on around him. Even while he appeared detached, his perceptive brown eyes missed nothing. Confound it, she had wanted Catlin's appearance to be a complete surprise, the unexpected kind that would sweep this handsome bachelor off his feet. Her lovely niece was to have made her regal entrance and Lucas was to have fallen in love at first sight. Well, he still didn't know who was coming to dinner, Martha consoled herself. Catlin's arrival would still make an impression on Lucas.

"Let's drink a toast to your purchase of the ranch and my new home in San Antonio," she enthused, purposely ignoring Lucas's question. "I've been three days without my nip of brandy. This seems to be the perfect time to enjoy it."

As Lucas was led away, his gaze darted back to the dining room table that was lit with candles. "You aren't trying to fix me up with another of your friend's eligible daughters, are you?" he wanted to know. "Isn't it enough that Dr. Blake has been pushing Ginger Hanley at me every chance he gets? *Et tu, Brute?*"

Martha waved him to silence. "You are much too suspicious," she fussed, pouring them both a drink. "And speaking of Ginger, are you still planning to escort her to my house-warming party next week?"

As much as Martha liked Dr. Blake's pretty assistant, she would prefer to see Cat dancing in Lucas's arms at the party. Ginger was a wonderful girl who had been forced to take on the lion's share of responsibility since her father's illness. Robert Hanley had worked for the Lewis Ranch several years ago, but consumption had finally made it impossible for him to hold down a job.

Martha regretted Robert's loss of health and she always stopped to check on him on her way to town, bearing gifts and needed supplies. At first Robert had been too proud to accept charity, but money was scarce and he had been forced to swallow his pride. Being an invalid, he had no choice but to allow Ginger to support him and to supply the medication that barely kept him alive. And as loving as Ginger had been to her father, Martha couldn't quite envision Ginger and Lucas together. She simply wasn't woman enough for him.

Catlin and Lucas were both driven by strong inner forces, and they were vital, dynamic individuals. As badly as Ginger needed a husband to help her bear her burdens, Lucas wasn't the right man, in Martha's opinion. And for the life of her, Martha couldn't imagine why Emmet Blake was trying to make a match of his lovely assistant and this brawny cowboy. He knew as well as she did that the couple was mismatched.

Lucas nodded affirmatively to Martha's prying question. "The truth is Dr. Blake asked Ginger in my behalf and then informed me later. Since I borrowed money from him to put this drive on the trail, he has taken advantage by requesting favors. One of them was to ensure that

Ginger thoroughly enjoyed herself at your house-warming party. He'd have me married to Ginger in a minute if he thought he could drag me to the altar." His twinkling brown eyes drifted to Martha, studying her pensive frown. "It seems my friends and acquaintances are more concerned about marrying me off than I am."

"You should be more concerned," Martha scolded him between sips of brandy. "A handsome man like yourself needs a good wife. You don't need to be pussyfooting from one woman to another."

"I thought I had been invited to dinner, not a lecture," Lucas chuckled.

"A little of both wouldn't hurt you," she declared with great conviction. "When you take possession of this ranch you'll have Flapjack Barnett doing your cooking for you and you'll shrivel up from malnutrition after eating a solid diet of those boiled beans which he insists on calling Pecos Strawberries."

A deep skirl of laughter echoed in his chest as he scrutinized Martha's disdainful frown. "I've managed well enough for the past thirty-one years by myself. I'm not sure I'm the marrying kind." Gracefully, he unfolded himself from the sofa and ambled across the room. "I've been fantasizing about steak for three days. Why don't we start without this mysterious but late guest of yours. . . ."

His voice trailed off into oblivion when he rounded the corner to see none other than Catlin Quinn scurrying down the steps, favoring her right leg—one that no longer was splinted.

"Hell's bells, of all the rotten luck . . ." Lucas grumbled. He had the inescapable feeling this wasn't going to be a calm, relaxed evening. He was right!

Chapter 6

Catlin glanced up when she heard the rich baritone voice mumbling below her in the hall. Her astonished gaze landed on the tall, muscular man who was garbed in a tan chambray shirt and black breeches that fit his masculine physique like a second set of skin. Her surprise transformed into blind fury within a heartbeat. Her fingers clenched as she started toward him like a charging rhinoceros, itching to tear that scoundrel limb from limb. But in her haste to satisfy her vengeance, Catlin tromped on the hem of her skirt. A shocked squawk broke from her lips when she lost her footing and teetered precariously on the step.

Like streaked lightning, Lucas was beside her in a flash, offering a supporting arm. It was at that exact moment when Martha waddled into the hall to determine what had provoked Catlin's loud yelp. To Martha's pleasure and relief, Lucas scooped Cat into his strong arms and set her to her feet at the bottom of the staircase.

"Catlin, this is the man I have been telling you about— Lucas Murdock," she introduced while Cat turned seven shades of fuming red. "And Lucas this is my sweet little niece from Louisiana who has come to live with me."

Sweet little niece? Lucas silently scoffed. Cat looked like

a one-woman war party and she wanted his scalp!

For a moment Lucas and Catlin stared at each other as if they each had brussel sprouts growing out their ears. But Lucas was the first to recover from astonishment. Wearing an ornery grin that infuriated Catlin to no end, he retreated a step, struck a dignified pose and then dropped into an exaggerated bow.

"It is a pleasure to make your acquaintance, Catlin," he purred in that low sexy voice that could send goose bumps ricocheting down a woman's spine. If Martha hadn't been standing there, Lucas was certain that Cat would have bitten a few chunks out of his hide and clawed out his eyes. She looked that furious!

And indeed she was. Catlin had spent the past few hours working up a murderous hatred for the man who had purposely made her the brunt of his prank. If not for Martha, Catlin would have been flying fur and bared claws. It was next to impossible to restrain herself when she was harboring spiteful methods of torturing this varmint.

In silent amusement, Lucas watched the curvaceous blond in elegant pink satin fight down the flaming blushes that scorched her cheeks. She was angry alright. Absolutely furious was nearer the mark, Lucas amended. If looks could kill he would have been drawn, quartered and roasted over the fiery pits of hell. Catlin's violet eyes were spitting flames that could have burned him to a crisp if he hadn't deflected her glower with a beaming smile.

"Dear me," Martha gasped. "I just noticed you were without your splint, Catlin. I thought you said your leg was broken."

Catlin punished Lucas with another glare that was meant to maim and mutilate. Then she mustered a smile to present to her aunt. "It seems the physician's first diagnosis was wrong. Actually, I'm only suffering a sprained knee. Doctor Blake removed the splint and told me to tread lightly for a few more days."

"Well, it's a good thing Lucas caught you before you stumbled down the steps," Martha breathed. "You might have wound up with more than a wrenched knee." Hurriedly, she scurried toward the kitchen to fetch the steaks, strategically leaving the couple alone for a few minutes.

"I'm going to wring your neck the first chance I get," Catlin spluttered into Lucas's grinning face.

Without preamble, Luke's sensuous lips swooped down on hers, stealing her breath and the protest she most certainly would have voiced. Although Lucas had been tremendously busy the past few days, the image of this amethyst-eyed spitfire had come uninvited into his thoughts. Being perfectly honest with himself (and he usually was) Lucas knew it was a waste of time to dwell on his first encounter with this bewitching minx. He had too much to do and not nearly enough time in which to do it. Therefore, fantasizing about Cat was a waste of precious time. She had taken up permanent residence in his mind whether he wanted her there or not. She had touched a part of him, filled part of the emptiness left by Elise's tormenting memory. But whether this relationship was going anywhere or not, Lucas was overwhelmed by the urge to take Catlin's honeyed lips under his the first chance he got. And so he did. . . .

His brain broke down when a flood of tantalizing sensations rippled through him. The sweet fragrance of jasmine fogged his senses and his arm involuntarily stole around the trim indentation of her waist, molding her rigid body familiarly against his. He was instantly intoxicated by the taste of her. The days he had gone without a woman had taken their toll. His male body instinctively responded and he deepened the kiss to ravish her mouth like a starving man devouring a long-awaited feast.

Catlin desperately needed air! The lack of oxygen in her brain left her suspended and without the ability to formulate a single thought. She was unaccustomed to these internal explosions when she found herself wrapped in a man's arms. But with Lucas it was as if she were sitting on a short fuse and his flaming kiss caused spontaneous combustion. Shock waves of unwanted pleasure undulated through her naive body, rising from deep inside her and splintering through every nerve ending.

It was impossible to explain why a man she detested could cause her to melt into a puddle of forbidden desire. When he enfolded her in those sinewy arms and absorbed her body into his, her will suddenly became his own. It was phenomenal what he could do to her. It rattled Catlin to realize how little control she had over her passions when Lucas aroused them.

Honest to goodness! One would have thought she had been a harlot in another lifetime and this demon had been her lover. Never in twenty-two years had Catlin felt the earth move beneath her feet when she was kissed. But it was moving!

The scent of the man and his musky cologne invaded her nostrils and fogged her brain. Each place his body touched left his searing imprint on her skin. Cat was a branded woman. For crying out loud, she had been branded by a man who represented everything she disliked. This was Lucas Murdock, the rapscallion who was trying to sell Aunt Martha short, the viper who had made a fool of her, and then laughed behind her back. Had she no pride? How could she stand here kissing this devil as if he were her long lost lover when she didn't even like the man? Lord, that blow to her skull really had addled her brain. She was a dizzy hypocrite, that's what she was!

Although Lucas knew Catlin was furious with him and would be even more so when he let her loose, it didn't matter just then. He was hopelessly lost to the wild tremors that riveted through his body. Kissing this sprite was as natural to him as breathing. She desperately needed to be kissed and he definitely needed to be the one to do it.

"Yoo-hoo! Dinner is on the table," Martha called.

A devilish smile pursed Martha's lips as she set the heaping bowl of potatoes beside Lucas's plate. Her attempt at matchmaking was working out splendidly. The fact that Catlin and Lucas weren't already seated at the table, awkwardly glancing in every direction except at each other was a good indication they were taken with each other. They had obviously struck up a private conversation in the foyer. Things were going superbly!

After Lucas took his Texas time about kissing Catlin blind, he withdrew to drag in a steadying breath. "I always did claim it was best to take dessert before supper."

"I hope you've been poisoned," Catlin muttered as she flounced toward the dining room. "I have never met a more rude, spiteful, inconsiderate, ornery man in all my life!"

Lucas's perceptive gaze wandered over Catlin's rigid back and the delicious curve of her hips. "And I've never met a woman who arouses me as quickly as you do. I would kiss you all over again if Martha wasn't waiting dinner."

His compliment and the seductive threat were not well-received. Catlin not only didn't want to be kissed again, but she didn't even want to discuss it! Lucas Murdock rattled her and he was virtually impossible to control. He was impulsive and forthright and passionate and Catlin couldn't handle that brawny giant. He was like a runaway locomotive—an unstoppable force that plowed through every barrier of her defenses.

Without Lucas's assistance, Catlin plunked down in the chair across from her aunt. She wasn't sure which position at the table would discomfort her the most—sitting beside that infuriating rake or across from him. Not having him there at all would have been best!

"Your niece is lovely," Lucas murmured as he agilely dropped into the chair beside Catlin. Purposely, his arm brushed against her shoulder, certain it would annoy her. It did.

Martha fairly beamed. "That she is, Lucas, and she is also a very assertive young woman. Of all the people on the stage that was robbed, Catlin was the only individual with enough gumption to stand up to the desperados."

One thick brow elevated acutely as he glanced at Catlin who had compressed her lips so tightly they looked as if they might split under the pressure. "Did she now?" His marveling tone was warped with sarcasm.

"She most certainly did," Martha affirmed. "According to the reports I've heard from the townspeople, the sheriff was astounded by her bravura. The incident left her with a sprained knee and a goose egg on her head, but she has already made a name for herself in San Antonio. Why, I wouldn't be surprised if Catlin has a string of suitors lined up to dance with her at my house-warming party."

"Nor would I," Lucas concurred in a glib tone. His lean fingers folded around the heaping bowl of potatoes upon which he feasted his hungry eyes.

"And my ambitious niece didn't tarry a moment before journeying into town to find herself a job so she could compensate for the loss of her stolen money," Martha boasted. "Jacob Ross hired her the instant he saw a sample of her writing."

"All this beauty and talent, too," Lucas proclaimed. His voice lacked sincerity. He seemed more concerned about stabbing at a steak than ogling Martha's bewitching niece.

Martha frowned disconcertedly. Lucas didn't seem as impressed as he should have been after all those glowing accolades. Perhaps his hunger pangs were distracting him. He would be more receptive to Catlin when his belly was full. Clinging to that encouraging thought, Martha focused her attention on Catlin who fiddled with her silverware and blushed up to her eyebrows—not from embarrassment, but rather from raw fury. But Martha didn't know that.

"And speaking of exceptional talent, wrapped in a handsome package," Martha commented between bites. "Lucas Murdock is the most eligible bachelor in town. . . ."

Lucas choked on his first nibble of steak as beneath the table, Cat's hand clamped onto his thigh and her long spiked nails penetrated his flesh like porcupine quills.

When Lucas sputtered to catch his breath, Catlin reached over to whack him between the shoulder blades. The blow was so forceful it knocked his chest into the edge of the table.

Once Luke recovered from his near brush with strangulation Martha continued to list his redeeming qualities for Catlin's benefit, even though she had been boasting the man's talents for four tiresome days.

"For several years now, Lucas has been trailing cattle herds all over the country. There isn't another man in Texas who knows how to handle cowboys, cattle, and horses better than Lucas. His men are staunchly loyal to him and he has earned the respect of every citizen in San Antonio because he is a man of many skills and he is capable of assuming a tremendous amount of responsibility."

"Pass the peas," Catlin requested absently.

Muttering under her breath, Martha complied. Apparently, Catlin had her heart set on resisting the lures of this handsome young man. Martha had been certain Catlin would buckle beneath Luke's charms when she finally got a look at him. Although Catlin resisted, Martha wasn't giving up easily. She was determined to make a match of these two willful individuals.

"Other ranchers entrust their cattle to Lucas, even when they know they won't be paid their profits until after the four month drives. And he is a wizard on the trail, believe you me," Martha added enthusiastically. "He can tell where to locate water on the Staked Plains by watching the flight of swallows. Lucas says when the birds are carrying mud in their beaks for their nests there are waterholes lying in the direction the birds have come. He also has noted that clumps of mesquite indicate nearby springs. Why, he is so trailwise that he can determine the freshness of an unidentified hoof print by counting the insects that have tracked across it."

"Pass the steak, please," Catlin murmured disinterestedly.

Martha glared at her stubborn niece as the steak plate exchanged hands. "When Lucas is tracking horses for his remuda he can tell by the prints if the mustangs are grazing, taking a slow walk to water or galloping away from trouble. He also looks at bent twigs to determine the amount of time that has passed since a wild herd of cattle or horses has passed through the area."

Her disappointed gaze bounced back and forth between Lucas and Catlin. If they were interested in each other, they were certainly keeping their own counsel. They both appeared far more engrossed in the meal than in the other person. Confound it, they both should have been paying more attention to each other!

"Lucas is even a doctor of sorts," Martha went on to say, growing more discouraged by the second. "On the trail Lucas's men come to him to be patched up and he tends the livestock, too. Why, he can take one look at a calf and tell by the way it's standing whether it has suffered a rattlesnake bite or is infected with screw worms. He knows the Southwest like the back of his hand and he can lead a herd to water better than a thirsty coyote."

"This steak is delicious," Catlin cut in, her tone

carefully void of the aggravation she was experiencing.

Frustrated, Martha slammed down her fork. "Is that all you have to say?" she questioned her unreceptive niece.

Catlin touched her napkin to her lips and displayed a mock innocent smile. "Oh, my no, Aunt Martha, the entire meal is scrumptious. I could easily gain ten pounds on your cooking."

"For crying out loud, that isn't what I meant," Martha snapped, unable to control her exasperation.

Catlin spared the brawny cowboy a brief glance. "Forgive me," she pleaded, her tone nowhere near apologetic. "I suppose I should be paying more attention since I have the divine privilege of sharing a meal with God's brother." Taunting violet eyes greeted Lucas's rugged face when he jerked up his head to frown at her snide remark. "Indeed, had I known a prophet was coming to dinner I would have garbed myself in my wings and halo." Catlin flashed him another goading smile. "Tell me, *Ducas*, will you be entertaining us with a few miracles after supper?"

It did Catlin's heart good to get his goat. For once Lucas looked as if he would have liked to pinch her head off instead of it being the other way around.

"The name is *Lucas*," he emphasized between gritted teeth. "Lucas Murdock. My friends call me Doc for short."

"How fascinating," she replied with a sugar-coated smile.

"Catlin Stewart Quinn! What has gotten into you?" Martha gasped. "Lucas is a guest in our home and there is no reason for you to malign his character with such mocking remarks. He is one of my most loyal and dependable friends. You have obviously misplaced the good manners my sister taught you."

Catlin made a stab at appearing repentant, difficult though it was. "I'm sorry, Aunt Martha," she apologized with exaggerated politeness.

"Well, I should hope so," Martha sniffed. "It would grieve me to no end if my two favorite people in the whole world couldn't be compatible for the short time it takes to consume a meal."

"Argh!" Lucas erupted suddenly. When Martha cast him a questioning glance he forced the semblance of a smile. "I twisted my back in the bush country yesterday," he explained. "Every time I move I'm plagued by an unexpected stab of pain."

Martha swallowed the lie. In actuality, Catlin had ground her heel in the toe of his boot and simultaneously gouged him beneath the table with her fork. But Lucas didn't tattle on the spiteful tigress so soon after Martha's lecture on being polite and cordial at the dinner table. Lucas vowed to get even with Cat later.

Both Cat and Lucas managed to suffer through the meal without another outburst. But when Martha sprang from her chair and waddled to the kitchen to fetch the apple pie, Catlin turned on Lucas.

"My aunt may be scheming to throw us together, but I want no more of you," she hissed venomously. "I know you are trying to cheat Martha out of a decent price for this ranch, one she has no business selling in the first place. You are preying on her kind nature like a parasite."

"Parasite?" Lucas growled, but quietly. "Lady, you don't know what the hell you're babbling about. I've been called a lot of things in my life, but never that! And I'll have you know I have been looking after your aunt when there was no one else around to do it."

"Just like you looked after me when Dr. Blake wasn't in his office to examine me?" Cat hurled at him with a contemptuous smirk. "You assured me my leg was broken and you put a confounded splint on it when it didn't need one."

"*You* assured me your leg was broken," Lucas clarified in a gruff voice. "And I make it a practice never to argue with a raving lunatic. You burst into the office like Madam Atilla, shooting orders like bullets. Stubborn as you are, you would have contradicted my diagnosis. And you got exactly what you deserved, Miss High and Mighty." His dark eyes flickered with irritation. "And if I'm God's brother, you're His sister!"

The creak of the kitchen door brought quick death to their spirited discussion on who was more arrogant than whom. Martha reappeared carrying Lucas's favorite dessert.

"You're too good to me," Lucas sighed appreciatively.

"Amen to that," Catlin sniffed sarcastically. "If I were she, I'd kick you out the door on your a—"

"Make mine a wide slice," Lucas requested as he stomped on Catlin's foot, causing her quiet voice to trail off in a pained gasp.

Oblivious to the private war that was being waged at the dinner table Martha sliced three pieces of pie. "When I get settled in town I hope you will come to visit me often, Lucas. Don't be a stranger to my doorstep."

Catlin clamped down on her tongue before she blurted out her wish that Lucas would make himself scarce, now and forevermore.

Martha scrunched into her chair and smiled appreciatively while Lucas "oohed" and "ahed" over her pie. "I may be talented in the culinary arts, but I have no savvy in business," she began, tactfully approaching a new topic of conversation. "I have decided to put Catlin in charge of finalizing the sale of the ranch. She has had more experience at that sort of thing."

Lucas swallowed with a gulp. Hell's bells, he was in serious trouble if he had to do business with this human wildcat. She was spoiling for a fight!

"In other words, Mr. *Murphy*, you'll have to go through me to get to my dear sweet aunt," Catlin inserted with a triumphant smile.

"Murdock. The name's *Murdock.* And dealing with you should prove an interesting experience," he managed to say without shouting in this minx's smug face.

"I intend to see that Aunt Martha gets everything she deserves," Catlin declared. "We all should from time to time, don't you think, Mr. *Murphy?* In fact, I am ever so anxious to see that you get what *you've* got coming."

"I'm sure you are," Lucas mumbled miserably. He peered at his slice of pie, knowing exactly what had happened to his appetite. Cat had spoiled it. Damn, dealing with this feisty shrew was going to test the limits of his patience. She was going to make the transaction difficult, if not impossible.

"I have a splendid idea," Martha announced as if the thought had just come to her. It hadn't. She had dreamed it up earlier in the afternoon. "Why don't you join us for dinner again day after tomorrow and you and Catlin can discuss the transaction. That will give you time to read over the contract Catlin has drawn up."

"Contract?" Lucas stared warily at the violet-eyed virago. "Martha and I thought a word of promise was contract enough." Damn, this hellion probably intended for him to sign his life away. And if something went wrong (God forbid), she would expect the termination of his life to compensate for the breach of contract. Double damn.

"Times have changed, *Ducas,*" Catlin remarked. "A written contract will state the stipulations of the sale and protect both the buyer and seller."

"I'll just bet it will," Lucas snorted acrimoniously. Rising from his chair, he snatched the paper Catlin had mischievously waved under his nose. Stiffly, he turned to his hostess. "Thank you for the meal, Martha. As always, it was delicious." His flashing brown eyes clashed with those taunting pools of amethyst. "Good night, Miss *Finn.*"

"Quinn," she corrected.

"Whatever . . ." he muttered as he stalked out of the room and slammed the front door behind him.

Martha glared disappointedly at her niece. "What has gotten into you, girl? I've never seen such a poor display of manners in all my born days. Lucas didn't deserve the hell you put him through."

"Didn't he? He was the one who—" Catlin snapped her mouth shut. It was a waste of time to discredit *Saint* Lucas. Martha worshipped the ground that weasel walked on. If Catlin insisted his name should have been *Lucifer* instead of *Lucas* and explained that Lucas was the quack doctor who splinted her leg, Martha would make excuses for his prank. "Oh, never mind . . ." Heaving a sigh, she hoisted herself from her chair. "I'm going to bed. It has been a long tiring day."

"I will expect you to be more courteous to Lucas when he returns day after tomorrow," Martha demanded, casting Catlin the evil eye. "He is a good man and I happen to like him. Once you get to know him you will, too."

Catlin doubted it, but she didn't argue the point. All she wanted was to return to her room and punch her pillow a couple of times, pretending it was Lucas Murdock. Discovering that the two men she disliked most in Texas were one and the same had her cursing vehemently. Martha may have thought Lucas was one of a kind, but in Cat's opinion he was just like the rest of the male gender. He was not to be trusted. He was sly and cunning and Catlin promised she would never let herself forget that. Damn that man! He made her so furious she could barely see straight!

Chapter 7

When Catlin lit the lantern in her boudoir, the darkness evaporated to reveal Lucas Murdock lounging on her bed as if he owned the place—which he didn't yet!

"How did you get in here?" she demanded, clutching her gown around her bosom. Catlin made a mental note never to begin undressing the moment she breezed through the door as she had done tonight, lest she run headlong into an uninvited guest.

Lucas hitched a thumb toward the window. "Another of my amazing talents," he mocked dryly. "I can climb trees like a monkey." His all-consuming gaze lingered on the bare flesh exposed by her sagging gown. He liked what he saw and he had no aversion to seeing more.

Catlin tilted an indignant chin and flung him a frigid glare. Apparently Lucas was immune to frostbite. If he hadn't been, he would have turned into a block of ice. Her glower was as cold as the arctic winds.

"Then you may go out the same way you came in," she snapped. "I have seen quite enough of you for one night."

"I'm not finished with you yet," Lucas insisted in a rumbling tone that Catlin couldn't quite decipher.

Gone was that rakish, teasing smile. Catlin was disturbed by the predatory stare she was receiving. She hadn't been successful in handling this man when he was in playful or amorous moods. She wasn't sure what mood he was in now, but his mere presence and his quiet, scrutinizing gaze worried her more than a mite.

"If you have come to discuss the contract . . ."

"I never discuss business in bedrooms." Lucas's voice was low, like the muffled purr of a panther. His dark eyes raked her with a mixture of irritation and unappeased desire.

Catlin finally detected the hunger in his eyes and she self-consciously wormed her arms back into her gown. "Then what is it you want from me?" As if she didn't know, lusty beast that he was.

The faintest hint of a smile quirked his lips as he gracefully rolled to his feet to loom over her. "I want you," he told her simply and directly. "You make me mad as hell sometimes, but I still want you in my arms. I want to feel you responding to my kiss and caress. . . ."

Her face flamed. "If you dare touch me, I'll scream," she threatened, standing her ground, but shakily. Never had Catlin found herself in such a compromising situation. It unnerved her.

"No, you won't," Lucas smirked, lifting a tanned hand to trace her exquisite features. "You're so proud and stubborn that you wouldn't lower yourself to call in reinforcements. It would crush your pride to rely on Martha or anyone else to save you, even from disaster. Your dealings with the desperados who robbed the stage lend testimony to that."

"Do you honestly think I desire a man who played me for a fool?" Catlin scoffed, her voice not as firm as she had hoped. "Do you think a tumble in bed will soften me so you can walk all over me as easily as you tromp on Aunt Martha?"

"This isn't about contracts and land sales and pranks." His voice dropped to a husky whisper and Cat's overworked heart leaped into triple time. "This is about you and me, violet eyes. I want to know if you can love as well as you fight. . . ."

His mouth took possession of hers. He didn't force himself on her, even though Catlin wished he would have. Then she would have had an excuse for accepting the feel of sensuous lips rolling masterfully over hers. But Lucas had alerted her to what he wanted in the way he focused on the curve of her mouth, the way he slowly lowered his raven head and enfolded her in his arms.

Catlin found herself a slave to her own curiosity and her own ungovernable passions. Resisting this infuriating man was like willing the sun not to shine. It couldn't be done. In her past dealings with men, Catlin had made the rules. She had been in command because she was strong-willed enough to get away with it. Most of her suitors, even her fiancé, had been gentlemen enough to respect the limitations and guidelines she set. But Lucas was one of those rare dynamic men who simply walked in and took over. He was honest and forthright and Catlin wasn't accustomed to dealing with this breed of man since there were so few of them around. She admired the strength of his personality, even though she was intimidated by it.

Although she knew she was flirting with disaster and warning signals were flashing in her head, there was no way to counter the onrush of unfamiliar sensations that channeled through her bloodstream. Wild tingles shot down her spine. His exploring hands mapped the curve of her hips and pressed her against his bold manhood, making her vividly aware of how she affected him. Suddenly Catlin couldn't breathe normally. Her heart was ramming against her ribs and the sensitivity of her skin increased tenfold.

"You provided the fire," Lucas breathed raggedly as his lips grazed her eyelids and cheeks. "Now feed the flame, Cat. I can't be satisfied until this blaze burns itself out."

Now a normal, level-headed woman would have run for her life, wouldn't she? Cat considered herself normal and level-headed, or at least she used to be. So why was she arching shamelessly toward the adventurous hands that were exploring previously unchartered territory? Why did her feminine body crave what her brain was sure she didn't need?

Lucas knew she had never been intimate with a man. He offered no commitment, no promise. That wasn't his style. He was a creature ruled by his instincts. Martha's boasts had already assured Catlin of that. He had the eyes of an eagle, ears like a fox, a nose like a bloodhound and the sexual appetite of a *cimarrone* bull. He was rough around the edges because he didn't give a whit about what was socially acceptable. He never asked when he could demand. He never used tact when being blunt sufficed. Lucas was his own man and he had tested his abilities to their very limits for the mere challenge of it.

And Catlin knew full well that this powerful lion of a man had very little sensitivity or respect for the female of the species. He wanted her only as another conquest. Desperately, she clung to that thought while the world careened crazily about her. She could feel her wild reaction to his skillful hands moving evocatively over her breasts to tease their throbbing peaks. She could feel the burgeoning ache that rose out of nowhere to consume her. And through the madness of awakened passion, Catlin valiantly battled to keep her wits about her.

"No," she gasped, twisting from his arms. Catlin inhaled a tremulous breath and fought for control. "No, Lucas. You can find passion anywhere, with any woman. Maybe my damnable pride refuses to let me call for help, but it is that same fierce sense of pride that cannot allow me to submit to you, simply because I want you—" Catlin slammed her mouth shut so quickly she nearly chipped a tooth. Blast it, her tongue had outdistanced her brain. She hadn't meant to say that! It was like aiding and abetting the enemy.

Lucas managed a smile, even though he was about to burn himself up in a frustrated pile of ashes and his blood pressure was so high he was dangerously close to springing a leak. "But you do want me, the same way I want you?" he prodded, causing her to blush crimson red.

Mustering her composure, Catlin lifted her gaze to meet his intense stare—one that could penetrate through bone and flesh to seek out the secret places inside her. "Yes, I see you as a dangerous temptation. But I am not impulsive when it comes to affairs of the heart. You see nothing wrong with satisfying your craving when the mood strikes. You may want no more than a warm body, but I expect far more than that from a man."

"His respect?" Lucas speculated, his probing gaze moving deliberately over the luscious curves he had dared to measure with his bold caresses, rattling Catlin more than she already was.

"Respect for my wants and needs and feelings," she qualified. "Maybe you can separate business contracts from personal desire, but I cannot. You tempt me to satisfy my feminine curiosity but there has to be more to it than that. And I cannot see you as two different men—the one I desire in my bed and the one who wants my aunt's ranch at the cheapest possible price. We have conflicts to resolve. You made a fool of me once and that makes a difference."

"It shouldn't," he said with great conviction.

"Why? Because you say so?" she countered caustically.

"Because the contract is business and the prank with your leg was your fault as much as it was mine. Those things have nothing to do with the magnetism between a man and a woman," he told her in plainspoken words.

If Catlin had known how much self-restraint it required for Lucas to stand there conversing when he wanted something far more intimate than conversation, she

98

would have pinned a medal on his chest. The mere fact that he didn't grab her to him again and kiss her into silence spoke volumes. She already had his respect, dammit! Now he wanted the delicious body attached to that willful, feisty personality. The truth was he had wanted her since the moment she stamped into Emmet Blake's office with her feathers ruffled and her jewel-like eyes sparking fire. It had been as simple as that, but Cat was trying to complicate matters.

Resigning himself to a battle lost, Lucas scooped up his discarded hat and trekked silently toward the window. "I admire you for giving as good as you get, for taking up this crusade you feel compelled to fight for Martha, even though I have no intention of giving her the short end of the bargain. I also admire your gumption in finding a job, even when you're nursing a sprained knee." He paused and half-turned, his dark gaze caressing her. His massive chest swelled as he heaved a frustrated sigh. "But most of all I respect you for admitting you want me in your bed. Most women aren't so honest with themselves. They accept the passion I offer and then convince themselves they have been overpowered."

Again those hypnotic brown eyes glided over her curvaceous figure, leaving her to tremble as if he had reached out to touch her. "I've already decided what I want, Cat. I want us to be as close as two people can get. Just let me know when you're ready for me to offer passion to you." The faintest hint of a smile bordered his lips as he studied the proud beauty whose round violet eyes dominated her face. "I have no intention of being rough with you. Never that. I would cherish you as if you were a special gift . . . because you are one."

Of all the things she expected this rake to say, that wasn't even on the list. Catlin stared back at him with speculative curiosity, wondering what it would be like to touch him as brazenly as he had touched her.

"Good night, violet eyes. You'll haunt my dreams. . . ."

And then he was gone, like a stirring breath of wind stealing silently through the night. For two full minutes Catlin stood frozen to the spot, marveling at the enigmatic man she swore she would never figure out. Her mind was in a whirl. First Lucas had unexpectedly arrived for dinner, kissed her senseless, waged verbal battle with her, and stomped off with the contract she had flaunted at him. Then he sneaked into her room as if nothing out of the ordinary had happened. With his usual amount of candor he had admitted he wanted her in his bed. Lord, she would never understand that man. How could he put aside their private battle in the dining room and reappear in her boudoir a few minutes later? He admitted he had no intention of solving their problems in bed. He was only setting them aside, as if one was an entirely different entity from the other. Honest to goodness, how could she deal with a man who had such incredible control over the various facets of his life? And how did he do that? she wondered. Catlin certainly hadn't learned the knack of turning one set of emotions off to engage another set!

Martha was right after all, Catlin realized. The man was amazing! But the most astounding fact of all was that Catlin was irresistibly drawn to that dark-eyed devil, even when she could list a zillion reasons why she shouldn't be. And on that unsettling thought, Catlin peeled off her gown. She cursed herself for wondering how it would feel to have Lucas lying beside her, and yet she contemplated it anyway!

Wearily, Lucas dropped into his chair to pour himself a drink. His thoughts centered around the fascinating but frustrating minx whose bedroom lantern light shone across the hillside like a compelling beacon shining through the moonshadows. Why in heaven's name did he feel such a fierce obsession for that jewel-eyed nymph who was every bit as strong-willed as he was? More so, he begrudgingly admitted to himself. He wasn't the one who said no; Cat was. He couldn't have formed that negative word on his lips if his very life depended on it. Cat had more willpower than any female he had ever met, Elise included.

Lucas helped himself to another drink. Passion was burning him alive, but he wasn't content to settle for just any woman. When a man had a craving for chocolate he wasn't likely to curb his hunger with boiled beans, for crying out loud!

In the past he had allowed himself to make substitutions for Elise, to envision her in his arms while he seduced other females. But it wasn't Elise he wanted now, incredible though it seemed after lusting after her for five tormenting years. He wanted that violet-eyed blond. Even the night Ginger Hanley had crept to his cottage, offering her body, Lucas had compared her to Elise. But Lucas had stopped comparing Catlin to Elise days ago. They were alike in many ways and yet so different. Lucas had already begun to imagine how it would feel to draw away the hindering garments that protected Catlin's luscious body from his devouring gaze. Touching her had aroused him to the limits of his sanity. Making love to her would be . . .

Expelling an exasperated breath, Lucas aimed himself toward bed. His imagination was running wild! Even now he could see that feisty kitten curled up in his bed, her expressive eyes glowing with desire, her long blond hair streaming across his pillow. . . .

His entire body throbbed in rhythm with his thudding heart. Elise's sultry features faded into the recesses of his mind and for the first time in five years there was a new face forming the perimeters of his forbidden dreams—one as elusive and unattainable as the first one.

Perhaps some men were never permitted to enjoy their fantasies, Lucas mused as he shucked his clothes. Women had always come to him with little more than an interested glance and occasionally without invitation, as Ginger had done the previous month. But it was impossible conquests like Elise and Catlin that left their haunting impressions on Luke.

A quiet smile tripped across Lucas's lips as he stretched out in bed, cushioning his head on his linked fingers. There was definitely something different about that she-Cat. That sprite had more will, more inner drive and determination than any female he had ever come across. But in less than two weeks he would strike off on a rigorous cattle drive that would span four months. And during that time he was going to have to convince himself that Catlin, like Elise, was the woman he couldn't have, no matter how badly he thought he wanted her.

Catlin probably wouldn't even want him once she got a good look at him, Lucas thought dispiritedly. Even after three years, Lucas was still hounded by self-consciousness when it came to his unsightly scars. Would a full-fledged lady like Catlin find it offensive touching him? There had been more than one woman in the past who had hesitated when they spied the crisscrossed slashes left by Yankee butchers. . . .

Lucas growled at himself for even speculating about Catlin's touch. She wasn't going to accept his invitation, at least not in this lifetime. He would be doing himself a great favor if he shoved her from his mind and forgot that curvaceous, violet-eyed minx lounging in her bed in the ranch house on the hill. Hell's bells, why did Cat have to be Martha's niece? Why couldn't she be somewhere else, living under someone else's roof? Lucas failed to formulate answers to those two frustrating questions before he fell into a fitful sleep that left him dreaming about a night of splendor that would never collide with reality.

Two hours later he woke up in a cold sweat and cursed the witch-angel who tormented his dreams.

Chapter 8

Carefully, Catlin eased from the carriage and reached back beneath the seat to retrieve the freshly baked pastries Martha had asked her to deliver to Ginger and Robert Hanley. Catlin peered at the dilapidated cottage that sat a half-mile from the outskirts of San Antonio. Still limping, but not nearly as badly, Catlin proceeded to the door. When Ginger greeted her, Catlin again noticed that mysterious woebegone expression that hung over the attractive brunette like a dark cloud. Even when the petite young woman smiled she looked faintly miserable. Why was that?

Catlin's heart lurched in sympathy when she was ushered inside to meet the gray-haired man who was ghastly white and alarmingly thin. It was evident that, without the assistance of loyal friends like Martha and his devoted daughter, Robert wouldn't have survived as long as he had. Robert sat before the hearth, cuddled beneath a lap quilt, staring expressionlessly out the window. It wasn't difficult to see why Ginger was burdened with sadness. Catlin was moved by the ailing man and Ginger's love for him. The situation reminded her of the torment she had endured when her father died and her mother sat like a statue, refusing to eat, staring into the distance, willing herself to shrivel up and die. She, too, had watched a loved one wither away, day by agonizing day, and she knew what Ginger was going through.

It was with a heavy heart that Catlin hobbled back to her carriage and drove into town. The dreary cottage and its pathetic inhabitant preyed on her mind all morning. When Catlin received her first paycheck at noon, she immediately cashed it, paid her debt to Dr. Blake and offered Ginger a gift of money.

"I can't accept this," Ginger insisted, her wide green eyes misty with unshed tears.

"I have been where you are now, living a hand-to-mouth existence," Catlin told her gently. "Take it, for your father's sake."

Hesitantly, Ginger accepted the generous donation. "You are very kind, Catlin," she murmured, eyes downcast, tears trickling over her cheeks. "If only my father were the only source of my problems. . . ."

The comment drew Catlin's inquisitive frown. "Is there something else I can do to help? Name it and I shall see it done."

Ginger shook her dark head, wiped away the tears and forced the semblance of a smile. "No one can help me. It is a burden I alone must bear."

Catlin held Ginger's trembling hands, giving them a comforting squeeze. "Then perhaps you would accept the advice of another woman who has been to hell and back. I have found that nothing comes easily these days, Ginger. Every moment is a challenge. There are a few friends you can count on, but most of all, you must depend on yourself to slay your dragons, no matter what hideous form they take."

The determination that had sustained Catlin the past two years poured forth in her unblinking stare. "When there is firm, unrelenting will, there is a way. And if you meet with defeat, you can walk away knowing you have done all that was humanly possible. Put yourself in charge of your difficulties and don't let them rule you."

Admiration glistened in Ginger's weepy gaze as she gave Catlin's hand a fond squeeze. "Thank you for understanding without prying."

As Catlin ambled back outside the office to inhale a deep breath, her eyes swung toward the cantina. And speaking of taking bulls by the horns . . . Catlin had assured her aunt that she would replenish her supply of brandy the moment she received her salary. Catlin didn't know Lucas had already seen to the matter and she didn't care who saw her march into the posada, even if she wasn't particularly welcome there.

Two of the steeds that were tied to the hitching post outside one of the many taverns that lined the street caught Catlin's attention. She had seen those mounts before—the day of the robbery. Suddenly, she had more than one reason for barging into the cantina. Unless her eyes were faulty (and she was sure they weren't) the mahogany bay gelding with its white stockings and the dappled gray mare belonged to two of the men who had robbed the stage. All she needed was a confirmation of her suspicions. If she recognized the men's voices and the one face she had seen when she clawed off the bandana, she would hotfoot it to the sheriff's office. Damn those thieves, they were going to rot in jail, just see if they didn't!

With her mouth set in a grim line, Catlin squared her shoulders and marched toward the posada. It was at that moment that Lucas arrived in town. He had intended to speak with Dr. Blake, but the sight of Catlin on her latest crusade caught his immediate attention. A wary frown knitted his brow when he spied Cat, with her back stiff as a flagpole, making a beeline for the saloon.

Had that minx lost her mind? Decent women didn't poke their noses in such places. What could she be thinking of? This was probably another of her crusades for

105

truth, justice and the rights of women, he thought with a disgusted snort. That she-male had more noble causes than a centipede had legs. Now it seemed she had taken up the crusade of temperance like Sarah Pellet who sought to outlaw liquor in California several years earlier.

Detouring past Emmet Blake's office, Lucas swung from the saddle and intently watched as Catlin stepped into the tavern. Demons of curiosity were dancing in his head. Lucas told himself to mind his own business, that Catlin wanted no help and expected none. Fighting her own battles was her way of life. And after hearing Martha's rendition of the stage holdup, Lucas knew for a fact that this independent firebrand wouldn't back down from the devil if he dared to cross her. Hell's bells, was there anything that harridan didn't think she couldn't do all by herself? The answer to that question provoked Lucas to quicken his step so he could take a closer look. Catlin Quinn may not have wanted assistance for whatever crazed crusade she had assumed, but she might need some. And Lucas vowed to be there to lend a hand, just in case this sassy wildcat took on more trouble than she was physically capable of handling.

With chin held high, Catlin breezed into the posada as if she belonged there. Two dozen pairs of eyes swung to the door when Catlin's appetizing figure was silhouetted by sunlight. The bartender gasped in astonishment when the shapely blond strode purposefully toward him.

"Lady, I think you must have made a wrong turn," he informed her, his gaze silently requesting her to reverse direction.

Catlin's narrowed eyes scanned the smoke-filled saloon, searching for the rugged face and bushy red hair that belonged to the man who had stolen her valuables and whacked her on the head. Recognition flashed in her eyes

106

when she spied the two desperados lounging at a table with their glasses of whiskey poised in their hands. Catlin glared at both men before giving the proprietor a hasty glance.

"Does this establishment serve whiskey to those who can afford to pay for it?" she questioned defiantly.

"Now look, lady, we don't want any trouble," the rotund tavern owner grumbled. "These men came in here for a drink, not a lecture on the evils of alcohol."

Swiftly, Catlin dug into her purse to fetch her coins. Dramatically, she plunked her money on the bar. "I would like a bottle of peach brandy, if you please."

Wearing a muddled frown, the bartender accommodated her.

"If you have an aversion to enduring a lecture on temperance, do you also have an aversion to harboring fugitives from the law?" she queried, turning to nail the two suspects to the wall with her accusing glare.

The silence in the saloon was deafening.

Catlin didn't blink or shrink away from the murderous glowers cast by the two buscaderos who had set their drinks aside and whose gun hands had mysteriously disappeared beneath the table.

"I don't take kindly to being labeled a thief, lady," the redheaded bandit growled threateningly.

Catlin not only recognized the face but also the voice. She had originally intended to make her exit to summon the sheriff at this point. But now that the moment was upon her—facing the man who had stolen her savings and clubbed her on the head—her feet refused to retreat. Surely there were those hereabout who would dash to the sheriff before the fireworks began.

"I don't recall naming names or pointing an accusing finger," Catlin taunted, her unrelenting gaze glued to the scowling desperado. "But if the boot fits . . ."

The screech of chairs scooting away from tables and the

sound of spurs clanking a swift retreat didn't distract Catlin. She stared the bandits down.

"Damn," Lucas muttered under his breath while he stood outside the door. Catlin had deputized herself as a one-woman posse. He admired her spunk, but her tactics left one helluva lot to be desired! What did she intend to do now that she had sniffed out the thieves who had victimized her? Lash them with her whip-like tongue? Chances were this daring vixen wasn't packing a pistol. And if she was, she better know how to use it. These men were not Southern gentlemen who fell to their knees apologizing. Confound it, Cat probably didn't even have a sling-shot stashed in her purse, although she was playing a superb part as David confronting Goliath.

"You never learn, do you, honey?" the redheaded desperado smirked.

Catlin didn't even blink at the intimidating expression on his craggy features. "I don't believe the scum of the earth should rule the rest of us. The planet belongs to law-abiding citizens and I have a low tolerance for thieves and parasites," she hissed.

Both men flinched as if they had been slapped in the face.

Hell, she was really asking for it! Lucas thought, rolling his eyes in disgust. If there was one thing Catlin Stewart Quinn wasn't, it was a shrinking Southern violet. She was a female daredevil!

Quietly, Lucas stepped back when four more men filed out the door. His keen gaze surveyed the posada, wondering if the three men, who chose to hold their ground, intended to aid that daring damsel who was soon to be in distress if she didn't stop badgering those two scraggly buscaderos.

All of Luke's senses came to life when the red-haired desperado rose to full stature. The pistol he had previously held under the table was now directed at Catlin's heaving bosom.

"Talk is cheap, honey," he goaded her with a mocking smile. "The question is . . . what do you plan to do about your accusations?"

Catlin stood her ground. It was her lot in life to be overcome with fury when normal individuals were hounded by fear. The threat didn't frighten her; it infuriated her. "I intend to press charges against you and your thieving friend," she informed him in a voice that quivered with barely restrained irritation. "My guess is that at least one of the men who slunk out of here had the good sense to summon the sheriff. When he arrives you can explain why you took offense to being called a bandit when I know absolutely certain you are."

The desperado had squared off against innumerable men during his life of crime, but never a defiant woman. The fact that Cat dared to challenge him caught him off stride. Killing a woman would be a first for him, but it would be a damned sight better than mildewing in jail.

The click of the trigger being cocked shattered the silence like a rock crashing through a window pane. But still Catlin didn't cower in fear.

"You're a fool, lady," the buscadero snarled at her.

Meanwhile, outside, Lucas was warding off a heart seizure. He couldn't remember being this frightened in all his life, even when a wild herd of stampeding cattle thundered off in the darkness, not even when he confronted Indian war parties or those damned Yankee butchers. But he was scared now, not for himself but for that reckless hellion who had pitted herself against impossible odds.

Inhaling a steadying breath, Lucas struggled to formulate his plan of action. If he burst upon the scene with pistol in hand, all hell would break loose and that sassy minx would wind up dead (even if she did deserve it, damn her courageous hide!). Finally an inspiration came to him.

Hurriedly, he unfastened the first few buttons of his shirt and left the hem dangling from his breeches. Quickly, he jammed his sombrero down around his ears and slammed himself against the outer wall of the tavern to announce his entrance. Like a half-blind, stumbling drunkard, Lucas weaved into the cantina, mumbling to himself.

"I'm buying rounds of drinks for everybody," he slurred out as he clomped across the room like a heavy-footed elephant.

The red-haired bandit surveyed the bungling fool who had barged into the posada. He didn't replace his pistol in his holster, but he didn't fire it either.

When Luke had strategically positioned himself between the two desperados and Catlin, pretending not to notice what was going on, he looked her up and down. "You don't look like no calico queen I ever saw, honey," he drawled sluggishly.

Catlin met the half-veiled eyes beneath the wide-rimmed sombrero and then watched in disbelief as Lucas staggered around as if he had not one tittle of coordination. "You're drunk," she declared for lack of anything else to say. What the blazes was he doing here, acting like an idiot?

Lucas wobbled on his legs, taking care not to remove himself from the bandits' line of fire. "Not as drunk as I'm gonna be, sweetheart," he babbled as his arm lazily circled the air to pluck up Catlin's newly purchased bottle of peach brandy. With a flair for the ridiculous, Lucas slouched against the bar and guzzled the liquor. Pushing himself upright once again, he stumbled across the room, taking another long swig of brandy. As if he had just noticed the two men behind him, he careened around to greet them with a droopy smile.

"Wanna drink, friends?" he questioned as he weaved toward the redheaded bandito who had relaxed enough to drop the barrel of his pistol.

"No, tha—"

The buscadero had only opened his mouth to respond when Lucas came uncoiled like a human spring, catching his victims flat-footed. Catlin would have tarried in mute amazement if she hadn't felt the urgency to lend a helping hand. The instant Lucas kicked the table into the seated bandit and launched himself toward the red-haired thief, Catlin shot across the room like a cannonball.

Lucas had purposely rammed the table into his challenger on his way to bury a meaty fist in the other outlaw's startled face. While one man staggered back, dazed by a blow powerful enough to fell a redwood tree, the other bandit squawked in surprise. His arms swished in the air like a windmill while he attempted to regain his balance in the chair that had reared up on its hind legs. While the seated buscadero was trying to stay atop his bucking chair, Catlin hurled a glass of whiskey in his face. His eyes burned like fire as he toppled backward, landing with the upturned table atop him. And still the flying mugs of liquor kept coming as Catlin approached, heaving one and then another grenade of abandoned whiskey.

Like a shot, Catlin darted toward the misfired pistol that had flown loose and discharged when the desperado slammed against the floor. The second Colt tumbled end over end when Lucas kicked it from the red-haired bandit's fingertips. With a roar, the outlaw hurled himself at Luke, matching fist with beefy fist. The sound of flesh cracking against flesh mingled with crashing whiskey glasses and the roars of the two men who were attempting to pound each other flat.

Another growl erupted from the redheaded bandit's curled lips. He swung wildly to counter the teeth-rattling blow that had catapulted him against the wall. Lucas blocked the oncoming fist with his forearm and delivered another punishing punch that knocked the man's navel

111

against his spine.

While Lucas was making his victim a human punching bag, Catlin scooped up an overturned chair and smashed it over the other desperado's head. He still flopped around on the floor like a gigantic overturned beetle, so Catlin grabbed another chair and clobbered him with it. The bandito's eyes rolled back in his head and he lay there like a wet noodle, not to rise again.

Wheeling about, Catlin kept the pistol trained on the two men who were still beating the tar out of each other. Although Lucas was managing quite well by himself, Catlin grabbed the barrel of the Colt in her hand and stalked forward, positioning herself behind the redheaded bandit who had clanked her skull during the robbery. In her estimation one brain-scrambling blow deserved another. Clinging to that vindictive theory, she parted the desperado's hair and his head the moment he staggered back in an attempt to recover from the jarring blow Lucas had planted on his jaw. It was difficult to determine whether the blow to the skull or the punch in the cheek felled the outlaw, but he teetered backward like a growling grizzly bear.

Catlin let out a yelp when the desperado's limp body collapsed against her, knocking both of them into the corner and pinning her to the floor.

Lucas would have stamped over to unearth Catlin from under the unconscious *hombre* if he hadn't been so furious with her for instigating this showdown. He let her buck and snort in an effort to rid herself of the body that mashed her into the floor and he cursed her but good all the while.

"What's going on here?" the sheriff questioned as he burst through the door of the cantina, pistol in hand, aiming all directions at once.

Finally, Catlin managed to worm out from under the dead weight that had held her fast. "You could have helped," she spewed at Lucas who looked positively murderous.

"You've already gotten all the help you're going to get from me, damn you," Lucas snarled as he wiped the drip of blood from his lips.

Preferring not to endure another second of Lucas's punishing looks, Catlin readjusted her calico gown and tested her tender leg. Raising her chin to a proud angle, she marched toward the puzzled sheriff. "These two men are part of the gang who robbed the stage in which I was riding last week," she told him matter-of-factly. "I want them arrested for robbery and for the physical attack on my person. And I would like you to have them shot and hanged at your earliest possible convenience."

The sheriff couldn't contain the amused smile that tugged the corner of his mouth. The posada was in shambles and the two banditos were lying in unconscious heaps. That wasn't particularly amusing, but finding this firebrand in the saloon with Lucas Murdock was. He still didn't have the foggiest notion who had started this ruckus but he could hazard a guess. And he didn't have to be a prophet to determine who had finished it. Lucas Murdock was adept with pistols and his fists.

His gaze flicked to Lucas for confirmation of Catlin's announcement. When Lucas nodded affirmatively Catlin compressed her lips, annoyed to no end that the sheriff wouldn't accept a woman's word without a man confirming it. Damn, men clung together like a den of thieves.

"I'll have these criminals behind bars in a few minutes and you can register your complaint, ma'am," the sheriff replied.

While the sheriff deputized a few of the onlookers to haul the desperados off to jail, Lucas clutched Catlin's arm to propel her back to the street. To his annoyance, she refused to budge from the spot. "Hell's bells, now what?"

113

he grumbled crankily.

"I came in here to restock Aunt Martha's supply of peach brandy." Her eyes fastened on the bottle that lay on the floor without a drop left in it. "You spilled it and you are responsible for replacing it."

Lucas gaped at her as if she were a weird creature who had just flown down from the moon. "You incited a barroom brawl that I had to finish for you because you weren't man enough to tackle the task all by yourself. Now you expect me to replace the liquor I spilled on my way to pound your enemies flat?" he hooted incredulously. "Dammit, I replaced Martha's brandy two days ago!"

Catlin blinked like a disturbed owl. "You did?" When Lucas nodded curtly, Cat mumbled a curse. "Well, nobody told me. You should have said something."

Flashing black eyes scorched her with a molten glare. Cat sounded suspiciously as if she was blaming him for the incident. "You could at least extend your gratitude for my assistance," he snapped, a distinctly unpleasant edge to his voice. "You could have gotten yourself killed."

"Consider yourself thanked," Catlin declared, tilting a smudged chin. "But I don't recall inviting you to rescue me. And if you had informed me that you had already bought the brandy I would never have glanced in the direction of the posada in the first place. Now kindly pay the barkeeper for another bottle so I can be on my way. I was due back at the newspaper office fifteen minutes ago."

This she-male beat anything he had ever seen! With a wordless scowl, Lucas navigated around the upended tables and chairs to purchase the brandy and then thrust it at Catlin.

"Thank you very much," she said in a voice that was nowhere near sincere.

"You are not the least bit welcome," Lucas muttered grumpily.

Neither Cat nor Luke glanced at each other as, side by side, they stalked out the door.

"Ah . . . miss?" the bartender called after her.

Catlin pirouetted in the opened portal and raised a curious brow. "Yes?"

"The next time you have a hankering for peach brandy, let me know." His gaze swept his ransacked cantina. "I'll have the bottle delivered."

"I appreciate your consideration, sir," she said courteously.

The bystanders who had congregated by the door parted like the Red Sea when Catlin and Lucas stormed out. Murmurs rippled through the crowd, but Catlin spared no one a glance as she walked straight ahead, favoring her sprained knee as little as possible.

"What next, Cyclone Catlin?" Lucas smirked out the side of his mouth that wasn't swollen. "Do you plan to set fire to the Market Plaza or blow up a couple of bordellos to put the finishing touches on this eventful day you've had?"

Catlin didn't dignify the asinine question with an answer. She simply strode down the boardwalk and veered into the newspaper office, slamming the door behind her. She had an article to write for the paper. And being an eyewitness, the report she penned earned her Jacob Ross's praise. It was a wonderful story which Jacob announced would be printed on the front page.

A concerned frown puckered Ginger's brow when Lucas ambled into Emmet Blake's office. Without asking how Luke sustained the split lip and bruised cheek, Ginger scurried into the examination room to summon Dr. Blake. The physician took one look at Lucas and requested that she fetch the antiseptic.

"How soon can I expect the other casualties of the brawl?" Emmet questioned as he inspected the cut on Lucas's lower lip.

"The two casualties were hauled off to jail," Lucas

explained, grinning out the unswollen side of his mouth. "I doubt those desperados are worth your medical attention. And all the money they have in their pockets probably belongs to Miss Quinn."

Emmet's brows elevated. The remark suggested Lucas had somehow managed to become acquainted with the saucy young woman he had met a few days earlier. "You are still taking Ginger to Mrs. Lewis's house-warming party, aren't you?" he questioned quickly.

Lucas looked surprised and then hurriedly composed himself. "You never have told me why you've decided to play the matchmaker. I've grown accustomed to getting my own dates."

"Ginger needs a man to help her carry the lion's share of responsibility." Emmet sighed as he stuffed his hands in his pockets and leaned a hip against the desk. "Is it asking too much of you to ensure she enjoys herself occasionally? If I am generous enough to offer you a loan for your trail drive, I should think you could grant me a few favors."

"I need more money than I previously thought," Lucas announced, cutting to the heart of the matter that had brought him into the office.

"And Ginger hasn't taken time out for lunch," Emmet declared with a cunning smile. "After you escort her to the restaurant and stop by her house to check on her father, we'll see what we can do about increasing the size of your loan."

"I think I should have contacted the bank," Lucas grumbled acrimoniously.

"You know the bank is barely back on its feet," Emmet chuckled. "Trail drives are risky business to banks who plummeted during the war. I'm the only private investor in the county who would offer you a loan, Luke."

When Ginger reappeared, Lucas allowed her to dab the stinging antiseptic on his lip and then he set the medication aside. "Come on, honey, I'll take you to lunch."

Although Ginger cast the doctor a disdainful frown, she spoke not a word. She knew Emmet was pushing her off on Lucas again. Not that she minded his company. He was the stuff dreams were made of, but she did not appreciate Emmet's intervention. After her conversation that morning with Catlin, Ginger intended to take the good advice to heart. Woman or no, she was going to assume control of her life—mess that it was. Yes, she had been intimate with Lucas, but she still had her pride!

"I have a matter to discuss with you when I return, Dr. Blake," she forewarned the physician as she breezed out the door.

Warily, Emmet peered at the petite brunette. "You'll have to wait your turn, my dear. Lucas and I have a business transaction to make when he returns."

The remarks that were tossed back and forth provoked Lucas to frown curiously. The moment they were outside Ginger lapsed into distracted silence. "Do you want to talk about it?" he murmured as they ambled past the newspaper office where Catlin was laboring over her articles.

Ginger mustered the semblance of a smile. "No, my problems are my own," she insisted, tilting a determined chin. "And thank you for inviting me to lunch, even if you were prompted to do it."

As Lucas and Ginger walked down the boardwalk, Catlin experienced an unfamiliar stab of pain in the pit of her belly. Why should she care if Luke was escorting Ginger down the street? She didn't, she convinced herself. Lucas meant nothing to her, nothing at all. Besides, Ginger and Lucas had probably seen a great deal of each other before Cat arrived on the scene. Cat only hoped Ginger was strong-willed enough to resist the lures of the midnight-haired devil. If not, she might find herself in serious trouble.

Catlin had met Lucas's type before, dozens of times. He was one of those lusty men whose aspiration in life was to populate the continent all by himself. There should have been a law against letting the devil's own temptation run around loose. That philanderer was a threat to women everywhere!

Forcefully, Catlin shoved all thoughts of Lucas aside and concentrated on her work. Lucas may have wanted her two nights earlier, but apparently his cravings were short-termed. Never mind that Catlin had lain awake for hours both nights, battling her womanly feelings—ones that she never knew she had until that dark-eyed demon opened Pandora's box of forbidden desire.

Honest to goodness, there was no reason why she should be so unwillingly compelled toward that infuriating man. But dammit, she was and pretending she wasn't did not make the yearnings go away. They only inflamed her when she saw Lucas courting Ginger Hanley.

Curse the man! He could have walked down the opposite side of the street so Cat wouldn't have had to see him usher Ginger into the restaurant. He had thrown a tantrum about replacing the overturned bottle of brandy, but Catlin bet her right arm Lucas wouldn't bat an eyelash at paying for Ginger's meal. Damn him. No, double damn him, she amended irritably.

Chapter 9

Although Lucas tried to persuade Ginger to discuss what was bothering her, she was as tight-lipped as a clam. When they had checked on her father, Lucas walked the sultry brunette back to the office and made his arrangements with Emmet Blake. Lucas strolled away with enough money to purchase the last of the necessary supplies and essentials for the trail drive to Colorado. But the agreement had strings attached. Lucas was requested to take Ginger out on the town when time permitted.

If Lucas hadn't needed the money he would have had a few choice words to make to Emmet about his attempted matchmaking. Lucas had been too proud and stubborn to write his brother, requesting his inheritance. He had been determined to make a fresh new start, to acquire land and cattle by his own devices. Now it was too late to change his mind and wire for the money he needed posthaste. He was left to deal with Emmet and his "favors."

Although Lucas liked Ginger well enough, there was another female on his mind, one who prevented him from spending too much time dwelling on Ginger's redeeming qualities. But Lucas did need money. The other ranchers who were entrusting their cattle herds to his care during the long drive had yet to pay his fee as drover and trail boss, nor would they until they received the profit from their beeves.

Since money was tight, Lucas had taken out a loan with Emmet. The doctor was one of the few men in the county who had acquired substantial amounts of cash and Lucas swore the physician still had the first cent he ever made. Because Emmet's patients could not always afford to pay for his services with cash, he had acquired ranch land, cattle and real estate. His investments paid off because Emmet was a shrewd man who always wound up on top, no matter what the situation. He maneuvered for position and power. Even though his rapport with the sick and ailing was legendary, there was another side to the doctor who had made himself a pillar in the community. Besides being a man of wealth and influence, Emmet had a violent temper when he was crossed. He tolerated no one's opinion but his own and he lived by the philosophy that there were two ways to do things—his way and the wrong way.

Lucas had witnessed Emmet's fiery temper on two occasions. Two years earlier, Emmet had left Ann Livingston, the young assistant who preceded Ginger, in another doctor's care while he and Mrs. Blake were out of town. Ann had unexpectedly died during Emmet's absence. When he learned of her death, Emmet flew into a demented rage, accusing the other physician of being his patient's cause of death. Emmet and the other physician had exchanged heated words and Emmet physically attacked his competition. He swore he would run the man out of town for malpractice. This Emmet proceeded to do, using his power, position, and influence.

Emmet contended that his young assistant had only suffered from the grippe and that the doctor who was left in charge was totally incompetent. The fact that Emmet and his competition had never gotten along was another reason Emmet wanted him out of town, Lucas mused.

The second time Lucas had seen Emmet come apart at the seams was at a community meeting. One of the other potentates in town contested Emmet's opinion on a civil matter. Again, Emmet launched himself at his challenger in blind fury and had to be pulled back and restrained.

For the most part, though, Emmet was well-respected and able to control himself. But it was that peculiar quirk of character that prevented Lucas from trusting Emmet completely. The doctor knew how to throw his weight around. And if Lucas hadn't felt compassion for Ginger he probably wouldn't have allowed Emmet to maneuver him, whether he needed the loan or not.

There was no harm done, Lucas assured himself. Ginger was pleasant company and there had been times when she needed a man around her home. Since her father was incapable of making repairs, Lucas lent a helping hand. And although Ginger had once come to him in the darkness, Lucas had never repeated the intimacy. That night had been . . .

His thoughts evaporated as he ambled into the newspaper office. Lucas had veered into the courthouse to post his trail brand and the Flying Spur brand in the county brand book. It was also standard procedure to place an ad in the local paper, designating both brands before the herds were put on the trail. The procedure prevented a duplication of brands and made it difficult for outlaws to sell stolen stock that carried a registered brand. Lucas wouldn't have minded seeing to his duties if he hadn't been forced to confront the violet-eyed rabble-rouser who had brewed trouble in the posada two hours earlier.

The mere sight of this curvaceous blond triggered a riptide of emotions in Lucas. He was vividly aware of her as a woman and mad as hell at her because of her reckless daring. Each time they crossed paths he had more difficulty separating his personal feelings from his business feelings. That was unnatural for Lucas. In the past he could erect a wall between personal and business matters, as in the case of Emmet Blake. But Catlin Stewart Quinn was another matter entirely.

The problem was Catlin had wedged herself into both facets of his life and she maintained that she couldn't view him in separate perspectives. And as much as Luke hated to admit it, he was having problems with the boundaries of their relationship himself. He looked at the shapely firebrand and he saw a lovely desirable woman . . . who had dragged him into a fist fight and thrust a contract at him that demanded payment for the ranch the moment the land was registered in his name! Hell's bells, this she-cat was giving him fits.

"To what misfortune do I owe this visit?" Catlin inquired in a haughty tone that counteracted the frustration of knowing Lucas had spent part of the afternoon with Ginger Hanley.

"It's strictly business," Lucas announced stiffly. Like hell it was. One look at this gorgeous minx and he ached for her up to his eyebrows. If he thought he could continue to separate his personal and business feelings for Cat he was a fool. She touched off too many emotions at once, damn her.

"Oh yes, how could I have forgotten," Catlin smirked, raking him up and down. "If you had come to seduce me you would have been wearing your other set of clothes."

The taunt struck like a well-aimed dagger in the chest. "I happen to own more than two sets of clothes and stop picking fights. You've done enough of that for one day," he growled down at her.

Although Cat was taller than average height, so was Lucas. When she vaulted to her feet, he still loomed over her like a granite mountain. Damn, what she wouldn't give for a step ladder so she could glare directly into his rugged features. "I suppose you have a separate set of garb for your business transactions and for each female you chase—" Catlin clamped her mouth shut and glanced the other way.

A wry grin dangled on the corner of his sensuous lips as he surveyed the blush that rapidly rose to her cheeks. So this minx had seen him with Ginger, had she? Good for her. "Jealous, Cat?" he teased unmercifully.

"Not hardly," she sniffed in contradiction. "I was only trying to differentiate between the cowboy, the business man, the skirt-chaser, and the knight in shining armor." Her tone had grown more caustic by the second. "You really should post a sign on your chest so I will know which one of your multiple personalities I am addressing."

Lucas heaved an annoyed sigh. This sassy sprite could drag him into an argument before he knew he was there. He had dozens of chores to attend, none of which included waging a verbal sparring match with this sharp-witted shrew.

"I want my brands posted in the newspaper," he announced in a business-like tone. "If you will kindly jot down the ad, I will be on my way."

"And I wouldn't want to detain you," she assured him, her voice carrying an underlying bite of sarcasm. "I'm sure you have at least a dozen other women to seduce before dark. All this trifle of business is probably getting in your way."

Brawny arms flinched as Lucas braced his hands on the front of her desk, granting her wish of staring him squarely in the eyes. Catlin didn't want to meet his fuming glower quite as badly as she first thought. He could rip holes in her composure with those penetrating dark eyes and he looked more than a little dangerous looming over her desk!

"You're the one I wanted in my bed," he told her without mincing words. "But you weren't prepared to accept me. For a female who displays such incredible amounts of courage in the face of adversity, you have a streak of cowardice when it comes to dealing with men."

Those piercing brown eyes bore through her garments, stripping her naked. Catlin felt the most peculiar need to cover herself.

"If you don't think you're woman enough to handle me in bed, then you shouldn't give a flying fig who can," he ridiculed her.

Catlin gasped at his audacity and his infernal bluntness. "Well, I have never in all my life—"

"I know," Lucas said with an intimidating snort. "That's the problem. I think you would be a helluva lot more comfortable with your femininity if you would cling a little less tightly to your virginity and stop trying to wear the breeches—"

WHACK! Her palm smacked against the left side of his cheek, temporarily mashing his nose onto the right side of his face and inflaming the horseshoe-shaped scar on his jaw. Catlin should have been satisfied with slapping him silly, but the smug expression on his features never altered, not even for a second. The taunting smile remained intact, even under the red welt he was now sporting. It was as if he had anticipated her assault and it hadn't fazed him in the least.

"The truth hurts you worse than a slap in the face," he mocked.

"I hate you . . . all of you: the cowboy, the business man, the lover, and the antagonist . . . especially the antagonist," she spumed furiously.

"And I still want you in my bed," he had the nerve to say. "You are using anger and sarcasm as a shield to protect yourself from me. And to tell the truth, I think you need to be in my bed as badly as I want you there."

WHACK! Catlin struck like a rattlesnake, but again Lucas didn't wince. If she owned a shotgun she swore she could have blown him to smithereens without one tittle of regret.

Drawing himself up to full stature, Lucas dug into his pocket for the coins to pay for the newspaper ad. Nonchalantly, he replaced the dark sombrero on his head and offered Cat a mock salute. "Good day, violet eyes. It was an experience seeing you again. Not a pleasant one, but an experience nonetheless."

As he sauntered out the door Catlin erupted in a rush of unprintable curses. If she lived to be one hundred she would never find the proper way to deal with that insufferable man. He provoked her to fury with his cutting insults and his outrageous honesty. She should invite him to her bed, she thought spitefully. Nothing would wound his stupendous male arrogance more than having a woman ridicule his prowess and virility. Indeed, that would wound him where he could be hurt the most—in his inflated male pride!

Lucas Murdock was probably a recklessly inconsiderate lover. He probably preyed on love-starved females who were content with whatever scraps of affection he could offer. He would unfold his sinewy body on a woman, taking possession. His sensuous lips would steal her breath. . . .

Catlin blushed up to the roots of her hair and quickly clamped down on that sordid thought. It was all too easy to imagine Lucas hovering over her, stripping her of her inhibitions. And just Catlin's luck that her vivid imagination had unleashed the forbidden sensations Lucas had aroused in her with his devastating kisses and soul-shattering caresses. She remembered the powerful cross-currents of emotion that swept through her when that raven-haired devil worked his sensual black magic on her. Cat went hot all over!

Don't think about such things! Catlin scolded herself harshly. She had to finish her story before Jacob returned from his tireless crusade of gathering news. She tried to fight down her wild blush and turn her thoughts away from that impossible man.

I don't need a man in my life to make my life complete, Catlin told herself firmly. She had survived quite nicely without surrendering to passion these past twenty-two years and she could survive another score without the complications caused by a man. Lucas Murdock couldn't give her what she wanted and needed. His arms wouldn't be tender and loving. He knew how to take, but he didn't know beans about giving of himself. Cat was prepared to bet what was left of her paycheck on that fact! If she submitted to Lucas she would have everything to lose and nothing to gain. And if she knew what was good for her she would never allow herself to forget that!

The last rays of sunshine sprinkled across the sky as Catlin climbed into the carriage and pointed herself toward the ranch. As she rumbled down the street she saw Ginger stomp from Emmet Blake's office and flounce into her rickety buggy. While Ginger shot off in a fast clip, Catlin followed at a more reasonable pace. For the life of her Catlin didn't know what could have put Ginger in a huff. She couldn't help but wonder if Lucas was the source of Ginger's underlying problem. He certainly was the crux of Catlin's. The man had taken up permanent residence in her mind, even when she spent hours telling herself she wanted nothing to do with him.

Every once in a while, Catlin drifted into a slump of depression. With her fierce will and determination it was the exception rather than the rule. But after a full day of battling a myriad of emotions, her weariness gave way to nostalgic thoughts and tears flooded her eyes.

Catlin thought about Ginger's burden and the anguish of watching a loved one wither away. It reminded Catlin of the months of agony she had endured when she lost her family, her fiancé, and her home. Oh, how much easier it would have been to deal with Benjamin Saunders than that billy goat of a man named Lucas Murdock. But that blasted war had destroyed Catlin's world. Now she was in Texas, trying to find a new lease on life and Lucas Murdock was here to torment her.

Lucas constantly tugged at her emotions, provoking sensations and frustrations Cat didn't want to cope with. She wished Luke could have been a little less honest and a lot more sensitive to her needs. Dammit, he should put himself in her place and see how he liked being pursued, propositioned, and intimidated by men who used their superior strength and powers to manipulate a woman.

Maybe Luke was right. Maybe she wasn't comfortable being a woman when she perceived men as having all the advantages in life. Maybe she needed to be less sensible and defensive and a little more impulsive. Maybe she should live one day at a time and stop fretting over her future. She had dedicated herself so completely to making a new start in life that she refused herself the slightest pleasures. The past week she had been invited out to supper and to the theater by several young bachelors, but she had rejected all invitations. Maybe she needed a distraction, she told herself.

Catlin stared at the silhouette of Lewis Ranch against the backdrop of a fiery crimson sunset. An appreciative smile hovered on her lips. It was time she pampered herself a bit and paused to enjoy life's simple pleasures. She would shrug off the chip on her shoulder and attempt to be less defensive when Luke came to dinner. They would discuss the contract like two reasonable individuals and she would enjoy his companionship—within the limited guidelines she set for herself, that is. For once she wouldn't dwell on the handsome rake's faults. She would learn to appreciate his saving graces. She would try to separate her personal feelings and concentrate on the business relationship between them. She and Luke could never be totally compatible, but she would make an attempt to bury the hatchet somewhere besides in his back.

Chomping on that noble thought, Catlin pulled the carriage to a halt in front of the barn. As she stepped down, a thirteen hundred pound longhorn trotted around the corner and Catlin very nearly lept out of her skin when the animal dashed right up to her.

A startled yelp burst from her lips when the stocky steer jerked to a halt a mere foot away from her. For a moment she peered into Spur's big brown eyes, wondering if he was contemplating goring her with his horns or if he had decided to settle for nothing more than plowing over the top of her.

"Come here, Spur," Lucas called as he ambled onto his stoop.

Catlin flinched when the broad head and wide-spread horns swung toward Lucas's voice. To her astonishment, the steer let out a bellow and trotted off like an obedient puppy—grossly oversized though he was. Curiously, Catlin walked over to watch Spur rub against Lucas's thigh. Chuckling, Luke stroked his muzzle and murmured affectionately to his unusual pet.

"Is this your steer?" Cat questioned, her gaze sweeping over the huge creature.

Luke nodded absently. "Spur is relatively harmless if you don't rile him," he explained as he ambled over to fetch the bucket of grain. "I found him minutes after he was born. I milked his mother and fed him as best I could. The only scent Spur knows is mine. And to this day he still thinks I'm his mama. When he was young I fed him from my employer's milk cow and he was allowed to graze with the flock of sheep. His only friend, other than me, was a flop-eared mutt. Poor old Spur still isn't sure if he's a lamb, a dog, or a human.

"And because Spur was the first longhorn I had to my name, I'm calling this the Flying Spur Ranch. He's the first thing that truly belonged to me and depended on me. He takes care of me and I take care of him," Lucas murmured, giving the steer an affectionate pat on the flank. "When it comes to leading a herd of cattle up the trail, Spur is a drover's dream. Without Spur there would be more stampedes and more problems. This steer saves me a lot of headaches."

A pensive frown furrowed Lucas's brow as he glanced over his shoulder at the shapely blond. "I didn't think you would be speaking to me after what I said this afternoon."

"I thought it over and decided you were right," Catlin admitted as she brushed her hand over Spur's sleek coat. "I suppose I envy a man's position in the world. I wind up striking out to compensate for the frustration of being confined to the restrictions of womanhood."

For a moment the defensive walls came down and Lucas marveled at the lovely vision whose features were caressed by the fading rays of sunset. Silently, he approached her, forcing her to lift those entrancing amethyst eyes—eyes that lured him like a ship following the magical melody of a sea siren.

"I was a mite too rough on you this afternoon. I'm sorry," he apologized. "I'm a bit frustrated too, Cat. For some reason you've become an incurable obsession with me." His lean fingertips limned her delicately carved features, marveling at the soft texture of her skin, the unique way her eyes darkened when he touched her. "But I told you before that I wouldn't force myself on you and I meant it. I have a lot of experience at denying myself women I crave most."

"Like Elise?" Catlin queried, searching his craggy features.

"Like Elise," he concurred, his voice so husky that Catlin's knees threatened to buckle, even while they were discussing the light and love of his life. "But with you, I wouldn't be pretending I wanted someone from my past. . . ."

Catlin stepped away, rattled by the shock waves caused by his caress, confused by her feminine longings and still too cynical of men in general to believe she wasn't a substitute for what Luke really wanted—Elise. Lucas was a dangerous man. He could be gentle and persuasive when it suited his purpose and he knew his way around a woman's anatomy better than a practicing physician. And if she didn't watch her step she would melt beneath his dark charm. Then where would she be?

"I . . . I had better go help Aunt Martha with dinner," she chirped, her voice quaking with the turbulent battle of mind over body.

Lucas could detect the confusion that flashed through those wide jewel-like eyes which dominated Cat's flawless face. "Until later . . ." he murmured, leaning leisurely against Spur.

Inhaling a steadying breath, Catlin ambulated up the hill to the house. Honest to goodness, that man came within ten feet of her and her emotions erupted—but never the same feelings that assaulted her during their previous encounter. With Lucas, each confrontation involved new, unexplainable emotions. They became stronger and more complicated with each passing day.

Catlin shook her head to untangle the complex cobwebs of her thoughts. What she needed was a swig of Aunt Martha's peach brandy. Hopefully, it would take the edge off her nerves that had been sorely put upon during the course of the day. With her heart set on a relaxing bath and a sip of brandy, Catlin aimed for the door. She wasn't sure if she was more anxious to soak in the tub or put a safe distance between her and the charismatic rake who rattled her so much she couldn't think straight.

Chapter 10

The evening meal went according to Martha's expectations. Lucas was the picture of manly attentiveness and Catlin was the epitome of feminine poise and politeness. Lucas offered a sketchy account of the incident at the cantina, taking care not to make Catlin's grandstand tactics sound as dangerous as they really were. As anticipated, Martha raved about Catlin's ability to slay her own dragons and Lucas's unique talent of taking care of every situation with quick efficiency.

Once they had consumed their meal, Martha insisted on seeing to the dishes while Catlin and Lucas ironed out the details of the contract. Catlin expected Lucas to put up a fuss over the stipulation of surrendering the down payment if he could not fulfill the contract upon his return from the trail drive. But he didn't. He sat calmly beside her on the sofa in the parlor, nodding agreeably. When Catlin asked for more than three dollars an acre Lucas stated that was the going rate and that both he and Martha had arrived at the price. Other than that, Lucas couldn't have been more pleasant and compatible.

"You are certainly in an agreeable mood tonight," Catlin observed as Lucas signed his signature on the contract.

A disarming smile quirked his lips. Lucas neatly folded the contract and placed it in Catlin's hand. "I'm usually an agreeable man . . . except when I get crossways of someone," he murmured in that soft husky voice that could send a herd of goose bumps galloping down her spine. "But I have never been one to hold a grudge."

The silky huskiness of his voice and his thorough perusal caused Catlin to blush. "Does this mean we can make a stab at being friends again?" she questioned for lack of much else to say.

A deep skirl of laughter reverberated in his chest. Distracted, Lucas reached out a tanned hand to smooth an unruly strand of blond hair away from her face. "I told you before, Cat . . ."

His voice was like a slow, lingering caress that intensified her awareness of him. (Which wasn't necessary. She was as aware of him as any woman could be, even though she fought the feelings with no success.)

"My desire to be your lover prevents me from stooping to being no more than a friend."

The evocative remark sent Catlin into her protective shell, but not as quickly as it had in the past. She had grown accustomed to his plainspoken comments. Her face didn't flush as red as it once did when Lucas assaulted her with his brash declarations. Cat wasn't sure she could deal with his straightforwardness, but she had come to anticipate it from this raven-haired rake.

Lucas refused to allow this elusive sprite to retreat behind her wall of self-imposed reserve. His hand came steadily toward her, alerting her to his intentions without frightening her. His dark, hypnotic eyes focused on her soft lips as if they were the first pair he had ever seen, as if he were intrigued by them. Catlin's heart missed several vital beats as his sensuous mouth rolled over hers. Her lips opened to him, as he taught it to do when he wanted more than a fleeting touch of a kiss. His hand tilted her head back to grant him free access and his fingertips monitored the accelerated beat of her pulse in her neck. Her legs turned to rubber and butterflies rioted in her stomach as his musky scent fogged her senses. While he savored the taste of her, strange unexplainable longings unfurled deep inside her. His darting tongue inflamed her. And even with her eyes closed she could see Luke's handsome visage through the cloudy fog that crowded in on her.

Catlin couldn't breathe without inhaling him, couldn't move without feeling his masculine presence beside her. A tiny moan that Catlin didn't remember emitting echoed beneath his nerve-shattering kiss. Catlin could feel his light caresses migrating over her ribs to brush against the sides of her breasts, but she was paralyzed by such tingling pleasure that she couldn't remove his straying hands. He knew just how and where to touch to set her on fire and each gasping breath she inhaled fed the flames that were beginning to burn out of control.

Lucas told himself that he had carried the kiss as far as it should go while Martha was in the kitchen, clanking her pots and pans. But damned if he could stop what he was doing. It would have taken a remuda of horses to drag him away from a pleasure so innocent and sweet that it shattered thought and stole his breath away.

Undulations of mounting desire crested in his blood like frothy white-capped waves. Lucas had to restrain himself from pulling Catlin full length beneath him— right smack dab in the middle of the parlor. God, he wanted this violet-eyed vixen! She was tormenting his male body without even trying, making him ache in places he had forgotten he had.

Like a starved tiger, Luke devoured her honeyed lips. His roaming hands set out on a journey of discovery, imagining what lay beneath the form-fitting gold gown. He was like a blind man feeling her tantalizing curves and swells, learning her by touch, taste and feel. He could close his eyes and conjure up this luscious angel while she was lying naked in his arms. She would be perfection. Her peaches and cream skin would glow in the candle light. And he would come gently to her, teaching her all the wondrous ways a man could pleasure and excite a woman.

"How about a steaming cup of coffee?" Martha announced long before she made her entrance into the parlor.

"How about a cold bath?" Lucas muttered as he pried himself away from the world's greatest temptation.

Catlin tried to look as if she were contemplating some deep philosophical thought and Lucas appeared as unruffled as a rooster perched on his nightly roost. But Martha wasn't fooled for a minute. Catlin had been soundly kissed. The telltale signs of partially swollen lips and mussed hair gave their secret away. Cat and Luke had been sparking on the sofa and the tension in the room was so thick Martha could have sliced it with a butcher knife.

"So, did we agree to the terms of the contract?" she questioned cheerfully.

Catlin collected her scattered wits and allowed her vocal apparatus a few more seconds of silence. She knew if she opened her mouth she would chirp like a sick cricket. When she finally felt confident to speak, she mustered a smile. "It all went without a hitch," she informed her aunt. "Lucas will grant you the down payment when he takes possession of the ranch. Upon his return from Colorado, you will be paid the remainder of the amount or he will forfeit the land and the initial payment."

"My, that sounds a mite drastic," Martha murmured between sips of coffee. "There are unseen hazards on the trail, unanticipated pitfalls that can cost hundreds of cattle their lives. Matthew always said a man was lucky indeed if he trailed a herd of three thousand and managed to lose only a third of the herd. That in itself could cut a gash in profits."

"Nevertheless, Cat is right," Lucas declared, his voice gravelly with the side effects of unappeased desire. "No matter what trials I face, I have an obligation to uphold the contract. My troubles aren't yours, Martha. Business and friendship are separate."

When Luke was sure he could stand without embarrassing himself by carrying a pillow over his lap, he gathered his long legs beneath him. "Tomorrow promises to be a long, tiring day. I have to gather Braxton and Gresham's herds, drive them to the holding pens my men have constructed beside the creek and brand them for the trail." He cast Martha a playful wink. "For the next several days I'll be stuck with Flapjack Barnett's cooking. Thanks for the grand meal before I resign myself to less-than-appetizing rations."

"I'll bring your breakfast down in the morning," Martha volunteered. "It may be the last decent meal you digest. I swear that man's cooking has caused as many injuries to cowboys as cattle stampedes."

"I won't tell him you said that," Lucas chuckled as he swaggered toward the door. Half-turning, he cast Catlin a parting glance that sent out invisible waves that rippled over her like a searing caress. "Good night, Catlin. Pleasant dreams."

The sheer impact of those glistening brown eyes caused Catlin to flinch. She could almost feel his touch from minutes before. His hands had been steady and sure, demanding things that Catlin wasn't sure she knew how to give, even if she wanted to.

"Good night, Lucas," she mumbled awkwardly.

When Lucas took his leave, Martha began chattering like a magpie. Catlin couldn't have repeated the conversation if her very life depended on it. Thankfully, she managed to appear reasonably interested in what Martha had said, even if her thoughts were on the ruggedly attractive rogue who left her to burn with a fever for which there was only one cure. Catlin did remember Martha asking her to deliver another basket of food to the Hanleys on her way to town the following morning. And that was about all Cat remembered. The rest of the colloquy was a

135

blur because Lucas Murdock's musky scent and the lingering taste of his explosive kisses had thoroughly shattered her composure and left her wanting things she knew she shouldn't have.

When Catlin eased her bedroom door shut an hour later, the silence crowded in on her. Trying not to dwell on that midnight-haired devil, Catlin trolled through a vast sea of memories—some pleasant, most of them not. She contemplated Ginger's unexplained dash from Dr. Blake's office and her difficult life with her ailing father. And then Cat pondered her own troubled past. Catlin had battled the system alone, holding down two jobs in hopes of keeping the plantation together. She had stood alone because there was no one to assist her. There had been times when she ached for her father's comforting arms to enfold her, to comfort and protect her. But there had been no one Catlin could lean on when the bottled up frustrations threatened to consume her. She had needed a man then, but her fiancé was dead and it had been a time of emotional upheaval. The other men who had courted her were not offering moral support or comfort. They had only wanted her body not the person she was.

Now she confronted a man who matched her fierce determination, a man who offered to pleasure her, to make the world go away, if only for the night. Catlin felt a need that had eluded her until this past week. She was confronted with a growing awareness of her desires. There was a time not so long ago when passion without commitment was unacceptable. But Lucas Murdock had a unique way of making her forget what was right and wrong. His touch had burned her blind with forbidden desire. He left her wanting to discover where these burgeoning sensations would lead. She knew Lucas was offering no more than a smile and a moment, but she found herself craving something so potent that it distorted logic. She didn't want to think past tonight. She was tired of being a tower of strength. The memories of the past

136

preyed heavily on her mind and Catlin needed to escape them before they depressed her more than she already was. . . .

Her gaze drifted toward the window. Involuntarily, her footsteps took her across the room to stare out into the night. The moonshadows clung to the outer walls of the two-room cottage below the hill. A warm shaft of golden light beckoned to her. Catlin could barely make out the motionless silhouette who had propped himself leisurely against the supporting beam of the porch. Her heart flip-flopped in her chest. She wondered fleetingly if Lucas could see her poised in front of her window, if it were his magical powers that had lured her to seek him out among the crisscrossed shadows.

Lucas could see her alright. Her tantalizing figure was framed by beams of light. He had silently called to her, willing her to shed her protective cocoon and fly down to him. But she didn't come. Lord, he would almost be thankful to bed down under the stars in the camp with the other cowboys for the next two nights. Standing sentinel on the stoop every evening, wishing upon a star, was driving him mad with wanting. He stood gazing at Catlin's window, waiting for the lantern to be swallowed by the darkness. It had become a nightly ritual, one that was getting him nowhere but fast!

But tonight, Catlin's curvaceous body lingered in the light, watching him watch her from a distance. If wishing would have made it so, he would have had the lovely butterfly spread her velvet wings and flutter down to fill his night with splendor.

His heart sank when Catlin turned away and disappeared from sight.

Heaving a melancholy sigh, Catlin had reversed direction to snuff the lantern. She sank onto the edge of the bed and pondered the silent darkness. The ghosts of her past were her companions, reminding her of the hell she had been through before she transplanted herself in Texas.

Texas . . . It seemed to stretch out forever in all directions and Catlin was like one insignificant star that twinkled on its wide horizon.

Silly fool, she scolded herself. She had Aunt Martha now. That was more than she had the past two years. But sometimes the companionship of family wasn't enough. Catlin squeezed her eyes shut, battling the longings that whispered through her mind. Lucas had become her shadow. His whispering voice was in the wind. When he walked away this evening he had taken a part of her with him, leaving her feeling half-alive, wanting him . . .

Catlin bounded to her feet and paced like a restless creature in captivity. She was not going to succumb to the wanton desires of the flesh. Wanting that dark-eyed devil wouldn't solve her problems. It would only create new ones. She had stood alone this long. She could endure the torments of wanting a man who would complicate her life.

With a frustrated groan, Catlin wheeled to pummel her pillow and cursed the betraying yearnings of her innocent body. Damn that Lucas Murdock. He had unleashed emotions Catlin hadn't realized existed. She had been able to combat the emptiness until he teased her with passion and left her to smolder!

With a muted growl, Lucas wormed from his clothes and carelessly tossed them aside. The moment the glowing light in the upper bedroom window faded, he felt as if a shade had been drawn over his eyes. It was Catlin's way of saying no. She had turned away from her window and shut him out, just as she always did. The look he had given her earlier had held intimate promises and unspoken invitations, but Catlin had declined them.

"Witch," he grumbled to the walls that were superimposed with flowing blond hair and lively amethyst eyes. Of all the females in the world, he had to find a spell-

138

casting sorceress in the house on the hill—a house that would soon belong to him. No doubt her bewitching spirit would be lurking in those halls, haunting him when he took possession—of the house, not Catlin.

Lucas chastised himself for lying awake when tomorrow would test his stamina and endurance. He and Old Bill would become Siamese twins and he would take on the same fragrance as his horse. So why was he staring at the shadows, counting the cracks in the ceiling? He could wish until he was blue in the face, but Catlin wasn't coming. She hadn't come the previous night or any of the ones before. And on that depressing thought, Lucas slammed his eyes and begged for sleep to satisfy the fantasies that eluded reality.

The timid touch of fingertips gliding across Lucas's shoulder brought him up from the groggy depths of sleep. His breath caught in his throat when he saw a vision of unrivaled beauty poised beside him. Moonshadows slanted across his room making a silvery pathway of light that streamed across the floor. Moonbeams glistened on Catlin's enchanting features and filtered through the sheer gown that formed a tempting wrapper on a gift of perfection. The pale light glistened in the long cape of blond hair that lay enticingly across her shoulders and Lucas struggled to inhale a breath before his hammering heart pounded him to death. He sensed that this cautious dove was poised for flight. If he made a sudden move the mystical lure that brought her here against her will would put wings on her feet.

And so Luke lay there, watching her watch him, gauging her reaction to the scars that marred his chest. Her light caress skimmed across the breadth of his bare shoulders and glided down his hair-matted chest. If she was offended by his scars she disguised it well. Her gaze was fixed on the rippling muscles. Her hands fluttered to and fro while she adjusted to the feel of a man's body beneath her fingertips.

It was all Luke could do to restrain himself from clutching this luscious angel to him, to explore every inch of her satiny flesh. Instead, he allowed Cat to investigate his masculine terrain, appeasing her curiosity about men.

Catlin wasn't sure why she had come. She had certainly told herself enough times that she wouldn't and shouldn't. But she was compelled to the cottage like a kite being tugged by the wind. She had never done anything like this before and it would have taken very little provocation to send her back where she belonged. Lucas seemed to sense that, she mused, as her inquisitive gaze followed the languid path of her hands over the muscled planes of his chest. Her heart went out to him as she traced the jagged scars, knowing he had suffered greatly because of them. But Catlin didn't shrink away from the sight of them. In fact, she felt closer to him, knowing they had both suffered because of the war. She had sustained invisible scars while Lucas plainly wore the atrocities of battle on his chest and back.

Luke lay perfectly still while Catlin appeased her feminine curiosity. He studied her with dark intense eyes that peered up from beneath a thick fringe of black lashes. The fact that she was here at all thrilled and excited him. The fact that she dared to touch him sent fires spiraling through his bloodstream.

Catlin marveled at the strength and vitality that lay in repose. She was moved by the longings that undulated inside her. Lucas was all man, every steel-honed inch of him. She could feel the whipcord muscles flex and relax beneath her inquiring caresses. He was like a sleek, powerful panther—a monument to masculinity in its purest, most elegant form.

Studying him as if he were a magnificent work of art, Catlin allowed her fingertips to drift lower, following the thick furring of hair that descended down his lean belly.

140

Her hands trembled as they migrated beneath the sheet to sketch the hard contours of his hips and thighs. Her pulse pattered like hailstones on a tin roof as she investigated his rugged masculine terrain. Ever so slowly, her caresses receded, rediscovering the warm hard flesh and finely tuned muscles from his knees to his shoulders.

Touching him was pleasure in itself, a rare privilege. Catlin trembled in response to the sensations that uncoiled inside her when she dared to learn the contours of his body better than she knew her own. But caressing him was no longer enough to appease the ache that mushroomed inside her. She needed to taste as well as touch him.

Her butterfly kisses skimmed his chest, swirling around each nipple, monitoring the rapid beat of his heart. Catlin withdrew to peer into those hypnotic eyes that glistened like ebony in the moonlight. How could he lie there motionless when his heart was thundering at the same accelerated rate as hers? She wouldn't have been able to, that was for sure!

Weren't men supposed to be wild, lusty creatures? If they all were, why did this one possess such amazing self-control? She knew he wanted her. The hunger was etched in his craggy features; it glowed in his eyes. Yet, he denied himself so she could discover the differences between a man and woman without being frightened away.

That thought tugged at Catlin's heartstrings. Beneath this rugged callused exterior was a man who was sensitive to her wants, her moods—a man who seemed to know what she needed better than she knew herself. He had reassured her by allowing her to touch him at will, allowing her to proceed at her own pace. Luke was comfortable with his masculinity, comfortable enough to allow Catlin to set her own rules and move at her own hesitant speed without feeling intimidated or wary of him.

Catlin spoke not a word to break the magical spell. Her lips returned to his skin, memorizing the feel of his masculine terrain. She inhaled the alluring scent that had clung to her since he had kissed her hours before. Her senses were overflowing with this powerful lion of a man. She could hear the rapid thud of his heart, feel his ragged breath, taste him, inhale him. . . .

This was the end, Lucas assured himself shakily. He was going to catch fire and burn alive any second now. Cat's worshipping kisses and adventurous caresses were going to kill him. Her name would be listed on his certificate under cause of death. Sweet mercy! He wanted her so badly his palpating heart was going to leap from his chest the moment before he went up in flames—cremated by frustrated passion.

A tormented groan rumbled in his throat when her untutored hands and exploring lips trailed lower and lower still. His breath stuck when her hands enfolded him and then drifted away. Lucas was suspended on a plateau of sweet agony. He couldn't breathe. The scent of jasmine clogged his lungs—lungs that were on the verge of bursting.

The instant before Luke whispered his last words and resigned himself to death by exquisite torment, Catlin withdrew. Like a hovering angel she rose up beside him. Her gaze never left his as she shrugged away the gossamer gown, letting it drift into a puddle at her feet.

And then Lucas sure enough couldn't breathe! His heart hung in his chest like a rock while he devoured a portrait of unparalleled loveliness. Catlin was even more exquisite than he had imagined. Her breasts were full; the rose-tipped crests begged for his touch. He could encircle the trim indentation of her waist with his hands. The gentle curve of her hips and thighs drew his eyes before they flooded over her again and again, afraid he had missed some minute detail in the moonlight.

Lucas deserved a medal for restraining himself from pouncing like a starved cougar. He could have so easily. But there was something in the hesitant, cautious way

Catlin peered at him that held him fast. He didn't want to frighten or hurt her. This feisty tigress was innocent of men and her mind was still warring with her feminine desires. Despite her reservations and better judgment she had come to him, offering him what no other man had been granted. Lucas accepted the treasure as if it were twenty-four karat gold. He longed to make this night a magical memory for her.

Slowly, his hand lifted, reaching out to her without touching her. Patiently, he waited for her to link her fingers into his. Tentatively, Catlin touched him, allowing him to draw her back to his side. A muffled gasp tripped from her lips when he pressed her quaking body against his hair-matted flesh. His sensuous lips slanted across hers as his caresses flowed over her skin like a tide rolling upon the shore. His hands and lips learned her feminine contours and Catlin's naive body burst into flame each place he touched. Her heart somersaulted around her chest, making it impossible to draw a breath.

Lord, she had never expected anything like this! Where were these soul-shattering sensations leading her? And would she survive them when they were already threatening to devastate her?

"Perfection . . ." Lucas whispered against the velvety texture of her skin. "There are not enough words to describe all the ways I burn when I touch you."

Catlin half-expected this swarthy giant to become a savage when she offered herself to him. But he was as gentle as the whisper of words that rippled over her skin. She couldn't imagine that such an awesome man could display such incredible tenderness. There was no rough urgency in his caress or kiss, only the quiet stirring of exploring hands and lips.

A tormented moan of pleasure bubbled from her throat when his caresses skied over the slope of her shoulder to draw lazy circles around her breasts. Catlin involuntarily arched toward him when his tongue flicked at each throbbing peak. Her skin quivered as his palm slid across her ribs and swirled across her belly to trace the clover-leaf birthmark on the sensitive flesh of her thighs.

The gnawing hunger built like a wild sweet crescendo. He teased her with his bold caresses, tantalized her with warm moist kisses. When his knowing fingers found her womanly softness, Catlin felt passion surge through her like a tidal wave. Her mind went blank. Her body suddenly possessed a will all its own, one so fierce and demanding that she could do nothing but surrender to the potent sensations that riveted her.

"Lucas . . ." His name fluttered from her lips in a breathless whisper. She didn't even know what she intended to say, only that she had to say something before she exploded like a geyser.

Catlin felt as if she were spinning in a whirlpool as he worked his seductive magic on her innocent body. He made her want him in the wildest ways. He siphoned her strength and left her trembling in his arms. White hot flames flickered in the core of her being and she knew, somehow, that this simmering caldron of untapped passion was going to erupt, just as surely as his name had tripped from her lips.

With a cry of frustrated pleasure Catlin looped her arms around his neck, bringing his face back to hers. Her lips parted beneath his, savoring the taste of him. And while he fervently kissed her his skillful fingers glided between her thighs, driving her mad with wanting. Catlin burned in places she didn't know she had. Instinctively, her naive body surged toward his masculine strength, feeling the need to absorb him, to become a part of this mass of boundless vitality.

Lucas had no experience with virgins, none at all. The magical inventiveness of Catlin's lovemaking had unleashed his ardor. But he had kept his sanity long enough to realize the critical moment of passion was upon them. If he didn't gently ease her over the hurdle of initiation, he would reaffirm her cynical opinion of men. What was meant to be a rapturous dream could quickly evolve into a painful nightmare for this innocent imp.

The responsibility he had assumed to appease his obsession for this lovely nymph made him shudder. He had never given much consideration to the women in his arms before this night. He had merely taken what was offered and dived headlong into passion's sensuous abyss. But with Catlin he had become an instructor who had to take one step at a time without rushing her over the waterfall into unbridled desire. He was giving of himself to ensure that her first taste of passion was sweet, not bitter.

Ever so slowly, his knees parted her thighs, letting her absorb the feel of a man's weight settling upon hers. He could feel her soft breasts mashing against his chest, her hips molding intimately to his. It was all he could do not to ravish her, but Lucas had made a promise he intended to keep—even if it killed him and he was sure it would.

God, he wanted her so badly his body shook like a leaf whipping in a windstorm. And Catlin had no idea that her frantic writhing was making it even more impossible for Luke to cling to his noble reserve. He could see the awakened passion shimmering in her wide eyes. He could feel her body quivering under his. But if he didn't take her gently, the splendor he anticipated would evaporate in a fog of fear and resentment.

"Lie still, Cat," he murmured against her quivering lips. "I want you desperately, but I don't want to hurt you." His muscular body took possession of hers and Catlin tensed at the sudden intimacy of being engulfed by this swarthy man. He caught her gasp in his kiss and then withdrew, but only for an instant. His hands slipped beneath her hips, gently holding her as he came to her, sharing the pleasure he longed to offer her.

Catlin's long nails dug into the taut muscles of his back, clinging to him in fear mingled with ardent desire. Her breath lodged in her chest when he moved inside her. She felt the flame billow until it burned like a bonfire. Passion, like a thick fog enshrouded her and the pain melted into a warm, pulsating pleasure. Catlin marveled at the wondrous sensations that drenched her body as he thrust against her. She could feel herself letting go, feel herself being towed into the sea of swirling flames. Although she clung to Lucas as if he were her lifeline, she was slipping into the dark dimensions that defied reality.

They were flesh to flesh, heart to heart, and Catlin cried out in the ecstasy of lovemaking. It wasn't anything like she thought it would be. The initial pain had bowed down to spine-tingling sensations that blew the stars around. She was part of his massive strength and he was the flame within her. They moved as one, soaring across the star-spangled heavens like an eagle in motionless flight.

One incredible sensation piled atop another, swelling like a thundercloud. Cat swore she would die in the pleasure of it all. She couldn't begin to translate her feelings into words because the sensations evolved with each demanding thrust, with each ragged breath. It was a kaleidoscope of rapture blending, swirling, twinkling like precious jewels in sunlight.

And then suddenly the most wondrous sensation of all burst inside her like a volcano. Catlin clung to this powerful man as passion poured forth like molten lava. The last ounce of strength seeped from her spent body as Lucas shuddered over her, whispering her name over and over again.

Catlin couldn't measure the length of time it required to descend from her dizzying orbit and reenter the perimeters of reality. It seemed forever before the haze of numbing pleasure rendered her body up to the stillness of the night.

Her lashes fluttered up to see Lucas's craggy features in the moonlight. A cryptic smile lingered on his lips as he bent to bless her with a tender kiss. There was no mocking slant to his mouth, no arrogant sparkle in his eyes. Catlin had never seen that expression before. It made her feel special and wanted, and if he didn't stop staring at her like that she was going to start reading more into that mysterious smile than was really there!

The soft purr of satisfaction rumbled in Lucas's chest. All these years he had flitted from one woman to another, appeasing his lusts. But if what he felt just now was satisfied passion, what the devil had he been doing for the past decade? It hadn't felt like this—this unexplainable pleasure that touched body, heart and soul. And he thought he knew all there was to know about passion. Ha! That was a laugh. Catlin had introduced him to a world of splendor that had somehow eluded him these past ten years. And having just found this last unexplored frontier, he was reluctant to give it up because he wasn't sure he would ever encounter it again.

"I desperately need my sleep," he rasped as he combed his fingers through the wild spray of blond hair that tumbled over his pillow. "But loving you only once isn't going to be enough, violet eyes . . ." His sensuous lips whispered over hers as his caresses rediscovered her luscious curves and swells. "I can't seem to get enough of you, Cat. You're in my blood now and the eternal flame is feeding upon itself . . ."

"Now?" she queried with wide-eyed innocence. "I don't think I could. . . ."

Her voice trailed off when his rumbling laughter interrupted her. Ah, this naive little sprite was a constant source of pleasure and amusement. "No?" he teased as his masterful hands sought out each ultrasensitive point and brought them back to life. "I think perhaps the lady underestimates herself. . . ."

Catlin might have questioned the recklessness of lingering in his bed longer than she had planned if she could have formulated another thought. But when Lucas wove another tapestry of intimate pleasure over her, her brain broke down. Leaving him when he was doing such impossible things to her body was inconceivable. Whatever this phenomenal lure he held over her, it was so ardent and intense that she could do nothing but respond to his touch.

Another round of giddy sensations began to blossom inside her. And this time she knew where the stepping stones of desire would lead—into a wild wondrous world that knew no time or space. She had reprimanded herself as she climbed down the tree outside her bedroom window to sneak to Lucas's cottage. But now that she was here, knowing the splendor that transpired between a man and woman, she couldn't tear herself away from him to return to her lonely bed.

With a quiet moan of surrender Catlin yielded to his familiar kisses and caresses. She returned the pleasure—touch for touch. This time she held nothing back. The first time she had been hesitant and unsure of herself and Lucas had been cautious and patient. But now the walls of reserve came tumbling down. They gave themselves up to the savagery of passion, allowing it to run its fervent course without restriction. It was a wild and breathless coming together—like two souls that had been separated for an eternity.

Catlin couldn't imagine herself doing the things she did. Modesty and inhibition flew out the window. Her bold caresses and eagerness left her to wonder if there had been another woman trapped beneath her shell of reserve all these years. She was like a starved creature whose cravings knew no limitations. She felt deliciously wicked and daring. When he had touched her she had gone mad with wanting. He had kissed her and she had ravished him, arching against his muscular flesh, needing him as desperately as she needed air to breathe.

This was passion in its rawest form, Catlin assured herself. Lucas had taught her the meaning of pleasure beyond bearing. This was like nothing her married friends had whispered about. There was nothing distasteful about the intimate communication between her and Lucas.

Obviously her friends had bedded the wrong man, Catlin mused as she soared in Lucas's sinewy arms. With this mystical wizard, passion was ecstasy. It was an incredible assault on every emotion. There was nothing to fear and no way to hold back when the feelings swept her away like a roaring river flooding from its banks.

Lucas marveled at the luscious creature in his arms. Catlin had come to life. She was a dozen kinds of passion seeking release and he was the recipient of her daring touch, her volatile kisses. She met each driving thrust, whispering his name, encouraging him. What Cat didn't know about lovemaking she compensated with lively imagination. Her caresses had sensitized every inch of his male body. And when she had glided her curvaceous body over his in a most inventive caress, Lucas had groaned in unholy torment. And when he took her the second time, he became her possession. He was a living breathing part of her and she had turned him wrong side out.

Lightning bolts shot through him as they blazed a fiery path across the black velvet sky. Passion had lifted its unruly head and gobbled him alive. He could feel the wild sensations converging, filling him to overflowing. His body shuddered convulsively and sweet release poured forth, draining his thoughts, his energy and his last ounce of strength.

Good gawd, he would need a crowbar to pry himself out of bed the following morning. There was nothing left, not even the will to move. He was now convinced that whatever he had been doing the past few years was not the same thing he was doing tonight. When he made wild sweet love to this vibrant nymph, he gave everything of himself and received all of her in return. Each ragged breath he inhaled was hers, each touch was soft pliant flesh molded intimately to his hard masculine contours. They were one essence and without her he was no longer whole. Whatever he once was, Catlin was now. What she had been he now understood. . . .

Hell's bells! He was making absolutely no sense at all. To be or not to be. Was not, but is now? What kind of crazy mumbo-jumbo was that? He was beginning to sound like a befuddled character out of a Shakespearean play, for crying out loud!

Lucas lost his grip on that thought when Cat's moist lips whispered over his. "No," he groaned tiredly. "I think we have both had enough lessons in love for one night. I don't think I have the energy to move, much less—"

Her adventurous hands strayed hither and yon, igniting fires Lucas was sure had burned themselves out. He was wrong.

"This time, my handsome rogue, I think you have underestimated yourself." She tossed his words back to him with a provocative smile. Her caresses flowed over him, taunting and tantalizing him. "If there is to be only one night for learning the lessons of love then I intend for this evening to last forever."

And sure enough it did.

Lucas soon realized that when this angel was in his arms nothing was impossible. She touched him and his soul sang. She kissed him and breathed life back into him. The dreams he had been having the past week could not compare to making love to this lively goddess. She satisfied him beyond his wildest imagination and Lucas really didn't care if he didn't sleep a wink. It wasn't every night that a man was visited by an angel who showed him the wondrous realm of paradise. Sweet mercy! If he had known lovemaking could be this good he wouldn't have wasted his time the past decade. Sailing in Catlin's arms was as good as it got. Catlin may not have realized that, but Lucas was experienced enough to know it beyond a doubt!

Chapter 11

The brisk rap at the door brought Lucas and Catlin awake with a start. Two pair of wide eyes locked in panic. Like bounding mountain goats they both leaped out of bed to gather their clothes.

Hell! It couldn't be morning already, Lucas thought as he shoved a bare leg into his breeches. "Damn, I forgot Martha promised to bring me breakfast," he muttered as he shrugged on his shirt.

In two swift strides he was at the window, quietly easing it open. The second Catlin threw on her dressing gown and tied it, Luke scooped her up and deposited her outside the window. His hand remained clamped on her elbow, spinning her about. With his head poked outside, Lucas swooped down to plant a hasty, but hungry kiss to her lips.

Another impatient tap at the door forced him to drag his lips away, although he would have preferred to continue kissing this adorable minx until midmorning.

"I wish your aunt (God love her) didn't have to get up with the chickens," Lucas scowled. "This isn't the way I envisioned telling you good-bye."

Wheeling about, Lucas stalked toward the adjoining room to answer Martha's knock. Catlin half-collapsed against the cottage and frantically gathered her wits. Her heart was still pounding like a drum. There was a vast difference between slowly rousing from sleep and being jarred to consciousness and being forced to dress and flee like an escaped convict.

When the piercing sunlight beat down on her face, Catlin was assaulted by harsh reality. A muted groan erupted from her lips as she stared at the window through which Lucas had hurriedly dumped her like a sack of dirty laundry. She could hear Luke's deep resonant voice mingling with Martha's chatter. Like a misbehaving child sneaking home after her nocturnal prowling, Catlin crept toward the ranch house, praying Martha wouldn't spot her.

Regret mingled with remembered passion, hounding Catlin every step of the way. She had found a pair of brawny arms to hold her, to chase the world away. But come dawn, life went on as usual. In a way, Cat was thankful she wouldn't have to face Lucas for the next few days. It would take her at least that long to come to grips with her reckless night of passion. Lord, the things she had done! And the things Lucas had done! Catlin blushed apple red.

What had seemed right and natural the previous night appeared careless and ill-advised in the light of day. Catlin had sacrificed her self-respect, just to appease her wanton desires. And magical though the night had been, nothing had changed . . . except that Lucas held her secret. He would look at her and know exactly what lay beneath her garments. He would know how shamelessly she had responded to his ardent lovemaking.

And the most depressing thing about their affair was that he was her first time and she was just another of the endless rabble of women who had succumbed to his powers of persuasion. What Lucas thought of her couldn't be worse than what she thought of herself. She was a tainted woman, a hypocrite, a harlot!

"Idiotic fool," Catlin muttered at herself as she breezed in the front door and whizzed up the steps two at a time. The previous week she had insisted that passion for passion's sake was beneath reproach. Now she was a party to the sins she had condemned. Was the pleasure she discovered in Luke's arms worth the price of humiliation, the price of knowing she couldn't trust herself where that raven-haired rake was concerned? Lucas loved a challenge. Catlin had been just that in the beginning. But now she was his conquest. As soon as another woman caught his roving eye, he would set his sights on a new conquest and she would be left to nurse her bruised pride.

That dispiriting thought caused Catlin to expel a raft of indecipherable curses. Oh, what did she care if Lucas focused his hunting instincts on another female? She hadn't expected his love or commitment. He was a dedicated bachelor, for Pete's sake. If he had wanted just one woman to become a part of his life, he would have settled down years ago. But he hadn't because the woman he wanted was married to his brother. Catlin had become another substitute for what Lucas really wanted and couldn't have.

Muttering disgustedly, Catlin wiggled into her muslin gown and flung her dressing gown aside. She had to get herself together and quickly. Martha would barge in any moment. Okay, so she had spent the night with Lucas. Cat squeezed her eyes shut and forced herself to face the mortifying reality. And yet, she had gone to Lucas of her own free will. He hadn't forced himself on her. Catlin gulped hard. Damn, it was difficult to cope with what she had done, not to mention the humiliation of facing Lucas again. She could just imagine the male arrogance in his grin the first time they met after his return from camp.

Catlin drew herself up and glared at herself in the mirror. She had her fling and now she knew what a man and woman shared in the whirlwind of lovemaking. She knew the feel of that lion's sleek muscles, the satisfaction of having his powerful body take po—

Heaven forbid that she should get carried away with arousing memories! It was over as quickly as it had begun, Catlin lectured herself sternly. She was not going to crawl to that handsome devil like a simpering twit, begging him to make a respectable woman of her. Lucas was obsessed with buying this ranch and making his operation the biggest and best in Texas. His plans did not include settling down, not when Elise's ghost still haunted him. . . .

"Well, good morning," Martha greeted enthusiastically. "You're up and around early."

"The circuit judge is due in town today," Catlin murmured as she brushed out her waist-length hair. "I have to testify against the thieves who stole my money and then I have to report to work."

"Surely you have time for breakfast," Martha said, tempting her niece with a tray of eggs and biscuits. "My goodness, you seem as eager to dash off as Lucas was."

Catlin wished Martha hadn't said that. It assured her Lucas was as eager to forget their tête-à-tête as she was. He had gotten what he wanted and now he was anxious to trot off on his merry way, never to spare Cat another thought. He would busy himself with his herd of cattle and she would be the furthest thing from his mind. Well, Cat wished she had a ranch and a herd of cattle to fuss over. But she had nothing, not even her innocence. Damn, what a fool she had been!

While she gobbled down her breakfast, Martha raved about what a wondrous day it was, what a fine man Lucas was. Catlin didn't share her enthusiasm, however, not when her pride was bruised black and blue.

Resolving to put the previous night behind her, Catlin pointed herself toward town with the basket of goodies Martha had baked for the Hanleys. Seeing Ginger's morose smile didn't improve Catlin's bleak mood. The sight of Ginger reminded Cat that she had bedded the man Ginger was also courting. She wondered if Ginger's sadness had anything to do with the depressing feelings Catlin was now experiencing. No doubt, Ginger had also fallen beneath Luke's devilish charms and now she found herself wanting more than that philanderer could give.

Catlin kicked herself all the way to town, certain she and Ginger were just two of the harem that Lucas kept at his beck and call. But it wasn't going to happen again, Catlin resolved for the umpteenth time. Only a fool would make the same mistake twice. She wasn't going to become sentimental and assure herself that Lucas cared deeply for her, to rationalize their night of lovemaking. Men didn't carry around these yokes of guilt and neither would she. Lucas was like a case of the grippe. Catlin had had him and now she was over him. She was immune . . . or at least she hoped she was. Just her luck that Lucas Murdock was as contagious as a cold, one that could be contracted time and time again!

Straining to hold the kicking, bawling calf in place, Lucas squatted down to press his knee against the animal's head. The calf bellowed as Lucas seared the road brand on the animal's hide. Bounding to his feet, Lucas freed the steer and strode over to brand another calf.

The sun had been beating down on Luke all afternoon and he shed his shirt. Perspiration streamed over him as he sank down to brand the calf two of his men were struggling to hold on the ground. After the brand was etched in the calf's hide, Bo marked another check in the roundup tally book and strode over beside Luke.

"It must have been one helluva cat fight," Bo Huxley snickered as his discerning gaze raced over the claw marks that mingled with the scars on Lucas's back.

The teasing remark caused Lucas to flinch and the branding iron he intended to poke into the fire grazed his thigh. Cursing a blue streak, Lucas twisted around to glower at Bo as if the accident were his fault. But Bo didn't cower from the maiming glare; he merely chomped on his oversized wad of tobacco.

"No work, no pay, Huxley," Lucas snapped grouchily. "Go find something to do besides keep the tally. I can do that myself." He gestured toward the heaping stock pens. "There are a thousand head of cattle that need branding. I'm not the only one around here who can tote a hot iron."

"Looks to me as if I should fetch the persylic ointment to tend your wounds. We wouldn't want them to get infected," Bo taunted relentlessly. "What was it? A two hundred pound leopard that got hold of you? Christ! I didn't even know those kind of cats were native to Texas."

Lucas brandished the hot iron in Bo's grinning face. "Unless you want your lips sealed shut, get to work," he roared.

Bo lifted his hands skyward. "Okay, Doc, no need to get riled. I only have your best interests at heart." His eyelids dropped into a teasing wink as he backed away. "Was she anybody I know?"

Lucas raised the glowing iron and Bo swaggered off, chuckling all the while. Grumbling under his breath, Lucas went back to his chore, wishing like hell that Cat's haunting image would go away and grant him a moment's peace.

He had seen the look of abandonment sweep across Cat's elegant features when he sat her outside his window. Ten to one, she was being hounded by regret. She was probably dreaming up reasons to avoid him like the plague when he returned to the ranch. There hadn't been time for lengthy good-byes, not with Martha pounding the damned door down.

Lucas sank down on the wriggling calf and cursed

fluently. After shuffling Martha out of his house, he had strode back to his bedroom to see the stained sheet. Thank God Cat hadn't noticed it in her rush to leave. If she had, she would have turned twelve shades of red. Dammit, he was the only man Cat had ever had and he had been forced to shove her out the window without discussing what they had shared. She probably felt cheap and unwanted.

Unwanted? Lucas vaulted to his feet and stalked over to brand another calf. Hell's bells, Cat had been his obsession. And once he had taken possession, he couldn't let go. Thrice hadn't been enough. It should have been but it wasn't. His craving was like an eternal spring that bubbled forth each time her image materialized above him. Lord, she had been a wild thing in his arms—all that fire and passion. Catlin was all woman, the kind who instinctively knew how to please a man. Lucas blazed like a torch, just remembering the sparks that had leaped between them.

He had the inescapable feeling Catlin wasn't the sort of woman who would accept their affair without blaming him and herself. She was too independent and feisty to let her emotions get the best of her. She would convince herself never to surrender to her desires again. Lucas was prepared to bet his life on it. Approaching that wary nymph when he returned to the ranch would be like starting all over again—wooing her, wanting her, wondering if he would ever get her back in his arms to recapture that night of ecstasy. Dammit, if only he would have had time to reassure her before he left—

"The idea is not to brand the poor calf all the way to the bone!" Bo growled harshly.

Lucas jerked back, so distracted by his thoughts of that violet-eyed elf that he had left the iron on the calf a second longer than necessary.

"She really must had been something else," Bo razzed Lucas with a naughty grin.

157

"She who?" Lucas inquired in mock innocence.

Agilely, the older cowboy rolled off the heifer he had branded and pivoted to poke the iron in the fire. "*She who* left her brand on you and has you wandering around with your head in the clouds, that's who."

"Go to hell, you nosey old codger," Lucas muttered in annoyance.

Bo threw back his red head and expelled a horselaugh. "A mite touchy, aren't we, Doc?"

"No, we are not." Lucas looked as if he wanted to bury Bo in the sand and sic a legion of ants on him.

Bo opened his mouth to fling a taunting remark, but the cook announced that supper was waiting. Hurling the ornery cowboy a mutinous glare, Lucas stalked toward the chuckwagon, vowing to converse with one of the other men during the meal. He was in no mood to tolerate Bo's jibes. But what bothered Lucas most was that he *was* touchy when it came to the subject of Catlin. If he had been with any of the other women who found her way to his arms the past few years, he could have shrugged off Bo's taunts. But Luke was frustrated as hell, wondering what Cat was thinking, wishing he could have told her she had fulfilled his wildest expectations. And by the time he reached the ranch house, she would not be receptive to any remarks referring to their rendezvous in the moonshadows. Cat would prefer to forget that night existed, sure as hell.

Damnation, if Martha had stayed in bed an hour longer, things would have been much better. Well meaning though the jolly old woman was, she had inadvertently driven a wedge between Lucas and that jewel-eyed she-Cat who had the pride of a lioness!

For six days Catlin had warded off thoughts of the raven-haired rake by working herself into exhaustion and dropping into bed each night, too tired to think. The trial in which she testified hadn't turned up the money she had lost, but she was offered the reward that was on the two desperados' heads. She intended to split the cash with Lucas since he was as responsible for their capture as she was. Although the bandits had been sent to prison, they refused to name the other men who had taken part in the robbery.

Catlin had taken her share of the reward money and purchased paint and new curtains to redecorate the Hanley's cottage. Although Ginger protested such generosity, Catlin arrived one evening after work with brush in hand. Together they moved Robert out on the stoop to enjoy an unhindered view of the landscape. Catlin delighted in having a friend her own age, one who unfortunately harbored the same secret Catlin kept hidden behind her rueful smile.

Unaware of Catlin's involvement, Ginger spoke of Lucas, mentioning the fact that he had invited her to Martha's house-warming party. The news stung like a wasp, but Catlin bore the pain without displaying her disappointment. Ginger had opened up enough to express her concern for her father and her fears for the future. But whatever was truly bothering Ginger was anybody's guess. Catlin had the sinking feeling it was the same nagging fear that had haunted her since the night she had spent in Lucas's arms. She could think of nothing worse than for both of them to be carrying the same man's child. Catlin hoped she was wrong on both counts. Babies should be born in wedlock and in mutual love, not in passion, Catlin reminded herself. And she was never going to let Lucas get that close again!

Resolving to forget her reckless indiscretion, Catlin accepted every invitation to be escorted about town by every respectable man who requested her companionship. She had been wined and dined and entertained at San Antonio's Casino Theater where the repertory company performed plays. She had danced at the Casino ballroom until her leg throbbed. She had dined on juicy steak at Casino Hall. She had viewed the rolling hills from carriages in the moonlight, but none of her suitors compared to the brawny cowboy who had taught her the meaning of passion in its purest, sweetest form. Catlin chided herself for measuring all other men by the standards of Lucas Murdock. But most men turned out to be the same. They uttered long lines of flattery in hopes of stealing a kiss or caress.

Catlin never thought she would long for Lucas's point-blank honesty, but she did. He was plainspoken and downright infuriating at times, but he was in a league all by himself. And the painful truth was she missed him! She knew he would be off limits because of Ginger, but that didn't stop her from missing that philandering rascal.

The date Cat had accepted with the young rancher named David Krause proved to be the closest thing to pleasant that she could remember before or after Lucas. The young man was four years her senior and had assumed the management of his father's ranch north of San Antonio. He was delightful company, a man of aspiration and he had a sense of humor. Like Lucas, he leaned toward straightforwardness in his intentions and he announced after their first date that he liked Catlin quite a lot. He also made it known, as he drove her home, that he was in the market for a wife. Catlin was his first choice and he didn't believe in long engagements or coquettish games. Although Catlin refused to accept the proposal after their first date she did agree to accompany David to Martha's party.

Things were going splendidly until David halted his carriage in front of the ranch house after their third date. While they sat there discussing a myriad of topics, Lucas appeared on the stoop. The forbidden feelings came rushing over Catlin and she flinched when the invisible tentacles reached across the distance to torment her. Purposely ignoring the brawny giant who loomed on the porch, Catlin concentrated on what David was saying.

Lucas silently fumed. He had knocked himself out gathering Braxton's and Gresham's herds, branding and corraling them in pens. He had worried himself sick wondering how Catlin was handling their secret rendezvous. The fact that she appeared to be handling it better than Lucas turned him inside out. He had been jealous of his brother when he courted and married Elise, but this was the first time in five years that possessiveness hounded him. Damn that minx. And she referred to him as a rogue. Ha! The pot was calling the kettle black.

Martha had made it a point to inform him of the string of suitors who had landed on the doorstep to court the lively Miss Quinn whose daring deeds were the talk of the town. Knowing Cat was seeing more men than he could shake a stick at wasn't half as frustrating as watching her with another man. And dammit, David Krause was a little too handsome and a lot too eligible!

Spurred by the green-eyed monster, Lucas strode off the porch to greet David, much to Catlin's chagrin. She looked in every direction except at Lucas. After a few minutes of small talk, Lucas, without forewarning, reached up to pluck Catlin from her perch and bid David a cordial but hasty good night. David declared he would return the same time tomorrow to take Cat to the new play that was opening at the Casino Theater and Lucas had to clamp his lips together to prevent voicing a loud and emphatic "Oh no you won't!"

"I do not need you to terminate my dates," Cat hissed as Lucas swept her along with his swift impatient strides. She wasn't sure if she was more irritated with herself for being so aware of this impossible man or at him for dismissing David.

"We need to talk and we can't do it with David

161

lollygagging around," Lucas muttered.

"There is nothing to say," Cat snapped brusquely.

"The hell there isn't. I'm just getting started," Luke growled.

"What a pity. I am already finished listening. Good ni—"

Lucas yanked her to his hard unyielding frame so quickly the last word was left dangling in midair. He didn't want to know how much kissing Cat and David had been doing before they returned to the house. But one thing was for sure, Lucas wanted his fiery kiss to be the one that lingered on this sassy woman's lips, the one that inflamed her dreams. His male pride was smarting. The only females he had seen in the last six days (other than Martha) were bawling heifers and they didn't count. Cat, on the other hand, had been going through men like an elephant through peanuts, damn her lovely hide!

Lucas felt as if he had been used—like one of many steeds in Cat's stable of studs. She hadn't wasted a second in replacing him the moment he was gone. The tormenting thought brought his lips down upon hers, stealing her breath, replacing David's kiss with that of his own. And for a full minute, Lucas devoured Catlin, compensating for all the times he had wanted to tug her into his arms and hadn't been able to do it.

"I thought you wanted to talk," Catlin gasped when Lucas finally allowed her to come up for air. "That didn't feel like talking."

Indeed, it didn't! The moment his warm greedy lips took possession of hers, Cat's knees buckled and her heart pole vaulted to her throat. Blast it, why did this man have to have the knack of waltzing up and kissing her until her mind turned to mush?

Lucas felt as if he had grabbed hold of a lightning bolt. Uncontrollable sensations sizzled through him. He had to inhale a steadying breath before he dared to speak. "Now

162

that I have your attention, what have you and David been doing? Studying human anatomy?" he demanded to know.

Catlin winced as if she had been slapped. So that's what he thought, did he? She had bedded him so naturally he anticipated that she would sleep with every man who courted her. How dare he suggest such a thing! Obviously, whatever respect he had for her before she surrendered to his passion was now nonexistent.

"Yes, as a matter of fact, we have, just like you and Ginger," she flung at him in childish vindictiveness.

"Ginger is another matter entirely," Lucas sneered into her defiant face.

"Another matter?" she parroted sarcastically. "Women are all the same to you."

"You were different," Lucas muttered, fighting like hell to keep from placing a stranglehold on this saucy sprite and shaking her until her teeth fell out.

"How stupid do you think I am?" Catlin blustered.

"Don't ask if you don't want to know," he shot back, his dark eyes flashing.

"Are you or are you not escorting Ginger to the house-warming party?" Cat challenged him.

"I am but—"

"I rest my case," she interrupted, her voice like the pounding of a gavel.

When Catlin launched herself from his arms, his hand snaked out to manacle her wrist. "I've missed you, dammit. I want what we had."

Violet eyes flickered with barely controlled fury. "I'm sure you can find what we had and more in any set of arms. I don't like being convenient!"

"Nobody said you were," Lucas gritted out. His handsome face twisted in an agitated scowl. "What we shared was special. Now that you have been around with every man in town you should know that."

Catlin took offense to everything he said, especially the bruising insults. It was the only way to prevent herself from buckling beneath his dark, magnetic charm. "I haven't been around. *You* have," she sniffed sarcastically. "Amazing how quickly your honesty falls by the wayside when lust overcomes you. What's the matter? Have you seen too many cows and not nearly enough women lately?"

"Woman, you drive me crazy," Lucas said with visible restraint.

Damn her, she had done it again. She had dragged him into an argument and accused him of misconduct when she was the one who should have been on trial!

"You're pretty hard on my sanity yourself," Cat countered in a caustic tone. In vain, she struggled to loose the hand that held her captive.

"Hell's bells, will you hold still?" Lucas grumbled.

"Not until you let go," Cat insisted and then she kicked him in the shin.

With a growl, Lucas pounced like a tiger. Catlin found herself imprisoned in his chaining arms. He swung her off the ground, slamming her body into his. The kiss he planted on her protesting lips carried enough heat to cremate the sun. White hot flames shot through her limbs. Catlin hadn't meant to return his fiery kiss, but responding to him had quickly become second nature. She didn't want to want him. But confound it, she did. The quivering sensations triggered forbidden memories of a night that had no place in her life. Suddenly, she was arching closer, aching to mold her flesh to his masculine contours. He could make her forget why she was so furious with him, forget her firm resolve to keep her distance.

Lucas couldn't formulate a sane thought himself. The feel of her curvaceous body left him burning on a hot flame. He touched her and he remembered the splendor, the wild uninhibited pleasure they had shared. He wanted to feel her silky flesh beneath his, to lose himself in the dark, sensual dimension of time that spanned eternity.

"You're not like the others, Cat," he assured her huskily. His lips hovered a hairbreadth away. "When I touch you I forget every woman I've ever known."

Catlin peered into the hypnotic brown eyes that were set amid a thick fringe of lashes. She wanted to believe him. But Lucas Murdock had already set a precedence of bedhopping. She hated to even hazard a guess as to the number of women who had lain in his arms. The population of San Antonio was more than six thousand. And if one-third of the citizens were females . . . Oh, for crying out loud, Catlin didn't want to think about it!

"Your coffee is getting cold, Lucas." Martha called from the partially opened door. A sly smile pursed her lips when Lucas and Catlin pried themselves apart. Things were looking up! Lucas was obviously jealous when she mentioned all the men who pursued Catlin. He hadn't wasted a second when he heard David's buggy roll into the yard. And she was delighted to find these two rambunctious individuals kissing. But Martha had to carefully monitor this budding romance. It was her responsibility to act as their chaperone. Had she known that this relationship had progressed far beyond a kiss in the moonlight, she would have dragged both of them to the Justice of the Peace and ordered an immediate wedding.

Rewinding her unraveled composure, Catlin wobbled on rubbery knees toward the door. Lucas, who wasn't navigating much better than Cat was, followed a respectable distance behind her.

After Catlin presented Lucas with his half of the reward money, she complained of a headache and retired to her room. Cat didn't want to put her emotions through the meat grinder another second. Lucas Murdock had given her a headache—a six-foot three inch, two hundred twenty pound headache. It was entirely possible that she would need to grow a thick shell to defend herself against his devilish charm. Blast it, she might have a chance at happiness with David Krause if Lucas would let her alone. She and David were compatible. He was interested in his ranch—something Catlin had lost and wanted to replace. If only David could appease these wild yearnings the way Lu—

Catlin shoved the thought aside and doffed her clothes. She wasn't going to think about any man tonight. She wasn't that crazy about men to begin with, she reminded herself cynically. They were all trouble. And on that sour note Catlin climbed into her bed and pulled the quilt over her head so Lucas Murdock's image couldn't materialize on the ceiling to torment her!

The feel of sensuous lips playing softly upon hers lured Catlin from her troubled dreams. Her tangled lashes swept up to see a bare-chested giant sitting on the edge of her bed. Catlin was all set to reject his midnight visit, but his index finger hovered over her mouth to shush her. The haunted expression on his shadowed features froze the words to her tongue.

"Don't deny me, Cat," he rasped as his hand drifted over the sheet, mapping her body with gentle caresses. "Please, not tonight. You're all I've thought about while I was away." His tousled raven head inched toward her again, his mouth courting hers with tenderness. "I need you, little nymph. You can make my dreams come true. . . ."

Now how was she supposed to put this tempting devil to flight when he kissed her so masterfully, when he awakened her slumbering passions with his featherlight caresses? She couldn't, Cat realized. Despite common sense, despite her noble vows, one night of passion only whetted her appetite instead of curbing her forbidden desires for this magnificent man.

When Lucas eased beneath the sheet to set his practiced hands upon her trembling flesh Cat lost the will to fight the sizzling sensations that ricocheted through her. Tonight would be the last night she spent in his sinewy arms, she promised herself. She would get this dark-eyed demon out of her system once and for all. Then he would no longer hold this mystical lure over her.

Catlin felt herself sinking into her mattress, as if it were a puffy white cloud. Ah, Lucas had the most incredible way about him. He spun a web of pleasure around her, creating silken threads that chained her to him. Instinctively, her body responded to the delicious magic of worshipping kisses and heart-stopping caresses.

The flickering flames burned hotter as his skillful hands tracked across her ribs to draw lazy circles around the pale pink tips of her breasts. His moist lips abandoned hers to glide over her collarbone and ski down the silky slope of her shoulder. The warm draft of his breath caressed her skin as he sought out the throbbing peaks, teasing them with his tongue, savoring their soft fragrant texture with his lips. Her traitorous body arched upward, craving more of the delectable pleasure he was bestowing on her with his masterful fondling.

The slow, erotic passage of his hands and lips were sweet compelling torment. They flooded over her quaking flesh like waves gently lapping against a sea shore. Giddy sensations splashed over Catlin, following in the wake of wondrous kisses and caresses. And when Lucas had coaxed her body into willing submission, he parted her thighs with his knees and levered himself above her. His lips returned to hers with whispers of his need, of pleasures to come. His hungry kiss stole the last of her breath and intensified the multitude of cravings that gnawed at her.

Catlin felt his powerful body surge upon hers and she knew she would sacrifice her own identity to become one with him. With a sigh of unbearable longing Cat broke every promise she had made when Lucas came to her, taking her to the heights of ecstasy. The hypnotic cadence of his lovemaking left Catlin diving and then skyrocketing through a world of ineffable sensations that stripped all thought from her mind. She was helpless, oblivious to all except the splendor that undulated through her.

And then it came, that wild, incredible feeling that shook the roots of her sanity. With a muffled cry of ecstasy, Catlin dug in her claws and held onto Lucas for dear life. Shock waves pelleted her and every soul-quaking sensation that had assaulted her suddenly converged to devastate her composure. And even when the rapturous feelings began to fade, there was still one thread of pleasure that streamed through her, refusing to allow her to unloose her grasp on the magical dream that Lucas had spun about her. She lay in his arms, marveling at the overwhelming feelings he instilled in her, reveling in the feel of his hair-matted body cuddled protectively against hers.

All through the night, Catlin awakened again and again to the feel of gentle hands. She could not think of one logical reason why she should reject the passion Lucas offered her. And worst of all, she didn't even try. He touched her and she automatically responded. There was no pretending she wasn't stirred by Luke's ardent lovemaking. He filled her with a need, one that blossomed and grew out of proportion. He had taught her all she knew about love and passion and he had branded his memory on her mind. This raven-haired devil had made her a slave to his desires and to her own awakened needs. To deny him was to deny herself the magic that compared to nothing in her life. Catlin seemed to have no willpower when she was in this man's arms.

But in the dark hour before dawn, her demon lover left her with a sizzling kiss and silently exited through the window. Swamped by a riptide of emotions Catlin watched Lucas disappear into the darkness, wondering how many lectures she would have to deliver to herself before she finally let go of this impossible dream. She couldn't keep this up, she mused, her body still tingling with the aftereffects of his potent lovemaking. She would be the one hurt by these amorous interludes, not Lucas. He saw her only as a conquest, one who had yet to whisper her undying love for him. Once he had taken her heart and soul he would turn his attention elsewhere, looking for another female to seize and conquer.

And Lucas was right about her, Catlin realized as she inhaled the musky scent that clung to her skin. She was a coward when it came to affairs of the heart. She knew how devastating it was to lose someone she loved. She was afraid to let anyone that close again. Lucas wasn't offering love or forever—only stolen moments of ecstasy.

This was the very last time she would revel in the splendor of his passion, she vowed firmly. It had to be. Luke would break her heart if she fell in love with him, just as he had broken the heart of every other woman who became a substitute for the one female Lucas wanted and couldn't have. Catlin knew she was every kind of fool if she didn't remember that Lucas was only satisfying his needs and pretending each of his lovers was Elise. If he hadn't stopped wanting his brother's wife after five long years, chances were he never would. No woman could measure up to Elise in Lucas's eyes and he was doomed to wander though life, searching for something he could never replace.

Catlin was sensible enough to know she couldn't compete with an elusive dream, especially if it had become bigger than life the past few years. It hurt to know she wasn't the woman Lucas wanted, even when he tried to convince her otherwise. He wanted her to share his passion, that was all, and he was willing to say most anything to lure her into his arms. Lucas looked at her and he saw Elise. Catlin was as certain of that as she was of her own name because she had seen Luke's face on every man she had courted for almost a week. It cut her to shreds to accept the fact that she was suffering the same torment Lucas experienced with his memories of Elise.

Better to be a realist than a fool, Catlin reminded herself gloomily. It was unsettling to know the best she could ever be in Lucas's eyes was second best, if even that. And considering her competition, she doubted she was even in the top ten on Lucas Murdock's "Most Wanted" list of lovers. Honest to goodness, she must have been crazy to get mixed up with that philandering rake in the first place. If she didn't watch her step Lucas Murdock would break her heart into a million pieces!

Chapter 12

'Catlin managed to avoid seeing Lucas for the next few days. He was busy rounding up other herds and branding the cattle he intended to put on the trail. If she could play these cat and mouse games for a little longer, Lucas would be out from underfoot for four months. Surely during that span of time she could convince her reckless heart to forget that raven-haired rake. Lucas was staying at the camp of tents the cowboys had pitched to stand watch over the huge herd. Catlin came and went without fear of confronting Lucas, without being reminded of the night he had crept to her room to teach her more about the ways of passion.

David Krause had become Catlin's constant companion. She tried to respond to his warm kisses, but there was no spark to set fire to her feminine desires. As compatible and considerate and attentive as David was, he wasn't Lucas. Catlin detested herself for wanting more than David had to offer. Honest to goodness, David was more than enough man to satisfy a woman. And he would have been enough to satisfy Catlin if she hadn't been caught in that devil's spell. Now that she had experienced Luke's brand of forbidden passion she couldn't be content with anything less.

The two times Lucas had come to town, Catlin saw him in Ginger's company. Catlin assured herself she didn't care but the words had a hollow ring to them. Yet, she kept repeating them each time Lucas and Ginger ambled past her office as if they were conducting a parade!

The day before the house-warming party, wagonloads of men arrived in town with Martha's furniture and belongings. With Martha giving direction as to where every object was to be placed, the wood-framed home was instantly livable. When Catlin arrived upon the scene, several cowboys were putting the finishing touches on each room, setting each piece of furniture just so, according to Martha's specifications. When Catlin rounded the corner to see her new room, she skidded to a halt. To her dismay, Lucas was tossing the pillows on her bed.

A mocking smile pursed his lips as he hitched his thumb toward the window. "I'm sorry there is no tree for you to scale when you are in the mood for nocturnal prowling. But considering the way you have been avoiding me, I don't suppose it will matter."

"No, I don't suppose it will," Catlin countered, tilting a proud chin. "I have given up doing things that make me ashamed of myself."

He moved toward her and the world shrank to a space no larger than the area Luke occupied. "I'm not ashamed of what we had," he murmured as his bronzed fingers cupped her chin, bringing it down a notch, forcing her to meet his dark, spellbinding eyes. "I hate for night to come, knowing I'll see you standing in the moonshadows, knowing you aren't really there. . . ."

Why did Lucas have to be the man who held the key that unlocked her hidden emotions? She knew she had been only a temporary physical release for his lust and that he was preying on her vulnerability. But all the passion in the world couldn't compensate for the devotion and respect she needed to make herself feel whole and alive and loved.

Catlin needed the same profound love her parents had shared. Down through the years they had grown together, sharing each other's hopes, disappointments and dreams. Lucas only spoke in terms of secluded rendezvous while he flaunted Ginger under her nose. He delighted in having a number of women on a string and Catlin detested knowing that her closest friend probably knew Lucas as well as she did and in the most intimate ways.

Lucas watched the conflicting emotions chase each other across Catlin's enchanting features. Cat was erecting that cussed stone wall between them again. He could feel the invisible partition going up. Cat was so cynical of men that she didn't know honesty when it stared her in the face. She didn't want to remember those special nights that he couldn't forget and that stoked the fires of his temper.

"But what do you care that I've missed you, that I still want you?" he grumbled resentfully. "You have David at your beck and call. He escorts you all over town, granting your every whim."

"He treats me like a lady," Cat snapped, brushing his lingering hand away from her face as if it were a pesky mosquito.

His brown eyes scrutinized her intently. "Maybe he can make a woman feel like a lady," he contended. "But the question is—can he make a lady feel like a woman?"

Catlin flushed up to the roots of her blond hair. "That is none of your concern," she spluttered, eyes snapping. "I haven't asked you how many times you've made a woman out of Ginger—" Catlin compressed her lips. It was obvious her tongue was not engaged to her brain. They were leading separate lives.

"I'll be glad to tell you. All you have to do is ask," Lucas taunted.

Ah, how he delighted in ruffling her feathers. He thrived on that living fire that flickered in her amethyst eyes. He loved to watch her coil like a tigress preparing

173

to strike.

Cat could have slapped him silly for that remark. Damn him. He was doing it again, flaunting his prowess with women in her face. Why, the man probably had to alphabetically categorize all his lovers to keep track of them. "I really couldn't care less what you've been doing and with whom," she declared with haughty conviction.

With that proclamation, Catlin sailed out the door. Lucas expelled a soundless expletive. Why did he always have to give way to the temptation of bombarding that firebrand with taunts? He knew she would explode. She was a walking grenade looking for a place to blow up.

Well, she had started it, Lucas thought self-righteously. He had admitted he missed her and that he wanted her and she had said nothing in return. She just stood there mistrusting all men in general and him in particular.

Just once before he pointed himself west with his sprawling herd of cattle, he would like to create another sweet memory. But Cat didn't want to believe she mattered to him because he didn't matter all that much to her. He had been her experiment with passion, a mistake she regretted making.

Growling at his preoccupation with a feisty sprite who had brushed him off like a bothersome insect, Lucas reversed direction to leave that stubborn minx a reminder he had been there, just in case she forgot he had.

With meticulous care, Catlin dressed for the evening. She had returned earlier that afternoon from the newspaper office to assist her aunt in preparing the refreshments for the party that would take place at the house, on the lawn, and in the street. Martha assured her that a party, Texas-style, compared to no other social event Catlin had ever attended. The musicians had already arrived and the music of Spanish guitars, fiddles, and harmonicas were already wafting their way through her window.

Catlin promised to enjoy herself, even if it killed her. She wasn't even going to notice Lucas and Ginger. Chomping on that stubborn thought, Catlin arranged her coiffure and double-checked her appearance in the mirror. The young woman who peered back at her had begun to take on the same underlying unhappiness Catlin had detected in Ginger Hanley. Sweet mercy, they hadn't both fallen in love with that rakehell, had they? At least Catlin was assured that she wasn't carrying Luke's child. It had come as a great relief, but she wasn't so sure about Ginger.

Yet, what truly disturbed Catlin was the expensive gift Lucas had left on her pillow the previous night. She wasn't certain where he had acquired the expensive jeweled ring and she didn't know whether to take the gift as a compliment or an insult. Was it to be compensation for the loss of her virginity? Did he usually leave trinkets for his lovers? And what had he given Ginger?

Well, whatever his ultimate purpose, Catlin wasn't accepting the gift, she decided. And if that raven-haired devil thought he could buy her body he had damned well better think again!

Martha's voice echoed in the hall, announcing David's arrival. Sliding the ring on her finger, Cat proceeded downstairs, making a mental note to return the ring the first chance she got.

Thrusting herself into the festive spirit, Cat dipped up a glass of punch and very nearly choked on her breath. She and Martha had mixed the fruit punch, but someone had obviously tampered with it.

Cat took another sip, finding the taste not as offensive after a few drinks. She was going to celebrate. It was to be the first time in over two years that she had consumed more than a nip of wine or brandy. And besides, the liquor would take the edge off her nerves, she convinced herself. She didn't need edgy nerves when she confronted Lucas Murdock while Ginger was on his arm.

For more than two hours Catlin and David milled

through the crowd that gathered on the lawn and danced in the street. Time and time again Catlin returned to the punch bowl, pretending not to notice how light Lucas was on his feet while he swirled Ginger around in his arms. She didn't even care that he looked incredibly sexy in his black breeches and matching jacket. David was every bit as attractive as Lucas with his blond hair and fair features. And David was a lot less dangerous. He didn't make mincemeat of her emotions the way that brown-eyed demon did.

Speak of the devil and he appeared. Catlin's long lashes swept up, peering at the stony face from over the rim of her punch glass.

Despite Luke's irritation over the fact that Catlin had been drinking steadily since she sailed out of the house, his brown eyes took inventory of the luscious witch-angel who stood before him. Catlin's blond hair had been fashionably pinned atop her head with soft wisps of curls dangling enticingly around her forehead and temples. The flickering torch light enhanced her peaches and cream complexion and her coiffure called attention to the swanlike column of her throat and the daring décolleté of her gown. Lucas found himself thinking this curvaceous pixie looked good enough to gobble alive. The deep crimson dress Cat had donned for the party accentuated the full swells of her breasts and the narrow indentation of her waist. Dainty lace adorned the frilly off-the-shoulder gown, leaving plenty of bare flesh to tempt any man who cared to look and scores of them did! Cat had been the object of many appreciative stares since she sashayed over to the refreshment table to guzzle one drink of spiked punch after another.

When Catlin gulped another drink, Lucas flung his meandering thoughts aside and awarded the saucy sprite with a condescending frown.

"You're drinking like a fish," Lucas observed disgustedly.

A lopsided smile dangled on the corner of Cat's mouth. Defiantly, she tipped up her glass and downed the remainder of her drink in one swallow. "I'm celebrating Aunt Martha's move to town and your departure," she declared, her voice slightly slurred.

Lucas snatched the glass from her fingertips, set it aside and ushered her to the dance area.

"I have an escort ... somewhere around here ... ," Catlin grumbled as Lucas enveloped her in his arms, making her a prisoner of her own wicked desires. Dammit all, she had purposely imbibed in drink to take the sting out of wanting a man she couldn't and shouldn't have. And here he was, holding her quaking body against his masculine frame, squeezing out the hauntingly sweet memories from the shadows of her heart.

"The spark is still there, isn't it, Cat?" he murmured in a voice that was low with caressing huskiness. He pressed her body even closer, making her throb with tormented pleasure.

The spark was there alright and if it got close to the liquor which she had partaken, combustion would take place. Catlin hated what he was doing to her. She was forced to compare her response to him with the one David evoked. It was no contest. But pride refused to put that confession to tongue. Cat would have died before she admitted the truth.

"Let me go. David is waiting for me to join him," she insisted, trying in vain to fling herself away without making a scene.

"You'll be easy prey for him if you don't leave that punch alone," Lucas warned her. "If he doesn't know the location of that clover-leaf birthmark yet, he will before the night is out. You're too drunk to reject him."

Her head snapped up, glaring at him through dulled eyes. "Your odd sense of possessiveness baffles me. Why should you care which man follows you when there are no strings between us?" Catlin said bitterly. She looked him up and down, searching for at least one flaw to criticize and finding none. Striking an arrogant pose, she stuck her nose in the air. "Does it put a dent in your male pride to know you were the first but you might not be the last lover I ever have?"

Catlin wasn't sure why she was goading him. Maybe she wanted to hurt him. Maybe she wanted to share the company misery loves so well. All the liquor in the punch bowl wouldn't make her forget the nights of splendor they had shared. She had tried every possible technique to exorcise him from her thoughts and her heart.

Lucas lips thinned in an annoyed scowl. It was all he could do to keep from shaking the stuffing out of Catlin for those taunting remarks.

While Lucas and Catlin were verbally waging war under the pretense of dancing, Martha Lewis was smiling like a Cheshire cat. Although her niece and Lucas had different escorts, the attraction between them drew them together. She had hoped they would make some sort of commitment to each other before Lucas set out on his trail drive to Colorado. If he didn't, Catlin might convince herself to marry David. That would never do!

"I think my niece and Lucas are quite taken with each other," Martha chortled to Dr. and Mrs. Emmet Blake, as she nodded toward the dance area.

Emmet's brow furrowed as he surveyed the shapely blond and her tall, dashingly attractive companion. His gaze circled the crowd to see Ginger standing like a wallflower beside the refreshment table. Excusing himself, he ambled over to demand a word with Lucas.

"Aren't you forgetting your date?" Emmet prompted, flashing Luke a condescending glance.

"I see no harm in dancing with Miss Quinn," Lucas contended, refusing to let Cat go, even when he knew she preferred to be anywhere except in his arms.

"You have a responsibility to Ginger," Emmet's dark brows came together as he stared pointedly at Lucas.

Catlin wasn't sure what Emmet's interest was in Lucas or Ginger's affair, but he appeared very firm in his opinion that Cat was unwelcomed on the third side of the eternal triangle. The doctor may have been a highly respected pillar of society, but Catlin didn't appreciate him meddling in her affairs. She didn't want to be in Lucas's arms, but neither did she want Emmet Blake's interference. She was accustomed to handling her own problems and she wasn't eliciting help.

"We are discussing the contract for the sale of Martha's ranch," Catlin lied. "There is no reason to fret, Dr. Blake. When we have worked out the last details, I will return to my escort and Lucas will eagerly return to his."

Dr. Blake glared at the shapely blond. She certainly wasn't afraid to speak for herself, even if she was addressing someone of the physician's position. "I certainly hope so, young lady. The two of you will have the gossips' tongues wagging."

When Emmet stalked away, Lucas peered down into Catlin's exquisite features. A wry smile pursed his lips. Wasn't it just like this rebellious minx to refuse assistance. It was obvious she wanted nothing to do with him, but she refused to let Blake interfere in her business. Slaying her own dragons was an admirable quality, but Lucas had seen this firebrand carrying her philosophy to dangerous extremes. And yet it was that daring courage that intrigued him . . . among other things.

The anger drained out of Lucas's body. This was not the time or place for an argument. There were obviously several pairs of eyes on them and he had no intention of spoiling Martha's party.

"I still want you, Cat," he whispered as he held her droopy gaze. "These verbal battles don't change the way I feel."

"Ah, yes," Catlin tittered bitterly. "The separate lives and loves of Lucas Murdock."

There she went again, trying to set him off. But Lucas

was not going to be dragged into another spirited debate. "Before I leave I need to know you aren't going to rush into a marriage with David. It would be a mistake. He isn't man enough to handle you."

Catlin gasped at his audacity. "David can provide security and pleasant company," Catlin bristled defensively. "I don't need you or anyone else telling me what I need and don't need. I have been on my own far too long to allow a man to do my thinking for me."

"He can't pleasure you in bed," Lucas had the nerve to say with his usual amount of candor. "You and I feed off each other's passions. You're not the kind of woman who could settle for less than what we share when we touch. When we are flesh to flesh . . ."

Shades of red flamed Catlin's already flushed cheeks. "Those two nights didn't happen," she muttered stubbornly.

"Didn't they?" One dark brow arched to a challenging angle. "If we weren't making wild sweet love in my bed and then in yours, what do you call what we were doing, violet eyes?"

Another blush stained her bewitching features. "I don't wish to discuss it."

"You always say that when I'm winning an argument," he taunted.

"Honest to goodness, Lucas. Sometimes you make me so furious I could strangle you!" Cat hissed resentfully.

"And you steal my breath away when we make love," he told her, his voice dropping to a seductive level that caused her pulse to leapfrog through her bloodstream. "In two days I'll be gone." His hand folded around her fingertips, calling her attention to the ring he had left in her room—a ring that had belonged to his mother, the same one he had intended to present to Elise the night his brother announced he had proposed to the sultry beauty. "Despite what you are probably thinking, this gift is a symbol of my affection and I want you to have it."

Catlin blinked like a disturbed owl. She wasn't sure if this was Luke's ploy to keep her dangling on a string while he was away or if he honestly meant what he said. For the most part, Lucas spoke his mind, but she had to be careful not to read more into the confession than he actually meant. He may have felt something for her, but he had made no commitment and there was still his relationship with Ginger to consider. How many other women had heard similar admissions? Maybe Lucas was one of those men who never met a woman he didn't like.

Cat needed to sort out the myriad of thoughts that converged on her, but Luke refused to grant her time to let her cynicism drive another wedge between them. He could tell her instincts were warring with her brain and he fueled her emotions with his candor.

"If you consent to marry David, what do you plan to do about me, violet eyes?" His probing stare held her hostage. "Once I walked away because my brother claimed the woman I wanted. The only reason I kept my distance is because Elise's husband was my own brother. But I feel no obligation to David. And when he can't give you what you need, I will be there waiting to recapture the splendor of having you in my arms, of rediscovering that delicious body of yours. . . ."

"Will you stop!" Catlin pulled away and this time Lucas let her go. But his dark eyes continued to penetrate the crumbling walls of her defenses. "You can hide behind a convenient marriage if you wish, but it won't keep me away from you. I have exhausted my supply of noble honor. I want you and I don't care who knows it, not your future husband, not Martha, and certainly not Emmet Blake who seems to have other plans for me. But make no mistake, Cat, I will not be manipulated. This time I'm going to take what I want."

Doing an about-face, Luke cut his way through the crowd to lead Ginger into the dance area that had been staked out in the street. On wobbly legs, Catlin aimed herself toward the punch bowl. Her mind was in a whirl, attempting to comprehend what Lucas had said. It sounded suspiciously like a threat. He had become possessive of her for some unknown reason, but he made no mention of marriage. If he had wanted that he would have said so, wouldn't he? When did the man ever refrain from speaking his mind—bluntly and directly?

It didn't sound as if he intended to buckle to Emmet Blake's blatant attempt at matchmaking either. But that was no surprise. Lucas Murdock was his own man and he lived his life his own way. Catlin supposed she should have been flattered that he wanted her. But there was a vast difference between wanting and loving. Catlin wasn't sure if she knew what love was or if what she felt for Lucas could be defined as love. Cat was an individual who considered her emotions carefully instead of constantly giving way to impulse. She would have to contemplate her feelings, to spread them out before her and analyze them one at a time before she knew for certain if it was love that tormented her so. Having never been in love before, it was difficult to say exactly what she felt. It was a pity love wasn't listed in a medical textbook with its symptoms and possible treatments. Then she could seek out a reference book to determine if she were lovesick or simply coming down with some dreaded disease.

Yes, she was unwillingly attracted to that sinewy giant. And yes, she wanted him physically. And yes, she was becoming emotionally involved with him. But their conflicting similarities and diametrical differences caused conflicts between them. She was stubborn and cynical and he was a strong-willed womanizer. He was his own man and she was her own woman. Luke was honest and plainspoken and she preferred tact and diplomacy unless all else failed. Cat needed all or nothing in a relationship with a man and Lucas was notorious for leaping from one shallow affair to another. He wanted her to do all the giving while he did all the taking.

Catlin gulped down another drink. When her glass went dry she refilled it again. Blast it, nothing could wash away the bittersweet memories of Lucas Murdock. She should be applauding his departure from Texas and from her life. But dammit, she was already missing him and he wasn't even gone!

While Catlin was battling a mental tug-of-war, Emmet Blake strode up beside her. The compassionate expression he wore while he tended his patients was gone, replaced by a hard, unrelenting stare.

"Keep your distance from Lucas," he warned in a low, threatening tone. "His place is with Ginger Hanley. They were seeing each other before you arrived to work your wiles on him."

In mute amazement, Cat stared dully at the physician. Was this the same compassionate man who had treated her sprained knee? Ginger had mentioned there was a flip side to Emmet's personality, a side that never showed until he was crossed. Cat didn't appreciate having opinions thrust on her. Neither did she appreciate the insinuation that she had wicked designs on Lucas. Feminine wiles indeed! Emmet Blake may have been an influential potentate but he wasn't pushing Catlin Quinn around.

"You presume too much, sir," Catlin growled. "You seem to think that I am influenced by your threats, but nothing could be further from the truth. Just because you have it in mind to marry your assistant off to Lucas doesn't mean you will be allowed to have your way in this or any other matter. You have overstepped your calling in life. It is your profession to save lives, not manipulate them."

Emmet puffed up with so much indignation he nearly popped the buttons on his shirt. "Your tongue is sharp and you have yet to learn your place, Miss Quinn," he sneered insultingly. "You seem to forget to whom you are speaking."

"I know and I don't care," she assured him hotly. "It is you who have forgotten that you are not God Almighty.

Your will does not necessarily need done."

Unable to control himself, Emmet latched onto the feisty firebrand's arm, cutting off her circulation. "Lucas and Ginger are going to be married. I will see to that. You stay away from him or I will make you regret it."

"So there you are, Catlin," David greeted as he ambled toward her. "I'm sorry I got tangled up in conversation with one of my ranch hands." He cast Emmet a smile, unaware of the volley of insults that had been tossed back and forth. "Luckily Catlin was in good hands while I was occupied."

Emmet regained his composure and flashed David an amiable smile. "It is not wise to leave your lady to her own devices," he commented. "There are a good many young men hereabout who would eagerly take your place. But now that you have returned, Miss Quinn no longer needs my protection. And I'm sure my wife would enjoy dancing." He dropped into a courteous bow and backed away. "I'll leave you to your lady while I return to mine."

Although David was apologizing all over himself for being detained, Catlin wasn't listening. Her eyes were focused on Emmet's departing back. The man puzzled her. She could understand his protective feelings for Ginger since they had worked together for almost two years. He knew of her troubles and her trials. But beneath that compassionate, concerned exterior lurked a man who was prone to violence when he found himself in a head-on collision with an opposing point of view. Emmet Blake saw himself as a demigod whose word was law. He used his position and influence in the community to get his way and he became indignant when others disagreed with his methods and opinions.

Heaving a frustrated sigh, Catlin pushed her thoughts aside. First she confronted Lucas, then she locked horns with Emmet Blake; all this while she was doing hand-to-hand combat with the spiked punch. Drinking and fighting didn't mix well and if she were smart she would engage in one without the other.

On that thought Catlin refilled her glass. She didn't want to think anymore. She wanted to forget everything that had any semblance to reality. She wanted to enjoy David's company. And so she did. Her blurry gaze focused on the handsome blond man who drew her into his arms to sway in rhythm with the music. But all the while, a pair of dancing brown eyes and a roguish grin kept cropping up in front of her. The arms that held her were all wrong. The fragrance that invaded her senses was pleasant, but another masculine scent clung to her skin. The feel of David's body brushing lightly against hers only served to remind her of the difference between his and Luke's lithe, swarthy physique.

And in the hours that followed, Catlin was plagued by forbidden memories, and the realization that Lucas would be gone an eternity. He may be gone, she mused bleakly, but this maddening ache wasn't going to go away. He had started a fire in her, a fire that only he could extinguish. What David had to offer could not compensate for wanting a man whose memory played a luring melody on her soul.

When the festivities finally wound down at midnight, Catlin accepted David's kiss and wandered unsteadily into the foyer of Martha's new home. Martha had retired the previous hour and Catlin was left to snuff the lanterns and struggle up the stairs to bed. Without undressing, she flounced onto the bed and muttered tangled curses at herself. But nothing helped. Restlessly, she swung her legs over the edge of her bed and paced the floor. The full moonlight lured her to the window and she stared out into the night, battling the confusion and the gnawing emptiness.

Before David had tenderly kissed her goodnight, he had proposed for the third time in a week. Cat could list a dozen reasons why she should accept, but her foolish heart overruled her head and the words refused to tumble from her lips. A month ago she had vowed to become a spinster, refusing to tolerate the presence of a man in her life. David was everything a woman could want. He was wealthy, responsible, caring—his redeeming qualities went on and on. But he wasn't Lucas and this star-crossed attraction between her and that brawny rake was condemned by a powerful, domineering physician. Cat knew Luke felt a certain sense of obligation because of the loan he had made from Emmet. And he was sensitive to Ginger's troubles. . . .

Catlin swore under her breath and wrapped her arms around herself. She felt so alone, so confused. She was tired of constant challenges. She didn't like living in town. The wide open spaces were crowded with houses and the bustle of activity in the streets. She needed her own space and she had none. This was Martha's home and Catlin had lost hers forever. She was like a tenant, living in the space of others. She was torn by logic and impulse. David wanted to marry her. Lucas wanted her—period. And Emmet Blake thought she was a trollop and he wanted her to keep her distance from Lucas. But no one really cared what Catlin wanted.

The pent-up frustration boiled down her cheeks in a river of tears. Catlin blinked through the mist in her eyes and stared at the twinkling stars. She was lonely, aching, yearning to escape her responsibilities, her obligations, the tangled confusion of being pushed and pulled in several directions at once. She wanted to spread her wings and soar, to forget what was troubling her, to find some small space in this universe that was hers to control and enjoy. . . .

The thought made her even more restless than she already was. Giving way to rare impulse, Catlin fled the confines of her room, following wherever her footsteps would lead.

Chapter 13

Lucas circumnavigated the sparsely furnished parlor that once held Martha's keepsakes. Now there was only a secondhand sofa and an end table. The dining room boasted nothing more than the crudely constructed table from the cottage. The kitchen was practically bare. His bedroom stood empty except for one feather bed and a dresser. The second bedroom had only the double bed Martha had left behind when she purchased a matching set for her new home.

For more than a year Luke had envisioned taking up residence in this ranch house and calling it his own. Now that he had, it was haunted by a lovely violet-eyed apparition. He could see Catlin gracefully moving from one room to another, hear her melodic voice calling to him like a siren in a sea of silence.

He had bid Ginger good night with a fiery kiss, hoping it would curb his hunger for that blond-haired vixen who had taken up permanent residence in his mind. When Emmet Blake had cornered him to suggest a hasty marriage to Ginger before he left town, Lucas had almost considered it. He was frustrated to no end and it would have been easy to compensate by wedding Ginger in a momentary lapse of sanity. If he did, he would only be striking out at Cat who fought so hard to deny the magnetic attraction between them. He couldn't marry any woman while he was beneath that witch's spell, no matter what his reasons. Ginger needed a man to provide for her and her father. But Lucas had vowed after his ill-fated love for Elise not to marry until he had buried the ghosts of his past. He had to be absolutely sure he wasn't transferring his love for Elise to someone else, just to compensate for what he had lost.

"Hell's bells," Lucas grumbled in exasperation. He should be sitting on top of the world. He had acquired this ranch without assistance from anyone. He was going to make a name for himself without touching the inheritance his parents had left for him. Once he had paid his debts by working to earn cash, he would have the calves he had weaned from the *cimarrone* heifers to start his herd. He would purchase other cows with the profits from the drive. And then, when he had made his own way all by himself, he would write to his brother, requesting him to send the inheritance money. Luke would have everything he wanted and he would have gotten where he wanted to be in his own way, without the inheritance.

So why didn't he feel elated? His dream was coming true. After years of wandering like a tumbleweed he had decided where he wanted to put down roots. He had waited for the opportunity and he had put the first phase of his long-term plan in motion. Everything was coming up roses, except for one aggravating thorn—Catlin Stewart Quinn. That belligerent, independent little elf had put a curse on him. Sure as hell, she was going to marry David Krause, just for spite. She wouldn't be happy with that mild-mannered rancher. Oh, she would pretend to be. She would reduce the wedding into a reasonable, sensible equation. She would make the best of her marriage because she was so damned practical and determined to make a new life for herself after she lost the old one to a bitter, brutal war. But she hadn't been around enough to know that passion was only good when two people were magnetically drawn together and held steadfast, even against their will. She could rationalize and analyze until she was blue in the face, but when David took her to his bed, she would realize she was settling for less than she needed to keep her content.

The creak of the front door caused Luke to spin about. Automatically, he grabbed for the pistol that hung on his hip. His breath stuck in his throat when his tormenting specter appeared in the flesh. Catlin's long blond hair was in tangles, as if she had been chasing the wind on a wild, reckless horseback ride (and that was exactly what she had been doing). Her violet eyes were misty with recently shed tears and red with too much drink. The provocative crimson, off-the-shoulder gown she had worn to the party drooped low on her breasts, exposing the soft, creamy swells to his all-consuming gaze.

"I know I'm going to hate myself in the morning." Her voice cracked and a tormented expression captured her flushed features. "But I need you tonight. I'm so confused. . . . I can't think straight. I know what I should do, but what I want to do keeps getting tangled in—" Catlin bit her trembling lips, fighting like hell for composure.

Lucas had never seen this staunchly independent minx so vulnerable. Usually she was a monument to rebellious spirit. He felt partially responsible for her condition. He had antagonized her plenty.

When Lucas merely stood there, staring through her to decipher the secrets of her soul, Catlin laughed bitterly. "You and your cussed confessions. Do you have any idea how many times I've been lied to by men who want to take one thing or another from me? You spoke but you didn't say much of anything. You claim you want me, but what have I to gain and how much will it cost me this time?"

189

Her accusing gaze riveted him. "All you want to do is torment me, to ensure that I won't marry David while you are traipsing across the plains with your herd of cattle." Catlin inhaled a hasty breath and plunged on before she crumbled before his very eyes. "But I should marry David, you know. I can't think of one practical reason why I shouldn't. And if I do, you will probably marry Ginger, as Dr. Blake would have you do. Then what shall we do about this ill-fated attraction? Cheat on our husbands and wives? Damn you, Lucas. Damn you for making me want you when logic tells me not to come near you!"

The tears spilled from her eyes and Catlin cursed for reducing herself to convulsive sobs in Luke's presence. "You just wanted me to bend until you saw me break, didn't you?" she questioned resentfully. "Well, I hope you're satisfied, Lucas Murdock. I hope you enjoy this because I'm not planning to break down ever again."

Her voice was becoming higher and wilder by the second. Seeing this vixen in tears tore at Lucas the way very few things could. She drew upon his sympathy, even while he was battling a hunger that only this sassy blond could appease. Instinctively, he closed the space between them, scooping her trembling body into his arms, comforting her with quiet whispers.

In long, graceful strides he carried her up the steps to the room she had once occupied—the room he had taken as his own. Catlin didn't protest. She needed him desperately, even while she cursed her lack of willpower. For more than a week she had fought the compelling magnetism, relying on her good sense. But the battle of mind over body had taken its toll. Lucas was right. She could solidify her future by accepting David's proposal, but she would be haunted by the man who knew how to unleash her secret desires and bring them to life. His memory would always stand between her and David. Catlin could never be a true wife to him, no matter how hard she tried.

Lord, she would never be able to undress again without remembering the scintillating way Lucas had removed her gown when he set her to her feet. His lips caressed every bare inch of flesh he exposed as his gentle hands pushed the garment lower. He sensitized her skin and left her dripping in puddles of liquid desire. His fingertips excited and aroused her. His kisses fanned the flames ignited by his touch.

When the gown and petticoats had fallen into a pool at her feet, Lucas laid her upon his bed. His dark glittering eyes roamed over her curvaceous body in total possession, memorizing each luscious curve and swell. She was breathtakingly lovely, he thought as he dragged in a ragged breath. Her skin was like velvet. She was perfectly formed—a goddess made for love. The wild spray of blond hair that framed her face flowed across his pillow like a glowing river of gold. She looked so vulnerable lying there, so utterly desirable and he was on fire for her.

As Lucas shucked his clothes, Catlin marveled at the sleek whipcord muscles that rippled beneath his bronzed flesh. Even the crisscrossed scars couldn't detract from his awesome appearance. He was a package of boundless energy and vitality. Cat knew she was selfish. Ginger needed Lucas more than she did. But Catlin was lured to this magnificent man. She had fought the attraction until there was no more will left to fight. She had discarded logic to enjoy this last night with him. And when it was over and Lucas had gone away, she would go back to her sensible world and live with the torment of submitting to her uninhibited passions.

A tender smile hovered on Luke's lips as he sank down, bracing his arms on either side of Catlin. Slowly, he lowered his raven head to press a light kiss to her petal-soft mouth. There were a hundred things he wanted to say to her, but words seemed so inadequate compared to the turmoil of emotions that hounded him. He needed to show her how he felt, to communicate in a physical way.

As his practiced hands rediscovered the delicious contours of her flesh, his lips set out on their own tantalizing journey. Catlin gasped at the intimacy of his touch, at the wild tremors that surged over her like a fleet of tidal waves. She didn't think about Ginger or David or Emmet while Luke's restless fingers aroused and explored. His prowling caresses and hot kisses stripped her of all thought. She could only feel and respond to his masterful lovemaking. She was aware of nothing but this strong, competent man.

Lucas had transformed seduction into a science. His skill had been perfected through years of practice and there was a mystical inventiveness in his touch that set him apart from all other men. Cat didn't have to lie with another man to know that. Intuition told her. Lucas had learned to read her moods amazingly well. He was sensitive to her needs and he satisfied them all. He claimed he couldn't be her friend when he was her lover, but in a way he was the best friend she had. When the world and her troubles crowded in on her and despair threatened to consume her, Catlin ran to him and no one else. She had come to know all the personalities Lucas tried to keep separate in his day-to-day dealings. But they were all a part of this complex creature who lured her and constantly fascinated her.

While his expert hands worked their sensual magic, Catlin lost herself in the haze of desire. The spiked punch she had consumed put the last of her inhibitions to flight and unchained the ardent passions that simmered beneath the surface. It was as it had been those two nights when they made love, and yet it was totally different. Each time Lucas wove his spell around her he led her down a unique avenue to the magical world of passion. The memories were there to entice her, but each sensation was new and his techniques were wondrous.

Catlin wasn't content to lie back and enjoy his intimate fondling. The intense crescendo of pleasure was meant to be shared. Her worshipping caresses migrated over the landscape of masculine terrain, reveling in the feel of his hair-roughened body, marveling at her ability to arouse him as thoroughly as he aroused her. Touching him was pure sweet ecstasy. He was one hundred percent male and Catlin adored caressing him.

They did set sparks in each other, she realized—a dozen kinds of sparks. She had never been able to control any of those volatile sparks—not the passion, the anger, the hidden jealousy, nothing. She would never be immune to this man when he had such a devastating effect on her.

Lucas groaned in tormented pleasure when lips as moist as morning dew lit on his cheek and shoulder. Feather-light caresses wandered everywhere at once, setting his nerve endings on fire. Desire throbbed in his loins while Catlin boldly touched him, bringing his need for her to a fervent pitch. She was driving him mad with wanting, doing the most amazing things to his body. Lucas had promised himself he would make their lovemaking last forever. But when Catlin unleashed his savage desires and passion channeled through every fiber of his being, he wasn't sure he could restrain himself.

As he rolled above her, his gentleness gave way to the ravenous longings that clouded sanity. He no longer wanted her; he *had* to have her, *had* to feel her silky body molded intimately to his. She was as vital to him as the oxygen he needed to breathe, as the nourishment required to sustain him.

Like an agile lion, he came upon all fours, towering over her. With eyes that blazed with wild hunger, he drew her to him. The swift eager descent of his mouth caught Catlin's breathless gasp. With a seductive growl, he took possession. He was famished for her—all of her. He needed her kiss, her body, and her soul, or he would surely go mad!

His hard demanding thrusts provoked her moan of surrender. Catlin gave herself up to the rapid cadence of his lovemaking, holding nothing back, wanting him in the same maddening way he wanted her. His muscular body became a part of hers and she accepted him, clutching her arms around him as if she never meant to let him go. He had become a sensual wild man and she was his equal match in the throes of mindless passion. Catlin swore she couldn't get close enough to the flame that burned her inside and out. He sought ultimate depths of intimacy and she reveled in the wild splendor of their union, nipping at his shoulder, rasping his name over and over again.

The fires blazed hotter and higher like a holocaust that consumed the sun. Catlin kept reaching up to grasp that elusive sensation that called to her through the wind and flames. Suddenly, she clutched that mystical feeling that transcended reality. She had shed the garments of the flesh and her soul unfurled its pinioned wings to find that special space in the universe where she could be at peace.

They were one beating breathing essence, gliding beyond the perimeters of the stars. The monstrous cravings were appeased and the emptiness was now overflowing with ecstatic sensations. For an eternity Catlin dangled in midair, marveling at the sublime joy of being encircled in Lucas's swarthy arms. This was that unique place for which she had searched when she fled her room. This was where she had wanted to be.

Catlin could feel Luke's heartbeat, feel the ragged draft of breath against her shoulder. Contentment was the warm pulse of masculinity that was molded so completely to her. Odd, two hours earlier she swore she was suffering all the tortures of the damned. Now she was drifting in paradise and no obstacle seemed insurmountable.

"I want you here with me," Lucas murmured in the aftermath of love. "We have only one day left, Cat. And when I return from Colorado, I want you here waiting for me."

Catlin smiled ruefully. Ah, what an impulsive man he could be at times. He expected her to disregard propriety and transplant herself on his ranch at the snap of his fingers. Lord, she could hear the rumors buzzing already. How could she explain to Aunt Martha and David and Ginger?

Slowly he raised his head to stare down into her bewitching face. "I need you to be here, violet eyes," he repeated huskily. "For one day we are going to set aside our conflicts and enjoy each other. I want to make love to you in broad daylight, beside the creek, basking in the sun. I want to show you every square inch of this ranch. I want it to be yours as well as mine—the dream you lost, the dream we can create together. Will you be waiting for me, Cat?"

Catlin blinked in bewilderment. "Are you proposing?" she chirped.

A deep skirl of laughter rumbled in his chest. "It certainly sounded like it. Are you avoiding the question?"

Catlin traced the rugged features that were hidden by moonshadows. "I'm not sure we can live together without . . ."

His lips grazed hers, silencing her. For the life of him he didn't know why he had made that request. It just seemed right and natural. Cat didn't love him and he wasn't sure he truly loved her. But the thought of this vixen married to David Krause turned him wrong side out. She had become Luke's obsession. He had taught her all she knew about passion. And if proposing would prevent her from turning to David until he returned, if the lure was still there, he would know if it was love that formed this strong bond between them, if they were meant to enjoy forever together.

"I'm not sure we can live together either, but neither am I sure I can live without you. Every relationship has its risks. Quit being so damned sensible and just say yes," he insisted.

Catlin needed to put distance between them and contemplate her feelings, but Lucas was giving her two minutes to make up her mind, not two months.

"Why do you want to marry me?" she questioned curiously. Had he decided to settle for second best since Elise was already married? Did he think a man of property also needed a wife? Or did Luke just want a warm body waiting for him when he returned from Colorado? Catlin needed to know for certain.

"If all prospective husbands are put through the third degree it's a wonder there are any marriages at all," Lucas grumbled.

"I want to know why," she prodded.

"Does there have to be a why?" Lucas countered before dropping a hasty kiss to her lips. "Don't be so damned inquisitive. Just say yes."

"But I—"

"Say yes, Cat," he growled as his body glided seductively over hers. "Stop being methodic and practical, for once. Consider what you *feel*, not what you *think*. . . ."

His hypnotic movements and the tormentingly sweet flow of caresses that were migrating over her flesh boggled her mind. She was rushing in where angels feared to tread. There was no hard and fast rule that stated Lucas would feel the same way about marriage when he returned. She knew this would be a trial period of sorts. But she would be the one to suffer humiliation and rejection if Luke decided not to marry her when he returned from the drive.

And what if she was asked to move out when he came back? How could she face her aunt and the vicious gossip? Where would she go from here when she would be too ashamed to stay in San Antonio?

"Say yes, Catlin," Lucas repeated as his lips grazed the rigid peaks of her breasts. "This is the last time I'll ask. . . ."

"Yes . . ." she answered, despite her reservations and because of the wondrous sensations that ricocheted through her body. He was doing it again, pleasing and tormenting her with his kisses and caresses. How could a woman hear herself think when her heart was pounding like thunder?

She was being lifted from one dizzying plateau to another, caught in the whirlwind of desire. The roar of turbulent winds engulfed her and Catlin responded as she always did—completely, wholeheartedly, needing no more than Lucas could give . . . and nothing less.

Catlin couldn't name another day in her life that compared to the one she enjoyed by Luke's side. He was playful and attentive and she felt incredibly alive, like a child again. Lucas had insisted that Flapjack Barnett pack a picnic lunch for them and when he returned from camp they rode off to explore the ranch. As he promised, they swam in the creek and made love in the grass before falling asleep in each other's arms. All the walls of defense came tumbling down and Catlin displayed the carefree facet of her personality for that space in time, oblivious to all except the man who had filled her world to overflowing. She and Luke wrestled on the creek bank and dashed across the plush meadow, their voices sparkling with laughter. Catlin had recaptured the pleasure-filled moments of her youth and had begun to believe in life again.

Her heart swelled with pride each time she peered at Lucas. This surely must be love, she mused as she closed her eyes and leaned back against the steed on which she had been riding. The touch of Lucas's hand on her cheek caused her lashes to flutter up. He stood before her, his brawny body eclipsing the sun.

"Tell me what's on your mind, minx," he requested curiously.

Catlin wasn't sure she could divulge her thoughts just yet. The feelings that tugged at her heartstrings needed to ferment and that would take time. Playfully, she tweaked the hair on his chest and then darted off. With a growl Lucas gave chase, capturing her in his arms. But the feel of her luscious body sidetracked him. Suddenly he didn't care what thoughts she harbored. He only wanted her. Time was so short and he was eager to squeeze a month of living into one day. One glance in those wide amethyst eyes and Lucas was lost.

He kissed her (devoured her was nearer the mark) and Catlin responded in wild abandon. They both sensed the urgency of living each moment to its fullest, of taking pleasure before it was snatched away.

While they made love, darkness crept onto the horizon, casting its deep purple shadows across the rolling hills. But Catlin never ever noticed until the wild sweet ecstasy had run its fiery course. They tarried by the creek which sparkled like silver in the moonlight, never speaking of tomorrow, only of the moments they had shared.

The ride back to the ranch house was a silent one. Lucas was hounded by his eagerness to put the cattle on the trail and his reluctance to leave Catlin behind. He was going to miss this mischievous imp. She breathed life back into him, filled the empty crevices that loving Elise had left behind. He wasn't sure if the tormenting memories of a love that could never be had finally faded with time or if Cat's presence in his life had simply overshadowed his yearnings. He would know for certain when he left Cat behind, he mused pensively. And hopefully, when he returned, Cat would know if she wanted him with her always. If this marriage was meant to be, neither of them would be plagued with doubts.

Four months was time enough, Luke assured himself. Now if only David Krause would gracefully bow out and give Cat time to think! Lucas grumbled at the thought. He hadn't given David that consideration. Why shouldn't he expect David to make a play for this saucy beauty? Luke certainly had taken advantage of opportunity.

Well, Luke wasn't going to waste these last precious hours worrying, that was for damned sure. He was going to sleep in Catlin's silky arms and love her for all the times he would want to hold her the next four months and couldn't. And so he did. He treasured each wondrous moment, committing the feel of her delectable body to memory, worshiping her with his kisses, taking absolute possession. Each time he roused from sleep, he came to her, whispering his need, and Catlin welcomed him, loving him as if the world were about to end.

And in the dim light that streamed through the window, Lucas pulled himself from bed, willing the slower parts of his body to wake up faster than usual. But it wouldn't matter, he supposed. In a few hours his stiff joints would be oiled by perspiration and the heat of the sun.

Quietly, he dressed for a long day's ride. He would have to push the herd to its limits, driving twenty to thirty miles, day and night without rest. If he didn't take the *cimarrones* far away from familiar territory they would attempt to turn back to bed down on their native ground. For two days he would force them to walk steadily without grazing, marching northwestward until San Antonio was a forgotten memory.

Ah, if only two days could make such a difference to him, Lucas mused with a melancholy sigh. Cat's memory would still be burning in his mind in two weeks. After that, he couldn't say for certain how he'd feel. Time and distance would give him the perspective he couldn't attain while he was this close to her. . . .

"I'll miss you." Sleepy eyes drifted over the chaps and deep-pocketed vest that clung to his muscular physique.

"Will you?" Lucas strapped his double holsters in place and sank down to stuff his foot in a boot. He tucked his pants deep in his boots. The high-heeled boots weren't much for walking but they prevented a man from slipping from the stirrup.

Mechanically, he strapped on his spurs with their star-shaped rowels, refusing to dart Catlin a glance. "You'll be surrounded by willing and eager men while I'm carrying on conversations with cattle. You probably won't even notice I'm gone."

Catlin levered up on an elbow to press a kiss to his bronzed cheek. "Now who's picking fights?"

He twisted to plant a passionate kiss to her parted lips. "You're contrariness is rubbing off on me. I was even-tempered until you came along," he insisted with a teasing grin.

Her gaze dropped to study the red flannel shirt beneath his leather vest. "If you have changed your mind about—"

"I have to go," he cut in, bounding to his feet. Damn, leaving her was even more difficult than he had anticipated. He felt as if he were leaving part of himself behind, just as he had when he left Elise. He was angry and frustrated and he didn't even know why.

Catlin blinked back the tears. If this wasn't love, it was an incredible likeness. She felt as if her heart was being ripped from her chest and she was expected to go on living and breathing.

How many women would he seduce when lust got the best of him? she wondered dispiritedly. Lucas was a muscular package of physical vitality and restless spirit who naturally attracted females. He was strong, capable, enduring and self-disciplined. He anticipated difficulty and danger and took them in stride. Women were drawn to these wild, sensual type of men.

Would Luke decline an amorous invitation if it was offered to him? Somehow Catlin doubted it. The true test of a man's fidelity was what he did when he didn't think he would get caught. And Catlin had no way of knowing if he was faithful to her.

As Luke strided out the door without another word, Catlin draped the sheet around her and sped after him. She caught up with him at the front door to send him off with a kiss that was hot enough to melt his metal spurs.

"Just so you don't forget. . . ." she murmured, retreating a step to blush self-consciously.

His dark eyes blazed over her makeshift garment, searing the flesh beneath it. "You're going to be positively dangerous when you finally realize what a sexy little seductress you are," he breathed, making another thorough sweep of her barely concealed figure. "And don't wear that sheet for anyone else but me, violet eyes." He bent to brush his lips over her petal-soft mouth. "Take care of yourself."

She watched him go, harboring a deep sense of loss. Catlin swore she was going to break down and cry again. It was killing her to watch him walk away. The way he looked in his Sugar-loaf sombrero and rugged clothes aroused her. He was so much a part of this wide, lawless land . . . so much a part of her.

A stab of pain knifed through her chest as she listened to the methodic click of his spurs. Lord, it had been a mistake to grant herself a full day with Lucas, learning his every mood. The hours and minutes would haunt her. How would she get through the next four months without seeing his handsome face, feeling his masterful hands upon her flesh?

And what if Lucas discovered *his* interest in her had faded with time and *her* affection had increased? She had a glimpse of paradise and she liked what she saw. It would be nothing short of hell to live without that man. Dammit, sometimes she wished she had never met him! She had been getting along just fine until he walked in and turned her logical, sensible world upside down.

Catlin inhaled a determined breath and marched upstairs to dress. She had skipped a day at work and now she would have to dream up an excuse and explain her disappearance to Aunt Martha. Honest to goodness, this wasn't like her to go off chasing rainbows for a day. And now that she had, she would have to explain herself.

Blast it, Lucas was the lucky one. He walked off without a word to anyone and she was left to announce their engagement. Catlin began to wonder if it might have been easier to chase three thousand steers for the next four months! Her aunt wasn't going to think highly of her for spending the night with Lucas. And then, of course, there was Ginger . . . Catlin dreaded informing her friend of the engagement. She felt as if she had betrayed Ginger and she had the feeling the news would not sit well with Emmet Blake. And she was absolutely right. Emmet was fit to be tied!

Chapter 14

Martha was beside herself when Catlin confessed she had spent the day, not to mention two nights with Lucas. She was, however, delighted by the news that her niece and Luke were seriously considering marriage. Catlin didn't bother to explain that she and Lucas were trying this engagement business out for size and that Lucas could easily change his mind by the time he returned from Colorado. Catlin decided to let Martha cross that bridge if and when she got to it.

For two days Catlin procrastinated in telling Ginger of her engagement to Lucas. But finally, afraid Ginger would find out from someone else, Catlin stopped by the shabby cottage. Ginger looked stunned but she accepted the information and wished Catlin well.

Catlin searched the young woman's green eyes, detecting the hint of tears she tried so desperately to hold in check. "Please believe that I never meant to hurt you, Ginger," she said gently. "But I—"

"You needn't say anything," Ginger insisted, her lips quivering. "I know Luke didn't truly care for me. We were . . ." Her gaze shifted from Catlin's face to focus on the freshly painted wall. "In the beginning I thought perhaps Lucas might feel something special for me. He is a fine man. I had hoped that my . . ." Her voice trailed off and she mustered a feeble smile. "I bear no grudge, Catlin, I hope you and Luke will be happy together."

There was something Ginger wasn't telling her. Cat could sense it. The teary-eyed brunette had never completely opened up to her, but Catlin was still harboring dark suspicions about how intimate Ginger and Lucas had been. They had known each other long before Catlin came to town and she had no right to speculate, but she was anyway.

Catlin thought her worst confrontation was over. She was wrong. Although David Krause was disappointed and insisted he would be waiting if she changed her mind, Emmet Blake was another matter entirely. The moment Catlin walked out of the newspaper office after a full day of work, Emmet approached like an invading army.

Raw fury twisted his features, giving him a diabolical appearance. As before, Emmet shackled Catlin's arm in a bone-crushing grasp and propelled her out of earshot of passersby. "You shameless trollop," he hissed furiously at her. "I knew you were an adventuress the moment I laid eyes on you. Now you have stolen Lucas away from Ginger when she needs him desperately."

Catlin never did appreciate being manhandled. Emmet's anger ignited her ire and she yanked away from his bruising grasp. Before she could malign his character with a suitably nasty rejoinder, he snarled maliciously at her.

"You may think you are going to become Mrs. Lucas Murdock and help him rule over his new ranch, but you're wrong. Lucas has other obligations. Ginger is carrying his child," he informed her harshly.

The news knocked Catlin to her knees. Emmet had just confirmed her worst suspicions and she simultaneously cursed the sneering physician *and* Lucas.

"But Ginger is too proud and noble to tell Lucas, to demand that he marry her. As if she doesn't have enough difficulty supporting her invalid father, there is a child on the way, a child who belongs to the man you stole away from her by flaunting your feminine charms," he growled in a disdainful tone. "Because of you, Ginger will be forced to bear her shame and shoulder another burden. I wanted her to go away to have this child but she refuses to leave her father."

Catlin staggered back as if he had slapped her across the cheek. Indeed he may as well have. The blow he struck could not have been more painful if he had delivered it with a double fist. Never had she experienced anything as agonizing as the gnawing torment that ate at her. Cat clamped her quivering lips shut, tormented by the vision of Ginger lying in Luke's arms.

"If you had one ounce of decency you would denounce your engagement and allow Lucas to accept his responsibility the moment he returns from the drive," Emmet demanded harshly. "But I'm not sure you are noble enough of character to find compassion for Ginger."

Fighting back a wave of tears, Catlin bolted to the street and ran as fast as her legs would carry her. Emmet's growling words echoed through her brain like resounding thunder. The day she and Lucas had spent together was their first and last, she realized gloomily. There was nothing else to do but go to Ginger and lie through her teeth. Cat would explain that Luke had sent a letter, stating that he had reconsidered his hasty proposal and that the engagement was off. Better that Ginger think the broken engagement was his idea.

She and Lucas could never marry, Catlin assured herself, battling her shattered emotions. Damn him! Damn him to hell and back!

The moment Catlin halted the carriage in front of the dilapidated cottage, she bounded to the ground. The door opened before Catlin had a chance to knock. A concerned frown knitted Ginger's brow when she noticed the distressed expression on Catlin's face. "What's wrong?"

"My engagement, short-termed though it was, is over," she blurted out. "I received a letter from Lucas this afternoon. It seems I have been played for a fool. He has decided not to marry me after all."

Dubiously, Ginger watched the comely blond compose herself enough to amble into the parlor to greet Robert. While Catlin conversed with Robert, Ginger studied her friend with a pensive frown. Sending a "Dear Jane" letter didn't sound like something Lucas would do, Ginger thought to herself. Ginger didn't have to be clairvoyant to predict what had happened. Emmet Blake was responsible for this, she would bet her life on it. She had told Emmet about the engagement earlier in the afternoon and he had hit the ceiling. Chances were, Emmet had confronted Catlin, forcing her to denounce the engagement. And chances also were that Catlin had concocted the story about the letter to spare Ginger's feelings.

While Ginger stood there speculating, Catlin bid Robert good night and murmured quietly to her friend before sweeping out the door. Once Catlin was outside the tears boiled down her cheeks. She felt betrayed and rejected and she shouldn't have. She knew there had been something going on between Ginger and Luke. But no physical pain could compare to the torment of caring for a man who owed an obligation to another woman, of knowing Ginger carried the child Catlin would have given Lucas in marriage. But now her dreams were a nightmare. She should accept David's proposal and marry him without wasting a moment. Then Ginger would feel no obligation to Catlin and she could marry Luke—the father of her child.

Shakily, she wiped the burning tears from her eyes and snapped the reins over the steed, sending him off in a canter. Catlin had to find a place to fall apart, to expel all these agonizing emotions, to exorcise that raven-haired demon from her soul now and forevermore. She had thought she was in love with that brown-eyed rake, but now she swore she hated him with every beat of her breaking heart. She and her lack of common sense! He and his promiscuity! Damn him. How many other women were in the same predicament Ginger was in? Lucas had never been forced to answer to his indiscretions before because he hadn't had Emmet Blake there to see that the reckless philanderer acknowledged his obligations. But Emmet would ensure Lucas married Ginger. He was too powerful and influential and Lucas was indebted to him.

Catlin didn't hear Ginger calling to her as she thundered down the road. She was too tormented with thoughts, too busy hating Lucas with every sobbing breath she inhaled.

Muttering, Ginger reversed direction to tend her father and then she clambered into her rickety buggy to confront Emmet Blake. They had clashed on this subject once before and Ginger decided it was time they did so again. Catlin had taught her to stand up for herself and by God she was going to make another attempt to resist Emmet's domination. He was not going to control her life, to make her decisions for her! She was going to do what she should have done in the first place!

Clinging to that determined thought, Ginger aimed herself toward Dr. Blake's office. Just see how he liked it when she interfered in his life and started telling him how he should behave! Curse him for upsetting Catlin. Curse him for manipulating her life, as well as Lucas and Catlin's. By damned, she would threaten him for a change and see how he liked it!

Aimlessly, Catlin wandered around the abandoned ranch, staring into the distance, seeing nothing. She had managed a greeting to Albert the stable boy who had remained behind to tend the ranch during Luke's absence.

But once Albert returned to the bunkhouse, Catlin fell apart and succumbed to convulsive sobs for two days. She had gone through the paces of living like a mindless puppet. And as much as she disliked the idea of leaving the wide open spaces, she knew she couldn't stay at the Flying Spur. The house was haunted by ghosts, by forbidden memories and by broken dreams.

It was time to swallow her humiliation and anger and take up residence with her aunt. She would give the news of her broken engagement to David and if he still wanted her, she intended to marry him—the sooner the better.

Resolutely, Catlin spun about and marched into the ranch house in swift precise strides. She would pack up and leave. It was going to kill her to explain to Aunt Martha that the engagement was off, but procrastination wouldn't help matters one whit. Catlin had already lingered two days after Emmet's crushing insults and shocking announcement.

Again Catlin had lost something precious and dear to her. It was becoming an unpleasant repetition of history. First it was her family and her plantation that had been stripped away. Now she had lost the man she could have loved and a ranch to replace what she had been swindled out of in Louisiana.

Hurriedly, Catlin stuffed her garments into her satchels and snuffed the lanterns. Without shedding another tear, she tossed her luggage into the buggy and pulled herself onto the seat. Never again would she set foot on this ranch. Never again would she allow memories of laughing brown eyes and a roguish grin to torment her. Lucas Murdock was a closed chapter of her life. She hated him, hated him for complicating her life as well as Ginger's.

Guided by moonlight, Catlin rode into town, mentally preparing herself for Aunt Martha's questions. Martha would have to be fed the same concocted story Cat had offered Ginger. It would make Catlin look the fool, but

Ginger deserved the most consideration, considering her plight. Once Catlin informed Martha of the broken engagement she would ride out to David Krause's ranch and hope for a reconciliation. David would be her salvation, her protection against the painful memories. . . .

Curiously, Catlin glanced over her shoulder when she heard the clatter of a carriage thundering into town. To her bemusement, she watched Ginger stamp on the brake and bound from her buggy, toting a pistol. What in heaven's name . . . ?

Quickly, Catlin reversed direction and halted her buggy a good distance away from Dr. Blake's office. Creeping along the boardwalk, Catlin pricked her ears to the sound of Ginger's wild voice shattering the night. Although Catlin was too far away to make out Ginger's words, it was obvious the young woman was furious with Emmet Blake and only God knew why.

Inching beneath the window, Catlin eavesdropped on the conversation.

"You bastard, you killed him," Ginger railed, waving the pistol at Emmet who had been taken completely by surprise.

"Ginger, get hold of yourself. What are you ranting about?" Emmet snapped, his wide eyes glued to the Colt she recklessly pointed at him.

"You killed my father, damn your wicked soul. You poisoned him!" Ginger hissed as the tears flooded down her cheeks.

"That's ridiculous," Emmet growled at her. "You know I have been treating your father without payment for almost two years. I have earned a reputation as a champion for the sick and ailing. How dare you suggest I ended your father's life!"

"But you did it, nonetheless. You are getting back at me for threatening you," she sneered hatefully. "You gave me a new bottle of medicine this morning. It was laced with arsenic, wasn't it?"

"You're mad," Emmet grunted. "You are so upset by your father's death that you are looking to place the blame on me simply because you are annoyed with me."

With her heart beating ninety miles a minute, Catlin scurried beneath the window in hopes of reaching the office door before Ginger did something she would later regret. If only Cat could open the portal without being overheard. She could cautiously tiptoe into the adjoining room and grab Ginger before she pulled the trigger.

"Let me fetch you a sedative to calm you down," Emmet suggested, carefully reaching toward his medical bag. "You are distraught and you don't know what you're saying."

"I'm in complete command of my senses," Ginger contradicted in a gritted snarl. Her green eyes snapped with fury. "You thought I would go away to have my baby if my father was dead, that I would marry Lucas after you forced Catlin to back away. You and your scheming! Well, you will manipulate no other lives, not mine or my child's or Catlin's.

While Ginger was ranting in outrage, Emmet reached into his medical bag, but not to retrieve medication. His hand folded around the scalpel, waiting to pounce on the woman who had become a raving lunatic. Her fury ignited his volatile temper. No one threatened or crossed Emmet Blake without facing the consequences. No one!

The rustle of skirts caught Ginger's attention. She whirled, half-crazed with grief and frustration. The moment she took her eyes off Emmet, he struck out with his scalpel. Ginger screeched in pain when the blade slashed across her ribs. Wildly, she wheeled on Emmet whose face was puckered in a murderous sneer. He lunged at her, but not before the revolver discharged, grazing his arm. The stinging pain sent him into a frenzied rage.

Swearing vehemently, he ripped the pistol loose, intent on returning the shot.

"No!" Catlin screamed as she hurled herself forward to push Ginger out of the way. As quick as Catlin was, she was too slow to prevent Ginger from taking a bullet in the leg. When Ginger buckled, yelping in agony, Catlin rushed over to steady her on her feet.

In horror, Catlin watched Emmet's malignant gaze fasten on her. "You caused this, you little bitch," he blared at her as he raised the barrel of his pistol.

Sweet mercy! The man had become a maniac! Groping behind her, Catlin clamped a shaky hand around the lantern and, in desperation, she hurled it at him before he squeezed the trigger. Emmet staggered back, his eyes burning with kerosene. An enraged howl erupted from his curled lips as he stamped out the flames that danced around his feet.

While Emmet was battling the fire and the kerosene in his eyes, Catlin assisted Ginger toward the door. She could hear Emmet cursing violently as she struggled outside. Catlin had to get help for Ginger. The other practicing physician lived on the south side of town and Catlin was eager to seek him out, especially since Emmet was on the rampage!

Dazed with pain, Ginger tried to pull herself into her buggy. But the moment she sank into the seat, darkness swirled like a looming vulture. "Take me home," she whimpered.

"But . . ."

Ginger shook her head and clutched Catlin's hands. "Take me home," she wailed, fighting the nausea that bubbled inside her.

As if Catlin didn't have enough trouble already, Emmet charged out the door spewing a string of curses. Frantic, Catlin popped the reins and darted off before Emmet could yank her from her seat.

Glancing frantically about him, Emmet spied Catlin's buggy. Breaking into a dead run, he barreled down the boardwalk and vaulted into the carriage to give chase.

Catlin swore her heart would pop from her chest as they clattered down the moonlit road in the dilapidated buggy. Although she willed the plodding mare to push herself to her limits, the steed was no match for the swift horse Lucas had given Catlin. And as fate would have it, Emmet was in control of the fastest steed. Try as she may, Catlin couldn't keep a safe distance between her and Emmet who was shouting epithets to her name. A terrified yelp burst from her lips when Emmet leaped from the carriage to attack her. Catlin tried to fight back, but Emmet backhanded her, knocking her atop Ginger who had fainted before they reached the outskirts of town. Struggling to gather her wits, Catlin pushed upright, only to be thrown into the front of the buggy when Emmet stamped on the brake. Halting the carriage in front of Ginger's home, Emmet motioned with the pistol for Catlin to climb down.

"Ginger might die if you don't tend her wounds," Catlin insisted, hoping to talk some sense into Emmet, but he was too consumed by fury to listen.

"Get inside before I decide to put a bullet through you here and now, bitch," he jeered at her.

Left with no alternative, Catlin approached the house with the same enthusiasm as a prisoner marching to the guillotine. In Emmet's present state of mind, Catlin calculated her chances of escaping with her life as slim to none. And that is exactly the same calculation at which Emmet had arrived. In his opinion, Catlin was responsible for this disaster and she was going to pay her dues.

The instant Catlin pushed open the door, Emmet raised the butt of the pistol and clubbed her from behind. Catlin pitched forward, fighting the pained darkness that sought to swallow her alive.

"Damn you . . ." Emmet growled as she collapsed in the

212

hall. "This is all your fault, bitch. You and your meddling . . ."

Spinning about, Emmet darted to the buggy to retrieve Ginger's limp body. He had to dispose of Catlin and Ginger before they exposed his part in this unfortunate nightmare. His reputation was at stake. If either of these sassy females survived, his life would be in jeopardy. He had to think of himself, his wife, and his patients who depended on him. He was an irreplaceable pillar of society and these two women were witches sent up from hell to destroy him.

Fire . . . That was it! A fire would destroy all evidence of this horrible night. Ginger, her father, and Catlin would all perish in the blaze. Before the citizens could reach the cottage that was situated a half-mile from town, the evidence would be no more than charred ashes.

With a demented stare, Emmet glanced toward town, thankful the ruckus had yet to rouse the citizens. Ignoring the throbbing bullet wound on his arm, Emmet stepped over Cat's sprawled form to place Ginger's unconscious body on the sofa in the parlor. Bent on his purpose, he scurried into Robert Hanley's room to see the corpse covered with a quilt. Half-crazed with panic and fear for his life and reputation, Emmet hurled the lantern against the wall and watched the flames inch their golden fingers across the room.

A cloud of smoke fogged the chamber. Sputtering to catch his breath, Emmet staggered out the door and scuttled to the kitchen to smash another lantern against the table. The crackling flames engulfed the brittle wood of the cottage, making it an instant inferno. Before Emmet could enter another room to start a fire, the ceiling threatened to collapse. Shielding his face against the intense heat, Emmet cursed vehemently. He had trapped himself in the kitchen! In panic, he grabbed a chair and hurled it through the window, providing himself with an escape route. Fighting the flames and fumes, Emmet clambered out the window before he became the fourth casualty of the fire.

Groaning in pain, Catlin pushed away from the floor and then caught her breath at the sight of the flaming walls and looming clouds of smoke that burgeoned over her like a fog of doom. Her lungs burned and her head throbbed in rhythm with her frantic heartbeat. Although the smoke stung her eyes and she wheezed to inhale a breath, Catlin instinctively crawled toward the front door.

I have to get Ginger to a doctor! her tortured mind screamed. Stumbling over the trailing hem of her skirt, Catlin scurried toward Ginger's buggy, but it stood empty! Her wild-eyed gaze circled back to the house that was now a holocaust of smoke and flames. Emmet Blake had gone stark raving mad! He had set the house and Robert and Ginger on fire to punish all of them. . . .

The sound of footsteps on the cobblestone walkway tore Catlin's thoughts from her mind. Her heart catapulted to her throat when the golden light of the fire beamed down on Emmet Blake. His revolver swung in her direction when he spied her poised beside Ginger's carriage.

"Curse your evil soul! You must have the nine lives of a cat!" Emmet roared over the sound of crackling flames.

In stupefied astonishment, Catlin watched him aim the Colt at her. Afraid for her life, Catlin dived beneath the buggy as the bullet barked in the night. This time she wouldn't make the mistake of clambering into Ginger's rickety carriage with its slow, plodding nag. If she did, Emmet would catch her and finish the job he had intended to do when he left her unconscious in the house.

Sobbing hysterically, Catlin crawled from the opposite side of the buggy and bounded toward her own carriage that sat beside Ginger's. Another shot rang out as Emmet raced after her, cursing a blue streak. Desperately, he bounded into Ginger's carriage to give chase to the fleeing witch who had brought the wrath of God down on him. He couldn't allow her to live and offer her rendition of this incident! That wicked woman was a threat to his very existence!

Catlin spared a quick glance over her shoulder as she sped down the path toward the Flying Spur Ranch. She swore Satan himself was in fast pursuit. Emmet was engulfed with demented fury and he had no intention of resting until he had destroyed her.

"You'll pay for this!" Emmet bellowed over the clattering of hooves. "Do you hear me, bitch? I will not only destroy you, but I will dispose of all of those you hold dear if you expose my part in this disaster."

Catlin grimaced at the roared vow that echoed in the night. Even if she did manage to escape with her life, Emmet would refuse to let her return to San Antonio, not when she could testify to his lapse of sanity, his violent struggle with Ginger. It was painfully obvious that there was a black side to Emmet's personality. When vengeance raised its hideous head, the man became a monster! If Catlin dared to defy him again he would vent his madness on Aunt Martha and maybe even Lucas. Neither of them would know why they were paying penance. Emmet would concoct a believable story or simply plead ignorance to Ginger's death. But he would manage to get back at Catlin by tormenting those she loved most in this world.

"By God, you'd better run for your life, bitch," Emmet snarled as he snapped the reins over the winded steed. "If you dare to show your face in San Antonio, I'll see that you are hanged for murdering Ginger and her father in a fit of jealousy. You wouldn't let Ginger have the man who carried her child. And I will take all those who are near and dear to you away from you if you dare return! You will be responsible for their deaths, just as you were responsible for Ginger's. I'll hunt you down. You can run now, but you won't escape me forever!"

The villainous threats resounded around Catlin like thunder. How could she fight a powerful, influential potentate like Emmet Blake and his bizarre brand of vengeance? He had been in San Antonio forever and she had been there less than a month. And she was also a woman. Her opinion and testimony against this well-known physician would count for nothing. Emmet would find a way to destroy her and all those she held dear—the same way he had taken Ginger's life when she wildly accused him of poisoning her father. The man was impossible to defeat. He had too much clout and credibility in San Antonio. No one would believe he had lapsed into such a murdering fit of temper.

Four days earlier, Catlin thought she was standing on the threshold of a new life. She had intended to marry Lucas and make the Flying Spur Ranch her new home, her dream. But then her world had gone up in flames and Ginger and Rober Hanley had perished in a blaze that still lit up the night sky.

Catlin squeezed her lips into a grim line and snapped the quirt above her horse. She was not only running for her life but for her aunt's and Lucas's. She had become a curse that destroyed Ginger and Robert Hanley and could destroy the two people she cared about most in the world. One person, Catlin quickly amended. Lucas was also to blame for this nightmare. His frivolous indiscretion was the root of this disaster. She didn't love him; she hated him. Loathed him would have been nearer the mark! Curse his careless soul.

Where could she go? What was she to do? Catlin blinked back the tears and fought to control the hysterical sobs that wretched her body. Emmet was still spouting vicious threats from a distance, promising to make her life a living hell. If she dared to circle back to town to take the stage he would discover her destination. And even before she could climb onto the stage he would probably spread his lies and she would be apprehended for murder. He would scour every community within a hundred miles of San Antonio until he located her and then he would—

Catlin refused to outguess that raving lunatic. There was no telling what hideous schemes were hatching in Emmet's mind. Would he really accuse her of setting the fire, claiming she was jealous and outraged? Would he point an accusing finger at her and insist that she had shot him when he tried to prevent her from setting the cottage ablaze? Catlin hated to hazard a guess, but she did recognize defeat when it stared her in the face. She had been forced to admit defeat when her devious lawyer saw to it that her property was taken out from under her. Now she faced another odious, manipulating man who had made her his sacrificial lamb. Catlin had fought tooth and nail, but a woman alone was no match for powerful men. Now her only alternative was to run, to admit defeat.

Where would she begin the next chapter in her life? California? And what if she met another manipulative man who decided she had crowded his space. What then? California was as far west as she could go without dropping into the Pacific.

Bitter laughter tumbled from her lips. Perhaps she should drown her troubles and end her misery. She couldn't write to Aunt Martha, offering any sort of explanation. Emmet Blake might see the innocent old woman as a threat and dispose of her as he promised.

Catlin Quinn no longer existed. She may as well have perished with the Hanleys in the fire. She could have no ties with her past. She had to put great distance between herself and San Antonio, never to be seen or heard from again. And she wouldn't, Catlin told herself as she left Emmet Blake far behind. She had escaped the disaster but the torment would hound her forevermore. Emmet may not have been able to keep up with her at the moment, but the haunting ghosts were following like her shadow. Catlin swore she would never forget this night. Each time she closed her eyes she would see the blistering flames and hear Emmet's malicious threats.

Emmet Blake cursed profusely when the laboring steed refused to stir another step. Catlin was still racing the wind to become a shadowy silhouette in the moon-shadows. By God, she had better not show her face in San Antonio again, he muttered stormily. He would crucify that troublemaker. No one would dispute the word of a well-respected physician. Catlin was the one who had initially upset Ginger and Catlin had caused the young woman's death, just as surely as if she had hurled the lanterns to ignite the blaze. Emmet vowed to see Catlin pay retribution some day, somehow. He wouldn't rest until she had perished from the face of the earth!

Part 2

It has been the providence of nature
to give this creature nine lives instead of one.
Pilpay—Fable

Chapter 15

Bo Huxley shifted uncomfortably in the saddle. His squinted gaze swung from the cloud of dust that loomed over the sprawling herd of cattle back to the tall figure of the man who approached from the left flank.

For almost two weeks the men had kept the herd strung out over two miles, walking four abreast behind the incessant clang of the bell that had been strapped around Spur's neck. The wild longhorns had once attempted to stampede back in the direction they had come, but the vaqueros had dissuaded them. Now the cattle had become "trail broke" and plodded along to the sound of Spur's bell, grazing occasionally and then moving forward like an infantry of horned soldiers.

When Lucas eased up beside him, Bo slung a muscled leg over the pommel of the saddle and leaned back to dig into his vest pocket for a chew of tobacco. "Things seem to be proceeding according to plan, Doc," he remarked before biting off a hunk of tobacco.

Lucas dragged the Sugar-loaf sombrero from his head, slapped away the dust and wiped the perspiration from his brow. "So far, so good," he said with a tired sigh. "I found a creek three miles ahead. We'll bed the herd down beside it after they quench their thirst."

Bo twisted around to stare off into the distance. "How long are you going to allow that lone rider to trail us before you find out what the hell he wants?" he questioned.

Lucas frowned. "He hasn't caused us any trouble and I doubt he's a one man raiding party. If he doesn't bother me I see no reason to bother him."

"If you ask me, you ought to ride up to him and demand to know his intentions. Maybe he's employing us as scouts on his trek west and maybe he isn't." Bo pulled his hat from his bushy red hair that was now plastered to his forehead with sweat. Absently, he mopped his brow and then sipped a swig of water from his canteen. "I must be more curious by nature than you are, Doc. I want to know what the blazes the man wants."

Lucas was curious, but he had met himself coming and going the past two weeks. Today he rolled out of his bedroll at five in the morning, gobbled down his breakfast and rode off to scout the trail for trouble and for much-needed water holes. When he returned to camp at noon and night to inspect the herd he found evidence that some of the stock was plagued with screw worms. Exhausted though he had been, he and Bo had cut out the calves to dab carbolic acid, persylic ointment and axle grease on their wounds. The acid killed the worms, the ointment healed the wound and the axle grease prevented the acid from blistering and complicating the infections. And then there were a few cowboys with sore muscles and sprains who needed his attention.

By the time Luke tended all the tasks required of him, he dropped on his pallet and prayed his aching bones and joints would wake up a mite faster than they had the previous morning. And if he didn't have enough difficulty tending ailing cattle and vaqueros and ramrodding a massive trail drive, Catlin's memory burned brands on his thoughts. Hell, he didn't have time to interrogate the cowboy who followed behind the herd. He had a zillion things on his mind.

"Maybe it's some kid who's looking for a job. Or maybe he's a tenderfoot who doesn't know beans about cattle, but he has his heart set on traveling west," Bo speculated jostling Lucas from his pensive contemplations.

"And what if he's a tenderfoot?" Lucas questioned. "Are you going to take him under your wing like a protective mother hen and teach him how to rope and trail a herd? I damned sure don't have time to wet nurse some scrawny greenhorn kid or an ignorant dandy."

Bo frowned at Luke's testy tone. "What the hell's eating you anyway?" he demanded to know. "You've had a thorn under your saddle since we started this drive."

"I'm ready to have the drive over with so I can return to the ranch," Lucas admitted, exploding like cannon.

"Now ain't that something," Bo smirked. "Doc is getting homesick and he has only been on the trail for two weeks. Have you got some sassy little she-male waiting for you or what?"

Lucas glared at Bo's ornery grin. "If you weren't so damned indispensable, I'd fire you on the spot," he threatened.

"And if you don't stop being so touchy I just might quit," Bo snorted. His gaze shifted to the lone rider who was making his way through the arid stretch of land that offered only buffalo grass and an occasional stream to quench his thirst. "Go talk to the man. He's probably starved for companionship and some of Flapjack Barnett's cooking."

Lucas glared at the silhouette who rippled with the heat waves that drifted over the plains. "Alright, dammit, but he's your responsibility if he turns out to be a know-nothing kid who wants a job trailing cattle."

Bo muttered under his breath when the same two yellow dun longhorn steers that had broken loose from the herd the previous day darted off again. "Damned trouble-makers," he grumbled. "If those two steers don't behave themselves I'm going to hook them up on a yoke beside Spur. He'll teach them some manners. I'm already tired of chasing these contrary critters to hell and back."

While Bo gouged his steed to prevent the animals from chasing off in the wrong direction, Lucas pointed himself toward the lone rider. It wasn't the first time a man had approached a moving herd. But usually a rider would come into camp to request a job or beg a meal before veering off. This particular rider simply followed in their wake like a ship navigating behind a fleet of longhorns.

Muttering, Luke pressed his heels to Old Bill's flanks and trotted off. Hell's bells, this was just what he didn't need—a freshly weaned, half-grown child who had left his mama's arms and had struck out in the world to prove his manhood. Well, if the kid wanted a job, he could have it, but he wasn't going to be paid a penny more than he was worth. And Bo was going to tuck this thumb-sucking infant into his bedroll every blessed night. Lucas was not going to concern himself with a greenhorn kid when he had a huge cattle herd to oversee!

Catlin tensed at the sight of the rider galloping toward her. Afraid to set out on a stagecoach for fear Emmet would track her down, Catlin had stopped at the Flying Spur Ranch long enough to fish out some of Lucas's over-sized clothes. Riding hell for leather, she galloped to Fort McKavett which sat on the right bank of the San Saba River. There, she swapped her steed for one Lucas wouldn't recognize and then purchased another set of clothes. Having nowhere else to go and no means of getting there, other than horseback, Catlin had decided to follow the tracks of the massive herd in her effort to elude Emmet.

The threat of impending doom had forced her to garb herself in men's clothes and keep her identity secret. Tempted though she was to dash into Luke's arms and explain her predicament, she couldn't, not after the spiteful threats Emmet had made on Martha and Luke's life. His ignorance of the incident and of her whereabouts was all that would spare Luke from Emmet's wrath. The raving physician had convinced Catlin with his vicious vows.

Although Catlin partially blamed Luke for this disaster, she couldn't involve him in her feud with Emmet. All she wanted was a knowledgeable guide across the sprawling land where a coyote would have a difficult time making a home for himself, much less a woman who had never tackled the frontier alone. But Catlin hadn't counted on being approached, especially by Lucas.

A muted growl erupted from her lips when Luke moved closer. She was unwillingly attracted, stirred by the way he sat so tall and confident in the saddle. Catlin couldn't imagine why the Comanches had earned the title of the Lords of the Plains when Lucas Murdock fit the description so perfectly. Lucas reminded her of a centaur who moved as one with his steed. He was poetry in motion.

Damn, of all the men on the trail drive she had to confront, why did it have to be Lucas? Honest to goodness, the only luck she had of late was rotten.

Luke yanked back on the reins, bringing Old Bill to a skidding halt. His gaze slid over the scrawny boy whose bowed head and broad-brimmed hat disguised his entire face. The lad was garbed in ill-fitting clothes that were obviously designed for his father or someone who was a damned sight larger than this skinny kid. The garments hung off his thin frame like laundry on a clothes line.

"Why are you trailing us?" Luke demanded in an impatient tone.

"There ain't no law that says a man cain't cross West Texas without 'splaining hisself," Catlin drawled in a deep, uncultured voice that sounded nothing like her own.

Lucas was in no frame of mind to converse with a smart-mouthed brat. "Look kid, I don't give a tinker's damn what you do as long as it doesn't affect me or my cattle herd. If you want a job, then say so. If you don't, then follow somebody else's tracks. I'm sure you can find several sets of Comanche prints to the north. I spotted a hunting party yesterday. Maybe they would be more to your liking."

That was not the sort of information Catlin needed to hear. Throwing herself into the Pacific Ocean was one thing, but being tortured and scalped by ruthless renegades was another matter entirely. Damn, maybe this wasn't such a good idea after all. But where else was she to go without Emmet finding her? There was no other place!

"I wanna job," she declared, her voice deep and carefully controlled. "I ain't anxious to meet up with no war party."

Lucas peered down at the boy whose hands were covered with worn gloves and who had yet to raise his face. Lucas wasn't sure the little bag of bones even had a face. If he did, he was obviously ashamed of it.

"If you aren't afraid of hard work and long hours, the job is yours for twenty dollars a month," he announced in a businesslike tone. "Bo Huxley is riding on the left flank. Go look him up and pay close attention to everything he tells you. From here on out, you stick to Bo like glue, kid. If he says jump, you politely ask him how high and then do it. Do you understand me, boy?"

"Yessir," Catlin acknowledged with a firm nod of her head.

Lucas glared at the crown of the brown sombrero. "Have you got a name, kid?"

"Yessir. It's Lin . . . Leonard," she floundered for a

suitable name to fit her new role as a country bumpkin—soon to be a cowhand. "Uh . . . Leonard Page." Page? Honest to goodness, why had she said that? Oh, what the hell. That name was as good as any. "Ah . . . uh . . . my friends just call me Lennie."

"My name is Lucas Murdock. My men call me Doc for short. I'm in charge of this drive and I do the hiring . . . and firing," he added in a meaningful tone.

Catlin didn't dare look up. Lucas would have recognized her in a second. Fortunately, he didn't seem too pleased about taking on a stray cowboy. With any luck at all, he would never be this close again and she wouldn't have to fret about being recognized. She had never met any of his men so they wouldn't know her from Adam. Well, except the scant few who had seen her when they unloaded Aunt Martha's belongings at her new home, Catlin amended. She would simply make it a point to take a wide berth around the familiar faces in camp.

Making a mental note to keep her distance from Luke in the future, Catlin shifted uneasily in the saddle. What if he did figure out who she really was? Lord, she would have to dream up a convincing lie! But hopefully, he would never know she had joined the drive for her personal protection. And the minute the herd reached its destination she would catch a stage west and Luke wouldn't know she had come and gone. Now all she had to do was forget her feelings for this powerful package of masculinity.

He doesn't mean anything to me anymore, Catlin assured herself fiercely. They had no future now. Emmet Blake would never allow her to live if she dared to return to San Antonio and she would never be able to keep quiet about what he did, even if she did return. They were bound to clash. What she and Lucas had shared was over. It had to be. He had fathered Ginger's child and Ginger and Robert were dead.

Cat had been a fool to get mixed up with Lucas

Murdock. His main concern was his cattle and his ranch. The women in his life only served one purpose—appeasing his lusts. If she had any sense she would never let herself forget that. Even if she had married Lucas she would have been his substitute for Elise, another piece of property he acquired to compensate for being unable to have the woman he wanted.

While Catlin sat with her head bowed, reinforcing her convictions to keep her identity secret, Lucas grew even more impatient. Without a word, he reined Old Bill around and trotted toward the herd's right flank. He had to ensure no wild creatures had approached the creek where the cattle were to drink and bed down. All it would take was a startled raft of ducks flapping about in the water and the cattle would bolt into a wild run. The longhorns were just settling into a peaceful routine, but it took little or nothing to set them off. Even the steady peal of the bell that hung around Spur's neck wouldn't calm a herd that turned back upon itself. The cattle would scatter in a thousand directions at once and it would take days to round them up. And once they stampeded around a water hole it would become a conditioned response. They would do it every cussed time.

If Luke would have known he had just carried on a conversation with Catlin he would have cursed her for shouldering another burden by herself. But he didn't know it was Cat beneath that oversized sombrero and she had no intention of allowing Luke to discover who she was. Catlin was accustomed to bearing her own troubles and fighting her own battles. The vicious vows of vengeance hung heavily on her mind and she couldn't bring herself to confide in the man who was partly responsible for the nightmare that hounded her every step like ghastly specters that loomed at her heels.

While Luke rode on ahead, Catlin followed at a slower pace. After posing a question to the young drag rider, Jesse

Lane, Catlin was pointed toward the stout, burly cowboy who had just returned from herding the two yellow dun steers back to the organized column of cattle.

"Bo Huxley. My name is Lennie Page," Catlin introduced, raising her head to survey the cowboy's leathery face. "The trail boss said I was to stick to you like glue and learn all you could teach me."

Bo spat tobacco out the side of his mouth and scrutinized the scrawny lad. Violet eyes peered at him from beneath the shaded brim of the sombrero. The boy looked young, damned young. And he had an effeminate face that was smudged with dirt and grime. Bo wondered if he hadn't bit off more than he could chew when he offered to teach this frail bundle of bones to herd cattle.

"What do you know about cattle, kid?" he questioned as he chomped on his tobacco.

"Not much, but I'm willing to learn," Catlin enthused.

The seasoned cowboy rolled his eyes heavenward. He was going to be playing nursemaid to a child. Damn him and his bright ideas! He should have kept his mouth shut.

"For starters, you had beeter learn to respect these longhorns. Many of them are *cimarrones*— fresh from the bush country. They are wilder and more deadly than a buffalo. Their sense of smell is as astute as a deer and they can run like antelopes when they're spooked. They can tear through briar and bramble like a panther through a jungle. Only a fool takes a longhorn for granted. When he does, he usually doesn't survive to correct his miscalculations."

Bo's pointed gaze probed the young attentive face. "The longhorns separate a man from his mistakes . . . permanently. These scarred, lanky animals can survive where most critters starve and die of thirst. They can fight off a pack of wolves and ward off heat, cold, and famine. They can smell water ten miles away and drink thirty gallons of it a day. And you had better not get in their way when they

229

charge toward a watering hole. If you do, you won't need a drink where you're going." Bo stood up in the stirrups to give his backside a rest. "Longhorns are wild by nature, aware and sensitive to their surroundings. They will raise their tails to take their first jump onto all fours and their second jump is to kingdom come. And it takes an eternity to gather them up and calm them down after they stampede."

"If they're such flighty animals, why do you bother with them?" Catlin questioned, eyeing the long, sharp horns warily. "It seems more domesticated stock would prove safer."

Bo spit an arc of tobacco juice and chuckled. "Longhorns are the only breed that can endure these long, tedious walks across *el desierto de los muertos*. That's the name we Texans have given this Godforsaken patch of land that stretches from south to west Texas. It's the land God gave to the devil, kid. Its Spanish translation is the desert of the dead. This is native ground to these *cimarrones*. If they can survive on it, they can endure most anything. They can trek across arid stretches and make a drink of water last two days if it has to. They can trudge through mountain passes without dropping from exhaustion. I knew a rancher who once bought some fancy bulls to breed to his longhorns. But the expensive bulls died and only the longhorns survived the rough winter."

While Bo continued to praise the long-legged creatures that trudged northwest, Catlin hung on his every word. She had to pay close attention and learn the ropes or she would run the risk of confronting Lucas again. As they worked beside the long string of longhorns, Catlin tried to mimic Bo's every move and mentally list his advice and suggestions.

Bo shouted instructions as the cattle quickened their pace to reach the stream. He warned her to keep the animals moving so the first ones in the water wouldn't linger too long and cause the ones behind them to spread and wander downstream.

Once the cattle had been sufficiently watered and allowed to graze, Lucas ordered them bedded down on the flat ground beyond the creek. The remuda of horses, or *caviada* as Bo preferred to call it, was then tended by the young wrangler Jesse Lane.

Catlin had just climbed from the saddle when Flapjack Barnett announced supper and she was eager for nourishment. With tin plate in hand, Catlin dropped down cross-legged to sample Flapjack's Sonofabitch Stew. Her gaze lifted to survey the stocky cook who had shocks of blond hair jutting out from his head in all directions. His facial features reminded Catlin of an exotic bird with his close-set black eyes, his long hooked beak and nonexistent chin. Around his broad midsection the cook had tied an apron that was splotched with globs of flour and smears of grease.

"This stew is quite good," Catlin complimented between bites.

"It oughta be," Flapjack declared as he propped himself against his throne of pots and utensils. "It's got half a calf's heart, testicles, a set of brains, marrow gut, and Louisiana hot sauce. All the proper fixings for stew."

Catlin stared at her plate as if the food was laced with poison. She suddenly wasn't as hungry as she first thought she was. Grimly, Catlin peered up at the chuckwagon—the stout canvas-covered carry-all against which Flapjack was leaning. Her eyes wandered over the box at the rear where the dishes, Dutch oven, frying pans, kettles, and coffee pot were stored. She wondered if she could find something else to curb her appetite. All the standard staples were in their exact places: gooseberry coffee, salt pork, corn meal, flour, and beans. A folding leg was attached to the chuck box lid, forming a table when one was needed. The main body of the wagon was packed with bedrolls, rain slickers and extra clothes. Fastened securely in front was a water barrel with a convenient spigot running through the side of the wagon. Beneath the bed was a cowhide sling for transporting dry wood and buffalo chips. And in a box below the driver's seat were the necessary tools—axes, hammers, and spades. But nowhere was a tasty snack on which Catlin could munch. Resolutely, she ate her stew, trying not to think which ingredients Flapjack had tossed into it.

While Catlin sat with her head poised over her plate, Lucas ambled over to Bo. "How did the kid do?" he questioned before sipping his coffee.

"He's a mite wet behind the ears and skinny as a starved coyote, but he's got a sharp mind and he learns fast," Bo replied eyeing the lad from a distance.

"Did he say where he came from or what he was doing out here by himself?" Lucas queried.

Bo shook his bushy red head. "Not a word. He could be from another planet for all I know."

Lucas stared at the scrawny lad from over the rim of his cup. In long graceful strides he ambled over to light his cigarillo at the fire and then prowled about camp. Occasionally he darted Lennie Page a speculative glance. But Catlin made it a point to keep her head bowed while Lucas circumnavigated the area like a posted sentinel. She was totally aware of the brawny cowboy, even when she had vowed to strike his name and his memory from the chronicles of her past. Telling herself she was over Lucas Murdock for good was a helluva lot easier than living up to that conviction. It would take time, she consoled herself. But she had made the right decision. The less Lucas knew the better.

Following that practical philosophy, Catlin stuck close to Bo and religiously avoided Lucas. But her eyes constantly followed him, watching him interact with the twenty vaqueros who worked for him. He had their respect; that was obvious. He was firm but rarely irate when something went wrong. Catlin admired his rapport with his men and his expertise with the country and the cattle. He had the knack of outguessing difficulty and bypassing it with meticulous calculation.

When dawn came, Lucas rolled to his feet to pace until his stiff joints loosened up. He wolfed down his breakfast, checked the cattle, and then rode off to scout the trail ahead of them. He searched for water, areas of good grazing, safe bedding ground, and then laid out the route for the herd to follow. He was like a restless cougar, constantly on the prowl. And it didn't help matters that Bo boasted of Luke's exceptional talents as much as Aunt Martha did. Catlin could see for herself that Lucas deserved the respect he was given. She didn't need to hear glowing accolades from Bo. Cat was having enough difficulty keeping her perspective as it was!

Catlin quickly became conditioned to the grueling routine of the drive. The long hours in the saddle prompted Catlin to give a new meaning to the term *rawhide*. The longhorns tested her stamina and endurance, but she never complained. She tolerated it because, of late, enduring had become a way of life.

When Flapjack Barnett clanged his pots and pans to signal breakfast, Catlin and the cowboys rolled from the pallets. Catlin had become accustomed to seeing the men in their underwear, but as for herself, she slept in her clothes for obvious reasons. After pulling on her boots, she washed her face from the spigot of the barrel on the chuckwagon and dried it with the community towel. At five o'clock (a most ungodly hour to rise, in Catlin's opinion) she sipped gooseberry coffee and gobbled down sourdough biscuits. The wrangler, Jesse Lane, hurried off to round up the remuda of one-hundred-fifty horses and herded them into the makeshift rope corral. Quietly,

Catlin strided alongside Bo to select her mount for the day. When she slid her rope around a roan gelding's neck, Bo gave his wiry red head a negative shake and indicated another dark steed that stood nearby.

"Take Black Jack," Bo suggested. "He's surefooted and he has quickly learned to herd cattle. What you haven't learned, Jack knows by pure instinct. If a steer cuts away, he'll take after the contrary animal and all you have to do is stay on his back. Black Jack will do the rest."

Catlin nodded agreeably, but Black Jack, for all his redeeming qualities, didn't like to be caught. He made a ritual of eluding his would-be rider. Staring the ornery mount squarely in the eye, Catlin approached him for the third time. "One of us is going to win this battle of wills and it ain't gonna be you," she told the contrary steed.

After the fourth attempt, Black Jack held his ground and allowed Catlin to slip the noose over his neck. Struggling with the fifty pound saddle, Catlin finally had her steed readied for another long day.

The next order of business was to toss the bedrolls into the chuckwagon whose tongue was always pointed toward the north star each night so the cowboys never lost their sense of direction. Once Flapjack Barnett had gathered his cooking utensils, he drove slowly through the herd of cattle that was climbing to their feet to face another day of walking. Flapjack pointed himself wagon-tongue north and then veered west to begin preparations for the noon meal at the location Lucas had designated.

Diligently, the vaqueros worked to squeeze the milling herd into formation. After an hour the column of longhorns began to march in rhythm with Spur's clanging bell. Flapjack Barnett and his chuckwagon and the *caviada* of extra horses led the procession from their bed ground. The cowboys who rode point guided the cattle in the proper direction, keeping an eye out for Lucas who relayed signals and orders with the wave of his hat.

The swing and flank riders eased alongside the longhorns to keep them from wandering off to the side of the procession.

On this particular day, Catlin and Bo took their turn as drag riders, trailing behind the herd, urging the bawling cows and their calves to file into line. Catlin drew her bandana over her face when the choking dust billowed around her. She accepted the worst position on the drive without uttering a discouraging word. It was far better than being cremated in Emmet Blake's raging fire, she kept telling herself as she rode through the wall of dust, trekking steadily northwest.

By the end of the day Catlin felt gritty and grimy and she would have sold her soul for a bath. She had been with the herd for over three days and she had yet to enjoy a moment's privacy. When the other vaqueros sank down in the creeks to cool and cleanse themselves, Catlin refrained. She was afraid the clinging clothes might reveal one too many curves or swells that the rest of the cowboys didn't have. She did however, employ Bo's technique of making the murky water acceptable to drink. Bo had showed her how to take the leaf of a cactus and sprinkle it in water that was full of sand. Within a minute the water she had scooped into her hat and had doctored with cactus juice was clean enough to drink.

When Cat was assigned to night watch, she silently planned to take a few minutes to swim in the spring Lucas had located earlier in the day. When Bo pointed out the best "night horse" in the *caviada*, Catlin saddled him. According to Bo, Cat-Eyes had sharp vision and he could locate a lost cow or pick his way through the darkness without stumbling or darting sideways. Cat-Eyes was so accustomed to the two-hour shifts that he refused to circle the herd after that amount of time. A man didn't need a timepiece to determine when two hours was up, Bo claimed. The horse was as good as any clock.

After circling the herd for a half-hour in a diminishing circle that kept the cattle congregated, Catlin slipped away while the other nighthawk reversed the circular direction, singing his doleful lullaby to the herd. A contented sigh escaped Catlin's lips when she sank into the cool water to cleanse herself. Ah, this was glorious! Never again would she take bathing for granted. Yes, she had waded into the stream earlier that day with the other cowboys, but she had only walked into the knee-deep water near the bank. But wading in the creek couldn't compare to shedding her garb and soaking to her heart's content. . . .

An eerie warhoop splintered the night and Catlin's blood ran cold. With her heart racing like a thoroughbred, Catlin grabbed the cloth she tied around her chest, mashing her breasts to conceal the swells. She darted a glance over the hill and decided she didn't have time to do anything more than poke her legs in her breeches and shrug on her shirt. Later, after she discovered what the whooping and hollering was all about, she would bind her breasts.

Another round of howls pierced the night and a rumble shook the ground. Catlin's pulse raced in grim anticipation. The cattle were on their feet, darting off in all directions at once, stampeded by a raiding party of Comanches who seized the opportunity to steal a few head of beeves.

Catlin vaulted into the saddle and the earth shook beneath her when three thousand frightened cattle lunged into the darkness. She could hear the curses of the cowboys who had saddled their horses in record time to charge after the stampeding herd. She could see the sparks flying from the tips of the horns as they clashed together in their wild run.

Pressing herself against her steed, Catlin tried to turn the herd back upon itself as Bo instructed her to do in case of stampede. But it was terrifying to see the long sharp horns darting every which way at once, threatening to gore her if she got in their way. The herd was like a monstrous force plunging through the darkness and Catlin gulped down her heart at the thought of stumbling beneath the wild animals. The weird flashes that quivered at the tips of their horns as they collided frightened the cattle more than they already were. A snake of apprehension slithered down Catlin's spine as she raced after the *cimarrones*.

Catlin knew any moment her steed would step in a prairie dog hole and she would become unrecognizable mush. But terrified though she was, she screamed at the thundering longhorns, forcing them to swerve to the right.

Voices resounded around her and pistols barked in the night as the other vaqueros swarmed in to assist her. Catlin swore she had ridden at breakneck speeds for an hour before the herd began to circle and slow their ground-shaking pace. And it was another hour before the longhorns had quieted enough to fall into step. It was a night Catlin swore she would never forget, another nightmare she would be forced to endure. Fires and stampedes. Lord, how she longed for just one sweet dream that wouldn't cause her to wake in a cold sweat!

Chapter 16

Catlin was totally exhausted by the time the cowboys had restored order and returned to their bedrolls to catch a few hours of much-needed sleep. As she trudged over to retrieve her pallet, Lucas's gruff baritone voice halted her in midstep.

"You are back on nightwatch, Lennie," he demanded. "Fetch a fresh horse." Lucas glared at the thin waddy who was partially responsible for the wounds and sprains he had just treated on several of his men. Lennie's punishment was to take a second turn as nighthawk.

Glumly, Catlin did as she was told. When she climbed into the saddle, Lucas eased his steed up beside her.

"I questioned the other nighthawk," he began in a gritted growl. "He admitted, though most reluctantly, that you were not in your position when he made his counterclockwise circle to meet you. Where the hell were you when the Comanches sneaked up to wave their blankets and startle the herd?"

"I'm sorry, Doc," Catlin apologized as she urged her steed forward. "It won't happen again."

Lucas's face twisted in a menacing scowl. "You're damned right it won't happen again, kid," he snapped. "You probably cost me twenty-five head of cattle and that cuts into my profit. Now what the blazes were you doing while you were supposed to be making your clockwise circle? Catching a nap?"

When Cat refused to answer the direct question a second time, Lucas muttered under his breath. Swinging from the saddle, he barked the order for one of the other cowboys to take Lennie Page's place. A surprised yelp burst from Catlin's lips when, without warning, Lucas reached up to grab the collar of her shirt and yanked her from the mount.

"By damned, you and I are going to have a talk, kid. And you better tell me where you were or I'm going to shake the information out of you," Lucas threatened as he stalked away from camp with the closemouthed boy in tow.

In swift, furious strides, Lucas shepherded the wriggling wrangler out of earshot of the other cowboys. When they were far enough away not to be overheard, he shook Catlin until her head snapped backwards. Catlin hadn't taken time to tie the bandana around her head when the stampede started. She had simply stuffed her hair under her hat and bounded to her steed. And when Lucas shook her so fiercely, the sombrero tumbled to the ground, causing the tangled mass of blond hair to cascade down to her waist.

"What the . . . ?" Lucas froze, staring bug-eyed at the masquerading wrangler.

He let go of Catlin as if he were touching live coals. She stumbled back, landing in an unladylike heap on the ground. Apprehensively, Catlin scraped herself up off the grass and waited for Luke to explode. And sure enough, he did!

"Are you nuts, woman?" he hooted in astonishment. "What the devil are you doing out here? Damn your hide, you could have gotten yourself trampled." His breath came out in a gritted snarl. "No wonder you haven't dared to look me squarely in the eye the past few days. What the sweet loving hell were you trying to prove and why didn't

239

you tell me who you were?"

Catlin glared back at him. "Which of those rapid-fire questions would you like for me to answer first?"

"All of them at once," he spouted like a geyser. "Dammit, Cat. This is no place for a woman. Stampeding cattle! Men running around in their underwear, conversing on subjects that aren't fit for a woman's ears. Hell's bells, how long did you think you could cling to your disguise without someone finding out the truth?"

Honest to goodness, just once she wished he would ask a question she could answer. How the blazes did she know she couldn't conceal her identity for three months? If Lucas hadn't shaken the stuffing out of her and knocked off her hat she might have fooled him for the duration of the drive. Who knew?

"Well?" Lucas muttered, crossing his arms over his chest.

"Well what?" she countered as she scooped up her hat.

"What was your intention?" he wanted to know that very second.

God, he had endured the shock of his life. The implication that Catlin didn't want him to know who she was rubbed him the wrong way. For more than two weeks he had been tormented by her memory, wondering if David Krause had decided all was fair in love and war and if he was actively courting this gorgeous minx. Lucas had ached for Cat up to his eyebrows. And now here she was, avoiding his questions, refusing to inform him of her intentions.

"All I wanted was a bath," Catlin sighed. "Riding drag is a dirty job and I didn't think it would hurt to leave my position for ten minutes. But then suddenly—"

"Didn't think it would hurt?" Lucas parroted sarcastically. "You don't go off and leave three thousand longhorns unattended, for Chrissake!"

"I already said it wouldn't happen again," she muttered resentfully.

"No, it won't because you aren't taking night duty," Lucas growled, "And if I thought I could point you toward San Antonio and you would arrive safely, I'd send you packing."

"I wouldn't go back," Catlin declared, tilting a stubborn chin.

The comment caught Luke off stride. Narrowed brown eyes swept over the ill-fitting clothes and then focused on her defiant stare. His temper was on a short fuse and Catlin's proclamation stung with implication. "Why not? Because *I* will be back again?"

Lucas was baffled by Catlin's attitude toward him. She was standoffish and aloof and he felt as if he were arguing with a stranger. The day before he left the Flying Spur Ranch he had enjoyed a vacation in paradise. And now, here was his angel, behaving like the very devil.

"Does this mean we are no longer engaged?" A mocking smile pursed his lips, concealing the sting of pride. "So the fickle butterfly decided to flit off somewhere else, did she? And if I hadn't discovered you were underfoot during the entire drive, did you plan to sashay away without bothering to tell me good-bye? Did you even bother to leave me a note at the ranch before you left or was I supposed to guess what had become of you?"

Catlin gritted her teeth and reminded herself there were times when one had to be cruel to be kind. This was one of those times. She couldn't tell Luke what had sent her fleeing from the ranch. "What difference would it have made? You wouldn't have missed me," she smirked. "This engagement was only a trial period for you. Admit it, you don't really want a wife when you can have any woman you want. If I wasn't there waiting for you, you would have found someone else to ease your lust. You strike me as the kind of man who has never been between women."

What the hades had come over this sassy sprite? Why was she treating him as if he were her enemy? My God, he thought there was a special bond between them and that she intended to wait until his return. From all indication, Catlin had played him for a fool. Women! He didn't know why he bothered with any of them. First it was Elise who tormented him. Now it was Cat. Damn her.

"I proposed to you, didn't I?" Lucas snorted caustically. "I would have noticed if my fiancée wasn't around when I got back. What did you do? Sit yourself down and analyze our engagement and then decide you could do better elsewhere?" His dark eyes raked her with scorn. "Now what? Do you plan to turn your charms on some miner who struck it rich in Colorado so he can support you in the manner to which you had grown accustomed before the war?"

"My only intention was to get the hell out of Texas!" Cat spumed. "And you know the only reason you're being snide and sarcastic is because I was the one who said it was over between us first. You wouldn't mind one whit if you had been the one to say it."

Lucas couldn't remember wanting to strike a woman before, but he was seriously contemplating it now. This vixen was a chameleon who changed the color of her moods with maddening inconsistency. She had never said so, but Lucas thought she felt something for him. Obviously, he was mistaken. Cat had only patronized him until he rode off into the sunset. Damn her. No, double damn her, he thought, giving the matter second consideration

Lucas reached out a lean hand to drag Catlin close, breathing down her neck. "I was willing to make a fresh new start with you, to put Elise out of my mind forever. I'm tired of Elise's memory hounding me and I would have been faithful to you—"

Catlin yanked her arm from his steely grasp and glared flaming arrows at him. "Faithful? You? Ha! I'm sure Ginger was counting on you to be loyal to her, too, but you don't have a devoted bone in your body and you will never

242

get over your precious Elise." Catlin could feel herself trembling with frustration—frustration that was growing out of proportion as flashbacks of the past and the nightmare rose up to torment her. "Ginger carried your child and now she is dead."

Catlin clamped her mouth shut and then cursed unintelligibly. She hadn't meant to say that, but Lucas had annoyed her and the incident exploded in her mind, putting words to tongue that should not have been there at all.

"What? Ginger is dead? Oh God," Lucas croaked like a startled bullfrog. "But the baby couldn't have been mine. . . ."

She wanted to slap him silly. "Did you or did you not sleep with her?" she interrogated him.

Lucas glared right back at her and refused to answer. Catlin, not to be put off, posed the question again.

"You are so proud of your honesty," she goaded him. "Now tell me the truth. Did you or did you not make love to Ginger?"

"Yes, once, but she came to my cottage," Lucas muttered sourly. "I wasn't even sure why she came. She had been crying and she asked for comfort."

Catlin exploded like a keg of gunpowder. "Honest to goodness, Lucas, how many times do you think it takes to make a baby?" she queried incredulously. "Once was obviously enough!"

His probing gaze riveted on her irate features. "And are you carrying my child, Cat? We have been lovers several times . . . or have you chosen to forget?"

Her face was as red as a beet. Not even the moonshadows could conceal the rise of color provoked by his candid remark. "I don't know," she mumbled, wheeling to stare off at some distant point. "It's too soon to tell after . . ."

"After we made love as if there was no tomorrow, after the last days and nights we spent together," he finished for her, his voice dropping to an intimate pitch. "And if we did create a child, would you have written me from only God knows where to inform me that I was a father?"

"Would you really care?" she flung at him. "Would you have wanted Ginger's child if she hadn't perished in the . . ."

Lucas was quiet and watchful, scrutinizing the turmoil of emotions that chased each other across Catlin's smudged features. Something was tormenting her, but she was reluctant to reveal the source of her frustration. He knew Ginger's death had upset her, just as it did him. But there was something more, something Cat was hesitant to confess to him.

"What happened, Cat?" he questioned in a gentler tone.

"The Hanley cottage caught on fire while Ginger and Robert were inside it," she admitted without confessing that she had come dangerously close to being cremated herself. She couldn't tell Lucas the whole truth, only what he needed to know.

His long lashes swept down and he let out his breath in a rush. The thought of the Hanley's enduring a fiery death grieved him. For several minutes he stood there, saying nothing, grappling with the news Catlin had given him. His child? Ginger had carried his child? God, why hadn't she told him? Was that why Catlin had left San Antonio? Had she cursed him because of his one night with Ginger?

Catlin squared her shoulders, fighting the urge to wrap herself in his sinewy arms. She was cold and tired and distraught. But she couldn't find consolation with Lucas, not anymore. She would only prolong the agony. They could never enjoy what they once had, not after what had happened. "If you are finished raking me over the coals for leaving my post to bathe, I would like to get some sleep. I have a job to do come first light."

"You are dismissed from your trail duties," Lucas told her, his eyes wandering at will, visualizing what lay

244

beneath the baggy garments.

"I need the money and I will do the jobs expected of me," she informed him crisply.

Lucas had had just about enough of her independent belligerence, but he hadn't had enough of Cat. He still wanted her. Nothing had changed. He looked at her and the memories burned like torches. "You will be paid," he assured her as he closed the distance between them. "But I'll decide what duties you will perform." His arm stole around her waist, molding her body to his masculine contours. "The first duty is to pleasure me. . . ."

Catlin gasped at the feel of his muscled body mashed familiarly to hers and at his infuriating audacity. She had told him it was over between them and he ignored her. She had told him about Ginger and although he did lament her death he didn't seem to think it made any difference between himself and her. Blast it, wasn't that just like this infuriating man who could separate one facet of his life from another? Well, maybe he could but she couldn't. The torment was too fresh on her mind and the invisible scars cut deep. And how dare he assign her the task of camp concubine!

Although Catlin tried to pry herself loose, Lucas's arms closed around her like a beaver trap. Catlin didn't want to tremble in response to the searing kiss that stripped her breath from her lungs, but she did. The forbidden memories came rushing back like a tidal wave. Lucas, devil that he was, could make her feel every inch a woman, make her aware of his masculine physique and the demanding pressure of his lips upon hers.

The instant her resistance dropped a notch, Lucas became gentler, savoring the thirst-quenching taste of kisses sweeter than wine. Lord, he could lose himself in this saucy sprite. They could quarrel until they were both blue in the face, but nothing could extinguish the fires ignited by their first kiss. It was as it had always been. He

245

touched Catlin and he forgot everything associated with reality. The world turned black as pitch and hot, compelling sensations sizzled through him.

Catlin may have scorned him because Ginger had carried his child, because Catlin could well be carrying his child herself. She may have decided to leave him, but she was here now and Lucas couldn't think past the moment. He couldn't breathe normally either. All he knew was that it had been two long weeks since he had touched this curvaceous nymph, since he had climbed the pyramid to the pinnacle of ecstasy. Catlin held the key that unlocked his desires.

The chain of burning memories formed a link that connected the past to the present. Luke ached for what they had once shared. He needed to feel her supple body beneath his. The memories intensified the cravings and Lucas shuddered uncontrollably as his questing hands delved beneath the baggy shirt to caress the warm, desirable woman beneath it.

Catlin couldn't draw a breath without suffocating on the manly scent of the man who kissed her until her brain broke down. She, too, became a prisoner of her desires, ones that had lain dormant, suppressed by fear and frustration. But Lucas was a magical wizard who could tap that deep well, sending a flood of emotions bubbling to the surface. His skillful hands could make mincemeat of her common sense. His hot greedy kisses transformed his will into her own.

And suddenly Catlin forgot she intended to reject his advances. She was as hungry for him as he was for her. Sparks leaped between them and back again as they exchanged kiss for kiss, touch for touch. The hindering garments melted in a pool as wandering hands glided over quaking flesh. Their lips twisted and slanted, desperate to devour, starved for the intoxicating brew of passion.

His body half-covered hers and Catlin moaned at the

feel of his hair-roughened flesh brushing provocatively against hers. Like a famished creature, she tasted him, touched him, rediscovered every inch of his virile flesh. She longed to become a part of him, to satisfy the gigantic need that had swallowed her alive. She reveled in the exquisite torture of his caresses roving over the dusky peaks of her breasts, her belly, her thighs. Each sensitive place he touched became a sizzling flame. Each moist intimate kiss provoked a tide of rapturous sensations that threatened to drown her.

Catlin felt like a floundering swimmer going down for the third and final time and she didn't want to be rescued. She would gladly sacrifice her last breath for a few wild, sublime moments of ecstasy. And all the while, as his masterful hands and lips covered her, he whispered his need for her and made intimate promises of pleasures to come. Catlin not only heard his words and became aroused by them, but she felt the tantalizing murmur of words on her skin.

When he finally braced himself above her, Catlin's tangled lashes swept up to peer into the craggy face above hers. The glistening moonlight danced in his dark eyes. He was a man caught in the throes of unbridled passion and his taut expression testified to the extent of his hunger. As his hair-matted body settled exactly upon hers, Catlin's eyes swept shut to block out the shrinking world.

"Look at me, violet eyes," he demanded huskily. He came to her, possessing her. "I want you to see what you do to me. I want to see what I do to you. And while I'm making wild sweet love to you, tell me again that it's over between us, that we don't feed off each other's fierce passions. . . ."

Catlin felt the warm soft flame inside her and moaned in pleasure when he set the slow, languid cadence of love. She watched him, felt him, and died a thousand times when the flood tide of rapture rose to engulf her. She was bobbing on a river of rapids, rushing toward a roaring waterfall. She clung to Lucas as if he were her life preserver, knowing nothing could save her from plummeting into the whirlpool of ecstasy. Each deep penetrating thrust brought her ever closer to the mindless fall through time and space. And as the earth slid out from under her, Cat dug in her claws and held on for dear life. His name gushed from her lips as the tumultuous sensations that had assaulted her one at a time converged to shatter her sanity. Her body quivered, shuddered. She could feel the lithe muscular man who clutched her possessively to him. She had absorbed his strength, but still it wasn't enough to save her from the potent shock waves of passion.

Lucas buried his head on her shoulder, nipping at her flesh as the ardent needs swamped and buffeted him. His body and brain were numb and it took forever to muster the energy to move. Their fervent lovemaking always had these devastating effects on him. Once he was beneath this sweet witch's spell he found himself melting into peach marmalade. And this sorceress kept him simmering in her caldron of passion until he dripped into puddles. Lord, she could have set a fire beneath him just then and he would have been fried to a burnt crisp long before he gathered the strength to roll away. . . .

"Doc?" Where the hell are you?" Bo's voice cracked the silence like a blaring bugle.

With a wordless scowl, Lucas groped for his discarded clothes and wiggled into them in record time.

"Doc? Are you out here?" Bo questioned the darkness.

Finally, Lucas appeared from behind a clump of brush and ambled toward him.

"What are you doing? And where the devil is Lennie?" Bo interrogated him.

"Lennie? How the hell do I know where he is?" Lucas grumbled, taking a quick glance at his torso to ensure he hadn't missed a button in his haste to fasten himself into his breeches and shirt.

Bo frowned bemusedly. "You dragged the kid out here to chew him up one side and down the other, didn't you?" His gaze whizzed across the star-lit horizon to probe the shadows. "I could have sworn Lennie was out here with you."

"He was," Lucas reluctantly admitted. "I said my piece and we parted company. Maybe he wandered off to sulk."

"You better not have been too rough on him," Bo threatened.

Rough on him? Lucas would have laughed out loud if Bo wouldn't have thought his trail boss was behaving more peculiar than he already was. Lucas couldn't very well tell Bo that he and Lennie had been lying beneath the stars, sharing a splendor that rivaled nothing in his experience. And besides, Lucas hadn't decided what he was going to do about that gorgeous nymph. If he told the rest of the men Lennie was a *she*, they would be trailing after her like starved kittens on the trail of fresh milk. And if he didn't tell them, they would be pealing off their clothes and talking the way men talked when they didn't think there was a woman around. Hell's bells . . .

"I didn't beat the tar out of the kid for leaving his post, if that's what you want to know," Lucas muttered as he barreled toward camp.

Bo stared after Lucas. Another puzzled frown puckered his bushy brows. His thoughts dispersed when he saw the frail figure in baggy clothes materializing from the shadows.

"Are you alright, kid?" Bo questioned as Lennie ambled toward him, head downcast.

No, she wasn't alright dammit! She had broken her vow to keep Lucas at arm's length, to forget the tempestuous hungers that gnawed at her. She had lost herself in Lucas's arms, finding passion and consolation from the night-

249

mares that haunted her.

"I'm okay," Cat drawled in a deep voice. "Doc bit my head off, but I deserved it."

Bo looped his arm around the boy's narrow shoulders to give him a consoling pat on the back. "Don't fret, kid. We all make a few mistakes in the beginning. The boss has been edgy since we left San Antonio. Considering his active love life, he's probably suffering withdrawal symptoms," he chuckled lightheartedly. "Doc bears the weight of tremendous responsibility and he's a man who demands perfection because he expects nothing less of himself during a drive. Once you learn the ropes, Doc will let up on you."

Catlin nodded mutely as they ambled back to camp. But she didn't glance in Luke's direction, nor he in hers. Mechanically, Cat crawled into her bedroll and cursed herself for submitting to that infuriating man.

Nothing had changed. It was still over, despite what Lucas said. They couldn't go back; Emmet Blake had spoiled any chance of that. Catlin had to let go of her dreams, to cast aside the plague of love. She was only going to make herself miserable if she didn't accept the fact that she and Luke had no future. Lucas may have been entertaining thoughts of another rendezvous in the bushes, but he was in for a disappointment. Catlin promised herself they had taken their last reckless tumble. If he needed physical release he could look elsewhere. Just where, Catlin didn't know and she didn't care, she convinced herself. There was nothing but miles of open range sprawling out in all directions. If Lucas wanted a woman he could go searching for one. And if he didn't find one in this forsaken patch of earth that God had given to the devil, that was his tough luck!

Chapter 17

Lucas wore a permanent scowl as he trotted ahead of the plodding infantry of longhorns. After discovering that Catlin was among his troops he had become aware and sensitive to his men's colorful comments about women and the finer pleasures of life. The fact that Cat was overhearing the ribald remarks annoyed him. The fact that she still treated him as if he had contracted leprosy irritated him.

He knew he should shrug her aside for trying to hornswoggle him, for leaving him without a word. But each time he fell into that trap of forbidden memories he was back to wanting that minx in the same wild ways. To make matters worse, Lucas lamented his one and only intimate contact with Ginger Hanley and her untimely death. It sickened him to think of the tragedies she and Robert had endured and that he was partially responsible for her woes. Dammit, why hadn't Ginger told him? And why had she told Catlin? Had Ginger expected him to return from the drive and accept his responsibilities? Was that why she had been so melancholy the previous month? For certain, Ginger's death had torn him and Catlin apart. She resented his recklessness and she intended to hold it over him for the rest of his life.

Lucas expelled an exasperated breath. He should let Cat go her own way when they reached New Mexico or Colorado. He had spoiled their chance at happiness. But dammit, he had come to depend on those radiant smiles, the living fire that sparkled in her amethyst eyes. He couldn't forget the wondrous day they had spent together at the ranch. She had become a habit he didn't want to break.

What was it that she wasn't telling him? Lucas swore Cat was keeping something from him. He could sense it. There was far more tormenting her than she was willing to admit. But whatever it was, she was keeping her own counsel, as usual. Catlin was the world's worst about shouldering her own burdens and fighting her own battles. She was determined to depend on no one but herself. Blast it, how could he solve the problems between them when he didn't know exactly what they were and Catlin refused to enlighten him? Damnation, that impossible she-male was making him crazy!

Forcefully, Lucas tucked his troubled thoughts in the closet of his mind and trotted his steed northward. He had enough difficulties without being sidetracked by that sassy sprite.

Fort Concho lay beyond the trudging herd, setting at the junction between the North and South Concho Rivers. It was the jumping off place for the eighty mile, waterless stretch of Llano Estacado that would test his men and the longhorn's endurance.

The Comanches called the Staked Plains of the Southwest "the land of the back shade folks." There were no trees, no shrubs, nor bushes to break the horizon or to shield travelers from the heat of the blistering sun. A man had to sit in the shade of his own back as he moved the longhorns toward their final destination. The vaqueros would have to trek through the dust beneath the baking sun for more than three days. They would push extra miles before they reached Horsehead Crossing—the only safe place to ford the Pecos River.

The sight of Fort Concho lying beside the desolate region ahead of him, brought a hint of a smile to Lucas's parched lips. Soon they could rest the cattle. He had moved the herd eighteen miles this day and his men would be rewarded with much-needed rest. They could take shifts to stand guard over the cattle while part of the men ventured to the fort to quench their thirst and satisfy their yearnings by keeping company with the camp laundresses who had no aversion to doing more than a man's laundry.

Wheeling his horse around, Lucas pulled his sombrero from his head, signaling the point riders to aim the herd toward the river and allow them to drink to their heart's content. Then they could graze on the bluestem, buffalo, and gamma grasses that carpeted the valley beside the river. While the herd was drinking its fill, Lucas trotted toward the fort to send a letter to his brother in Georgia. Hopefully, by the time he returned from the drive, Andrew would have wired the inheritance money to Martha Lewis, and Lucas could purchase more stock for the ranch.

Once the cattle were bedded down for the night, Lucas announced they would graze and water the herd for two days before starting onto the waterless plains. The cowboys could sit back and catch their breath before beginning the next cruelling leg of their journey.

Each time the conversation in camp veered toward the subject of women or boasts of prowess in bed, Lucas grumbled under his breath. He wasn't sure he wanted Catlin overhearing another round of "man-talk." She was cynical of the male of the species already. His frustration had begun to show in the way he shifted uneasily from one foot to the other as he leaned against the chuckwagon. But when Bo started teasing him about his love life, Lucas lost the reins to his temper.

"Talk about a man who knows his way around

women," Bo was saying with an ornery snicker. "Doc has been in more beds than you could find in a hospital."

"That's enough!" Lucas growled in a tone that brooked no argument, but Bo was not to be silenced.

"Women flock to him like flies after sugar," he chuckled, shrugging off the menacing glare. "Ah, that I should have those problems. In fact I recall one time when we were passing through Sante Fe that he had three . . ."

"Bo!" Lucas snapped gruffly.

". . . Women in one night and . . . Ouch! What the devil did you do that for?" Bo squawked when Lucas stamped over to kick him in the shin. "Damn, you're touchy when you go a few weeks without a woman."

Muttering under his breath, Lucas pivoted on his heels and made a beeline for Catlin who was growing madder by the minute. He reached down and hoisted her to her feet so quickly it made her head spin. Roughly, he yanked the sombrero and concealing bandana from the mass of blond hair, causing it to cascade down her back. Every pair of eyes in camp bulged from their sockets when they spied the tangled strands of gold.

"This is why I kicked you," Lucas muttered. "This is not Lennie Page. This is Catlin Quinn and she happens to be my fiancée. She doesn't need to hear all the off-color stories you were intent on telling." His stern gaze circled the thunderstruck cowboys. "And if any of you touch Catlin I'll blow your hands off. Is that understood?"

Catlin's face turned crimson red when all eyes fastened on her, wandering down her concealed figure in silent speculation. She felt the need to cover herself from the probing stares. Thanks to Lucas she had become a statue on display and she would have preferred to keep her identity a secret even if it meant overhearing sordid conversations about the gentler sex.

Bo plunked to the ground, his face paralyzed in an expression of disbelief. He had thought Lennie Page was an effeminate looking lad, but he never dreamed . . . "Well, I'll be damned!" Hurriedly, he clambered back to his feet to bow before her. "Excuse my language, Miss Quinn. Looks like I forgot myself again."

"You can all ride to the fort for the evening," Lucas offered. "Except for Bo and Jesse who will take the first night shift. You can draw straws to see who takes the other shifts. But you had better behave yourselves at the fort. If I hear one complaint from the commander, you'll be riding drag until we reach Colorado."

The vaqueros stumbled to their feet, removed their grimy hats and filed past Catlin, offering her a respectful greeting. When the men rode off to Fort Concho, Bo leaned negligently against the chuckwagon and displayed a grin as wide as the Staked Plains they were about to cross.

"Your fiancée?" he queried skeptically.

"Yes . . . No," Lucas and Catlin declared simultaneously.

Bo's gaze bounced from one glaring face to the other. "Well, which is it?" he wanted to know.

"Yes, Catlin is my fiancée," Lucas repeated, pinching Catlin's arm when she opened her mouth to contest his announcement. "And while we are having a private conversation you keep a close watch on the herd."

With that, Lucas propelled Catlin away from the campfire and aimed her toward the river.

"We are no longer engaged and I wish no private conversation with you," she sputtered, attempting to free herself from his firm grasp. It was a waste of energy.

"Whether we are or aren't is academic," Lucas declared sharply. "I want my men to think we are engaged and you are not going to dispute my word. It's for your own protection. If they think you are fair game for their starved affection, you may have more trouble on your hands than even *you* can handle."

Catlin couldn't argue with him when he made perfect

sense, although she would have liked to. She was more comfortable when they were at odds. And when they weren't, she always found herself swept off her feet by her forbidden desires and his fiery passions.

"Very well then, for appearance's sake and for my safety we will remain engaged," she begrudgingly allowed. "But there will be no private conversations. They always get out of hand."

A wry smile pursed his lips as he reached out to smooth away her stubborn frown. "I brought you out here because I thought you might like to take a bath without fretting over your privacy or the possibility of another stampede."

Catlin eyed him warily. "No thank you, I prefer to share the aroma of my horse."

Damned stubborn ungrateful female! He was trying to be considerate of her needs and she wouldn't let him. Okay, so he did have an ulterior motive for wanting to be alone with her. But blast it, she didn't have to be so cynical and defensive.

Without forewarning, Lucas scooped her up in his arms and heaved her into the river. It was fortunate the cattle were bedded down a good distance away or they would have bounded to their feet and thundered off when Catlin expelled a startled yelp.

"Lucas Murdock, I despise you," Catlin sputtered as she struggled to stand up in midstream. "I'll take a bath when I'm damned good and ready and not a moment before!"

She wiped the water from her eyes to see that Lucas had vanished into thin air. His absence provoked Catlin to sigh in relief. Now she could have her bath without being hounded by that exasperating rake. Catlin waded ashore to strip from her garb. When she walked back into the water, a soft moan bubbled from her lips. Lord, it felt good to stretch out and swim in the cool refreshing river. Ah, this was heaven. . . .

A frightened squawk erupted when something latched onto her bare leg, towing her under. Unseen hands migrated over her body while she was submerged. Either she had become a victim for the devil of the deep or that ornery Lucas had sneaked up on her.

When Catlin burst to the surface to gasp for breath, Lucas's dark head rose beside her. His sinewy arms encircled her waist, pulling her full length against him.

"You said I could have a private bath," she grumbled, pushing away as far as his chaining arms would allow.

"And you said you didn't want to take one," he reminded her as his lips moved deliberately toward hers. "What do you want, Cat?"

"Not this—"

The words were barely out before he kissed her senseless. Catlin could feel his muscular body gliding provocatively against hers. All the water in the river couldn't extinguish the flame he ignited in her. Try as she may, she couldn't stop herself from wanting this mischievous devil. Catlin could list a million reasons why she shouldn't love him. But she did, dammit. Love made no sense at all. It was totally irrational and so was she.

They couldn't enjoy a future together and Lucas didn't really need her to make his life complete. Bo was right. Women flocked to this dark-eyed devil and Catlin had always been a little too convenient. He was still harboring an unrequited love for Elise and he would never get over his forbidden dreams. . . .

Lord, he was doing the most incredible things to her body! He knew just where and how to touch to crumble the barriers of her defenses. Her chest caved in when her heart hammered furiously against it. Catlin could no longer hear herself think.

The sweet memories that loomed in the shadows of her heart rose to torment her. His exploring hands excited and aroused, luring her deeper into his spell of passion. The past mingled with the present and Catlin felt herself giving way to the exquisite pleasure of his touch. She was every kind of a fool and she knew it, but she wanted him, just as she always did.

Lucas located each ultrasensitive point on her body and brought it to life. And as he kissed and caressed her, Catlin felt the need to touch him, to investigate his powerful physique. Her hands glided over the muscled planes and sinewy contours of the one man who had the power to make her forget her firm resolutions. Touching his lean hard body gave her immense pleasure. She could feel the columns of muscles rippling beneath her migrating fingertips, feel his heart thudding against her breasts.

Her butterfly caresses caused Lucas to groan in unholy torment. God, he could never control himself when he was within ten feet of this captivating vixen. Trembling with awakened passion, Lucas shifted in the waist-deep water. His lips skied across her silky flesh to seek out the taut peaks of her breasts while his roaming hands cupped the ripe mounds that begged for his touch. His fingertips and mouth took possession of her flesh, loving the feel of her, adoring the exquisite texture of her skin. Ah, he could go on forever, mapping her curvaceous body, memorizing the feel of her elegantly sculptured curves and swells. She was made for love. She was the personification of perfection.

As his adventurous hand slid over the clover-leaf birthmark to guide her thighs apart, Catlin gasped for breath. His intimate fondling was sweet torment. He made her burn with desire. And suddenly she had to have all of him. His touch was not enough. He was the very essence of life and she wanted him with every fiber of her being. Shamelessly, Catlin arched toward him, her body caressing his. She whispered his name and her need for him without taking time out to curse her lack of willpower. When he was this close she couldn't fight the marvelous sensations he evoked. When he devoured her with his ravishing kiss she knew she would never get over wanting

258

this remarkable man. Every memory, every emotion had his name attached to it. She couldn't think without visualizing the rugged bronzed features of his face, that unique horse-shaped scar of his chin. She remembered the way his sensuous lips curved into a roguish smile and how they felt as they whispered enticingly across her skin.

"Love me, Cat," he demanded in a purring growl.

"I do . . . ," she murmured, unaware that she had voiced her secret. All she knew was that if he didn't take her she would die of wanting.

And when he did come to her, lifting her against his sleek, masculine frame, Catlin went wild with abandon. The hungry surge of his body against hers was her undoing. She clung to him, reveling in the joy of their union, overwhelmed by the undulating pleasure that rushed through her like a series of devastating tidal waves. All inhibition fled as Lucas took her higher and higher without allowing her to escape his encircling arms. Her body quivered uncontrollably as white-hot fire engulfed her. Desperately, she clung to him, meeting each hard thrust, devouring his lips, making his body as her own.

Lucas swore he was about to split apart at the seams when Catlin moved against him. He was no longer the possessor but rather the possession. He had become each breath she took and he shared each splendorous sensation that ricocheted through her while they spiraled through the sea of twinkling stars to measure eternity.

From deep inside him, the last wave of passion rolled upward, cresting upon him. A hoarse groan spilled from his lips as his body shuddered against her. There was no way to describe the sensations that toppled upon him. He had simply enjoyed the quintessence of pleasure that transcended the realm of reality. He was held aloft in a dark, electrifying dimension of time. Rainbows appeared above the black abyss of ineffable rapture. Lucas could feel the heat of colors splashing down upon him, shading his mind and body in a spectrum of wild splendor.

As the speckled beams of light faded, Lucas dropped a kiss to Catlin's lips. But he couldn't let her go. He held her intimately to him, watching the embers of passion glow in her eyes. They still stood waist-deep in a river of rippling silver, enfolded in each other's arms, waiting for the last shades of passion to ebb.

When Catlin finally regained her senses, an embarrassed blush stained her cheeks. It wasn't wise for Lucas to know how thoroughly he devastated her, how she reveled in his lovemaking. Wriggling free, Cat glided across the river, mustering her defenses and cursing herself for being so transparent in her desire for him.

"Cat, did you mean what you said?" His husky voice drifted across the silvery water, touching her like a leisurely caress.

"Did I mean what I said about what?" she questioned his question. Honest to goodness, she couldn't remember anything except the wondrous pleasures that had consumed her.

"You said you loved me," he prompted her, gauging her reaction with a hawkish stare. "Did you mean it?"

Catlin tucked her legs beneath her and spun about, her eyes wide as saucers. "I said no such thing," she protested. Sweet mercy, surely she hadn't betrayed herself by voicing the words!

A deep skirl of laughter rumbled in his chest as he walked through the water. "There is nothing wrong with my ears, violet eyes. I asked you to love me and you said you did." His expression sobered. Gently, he cupped her chin, forcing her to meet his penetrating gaze. "If you love me, why are you running from me?"

Catlin longed to unburden her mind and confide in him, to confess the atrocious nightmare that had ended in fire and death. But she could vividly remember Emmet Blake's vows as she rode off into the night, barely escaping with her life. The man was a murdering maniac! Emmet had proven himself capable of extreme violence and insanity. With his influence and power he could destroy her and Lucas. And loving Luke as she did, she could not bring herself to involve him in her secret feud against Emmet. In her effort to see justice served Martha and Lucas could lose their lives. Catlin couldn't take that risk. She would not jeopardize the only two people she had left in the world.

"Answer me," Lucas demanded, jerking Cat from the depths of pensive reverie.

"I can't," she insisted, pushing his hand away from her face. "I can't and that's that."

Lucas gnashed his teeth. Why was she being so elusive? She was driving him crazy. She always drove him crazy. It was her greatest aspiration in life.

"You can't or you won't?" he queried, his tone bearing evidence of his mounting frustration.

"Both and don't ask me to explain," she pleaded, presenting her back. "And if you want me, I will no longer deny my feelings for you. But when we reach Colorado we will go our separate ways because that is the way it has to be."

Lucas was dangerously close to pulling out his hair, strand by strand. Cat finally admitted she cared for him, but apparently it wasn't the strong lasting emotion that compelled her to reveal her inner thoughts or the kind that provoked her to stay with him forever. Love with stipulations. Just what he needed, Lucas thought sardonically.

"If I said I loved you, would it matter, Cat?" he asked her, fighting like hell to curtail his exasperation.

He may as well have cut out her heart. She couldn't hurt anymore than she did now. Of course it mattered how he felt! But it didn't change anything. "Do you, Lucas? Truly?"

His arms slid around her, pulling her back against his

261

scarred chest. His lips grazed her shoulder. "I do," he confessed. "I want you with me. I want you to belong to me and to no one else."

Catlin squeezed her eyes shut, fighting the tears, and reached back to cup the side of his face. "Enough to let me go when I say I must, enough to accept what I cannot explain?"

Lucas withdrew to heave a harsh sigh. "Obviously you don't care enough to trust me or to depend on me. What could possibly be so wrong?" he interrogated her. "What aren't you telling me?"

"I'm getting cold," Catlin announced as she waded ashore, avoiding his probing question.

"You know you're driving me insane, don't you?" he growled at her rigid back.

"Better insane than d—" Cat caught herself in the nick of time. Hurriedly, she wormed into her garments. "I'm offering you passion until you want no more of it. We have a little more than two months to enjoy with each other. But when it's time for me to go, I must go. Take it or leave it, Luke."

"That's it? Your way or no way at all?" he spewed as he stamped up the bank to breathe down her neck. "What kind of love is it that slips so nicely into your designated time slot? Well, thanks a helluva lot, but the answer is no. I don't want to be the time you're killing before you reach Colorado! I'd rather starve to death from the lack of your affection which, by the way, seems to be pretty damned shallow, if you ask me!"

"I happen to love you a lot more than you could ever love me," Catlin spouted, glaring daggers at him.

"Well, you've got the most peculiar way of showing it," Lucas snorted as he thrust his leg into his breeches. "I seem to be a miserable judge of women. Twice in my life I have wanted to settle down and twice I have wound up empty-handed. You offer me your body for two months, as if you were making some supreme sacrifice. If that's all you think love is, I don't want any part of it." His dark eyes blazed over her. "And maybe I don't love you after all. Maybe I mistook love for passion. But if you are that cold-blooded and hardhearted, I'd rather become a celibate monk. Hell's bell's, Cat, you are absolutely impossible!"

When Lucas stomped off, Catlin let her breath out in a rush. Confound it, he didn't understand and she couldn't explain. If they were both fortunate to wind up in heaven she would look him up and tell him why she had to be so logical and sensible. Not that he would care to know by then, she thought bitterly. By the time he reached the pearly gates, he would have forgotten her name. And he didn't love her, even if he said he did. In fact, she was willing to bet he had said he loved her because he thought it was what she wanted to hear. If he did love her he would have been a lot more understanding and a lot less condemning.

Men! She had sworn off them for the last time. She was going to live her life without being influenced by anything in breeches. She would enter a convent, that's what she'd do! She would spend her years in solitude, praying that raven-haired devil would no longer haunt her thoughts.

Lucas didn't really love her, Cat convinced herself. He was still carrying a torch for Elise and he had simply decided to settle for less than his heart's desire because he wanted to put down roots on his new ranch. Given six months, he would have a wife if he decided he really needed one at all. What he really wanted and needed from a woman could be satisfied in bed, whether it was Cat or someone else. He wasn't willing to allow a woman to share his thoughts and his life. She would be just another of his possessions, just like his confounded cattle and horses.

This time it was really over for good, Cat told herself

firmly. It was better this way. She and Lucas could part company disliking each other. That would ease the pain, she hoped.

By the time Lucas stormed back to camp, he was as ill-tempered as a grizzly bear that had been roused from hibernation. But Bo wasn't discouraged by Lucas's mutinous expression. Bo had faced worse, lots of times.

"Trouble in paradise?" Bo queried. He was met with a wordless scowl. "Do you want me to speak to Catlin in your behalf?"

"No," Luke exploded as he sloshed whiskey in his coffee and downed it in one gulp. After lighting his cheroot, he puffed and puffed until he had enshrouded himself in a cloud of smoke. "There is no reasoning with that independent, stubborn female. She is so reasonable and practical that—"

"I thought you said you couldn't reason with her," Bo broke in when Lucas contradicted himself.

"I can't!" he muttered, pouring himself another drink. "Her mind is a steel trap. She sets her own standards as to what is reasonable and practical and you couldn't convince her otherwise, even if you argued with her until you were blue in the face."

"So the engagement is off again," Bo speculated.

"Yes—I mean no . . ." Lucas spewed. "We'll be engaged forever, but she says she won't marry me."

Bo scratched his fuzzy head and smiled at Lucas. He had never seen the man in such a snit over a woman. This saucy she-male had obviously tied him in knots. "Has she got something against marriage?"

"No, she's all for it," Lucas grumbled, pacing back and forth like a restless tiger. "As long as I have no part in it." He wheeled about to stare at Bo. "She doesn't trust me and she won't tell me why we can't get married, only that we can't. And to quote little Miss Stubborn and Independent,

'That is that!' "

"You're getting what you deserve, you know," Bo snickered. "For all the times you have left women behind without a backward glance, you're getting a taste of your own medicine, Doc."

"Thanks a lot. I knew I could count on you to cheer me up," Lucas grunted sarcastically.

"Just give her a little space and she'll come around," Bo advised.

"Cat could have all the space in Texas and it wouldn't help matters," he scowled acrimoniously. "She said it was over and it's over."

"I thought you said you were still engaged." Bo frowned, befuddled.

Lucas threw up his hand in a gesture of frustration. "How do I know what I said? That woman is making me crazy!"

The crackle of twigs caused Lucas to snap his mouth shut like a clam. He watched in exasperation as Catlin marched past him to grace Bo with a smile. Without ado, she crawled into her bedroll.

Sporting an amused grin, Bo pushed away from the chuckwagon. "Jesse and I will take another watch and relieve Sam and Frank," he announced.

As Bo swaggered away, Lucas stamped out his cigarillo and glared holes in the cocoon of quilts. "I hope you suffocate," he muttered spitefully to Cat.

Catlin poked her head out to glower poison arrows at Luke. "And I hope a rattlesnake crawls into your pallet and makes a meal of you," she said nastily.

"Damned woman."

"Horrible man."

Lucas stalked over, plunked down on the ground and covered himself up, swearing to hate that impossible minx for the rest of his natural life while Catlin was vowing the same thing in reverse.

Chapter 18

For two days the herd of longhorns grazed on the plush grass beside the river and drank their fill. Bo had assured Catlin that a steer could consume as much as thirty gallons of water a day and she was sure he was right. She stood over the herd, watching them slurp and drink for hours. Cat preferred to stand watch rather than suffer Luke's presence. Their relationship was strained at best. He marched around camp avoiding her, refusing to glance in her direction. Not that she wanted his attention, mind you. But he didn't have to be so obvious about ignoring her!

When Catlin returned from her double watch, Lucas was riding back from Fort Concho. Without a word, he tossed her a new set of clothes, ones that fit far better than the baggy garb she had been wearing.

"Thank you," she murmured with exaggerated politeness.

"You're welcome."

His dark eyes drifted over her head to scrutinize the lone rider who had come from the direction of the fort. With a critical eye, Lucas watched the man draw his strawberry roan mount to a halt. The stranger's cobalt blue eyes settled on Catlin's trailing mass of blond hair and then slid down her concealed figure. When he had given her the once over, he tipped his hat to her and then focused his attention on Lucas.

"Are you the trail boss?" he questioned in an unhurried drawl.

"I am." Lucas replied, studying the stranger's buckskin clothes. He gave particular attention to the well-used Colts that hung on each side of the man's hips and the Winchester rifle that dangled in the sling on the saddle.

"I'm heading west. If you don't mind the company, I'd like to ride with you. I've heard the reports of raiding Comanches on *Llano Estacado* and I don't relish losing my scalp while I still have use for it."

Catlin was also assessing the new arrival with a scrutinizing gaze. The man's features were harsh and weather-beaten and there was something foreboding about him. The presence of the two revolvers slung low on his hips left her wondering if this *hombre* lived by his gun. He certainly looked the part of a gunslinger.

"Where are you headed . . . exactly?" Lucas questioned point-blank.

"Denver. I have business there." With lithe grace the *hombre* swung from the saddle to extend a callused hand. "The name is Jace Osborn," he introduced. "I'm not asking for a job, only an escort through rugged territory. My Colts are yours . . . if you have a need of extra guns. I've also trailed cattle a time or two, if you need an extra hand."

Lucas stared at Jace's craggy features and the whisps of chestnut brown hair that peeked from the edge of his hat. He was a gunfighter or gambler or both, Luke guessed. But he, too, had heard the report that Charles Goodnight and Oliver Loving, the two men who had blazed this trail northwest, had been attacked by Comanches not long ago. Oliver Loving, wily and trailwise though he was, had been wounded and had died three weeks later of gangrene. Jace Osborn's gun hand might spare a few lives if they met with trouble.

The faintest hint of a smile pursed Luke's lips as he accepted Jace's proffered hand. "What business did you say you were in, Osborn?" he questioned conversationally.

Jace returned the grin. "I didn't say and you damned well know it, Murdock," he replied.

The use of his name assured Lucas that Jace Osborn had interrogated the fort commander about the trail boss who was responsible for the herd of cattle that grazed near the river. After staring Jace squarely in the eye for a long moment, Lucas nodded his consent. "You can ride with us. In exchange for your assistance in case of trouble, I'll provide your meals. But I don't allow my men to gamble in camp. If you make trouble, you'll answer to me." His dark eyes slid to the revolvers on his own hips. "My Colts aren't ornaments either, Osborn."

Jace smiled respectfully at the blunt message Lucas had just delivered. "Sounds fair enough to me," he agreed before his steely blue eyes shifted back to Catlin, quietly undressing her with his piercing gaze.

A feeling of fierce possessiveness overcame Lucas when he noted where Jace's attention had strayed. "The lady's name is Catlin Quinn. She's my fiancée."

Jace's gaze circled back to the pair of narrowed brown eyes that were fixed on him. "I'll remember that, Murdock."

When Jace tipped his hat again and strode over to beg a cup of coffee from Flapjack Barnett, Catlin stared after him. There was something about Jace's penetrating gaze that made her wary. It wasn't because he had been plagued with a plain, rugged face. Catlin knew beauty was only skin deep at best. But the way Jace stared at her made her uneasy. There was something faintly predatory in his gaze—like a hunter on the trail of his quarry.

"I don't like him," Catlin mused aloud.

"Of course, you don't. He's a man, isn't he?" Lucas

smirked sarcastically before striding off to give orders to his men.

In the late afternoon, Lucas led his vaqueros in gathering the herd into formation. They began their grueling journey across the eighty-mile stretch of barren land that lay between the Concho and the thirst-quenching waters of the Pecos River. Taking advantage of the cool evening air, Lucas kept the longhorns marching until long after dark.

Bo had warned Catlin of the trials that lay ahead of them during this leg of the journey, but she was unprepared for the tedious trek across the arid plains. When she finally sank down on her pallet her gaze flooded over the treeless land. Only a distant cicada's lonely song whispered over the dry terrain. A silent breath of wind drifted past her face and swept the desolate country that looked pale and ashen in the full moonlight. The land had the look of death and its eerie silence hung in the darkness like a curse. The *Llano Estacado* offered no welcome to man or beast. It seemed old and unforgiving and Catlin dreaded the next few days of fighting and choking dust and sweltering heat.

Catlin lay down to sleep, but it seemed only a few short hours had passed before Flapjack clanged on his pots and pans, dragging her from her troubled dreams. After she finished her breakfast, she ambled back to retrieve her bedroll. The deadly rattle of a snake caused her to jump straight up in the air like a mountain goat. As the viper slithered from her bedroll, a pistol barked behind her. Shakily, Catlin watched the snake coil beside her boot before it lay motionless on the ground. Ah, how vividly she remembered wishing a serpent would slither into Lucas's bedroll. It seemed her spiteful curse had bounced off Lucas and stuck to her!

When Lucas stalked forward, his smoking pistol in

hand, Catlin peered at him in mute amazement. She had never seen Lucas display his lightning-quick draw but she was ever so glad he had. If not, she would have been bitten. Not that he would have cared, she thought bitterly, but he would have had to take time out to tend her wounds before putting his cattle into formation.

"Not bad," Jace murmured as he swaggered over to retrieve the snake. "Catlin is fortunate you are so handy with a pistol, Murdock. Your fiancée could have died of a snakebite."

In one fluid motion, Lucas stuffed his Colt back in its holster. "I doubt it," he scoffed, his gaze darting momentarily to Catlin whose face was white as flour. "Cat has been appropriately named and she seems to have been blessed with nine lives. It's not the first time I've seen her emerge from a life-threatening situation unscathed."

Grinning wryly, Jace held the rattler up for Flapjack Barnett's inspection. "How are you at cooking snake steak?"

"No good," Flapjack grunted, eyeing the viper distastefully. "And I ain't cooking it."

With a careless shrug, Jace hurled the snake away. His piercing blue eyes fastened on Catlin. "You were lucky, Cat. Murdock seems to keep a sharp lookout for you," he drawled before he strode away.

Catlin had no time to ponder her near brush with catastrophe. There were cattle to put on the trail in order to take advantage of the cool morning air. But it wasn't long before the oppressive heat bore down on them and the dust swirled up in a three-mile-long cloud. Lucas had cautioned his men to drink sparingly from the canteens they had filled before leaving the Concho River, but it was difficult not to take an occasional sip when thirst overwhelmed them. Catlin employed Bo's suggestion of sucking on a bullet to ward off her craving for water. When Flapjack passed out cans of tomato juice, she took a few sips and then wiped the juice over the cuts and scratches caused by the alkali dust, biting wind, and burning sun, just as Bo had instructed her to do. Her reddened eyes stung as if they were floating with salt and her lips cracked each time she dared to speak. Nothing seemed to ease the agony of trekking through this rugged patch of land.

After the first tedious day, Catlin already had enough of this desolate stretch of land. But the worst was yet to come. When they finally halted the procession long after dark, the thirsty herd refused to bed down. Even Spur milled about and plodded into camp to beg a drink from Lucas. He gulped down the sparse sips Lucas poured from his own canteen into his sombrero. When Lucas refused to give him more, Spur stamped over to each cowboy to beg another drink. Catlin, however, was the only one who gave the bawling steer another sip of refreshing water.

It took twice the usual number of nighthawks to hold the fidgety herd and Lucas allowed his men only a few hours of rest before aiming the cattle west again. As the day wore on, several steers tried to break and head back for the last remembered water at the Concho. Two of the culprits were the yellow duns that Bo had been cursing for over a week. Annoyed with the contrary creatures, Bo did as he had threatened. He roped the misbehaving steers and hooked them to a yoke on either side of Spur. The steers kicked and snorted until Spur lost his good disposition. Spur knocked one of the steers down and dragged him a quarter of mile. When the other yellow dun steer set his feet and refused to budge from his spot, Spur gored him with his horns until the contrary creature trotted at the swift pace Spur set. By the end of the day, the two steers had gained a great deal of respect for Spur and they trudged alongside the gigantic longhorn without putting up a fuss.

When Catlin wheeled her steed to give chase to three other desperate cows who craved water, her saddle slid

271

sideways. Her steed, alarmed by the sudden shift of weight, reared and bolted forward. Catlin fought to cling to the horse's back when he swerved to miss the cattle he had been chasing. A terrified shriek erupted from Cat's lips when she felt herself plummeting toward the sharp horns of the galloping steers. Wildly, she clawed to regain her balance, but the saddle shifted onto her mount's flank and the ground flew up at her with amazing speed. Her breath came out in a muffled groan when she collided broadside with one of the charging steers. The air gushed from her lungs in a "whoosh" when she bounced against the ground. Catlin swore it was only her quickly uttered prayer that spared her from the deadly horns. Without being gored, she skidded across the ground, sputtering on the taste of dirt.

The stars were still spinning around her head when Bo reached her. His silver-gray eyes were wide with concern as he checked for wounds and broken bones. Assuring himself that Cat had only taken a bone-jarring spill, he twisted on his haunches to survey the dangling cinch. Scooping Cat in his arms, Bo strided over to set her on his mount and then grabbed her steed's reins.

"Your girth strap must have worn through," he informed her grimly. "Doc was right." Bo spit out the tobacco he had very nearly swallowed when he saw Catlin plunge down beside the stampeding steers. Grabbing the pommel, Bo swung up behind her on his steed. "You do seem to have as many lives as a cat. But you better take care not to use them all up in one week. This time you were one lucky lady."

Catlin didn't feel lucky; she felt rattled. Every bone in her body was still vibrating. Moaning, she cuddled up in Bo's arms, thankful for his compassion.

While two vaqueros chased down the runaway steers, Bo trotted Catlin's horse around the herd to catch up with the chuckwagon. Flapjack always kept strips of rawhide in case of emergencies such as this. Bo had no intention of setting Catlin back on her own saddle until he saw to it that her cinch had been replaced.

The moment Luke spied Bo cradling Catlin against him, he jerked his horse around and aimed himself toward the seasoned cowboy. His expression testified to the extent of his concern. Although Luke had kept his distance from Cat, she was constantly in his thoughts. There had been times in the past when he could have cheerfully choked her for being so stubborn, but he didn't want her to perish or to be crippled for life.

"The girth strap broke and Catlin fell beside the runaway steers," Bo reported as he shifted Catlin over to Lucas's arms—the last place she wanted to be. "I'll go fetch some rawhide and make the repairs."

Catlin twisted to sit upright, even though Luke tried to keep her half-reclined on his lap.

"Hold still, dammit," he ordered gruffly.

"I'm perfectly all right," Catlin insisted as she pushed away from his solid chest. "It isn't the first time I've taken a spill and there is no need to pamper me."

"But this is the first time you've tumbled into the path of charging longhorns," he contended. "From now on, you are riding in the chuckwagon beside Flapjack."

"I most certainly am not!" she assured him in no uncertain terms.

"Woman, I swear you would get yourself killed, just to spite me," he grumbled sourly.

"Don't flatter yourself," Catlin sniffed, tilting her chin to an aloof angle.

Lucas swore under his breath. This she-male was absolutely impossible! "If you don't care what happens to you, at least consider my feelings."

"I have been," Catlin sighed dispiritedly.

A muddled frown plowed his brow. "What is that supposed to mean?"

273

"Nothing," she muttered. "Just put me down. I'll walk until Bo repairs my saddle."

Lucas set her to her feet and then stared down at her for a long, silent moment. "I'm ready to settle for the bargain you offered me," he told her somberly.

The unexpected remark set Catlin back on her heels. Her gaze lifted and the intensity of his dark eyes seared her flesh. Helplessly, Catlin fell into those bottomless chocolate brown pools. Even when they were at odds, Luke had the ability to stir her.

"Did you hear me, Cat?" Lucas questioned, studying her shapely profile that was emphasized by the trim-fitting garments he had purchased for her. In spite of everything, he couldn't get over wanting this saucy enchantress and nothing could make the ache go away.

"There is nothing wrong with my ears either, Lucas," she insisted, fighting for hard-won composure. "I heard you."

"Tomorrow night, Cat," he murmured huskily. "When we reach the Pecos. . . ."

He wasn't even going to allow her to escape with a shred of pride, she realized. They had parted on a sour note after she offered to love him until it was time for her to go. Lucas had avoided her until lust got the best of him. She had made her offer because she loved him and now he was accepting it because he wanted her body. She had become just like the other women in his life, an object of pleasure. The affection he claimed to feel for her had withered and died. If it had truly been there at all, she mused skeptically.

When Luke rode away, Catlin's shoulders slumped. Why hadn't she kept her mouth shut in the first place? Because she had wanted to love him for as long as it could last. Was that asking so much? Well, if he wanted passion she would give him what he wanted and when they parted he would remember her in the year's to come, she promised herself. She would brand her memory on his mind and they would both share the company misery loves so well, even while they were worlds apart.

A startled squeak spouted from Catlin's lips when Jace Osborn's lean fingers fastened around her ribs, lifting her from the ground. Catlin found herself deposited behind Jace's saddle and forced to clamp her hand on his waist to prevent tumbling off.

"What kind of a fiancé leaves you to walk like one of the longhorns?" Jace drawled as he glanced back to survey the flushed-face beauty behind him. "I haven't quite figured out what's going on between you and Murdock."

Quiet laughter echoed in the still air. "When you figure it out, let me know," Catlin requested ruefully. "I haven't figured it out either."

"When did you decide to marry Murdock?" Jace interrogated out of the blue.

Catlin's brows knitted in a frown. That seemed a rather odd question. Jace hadn't asked *why* but rather *when*. "I didn't decide. He did," she hedged, purposely omitting the how, why, when, and where.

It was Jace's turn to frown curiously. Although he was trying to pry information from this mysterious minx she was too quick-witted and wary to discuss her private affairs. Jace relinquished his attempt at cross-examining her. He found himself unwillingly enjoying the feel of Catlin's hands clamped to his waist and the feminine scent that invaded his senses.

It was late in the night when Lucas called a halt to the drive. The weaker cattle had to be whipped for the past two hours to get them to quicken their step. The leaders, Spur included, had to be restrained from dragging the herd out over three miles. Canteens had gone dry and the water barrels barely contained enough of the precious liquid for cooking. Wild-eyed calves wailed and bawled for a drink of water and once again they balked at bedding down. The cowboy's tempers were short. Their lips were cracked and their eyelids puffy from the irritation of wind, sun and dust. Every creature on two and four legs was feeling the effects of the waterless plains and blistering heat.

It was too hot to sleep and the cattle continued to mill. Lucas decided to drive through the night before the longhorns wasted their energy by futilely circling in their search for water.

Bo worked relentlessly at drag, trying to save every animal, keeping the reluctant steers moving. Catlin rode beside him, near exhaustion. Her weary steed stumbled and Catlin was helpless to do more than cling to his back as he staggered to maintain his balance.

A few animals dropped to the ground and no method of encouragement could force them back to their feet. Catlin did everything she could think of to rouse the pitiful creatures, knowing those who were left behind would undoubtedly perish.

Scowling, Lucas swung back and forth, monitoring the progress of the herd. His men were about to give out and Catlin looked as though she were about to drop off her saddle. Gathering all the empty canteens, Luke headed for the Pecos, urging his reluctant steed into a gallop. The horse stumbled, but Lucas jerked his head up before he toppled over.

After Lucas forced his reluctant steed to keep moving forward, the animal smelled water and went on his own accord. When his horse had drunk his fill, Lucas replenished the canteens and rode back in the direction he had come. Several of the men had been overcome by heat and exhaustion. Leaving them with full canteens, Luke instructed the staggering cowboys to follow at their own pace while he pushed the core of the herd toward the river.

Within forty-five minutes, the front line of the thirsty infantry smelled the Pecos. Bawling in anticipation they ran as fast as their wobbly legs would carry them. The few men who remained in the saddle tried to keep the herd strung out, but the enticement of water sent the entire herd thundering forward.

Cursing, Lucas cracked his whip over the lead steers who had plunged into the river. Yelling at the thirsty animals, Luke forced them to move through the river before the back ranks of longhorns stampeded over the top of them.

Exhausted though Catlin was, she sensed disaster. When the front line of the herd formed a living wall in the river, the last of the cattle plunged over the steep banks to quench their thirst. The confused herd spread outward like a gigantic fan and the weaker animals floundered in quicksand.

Catlin blinked, trying to moisten her scorched eyes, listening to Lucas shout instructions. But pandemonium broke loose. Horns—like deadly spears—poked and prodded. Suddenly Catlin found herself surrounded by bawling, floundering longhorns that rammed her broadside. She heard the whinny of another horse, but she was too intent on moving the stalled cattle toward the opposite bank to glance behind her.

Suddenly, her horse staggered, when he was rammed from behind. The steed fought for position but he was mashed against the longhorns that clogged the river. Catlin's frightened scream drowned beneath the barking pistols, the sharp whistles of the vaqueros and the bawling cattle that were jammed up like sardines. Unable to maintain her position atop her writhing mount, Cat plunged into the river, swearing there were a million legs waiting to trample her. She fought to find the surface, but the living wall of cattle prevented her from gasping for a much-needed breath of air.

Lucas wheeled his steed, shouting for Bo to keep the herd from floundering on the sand bars. When he spied Catlin's horse staggering back to its feet, its coat dripping wet, Lucas's heart ceased beating. With no concern for his own safety, he kicked his mount, forcing him to wedge his way through the dam of cattle that stood between him and the riderless horse.

"Catlin went down!" Luke bellowed at Jace Osborn who was the closest man to him. "Help me split the cattle."

Jace obliged, forcing the cattle apart. Luke dived from his horse, groping in the muddy depths for Catlin's body. He was sure he had searched for an eternity before his hand struck human flesh. Shoving his shoulder against the steer that stood in his way, Lucas dragged Catlin's limp body to the surface.

"Oh my God," he breathed as he peered down at her bruised cheeks. Obviously the steers had stomped on her after they gouged her in the hip. Cradling Catlin protectively against him, Lucas hurried ashore and sank down on top of her to force the water from her lungs. While he was diligently working to revive her, Bo took command of the field, barking orders, pushing the entire herd to the far side of the river.

When Jace rode up to check on Catlin, Lucas glowered at him. "You should have been the one to reach her first," he growled hatefully. "You were the closest one to her."

"I didn't see her," Jace defended. "I had a fight on my hands, just keeping my seat among the hoard of panicky cattle. If I had known she had fallen I would have been there."

Lucas dropped his head and breathed an exasperated sigh while he tended Catlin. Silently, he willed her to breathe on her own accord. "I'm sorry for snapping at you," he apologized.

"It's already forgotten," Jace replied. "I can see you are worried about your fiancée."

While Jace trotted off to pull two steers from the quicksand, Lucas tirelessly pressed his hands against Catlin's shoulder blades. After several anguishing minutes, Catlin wheezed and expelled a breath. Lucas sank back on his haunches to breathe a sigh of relief. He hated this intense, unnerving fear that overwhelmed him when Catlin was in danger. Nothing had ever frightened him until he faced the possibility of losing her. And even now, although she was breathing on her own, she was still unconscious and he was as shaky as a newborn calf. If he didn't get a firm grip on his emotions he would be of no use to anyone, especially not this feisty female who didn't know her place and wouldn't have stayed in it, even if she did.

Cursing a blue streak, Lucas lifted Catlin into his arms. Her wild mass of blond hair spilled over his arm as he carried her toward the chuckwagon to retrieve the small tent Flapjack kept tucked with his supplies. Rapping out orders like bullets, Lucas demanded the tent be pitched away from the milling herd. When the soft pallet was put in place, Lucas gently eased Cat out of her wet clothes and tucked her under a blanket.

Carefully, he inspected the other hoof prints that marred her skin and the puncture wound on her hip. Miraculously, Catlin had escaped with only a few injuries instead of losing her life. Lord, how pale and vulnerable she looked after swallowing half the Pecos River. This sassy vixen seemed unnatural lying there so still, so silent.

"What happened?" Bo questioned breathlessly, craning his neck around the tent flap.

"She practically drowned, not to mention getting stepped on like a damned doormat," Luke grumbled bleakly.

"If I were superstitious I'd swear she's been jinxed," Bo remarked, ruefully shaking his head. "She's been plagued with accidents since you announced Lennie Page was a *she*."

The comment cut Lucas to the quick. Come to think of it, Catlin had been getting along fine until he revealed her true identity, until their lover's spat. Geezus, he had wished the wrath of God on her when she made him so furious with her stubbornness and her refusal to take him into her confidence. He hadn't meant to curse her! He didn't really want anything to happen to her, even if he had wanted to strangle her a couple of times.

"Take charge, will you, Bo?" Lucas requested, never taking his eyes off Catlin's wan features. "I want to stay with her until she rouses."

"Sure, Doc," Bo murmured. He was moved by the unusual way Lucas was gazing down at Catlin's lifeless form. Never had he seen so much emotion on Luke's face. But it was there, making this rugged cowboy extremely transparent. Lucas cared deeply for this high-spirited beauty, even if he had been annoyed with her, even if he refused to spare her more than an occasional glance.

When Bo took his leave, Lucas expelled a weary sigh. He was completely strung out. First he had been forced to accept the fact that he would lose a few head of cattle while they battled the dry plains to reach the Pecos River. Then the cattle had stampeded over each other to drink. And now Catlin had become a victim of disaster. Hell's bells, what else could go wrong?

Lucas glanced upward, silently retracting that question. He wasn't sure he wanted to know the answer. It would probably depress him. After the grueling days of driving the thirsty, starved herd and watching Catlin court catastrophe for the third time, Luke was worn out. He felt as if he had been riding an emotional seesaw. When he finished dabbing persylic ointment on Catlin's flesh wound, he stretched out beside her. He needed to hold her, to ensure she was alive. Not well, but at least alive, he thought glumly. And from now on she was riding with Flapjack Barnett in the chuckwagon, even if he had to nail her to the seat!

*　　　*　　　*

A muffled groan tumbled from Catlin's lips as she battled her way through tangled dreams. Frantically, she struggled to crawl from the holocaust of flames. Coughing and choking, she clawed her way to the door, but the instant she managed to drag herself outside the blazing inferno she found her exit blocked by a nest of hissing vipers. The eerie hiss of rattlers died beneath the sound of thundering cattle. Catlin yelped hysterically when the blurred image of a man flashed before her eyes. And then suddenly she felt herself plunging into a frothy river beneath a thousand stamping hooves. She thrashed to reach the surface to grasp a precious breath of air, but she was shoved down again and again. Her lungs were dangerously close to bursting and panic set in. Wildly she fought for her life—

"Cat!" Lucas's sharp voice finally penetrated the harrowing darkness of her jumbled nightmares.

Her moist lashes swept up to see Luke poised above her. Was it his face she had seen leaping past her line of vision the split-second before she floundered in the water? Catlin couldn't say for certain. But at the moment it didn't really matter what she thought she had seen. She needed the comfort Luke could offer. Instinctively, she wrapped her arms around him, her body racked with hysterical sobs.

"Hold me," she managed to get out between the eruption of convulsive tears.

Lucas cuddled her quaking body to his and pressed a kiss to her perspiring brow. His hand moved over her bare flesh in a slow, comforting massage while he rocked and consoled her.

"It's all right now," he whispered sympathetically. "I'm here. I won't leave you. Sleep, violet eyes, sleep. . . ."

After several minutes Catlin relaxed in his arms and drifted from one terrifying nightmare to another. But Lucas was there each time the tormenting specters leaped out at her. He listened to her mumbled ravings, assuring her she was safe with him. But it was dawn before Catlin collapsed in total exhaustion and slept peacefully.

Looking every bit as haggard and haunted as he felt, Lucas unfolded himself from the mat and trudged outside to eat breakfast with his men. With tin plate in hand, he plunked down beside Bo.

"How many head did we lose?" Lucas questioned tiredly.

Bo swallowed his mouthful of sourdough biscuits. "Ten in the quicksand, four more that never made it to the river, plus the twenty-five head the Comanches stole from us," he informed Luke. "It could have been worse."

Lucas nodded his tousled head in agreement. "If the army at Fort Sumner is still willing to pay eight cents a pound for the beeves and the miners in Colorado give us a hundred dollars a head, we will still turn a tidy profit."

Bo mentally calculated the amount of money they were discussing. "If we pay the Texas ranchers the going rate of seven dollars a head for their cattle and, figuring the cost of a dollar a mile to trail each steer to market, you'll still have more than enough to pay off Dr. Blake and Martha Lewis."

That was exactly how Lucas had it figured. But he fully intended to give his men a bonus. The trek from Fort Concho to Horsehead Crossing on the Pecos had been worse than the last drive. The weather had been unseasonably dry and there had been no water standing in the creek beds and arroyos as there had been during their last journey across *Llano Estacado*. The barren land had soaked up what little moisture there was to be had like a sponge and the journey had been nothing short of a trek through hell.

"How's Catlin?" Bo queried apprehensively.

"Resting comfortably at last," Lucas sighed. "She was a prisoner of nightmares most of the night." His gaze swung to the herd of cattle that had begun to graze in the carpet of grass that lined the river. "We'll take the day to rest.

Remind the men to keep an eye out for patches of Loco weed, larkspur, and snakeroot. The last thing these longhorns need is to be poisoned and paralyzed after their recent ordeal.''

Loco weed affected a horse's eye sight; larkspur paralyzed cattle; snakeroot poisoned cow's milk. Lucas had noticed a sparse smattering of all three weeds sprinkled among the grasses on the east bank of the river. Chances were there was more on the west bank where the herd was grazing. What they didn't need right now was half-crazed horses stumbling around, sick calves, and cows that couldn't stir a step to save their lives.

"Don't worry about a thing," Bo insisted as he rolled to his feet. "You keep an eye on Catlin and I'll see that these longhorns stay healthy.''

When Bo strode away, the other men converged on Lucas to inquire about Catlin. Lucas assured the vaqueros that she would be up and around after a few days' rest. Once they learned of Catlin's condition they were satisfied to tend their chores.

Before returning to the tent, Lucas ambled about camp and then paused to stare southeast while he sipped his coffee. For several minutes he contemplated the past few weeks, mulling over the dozen thoughts that had selected this particular moment to converge on him. Finally he cast his troubled musings aside and strolled back to the tent to check on Catlin.

A tender smile hovered on his lips as he peered into her exquisite but bruised face. Lord, what a beauty she was, he thought to himself. She was all fire and firm will. There were a score of lively passions seeking release from that gorgeous body of hers. Catlin gave new meaning to lovemaking and to spirited debates. Sometimes this saucy sprite made him so furious he saw red and sometimes she left him dangling beside the stars in moments of unrivaled splendor. But their affair had never been fire and ice, only fire: hot consuming passion and fiery arguments. There was no in-between, no frigid disinterest where Cat was concerned, even if he pretended there was.

Lucas was constantly aware of this amethyst-eyed blond. She had become every breath he inhaled. She colored all conversation and stained his every thought. When she was wounded, he bled. When she was tormented by nightmares, he suffered. Ah, what turbulent dreams she had endured the previous night. They had worried him to no end.

His thoughts trailed off when Catlin squirmed to her side and pried open her eyes—eyes like a mountain meadow of columbines waving in the breeze. Adoringly, he smoothed the renegade strands of hair from her bruised cheek and greeted her with a smile.

"Feeling better?" he queried softly.

"I think I would have to be dead for a week to feel better," Catlin croaked. "I'm thirsty."

"How could you be?" he teased gently. "You already drank half the Pecos." When she frowned at his flimsy attempt to humor her, Lucas agilely bounded to his feet. "I'll fetch some water."

In less than two minutes he returned to her side, offering her a sip from a tin cup. "From now on, you are riding in the chuckwagon and helping Flapjack prepare the meals." When Catlin tried to protest, Lucas pressed the cup to her lips, forcing her to take another drink. "I am not opening this subject to discussion. You have become accident prone of late and my frazzled nerves can't take much more of this before they snap."

His eyes probed hers and he was silent for a moment before he spoke again. "Tell me about the fire at the Hanley's cottage, Cat."

The unexpected request caused Catlin to choke on her drink. Why had he asked her that out of the blue? "What is there to say about a fire?" she murmured in mock innocence. "It is deadly and hot."

Lucas heaved a heavy sigh. "While you were delirious, you mumbled about the fire."

Catlin looked the other way. "Did I? I don't remember. But I imagine all my haunted dreams got tangled up with each other."

"I'm sure they did," Lucas patronized her, wishing she would confide in him.

Slowly, he climbed to his feet to tower over her. "We are spending the day here, so the cattle can graze and rest. When you feel up to eating . . ."

His voice trailed off when Jace Osborn poked his head inside to offer Catlin a hint of a smile. "I just wanted to see for myself that you're all right," he said. "You took quite a spill in the river."

When Jace backed away, a startled yelp echoed in his chest. Behind him stood Spur who had come to seek out his best friend, the one who had been neglecting him. In mute amazement Jace watched Spur flip the flap of the tent out of his way with his horns and then stamp forward to bellow indignantly. Catlin chuckled and then groaned when the muscles around her tender ribs complained. It was difficult not to laugh when Spur barged in to shake the canvas walls with his bugle-like bellow.

"Get out," Lucas growled. "I'll feed you in a minute."

Spur objected and he said so with a disgusted snort and an impatient stamp.

"Alright, alright, you spoiled brat," Lucas muttered as he placed both hands on the wide-spread horns and backed the steer from the tent.

When Cat was left alone, a quiet smile pursed her lips. Seeing Lucas play the nursemaid for her and watching that overgrown steer who thought he was a puppy amused her. Honest to goodness, she would never get over loving Lucas Murdock. He had attached himself to every memory. She wouldn't be able to think a single thought

285

without his handsome face materializing before her.

A weary sigh tripped from her lips and her long lashes swept down to her cheeks. She was too tired to battle the riptide of emotions that hounded her when she contemplated that midnight-haired rake. It was a shame Luke hadn't permitted her to drown. She would have died, carrying her haunting secret. Emmet Blake would have been happy and Luke would have been rid of her and her rash of accidents.

While Catlin begged for sleep, a peculiar scene kept skipping across her mind. She was falling and there was a dark face on the other side of the wall of water. Eyes flashed. . . . She was screaming. . . . Catlin couldn't quite put the incident in its proper sequence. Had it been Emmet's face that she imagined she saw when she fell in the water? Had that thought become entangled with the vision of seeing Emmet as she collapsed on the floor of the Hanley's cottage? It must have been, she told herself. And yet, she had seen a splatter of blues and grays, felt the rush of—

Catlin shook her head, trying to hack her way through the jungle of tangled thoughts. Perhaps she was only recalling bits and pieces of hallucinations and attempting to haphazardly glue them together. Lucas said she had been delirious during the night. It was difficult to determine dreams from reality when she was weak and groggy. For now she would sleep. And when her mind was clear she would delve into these tangled dreams to separate the nightmares from reality . . . if they weren't one and the same.

Chapter 19

Despite Catlin's fierce protests, Lucas deposited her on the seat beside Flapjack Barnett and ordered her to assist with the noon meal. Pouting, Catlin crossed her arms beneath her breasts and stared straight ahead until Lucas stepped up to plant a kiss to her compressed lips—with Flapjack as witness.

"You'll live a lot longer if you stick with Flapjack," Lucas murmured, withdrawing far enough to stare into the violet eyes that dominated her bruised face. "I don't want to spend the day fretting over you."

Catlin gave way to the goose bumps that trickled across her skin after Lucas kissed her into submission. "I'm giving you your way this time," she granted him, breaking into a mischeivous smile. "But I'll see to it that your dinner is properly poisoned."

She was feeling her old self again, Lucas diagnosed as he hopped to the ground. She was as sassy as ever.

"Go easy on the arsenic, sweetheart," Lucas requested, his eyelid dropping into a playful wink. "I have a herd of cattle to drive north, you know."

Catlin pulled a face as he pivoted away.

"I saw that," Luke chuckled.

"Good," she grumbled and then stuck out her tongue at

287

him for good measure.

While Catlin sat on her wooden throne, Luke and his men moved the longhorns into an orderly formation to begin another leg of their journey across *Llano Estacado*. The day progressed without a hitch as Spur and his clanging bell kept the cattle marching like a well-drilled army. Catlin assisted Flapjack in cooking his specialty of Pecos Strawberries and Overland Trout—the glorified names for beans and bacon.

By the time the herd paused to graze at high noon, the meal was ready and waiting. Catlin didn't mind her new duty, but compared to sitting on horseback and herding cattle it was far cry from exciting. All that kept the hours from crawling along at a snail's pace was Flapjack's tall tales of previous trail drives. The man was a natural storyteller. As the days progressed Catlin learned more and more about the man she couldn't get over loving. Flapjack boasted of Lucas's savvy in the wild untamed country and of his miraculous feats that had saved them from impending doom.

Now how was a woman supposed to forget the man she loved when she was subjected to another round of boasts of Luke's exceptional talents? And how was she to forget the wondrous dreams they had created when Lucas swaggered past her from time to time, flashing her roguish smiles that held intimate promises? She couldn't. His flirtatious attention reminded her of the first day they had met and he had mischievously placed her leg in a splint. Cat could list umpteen instances that drew her to his charismatic charm. Lucas Murdock was simply one of those men that a woman could not forget.

That evening when Luke came to check on her, Catlin was spreading out her bedroll in the tent he had insisted she use since her fall into the Pecos. The look in his eyes revealed his intentions without Catlin having to pose a question. Lucas spoke not a word as he snuffed the lantern and gathered Catlin in his arms. In less than a heartbeat his warm, demanding lips took possession and Catlin melted into puddles. The uninhibited passage of his hands over her skin was wildly exciting. Butterfly kisses fluttered against her flesh and Catlin's breath came out in ragged spurts.

It seemed months since she had experienced this overflow of bubbling sensations. But Lucas had perfect recall. His masterful caresses sought out each sensitive point and created the familiar hungers that mushroomed into gigantic cravings. He could make her want him with every fiber of her being. And want him she did! She *needed* to touch him, to taste him, to hold him.

Twisting away, Catlin came upon her knees to caress his scarred chest. He was like a sleek lion. Whipcord muscles rippled beneath his bronzed skin. Catlin worshipped him, exploring every steel honed inch of his masculine torso, leaving him moaning with the intense pleasure of her touch.

Lucas swore he would burn alive when Cat employed her silky body to caress him. He could feel the taut peaks of her breasts brushing upward from his belly to tease his chest. He dragged in a shuddering breath when the titillating caresses receded and her hand folded around him, bringing his passions to a fervent pitch.

With a seductive growl, he pressed her to her back. Luke closed his eyes and mind to all except the sublime rapture of being one with this delicious package of beauty and spirit. If he didn't take her this instant he feared he would explode in unappeased passion. As his mouth took possession of her lips, his masculine body glided upon hers, setting the frantic cadence of lovemaking. His hands entwined with hers as he sought ultimate depths of intimacy. The feel of her supple body moving in perfect rhythm with his drove him to the brink of insanity. A hostage of his wild innate needs, Lucas clung to her, lifting them from one ecstatic plateau to another.

And then the dark, sensual world exploded. Flashes of silver-white light speared the darkness. Passion bubbled forth like molten lava. Lucas shuddered as if besieged by an earthquake. He swore the ground had moved beneath him and thunder rumbled above him.

As he slowly drifted back to reality, he realized the lightning and thunder weren't figments of his imagination. Although he longed to remain in the unending circle of this angel's arms, he had to ensure the approaching storm didn't incite a stampede. Reluctantly, he withdrew to press a parting kiss to her honeyed lips.

"Don't leave me, Lucas," Catlin murmured as she traced his shadowed features.

"Had I a choice, I would make love to you all through the night," he confessed in a voice that was husky with the effects of passion. "But the storm might frighten the herd. And if it does, you better take care of yourself. You have already used up several of your nine lives."

Catlin levered up on an elbow while Lucas donned his clothes. "Luke, I . . ." Her voice trailed off as another peal of thunder clattered above them.

By the time Lucas dashed back to camp, the flashes of lightning gave him a glimpse of the men who had rolled to their feet to dress. Jesse Lane had already herded the remuda of horses into a rope pen and cowboys were throwing their saddles on the first mount within reach.

Another rattle of thunder shook the earth and Lucas bounded into the saddle. As he raced toward the herd that had bolted to their feet and had begun to mill, a great flash of blinding blue-white light tore holes in the towering clouds.

"Circle the herd," Lucas roared over the howling wind that signaled the descent of the thunderstorm.

His heart pounded in furious rhythm as he swept the perimeters of the herd, forcing the cattle to circulate clockwise. Lightning flashed again and Lucas swore under his breath. The cattle were climbing all over each other in confusion, startled by the balls of fire that sparked at the tips of their horns. Even Spur seemed unnerved by the ground-shaking thunder and huge bolts of lightning that sizzled overhead. When Spur became uneasy it was a sure sign that this was no mild-mannered rain shower with which they were about to contend. Trouble was brewing.

When the right flank of the herd tried to break and run, Luke and Bo pulled their revolvers to fire above their heads, forcing the cattle to rejoin the milling circle. The churning mass of cattle emitted waves of heat that were almost scorching. But Lucas worked relentlessly, circling the startled mob. The vaqueros formed a ring around the frightened longhorns, ensuring they moved without going anywhere.

The patter of huge raindrops lessened the heat given off by the bunched herd. The rain gave way to the furious thump of hailstones beating down from the flashing sky. The cowboys were forced to climb from their horses to take refuge under their saddles. Although the men tried to hold their positions, the herd began to drift, bawling in complaint when they were pelleted by stones of ice that were as big as quail eggs.

Lucas was sure the storm would last forever. He had already stood an eternity with his saddle braced over his head, holding the reins to a horse that wished to be anywhere except beneath a shower of hail. Shouting orders that were passed from one lookout point to another, the vaqueros squeezed the drifting herd back into one milling core. Finally the hail passed over them and a steady drizzle of rain followed the wake of the storm.

For another hour the procession of men encircled the herd, singing lullabies to calm them. Only when the longhorns were content to bed down did Lucas call a halt to the constant vigil. He sent half of the men back to camp to nurse their bruises while the other remained on watch.

After longhorns endured such a violent storm it would take only one unidentified sound or unruly steer to put them back on their feet. Knowing an ounce of prevention was worth ten pounds of cure Lucas remained with the herd throughout the night while his men worked in shifts. He had no intention of allowing trouble to take root if he could possibly avoid it.

When Bo returned from guard duty, Catlin was poised beside the chuckwagon. Her anxious features glowed in the dim campfire which Flapjack had ignited with his supply of the dry kindling he kept in a sling under the chuckwagon.

"Doc is all right," Bo assured Catlin before she could pose the question that was written all over her face.

Catlin would have preferred to see for herself, but Bo refused to permit her to climb on his horse and check on Lucas.

"You go back to your tent, little lady," he demanded sternly. "Doc has enough to worry about without wondering if you're prowling in the night."

"My tent is no longer a tent," Catlin informed him. "The hail cut the canvas to shreds."

"Then tuck your bedroll under the wagon. But don't you dare ride out with the herd. Doc will have my head, as well as yours."

When Catlin looked as if she meant to object, Bo breathed down her neck. "I want your word, Catlin," he demanded. "Promise me you'll stay here."

Heaving a defeated sigh, Catlin nodded compliance. "Very well, I'll stay, but I'd rather—"

"Yeah and I'd rather be in some cozy hotel, sleeping on a feather bed," Bo cut in, sliding her a teasing smile. "But we're not, so we'll do what we have to do."

Resigning herself to the fact that she wouldn't get near

Lucas to determine if he had been beaten black and blue, Catlin continued making her rounds to ensure the other vaqueros had properly cared for their injuries. When she paused to inquire how Jace Osborn had fared during the storm, he eyed her for a long, pensive moment. Catlin usually had the feeling Jace didn't trust her intentions any more than she trusted him. But tonight his attitude toward her was different somehow. She had seen him watching her the past few days. Each time she glanced in his direction she was met by his probing stare. But now there was not one iota of hostility or skepticism in his plain features.

When Catlin dabbed ointment on the slash on his cheek, Jace grabbed her wrist and looked her squarely in the eye. "Why are you playing my nursemaid?" he wanted to know.

Catlin peered into those cobalt blue eyes that were usually penetrating through her like a sword. Now they were gentle and inquiring . . . and only God knew why. Cat certainly couldn't explain his metamorphosis.

"Because you and the other men have had a harrowing night and you were practically beat to death by hail," she explained as she wormed her hand loose to treat the gash on his craggy cheek.

"You puzzle me, Cat," Jace murmured as his gaze drifted over the damp clothes that emphasized her curvaceous figure. "I don't think you are what I first thought you were."

Catlin graced Jace with an impish smile. "That makes us even," she said saucily. "I don't think I have you figured out as well as I thought I did."

With that, Catlin moved on to her next patient. Each time Catlin glanced in the direction of the herd, wondering when Luke would return, she found Jace staring meditatively at her. My, the man was behaving strangely, she thought to herself. She had the most peculiar feeling that Jace had become interested in her as a woman. Now why was that? For the first week he seemed cautious and watchful and leery of her, even while she could detect a hint of lust in those piercing blue eyes. Catlin couldn't imagine what she had done differently to change his attitude toward her. It was as if he were viewing her in a new light and Catlin wasn't sure that was good either! After all, Jace was a man and that was one strike against him.

Wearily, Lucas swung from his saddle after a sleepless night of standing sentinel over the longhorns. No sooner had his foot touched the ground than Catlin flew into his arms to greet him with an overzealous kiss. Two dark brows jackknifed in disbelief when Cat squeezed the stuffing out of him—right smack dab in front of anyone who cared to watch.

The instant Catlin realized she was making a spectacle of herself, she backed away and blushed profusely. A wry smile quirked Luke's lips as he cupped her chin, raising her gaze to his chocolate brown eyes.

"Isn't it a bit out of character for you to throw yourself in my arms, minx?" he teased softly. "Not that I mind, you understand, but I didn't think you loved me all that much."

The taunt caused Cat to stiffen like a ramrod. For months Lucas had mocked her lack of impulsiveness and spontaneity. He accused her of being too methodic and sensible. And the one time she ignored her inhibitions and followed her heart, he teased her unmercifully.

"I was worried about you," she said in a tone that sounded far from concerned. "Some of us don't have sense enough to come in out of the hail."

"I'm fine," Luke assured her, melting her ire with his provocative baritone voice. "But I would be a helluva lot better if I could have another of your tantalizing kisses.

His mouth slanted across hers, savoring the soft texture of her lips that reminded him of delicate rose petals. The world shrank to fill a space the size this bewitching elf occupied. Lucas didn't care that he was providing a show for his men, that they were all wishing to be in his boots at the moment. Catlin had become his obsession. Knowing she intended to leave him the minute they set foot in Denver made each moment with her as precious as gold.

Dammit, if only she would trust him enough to confess why she wanted to leave him. For the first time in more than five years Elise's memory didn't torment him. Wide violet eyes had replaced the dark sultry pools that had once haunted his dreams. Of all the women he could have had, the two he wanted were always out of his reach, just like an elusive dream.

Clearing his throat to make his presence known, Bo waited for Lucas to finish what he was doing. An amused grin dangled on the corner of his mouth as he watched Lucas struggle to compose himself after his steamy kiss.

"Why don't you let me scout the trail ahead of us today while you take a rest." His silver-gray eyes twinkled with unspoken innuendos. "You and Catlin can rejoin the drive after you've caught up on your sleep. Since we have Jace Osborn as an extra hand, we can spare you for a day or two.

When Lucas glanced down into Catlin's exquisite features, he knew what his answer would be. He had less than a month to convince this independent beauty to return to Texas with him and there was so little opportunity for privacy.

"Thanks, Bo, I could use a rest," Lucas admitted, never taking his eyes off Catlin.

When Bo pivoted on his heels to take command of the drive and put the herd on the trail, Lucas strode off to fetch two fresh horses from the *caviada*. After he had hurriedly swallowed his breakfast and gave Flapjack directions to a suitable camp sight, he turned back to Catlin.

Wearing a roguish grin, Lucas swept Cat off her feet and deposited her in the saddle. Catlin gaped at him. They had only one bedroll between them and no food except the pemmican she had stashed in her pocket. All Lucas had for protection was a Winchester rifle and his two Colts. As much as she relished being alone with him, he seemed to be very impractical in gathering their provisions and she proceeded to tell him so.

"Ah, now we're back to being sensible again, are we?" Lucas tittered as he aimed himself northwest. "A pity that. I rather liked the spontaneity of your kiss awhile ago."

"You have to admit it is dangerous to be out here without much protection," Catlin sniffed. "We could starve to death unless you are a magician who can pull rabbits out of his hat to feed us."

"You're body is all the nourishment I need," Lucas assured her with a roguish wink.

Catlin rolled her eyes skyward. Why had she fallen in love with this impossible man? She had almost gotten herself killed three times already. And now Lucas was practically daring disaster to strike them. In her opinion he should have come prepared. There was no telling what dangers they might face alone in the wilds.

Despite Cat's reservations, Luke led them to the Pecos River which they had followed north from Texas into New Mexico Territory. After an hour, Lucas spotted a bend in the river that formed a cove which was surrounded by a natural fort of trees. The water was exceptionally clear and inviting and he wasted no time in stepping from his stirrup to strip stark naked.

While Cat gaped at him as if he were a creature from outer space, Lucas dived in. One too many hailstones had pounded his brain to mush, she decided. Here he was, as if he didn't have a care or responsibility in the world, swimming and diving in and out of the water like a porpoise. Catlin's gaze circled their surroundings, wondering just when disaster would strike. She had come to expect it of late.

Torn between the temptation of a swim and the anticipation of trouble, Catlin finally expelled a resigning sigh. Ah well, if they were attacked by Comanche raiders or Comancheros, at least she would have had a bath and swim first.

When Catlin peeled off her trim-fitting breeches, Lucas let go with a wolfish whistle. Catlin tried to fling him a condescending frown, but she couldn't cast the smallest shadow on that blinding grin that cut crinkles in his ruggedly handsome features.

A tremor of pleasure flooded over Luke as the sun sparkled over Catlin's honeyed flesh. Lord, she was gorgeous! There was no other adjective to describe Catlin. Some women possessed a natural beauty that nothing could disguise. Cat was one of those rare females who looked divine, no matter what she was or wasn't wearing—except maybe an oversized sombrero and baggy clothes that concealed her unparalleled beauty. Some women had to resort to garments that hid the flaws of their figures or rouge and powder to tone down the features that were less attractive. But that was not the case with Catlin Stewart Quinn. There was a unique radiance about her. She had the face of an angel and the body of a Greek goddess. What she didn't have, a woman didn't need. His hungry eyes fell to the clover-leaf birthmark on her shapely thigh, aching to possess what his eyes devoured.

Lucas forgot all about his leisurely swim. The previous night he had been stripped from Catlin's arms and forced to battle the herd of frightened longhorns. Now he had this curvaceous nymph all to himself and he wasn't wasting a minute.

"Come here, Cat," he growled seductively.

"I thought you wanted to swim," Catlin teased as she sashayed to the shore to test the water.

"One look at you changed my mind," he assured her huskily.

When Lucas cut through the water like a hungry shark, Catlin bubbled with blithe laughter. Like a gazelle, she shot down the river bank, her blond hair trailing wildly behind her. Lucas was reminded of the day at the ranch when Catlin had shed the shell of feminine reserve and had become a playful child. Too often she locked her emotions behind that self-imposed wall. But now she was a carefree butterfly who had emerged from her cocoon to flutter beside the river. Her reckless giggle was sweet music to his ears.

When Luke caught up with her and tugged her into his sinewy arms, Catlin squealed playfully. Breathless from sprinting naked in the sun, Catlin wormed for freedom and dove into the river. When she resurfaced she was ready and waiting for the raven-haired barracuda to emerge from the crystal depths. Catlin pounced before Lucas could inhale a breath, forcing his head under. Her body glided down his until her face was a hairbreadth from his tanned features.

Her lips drifted over his in a most provocative kind of kiss. Luke felt like an underwater volcano that was about to erupt. The feel of her silky body moving familiarly against his ignited a fire that all the water in the Pecos couldn't smother. The feel of her lips playing evocatively against his left him burning on a hot flame.

Like a whale spouting to the surface, Lucas finally came up for air. But it was difficult to draw a breath when his heart was hammering with the vigor of a carpenter driving nails. Luke drew Catlin from the depths of the channel and tugged her down into the shallow water that caressed the sandy shore.

His dark eyes glittered down on her as his hands

wandered to and fro, watching her flesh sparkle with drops of diamonds. Ah, how he adored mapping her luscious figure with his exploring caresses. She was exquisite and he ached for her. Time hadn't diminished his hunger for her. Catlin's stubborn independence hadn't stopped him from wanting to keep her as his own. Each time he touched her was like the very first time. Those wild needs and the excitement was still there. He delighted in inventing new ways to please and arouse her.

A moan of surrender tripped from her lips as his skillful hands swam over her ultrasensitive flesh. A ripple of pleasure undulated through her when he lowered his head to flick the tip of her breast with his tongue. Instinctively, she arched toward his warm lips, begging for more. And Lucas eagerly complied. His kisses scaled each peak while his caresses migrated up her belly to cup her full breasts. Before she could recover from his tantalizing fondling, his hand skied down her ribs to swirl across her abdomen. His fingertips brushed her inner thighs and then receded to trace the same sweet tormenting path to the throbbing tip of her breast. Not once but over and over again, Luke spread waves of pleasure over her sensitized flesh. His hands and lips toured her body until he knew her by taste and touch and she was trembling with the want of him.

A quiet whimper bubbled in her chest when his fingertips delved deeper, making her ache to the core of her being. And when Catlin swore she would die in the wild splendor of having him so close and yet so maddeningly far away, he came to her, appeasing the monstrous craving he had instilled in her. They were flesh to flesh, their hearts beating in frantic harmony. Catlin clutched him even closer, knowing what was to come, knowing soon she would feel the world split asunder. Her emotions would shatter and the love she felt for this incredibly tender man would pour forth, just as it always did. She couldn't hide her love for him when he opened wide the flood gates of passion.

Catlin felt the surge of ineffable rapture stream through her and the words she tried to hold in check spilled from her lips. "I love you, Lucas."

He heard her softly uttered confession as the universe splintered with shimmering white light. With a shuddering groan Luke rode out the cresting waves that tumbled back to reality's shore. He would never grow tired of this enchanting nymph. She always left him marveling at the sensations she aroused in him, the rare ecstasy they shared.

His lips whispered over the swanlike column of her throat as his hands slid over her pliant curves. "Then stay with me and be my only love," he murmured hoarsely.

"Please don't spoil the moment with impossible requests," Catlin beseeched him, her voice thick with the aftereffects of passion.

"Why shouldn't I?" Lucas laughed bitterly as he rolled away to loom over her. "You're spoiling our future."

"I can't go back," Catlin blurted out. "And even if I could I wouldn't want to settle for being second best."

Two thick brows formed one line across his forehead. "What the sweet loving hell is that supposed to mean?"

"It means that since you can't have Elise you have decided second best isn't such a bad bargain." Catlin replied as she rose to her feet to walk into the water. "I don't want to be a substitute for the light and love of your life, Lucas."

"You are not my consolation prize, dammit!" Lucas growled, watching her glide across the river like a swan . . . whose neck he would like to wring for being so confounded bullheaded.

"Aren't I?" Catlin's lips curved into a melancholy smile. "I love you and all the memories we've made together. I have experienced a maelstrom of emotions because of you. If I were to give myself to another man, then he would become a substitute for what I have come to need from you.

300

Old flames never die and some memories never fade with time. That is how it is with you and Elise and how it is for me with you. The emotions I experienced with another man would be like fitting myself into a garment designed for someone else. It just wouldn't be right, even if I tried to make alterations."

"You realize, of course, that you are making absolutely no sense," Lucas muttered, annoyed that Cat was reducing love to tailored dresses. Hell's bells, how could he argue with her when he didn't know where to begin to counter her weird analogies? "First you say you love me and in the same breath you insist you are going away. If you care so much you couldn't leave me!"

"I am making perfect sense," Catlin declared with great conviction. "You loved Elise enough to leave her, didn't you? For five years you have carried her image in your heart. Men, being the lusty creatures they are, finally buckle to their innate needs. They seek to replace what they truly want with what they can have. Men are more prone to settle for substitutes than women are."

Finally, she met his irritated gaze. Her eyes glistened with the forbidden love that would never be allowed to fully blossom and grow. "You are my first love, Lucas. I'm like a prisoner serving a sentence without parole. I will love you for the rest of my life. But you will get over me because I am only a substitute for your true love. I know I will never forget how I feel about you. And knowing that, I understand the tender emotions you still harbor for Elise. I could never drive her memory away, just as no man can tear your memory from me. The taproot runs too deep."

"Since when did you become an authority on men?" he spouted in frustration. "I will thank you not to tell me what I think and feel, Miss know-it-all!"

Lucas stamped to the shore and jumped in feet first, cursing a blue streak. Cat was driving him nuts again. She confessed she loved him, but she was making no plans to stay and she had convinced herself that he saw her only as a substitute for Elise. Well, maybe there was still a tender place in his heart for Elise, but that didn't mean there wasn't room for this blond-haired hellion. Geezus! How could he reassure her when she had made up her mind that she could never replace Elise in his eyes?

Still muttering a string of profanity, Lucas stomped back to the bank to tug on his clothes. "If you ask me, your reasons for leaving me have more to do with Ginger Hanley than Elise." His pointed gaze sought out the mermaid who was drifting amid sparkling waves. "There is something you are not telling me about her death. When are you going to trust me enough to explain what really happened?"

Catlin winced as if she had been stabbed in the back. Lucas was far too perceptive. He could read between the lines, knowing his preoccupation with his brother's wife was only part of the problem between them. And Lucas relentlessly probed, demanding information Catlin couldn't give without jeopardizing his and Martha's lives.

"There is nothing else to tell," Catlin lied for his own good.

Lucas expelled a few more unprintable curses as he stretched his long lithe body in the grass to rest. "Of course, there isn't," he snorted derisively. "And donkeys fly."

Crestfallen, Catlin waded ashore. There would always be obstacles between them, preventing them from fully enjoying the precious time they had left together. Lucas would not accept what she offered until the day she was forced to walk out of his life. He wanted to separate his unrequited love for Elise and his affair with Ginger as if they had no influence over his relationship with Cat. But it wasn't that easy. She loved the man he was. And he was what he was because of his past. But his past held complications neither of them could solve. It was a hopeless cause.

Catlin would never let herself believe that Lucas shared the same unselfish love she felt for him. He couldn't. He was a man—a man who had long loved a woman he could never have. He had accepted that fact but he hadn't really stopped loving Elise. Catlin couldn't help but wonder what would happen if Elise left her husband and came looking for Lucas. Faced with a choice, she knew Lucas would choose Elise. He might apologize for hurting Catlin, but she would have to walk out of his life nonetheless.

As Catlin shrugged on her clothes, the recurring vision that hounded her the past few days came again, just as it had so often since her fall into the river. A snake of uneasiness slithered down her spine. There was something strange in that vision that had become entangled with her nightmares. Catlin couldn't quite put her finger on the source of her uneasiness. The link in the chain of events on the day she was catapulted into the river still eluded her. Perhaps it was simply a fleeting hallucination caused by her delirious dreams. After nearly drowning, bits and pieces of memories had become entwined and she couldn't separate reality from the hallucinations. In that moment before anticipated death, her life had flashed before her eyes. And if not for Lucas she would have perished.

Lucas . . . Catlin frowned when the fuzzy image of a man's face streaked through her mind again. Was it Lucas she vaguely remembered glimpsing behind the wall of water? Heaving a confused sigh, Catlin eased to her back to bask in the sun. Her lashes fluttered down and she became a prisoner of her tangled dreams.

Chapter 20

Lucas was jostled awake by the sound of an alarmed shriek. Reflexively, he reached for his revolver. His body relaxed slightly when he realized the distressed sound had come from Catlin. Again her near brush with disaster had converged into nightmares.

Tenderly, he sank down to draw her onto his lap, soothing her with featherlight kisses. "Please tell me what torments you so," he pleaded.

Catlin felt the confining chains of her dreams melt away when Lucas spread gentle kisses across her tear-stained cheeks. Like a frightened child, she cuddled deeper in his arms, thankful for his protection. "I saw myself falling into the river again," she hedged. That was only part of the haunting vision that had come dangerously close to taking her life.

It stung his pride to know that, after all they had been through together, she still wouldn't confide in him. Hell's bells, what did it take to pry the dark secrets from her troubled soul?

"Catlin, nothing is so terrible that you and I can't face it together," he murmured, brushing away her lingering tears.

Her forefinger lined his bronzed features, committing

each one to memory. "You demand my trust but you don't trust me enough to accept the fact that you know all you need to know."

"The crux of the problem has something to do with Ginger, doesn't it?" he prodded, carefully gauging her reaction. "And Emmit Blake was somehow involved. I heard you utter his name the night you became delirious." Knowing Emmit had approached Cat at Martha's housewarming party was reason enough to suspect the meddling doctor had issued some sort of ultimatum. But what difference would it make after Ginger's death? Lucas couldn't puzzle it out.

Catlin pushed her palms against his scarred chest and leaned back in his encircling arms. He could never guess the horrors she had suffered, she assured herself. Even her troubled mumblings wouldn't betray her. He was only grasping at speculations.

"I'm famished," she insisted, purposely changing the subject. "What do you intend for us to eat while we sojourn beside the Pecos, Great White Hunter?"

Lucas reluctantly admitted defeat. He might as well try to pry information from a clam.

After they got dressed, Lucas focused his thoughts on the problem at hand. When Catlin had gathered wood for the fire, Lucas poured gunpowder into his pistol, wadded it loosely, and then fired it into the dry kindling. Poof! Flames crackled over the wood.

Catlin gaped at him in amazement. She had never seen such a technique for starting a campfire. What other tricks did this resourceful magician have up his sleeve?

Leaving Cat to tend the fire, Lucas disappeared into the trees and brush that hugged the cove. Half an hour later he returned with a fish and a jackrabbit. Now, why had she doubted that he could provide food as easily as he provided passion? Was there nothing this man couldn't do? He knew the land like the back of his hand. He had great strength of character and he could usually second-guess trouble before it could sneak up on him. He might even be able to encounter Emmet Blake and manage to—

Catlin clamped down on that whimsical thought. If she told Lucas the truth, she would be pitting him against the powerful physician who would do anything to protect himself and his reputation. Involving Lucas would only create more problems. This was one secret she had to carry to her grave. Emmet Blake would pay for his crime by roasting in hell one fine day, she consoled herself. In the meantime the innocent victims would be forced to suffer.

While Cat and Luke took their midafternoon meal, he discussed the changes he intended to make in the ranch. Catlin listened, wishing she could be a part of Luke's new life. But she knew it was only an elusive dream. She could only visualize the new corrals and stock pens Lucas described and the remodeling ideas he had in mind for the ranch house.

When they finished their meal, Lucas filled the canteens and swung into the saddle to catch up with the herd. As they rode north across New Mexico Territory, Catlin felt a tingle of excitement when she spied the Sangre de Cristo Mountains in the distance. There was something alluring about the soft blue-gray peaks that reached toward the sky.

"Will we be trailing through the mountain passes?" she questioned curiously.

Lucas shook his head. "The herd should reach Fort Sumner by late afternoon tomorrow," he calculated. "When I fulfill my contract by delivering fifteen hundred beeves to the army to feed soldiers, and the Navajo and Apaches who have been confined to the reservation at Bosque Redondo, we'll skirt the east side of the mountains to avoid Raton Pass. A man named Rickens Lacy Wootton, better known as Uncle Dick built a twenty-seven mile stretch of road from the southern border of Colorado to New Mexico."

A disgusted snort erupted from his lips as he shifted in the saddle. "I trailed cattle through the pass last year and dear Uncle Dick was charging a toll of one dollar and fifty cents per wagon, twenty-five cents per rider and five cents for cattle, sheep and horses. It was highway robbery."

Catlin quickly estimated how much it would cost Lucas to take the herd and the men through the shortcut. "Why, that is outrageous!" Catlin sniffed.

"That's what I told Uncle Dick last year," Lucas grunted. "But he is two hundred pounds of hard muscle with a wild shock of bristly hair and he has no qualms about collecting the toll at gunpoint. Since I didn't relish watching him start a stampede on the perilous ridges where the thin air made breathing difficult, I paid him. Reversing direction and sweeping around the mountains would have taken too much time."

Lucas removed his hat to mop the perspiration from his brow with his shirt sleeve. "This year we will veer east from Fort Sumner and sell a few hundred head of beeves at Fort Lyons. Then we will trail them to Pueblo and Fort Reynolds that lay on the plateau beside the Arkansas River. Whatever is left of the herd will be sold in Denver. . . ."

His voice trailed off. He didn't want to think about arriving in Denver just yet. That was weeks away and he hoped to convince Catlin to return to Texas by the time they reached Colorado. If not, he was going to sit himself down at one of Denver's many saloons and sulk. He would distract himself by watching the Hurdy Gurdy girls and listening to the orchestra, complete with its fiddle, banjo, and off-key piano. And he would get himself rip-roaring drunk on the imported whiskey the miners referred to as Taos Lightning. For sure, a couple of gallons of liquor would be all that could make him forget this curvaceous blond whose mystical violet eyes formed the dimensions of his fantasies. Dammit, why wouldn't she tell him why she refused to return to Texas? The not knowing was driving him up the wall!

As the sun dipped low on the horizon, bathing the world in shades of crimson, blue, and gold, Lucas called a halt to their traveling. He intended to spend one last night alone with Cat before they rejoined the herd the following afternoon. Lucas planned to make love to her until he depleted his last ounce of strength. And if he couldn't convince her that she was making a grave mistake by turning her back on the future they could build together he would—

Lucas expelled a frustrated breath. Hell's bells, he didn't know what he would do. At the moment, binding and gagging this stubborn vixen and toting her back to Texas had an appealing ring to it.

After building a fire in the same manner he had employed earlier, Lucas wandered off to hunt game while Catlin treated herself to another swim in the river. And when darkness settled over the plains, Lucas gave Catlin a dozen reasons why she should remain with him—beginning with a kiss more intoxicating than wine. For those splendorous hours, Catlin enjoyed a lifetime in Lucas's swarthy arms. She held nothing back when they made love and he chased away her fears and took her to paradise.

But Catlin, who had adapted the theory that if anything could go wrong it would, found disaster returning to torment her. While she and Lucas lay entwined in each other's arms, the whinny of an unidentified horse shattered the silence. Cautiously, she sat up beside Lucas who had discreetly reached for his rifle. Just as Catlin stretched out to grab her pistol, a rifle cracked in the night. The bullet whizzed past her shoulder, skidded off the ground and lodged itself in Lucas's thigh. With a growl that sounded inhuman, Luke rolled to his knees, jerking

308

his weapon against his shoulder. His target was the clump of underbrush where he had seen the sparks caused by their would-be assailant's discharging rifle.

"Stay down," Lucas snapped when Catlin reared up to fire her pistol. "You'll get yourself ki—"

Another shot rang through the air, scattering the dirt that lay a scant few inches from Lucas's hip. Lucas answered the singing bullet with two repetitive shots of his Winchester. And then the thunder of hooves heralded the departure of whomever had attempted to bushwhack them. When Lucas tried to give chase, Catlin sprawled on top of him. She well-remembered what Lucas had told her about Oliver Loving being wounded and dying of gangrene after his ordeal with Comanches. Luke was not going to dash off before his wound had been tended and that was that!

"Get off me!" he muttered. "He's getting away!"

"You aren't moving until your leg is treated to my satisfaction," she told him firmly.

"What the hell do you care if I bleed to death?" he growled in a bitter tone. "You're planning to leave me anyway."

"I don't want you to die because I love you," Catlin snapped back as she grabbed his Bowie knife from his belt to cut away his breeches.

"You love me enough to leave me," he scowled resentfully. "Why doesn't that make me feel better . . . Ouch! Dammit! That hurts!"

Catlin tried to be gentle but her hands trembled and it was difficult to prevent gouging his tender flesh.

"Fetch a bottle of whiskey from my saddlebag," he commanded, pushing her shaky hands away.

On wobbly legs, Catlin scurried over to do as she was told. Dropping down on her knees, she extended the bottle, but then she snatched it back to take a sip herself.

Through the grimace that thinned his lips, Luke

managed a faint smile. Catlin looked bewitching in the moonlight. In her frantic state, she had forgotten to finish dressing. She sat there with her shirt gaping wide open, her tangled hair cascading to her waist, tipping a bottle to steady her nerves.

Once she had downed the potent whiskey, she sloshed it on Luke's leg. He let out a howl that would have raised the dead.

"You'll never get a job as a nurse," he hissed, clutching his stinging thigh. Grimly, he peered into her peaked face, watching the light cast by the flames of the campfire flicker on her haunted features. "But for the time being, you'll have to become both a doctor and nurse—despite your lack of skills."

"Me?" Catlin chirped incredulously.

"Sterilize the knife," he instructed. "The bullet has to come out. Now."

Suddenly aware of her state of undress, Catlin fumbled to fasten her clothes. And Lucas expected her to perform surgery? Honest to goodness, she could barely manage the buttons on her shirt. She would probably kill him with her fumbling fingers!

Inhaling several deep breaths, Catlin sterilized the knife. After gulping down her heart, Catlin listened to Lucas instruct her in pulling back the jagged flesh to seek out the lodged bullet. A hiss of pain erupted from his lips when the knife jabbed his thigh. Hurriedly, he grabbed the whiskey and guzzled it down. Judging by the look on Catlin's face, she needed another drink as badly as he did.

"Here." He thrust the bottle at her.

Catlin gulped down the brew and handed it back to Luke before making another clumsy stab for the bullet.

"Damn that hurts!" Lucas crowed and then chugged another drink.

"I'm doing the best I can," she defended before she snatched the bottle away to help herself to a third drink.

"It isn't that easy, you know."

"Lord, what I wouldn't give to have Dr. Blake here," Lucas groaned as Catlin poked his tender flesh.

That remark had a quieting effect on Catlin. The very last person she ever wanted to see was that maniac Emmet Blake! Diligently, she concentrated on her task and within a few minutes she located the bullet. After tucking it in her pocket, she cleansed the wound and then retrieved the thread and persylic ointment as Lucas told her to do. It was the first time in Cat's life that she saw a constructive use for the stitchery her mother had insisted she learn.

When the makeshift bandages were in place, Catlin collapsed beside Lucas, who, by that time, had consumed so much whiskey he couldn't tell which of the two blurred images that were floating before his eyes was the real Catlin Quinn. And Catlin, rattled by her first attempt at primitive surgery, chose to forget the incident by polishing off the rest of the bottle. Lord, her nerves were as tangled as twine!

A fine pair they made—both drunk as skunks. Bubbling in slurred sentences, Lucas demanded that Catlin saddle their horses. She blinked at him like a disturbed owl.

"You can't be serious. You can't ride. You could still bleed to death," she predicted over her thick tongue.

"I want to reach camp," Luke insisted sluggishly.

"You're crazy," Catlin protested. "If you . . ." She hiccupped and then giggled. "'Scuse me. If you die I'll hold it over you for the rest of your life."

Lucas snickered at the drunken imp who wasn't making any sense. At least he didn't think she was. In his inebriated condition, he couldn't be certain. He wasn't thinking too clearly himself.

"And what if our would-be assailant is out there somewhere, waiting to finish off his fiendish deed?" Catlin questioned thickly.

"He isn't," Lucas assured her.

"How do you know, oh wise and wonderful wizard?" she smirked.

"Because there is nothing to hide behind once a man veers away from the river," he declared. "Our bushwhacker had his chance and he knows it. Now go saddle the horses."

With very little coordination, Catlin struggled to her feet and waited for the world to stop spinning. She swore the fifty pound saddles were twice as heavy as usual when she attempted to lift them. Gritting her teeth, she swung the second saddle into place, but she had stepped on the dangling girth strap, throwing her off balance. A startled yelp burst from her lips when she kerplopped on the ground with the saddle atop her.

The uproarious laughter behind her brought her head around to glare at Lucas. Mustering what was left of her dignity, Catlin wrestled out from under the saddle and heaved it over Luke's horse. When both horses were readied, she wobbled back to Lucas who had crawled over to fish another bottle of whiskey from his saddlebags. He hadn't brought much in the way of food, but the liquor was certainly plentiful!

Catlin frowned as he chugged another drink and then offered it to her. With a what-the-hell shrug Catlin accepted the bottle. She and Lucas were both mad, she decided. He had been shot and she had removed the bullet as best she could. Now they were both guzzling liquor like thirsty camels. In her opinion, they were both behaving like idiots!

Stumbling, Lucas clamped onto the pommel of his saddle to steady himself. With Catlin's assistance he managed to slide onto his mount. But his forward momentum caused her to topple backward in the dirt. Grinning, Lucas peered down at the fuzzy image he had sent sprawling when he pushed away from her helping hands.

After scraping herself off the ground, Catlin struggled onto her horse. Lord, the world was still spinning furiously about her and the stars were revolving in the sky. Catlin sincerely hoped Lucas knew which direction he was heading because she didn't have a clue. But they plodded across the plains, arguing inconclusively about whether the person in the moon looked more like a *he* or a *she*. Personally, Catlin thought the moon's features resembled a witch, but Luke was of a different opinion. But the longer they drank, the more difficult it was to tell whether there was a moon in the sky at all.

Chapter 21

The sound of slurred voices lifted in nonsensical song brought Bo awake with a start. Sitting up, he glanced first in one direction and then the other. "What the hell . . . ?"

Pulling on his breeches, Bo stalked across camp, stepping around the sleeping forms that lay in his path. Again, he heard harmonic laughter wafting through the night. Grabbing a lantern, Bo marched into the darkness.

"Hark, what light through yonder window shines?" Lucas slurred as he teetered drunkenly in his saddle.

"You stole that from Shakespeare," Catlin giggled. She stuffed the cork back in the bottle and leaned out to return the whiskey to Lucas.

"I thought I had heard that somewhere before." Lucas grabbed the bottle and helped himself to another drink.

"Sh . . . sh." Catlin blinked and then peered across the plains. I think it really is a light."

Squinting, Lucas focused on the golden glow that swung a few feet from the ground. "Biggest damned firefly I ever did see."

Catlin snickered at the remark. Her laughter was contagious and Lucas guffawed, very nearly toppling himself off his horse.

"Holy Jehosephat!" Bo muttered when he recognized

the two figures that swayed precariously on the backs of the approaching horses. Cursing under his breath, Bo stamped forward. "What in heaven's name are you two doing?"

Lucas straightened in the saddle when he recognized Bo's voice. But within a few seconds he burst into snickers.

"You're both rip-roaring drunk," Bo snapped crossly. "For crying out loud, Doc, what did you do to Catlin?"

"What did I do to her?" Lucas croaked as he indicated his numb leg. "Look what she did to me!"

Bo lifted the lantern to survey the blood-stained bandage. "She shot you?" he hooted in disbelief.

"Did I?" Catlin peered at Lucas through glazed eyes. She could barely remember her own name, much less why she had been drinking steadily for more than four hours. That, after all, was the point of guzzling whiskey—to forget what one preferred not to remember.

Cursing in fluent profanity, Bo grabbed Lucas's reins and led his horse back to camp. Firing orders, he sent the vaqueros scurrying to prepare a pallet for their injured trail boss.

After Jace Osborn helped Bo lift Lucas from the saddle, they carefully eased him onto the pallet.

"How many were there?" Jace questioned as he inspected Luke's leg and then glanced at Catlin.

"Only one," Cat answered for Lucas who was grimacing at the new position his stiff leg had been forced into.

"What did he want?" Bo queried, shoving a rolled quilt under Luke's head.

"I didn't have the chance to ask him," Lucas slurred out. "But more than likely he wanted me out of the way so he could have Cat. Some men will do most anything to get their hands on a woman in country where there are so few of them around."

The comment had a sobering effect on Catlin. Maybe Lucas had partially hit upon the truth. Maybe the sniper

315

had wanted to dispose of her and Lucas had accidentally gotten in the way . . . The dismal thought made her gulp over the lump that suddenly collected in her throat. Emmet Blake's harsh vow echoed in her ears. He swore he would hunt her down and dispose of her.

Catlin's wary gaze searched the shadows. Was that lunatic out there somewhere, trailing after her? Surely not! A shudder ricocheted through her soul. If Emmet had checked with the stage company to learn she hadn't resorted to that mode of transportation, he might have surmised that she had followed after Lucas for protection. Had he hired someone to dispose of her? Did he suspect that Catlin would confide in Lucas? She squeezed her eyes shut. Her association with Lucas could have put that maniac's henchman on her heels. She had to leave Lucas as soon as possible! Her very presence was endangering his life.

While Jace and Bo changed the dressing on the wound and wrapped it with fresh bandages, Catlin retrieved her bedroll and collapsed upon it. She shouldn't have partaken of so much whiskey, she scolded herself. Her thoughts were becoming more entangled by the second. Emmet's snarling face, Lucas's handsome features and the fuzzy image from her nightmare were there to torment her. Catlin couldn't quite sort out her contemplations before they all blended together. And gladly, she drifted off into a world in which she had only to contend with her subconscious. Which was just as well. Her conscious mind had been pickled by one too may swigs of whiskey.

A groggy moan tumbled from Catlin's lips when Flapjack's trumpet-like voice shattered the darkness. God, it couldn't be five o'clock already! Catlin cupped her hands over her ears and winced when Flapjack belted out his second and last call to breakfast.

With considerable effort, Catlin pried one puffy eye open and then flinched when a shadow fell over her. The face that loomed above her was big and broad and had a wet black nose. When Catlin recognized Spur she half-collapsed on her bedroll. She had become as jumpy as a grasshopper of late. Danger seemed to be lurking in every shadow. And wondering if that lunatic Emmet Blake had sent someone to track her wasn't helping matters one tittle.

A faint smile pursed Catlin's mouth as she propped herself up to stroke Spur's muzzle. Realizing Catlin had no treats to offer him, Spur finally wandered over to bellow at Lucas. Catlin winced again when another face appeared from the skipping shadows cast by the campfire.

"I thought you might need some coffee, Cat," Jace Osborn murmured as he extended a tin cup.

"Thank you," Catlin said hoarsely. With caution, she tasted the steamy brew.

"It must have been terrifying to find yourself attacked," Jace speculated as his blue eyes swam over Catlin's enchanting features.

She nodded mutely before taking another sip of gooseberry coffee.

"You've had one catastrophe after another strike you," Jace remarked. He peered at Catlin over the rim of his own cup. "It could have been you who wound up with a bullet in your thigh instead of Murdock."

Catlin stared up into Jace's weathered features that gave him a dark, foreboding appearance. The man probably had a heart of gold but he was such a rugged looking individual and he kept to himself so much it was difficult to tell. But he was more friendly and receptive than he had been when he first rode into camp. Catlin let her guard completely down and blessed Jace with an elfish grin.

"Knowing I'm jinxed, don't you think it wise to give me a wide berth?" she questioned. "My curse might rub off

317

on you."

Tenderly, Jace reached out to trace the heart-shaped curve of her lips. "If you find yourself in need of a body guard, pretty lady, I'd like the job. I wouldn't mind taking my chances with you.

When Jace rose to amble away, Catlin peered thoughtfully after him. If she didn't know better, she would swear that taciturn gunslinger, or whatever he was, had begun to warm to her. What had she done to earn his respect that she hadn't done when they first met? Not a thing Catlin could think of!

A struggle though it was, Catlin climbed to her feet to be hit by a wave of nausea. Weakly, she weaved toward the chuckwagon to fetch a biscuit. Once her stomach had settled, she walked over to check on Luke's wound, praying infection hadn't set in.

"I'm fine," Lucas assured her when she tried to unwrap the bandage. "Bo already put fresh salve on the stitches." His bloodshot eyes searched Catlin's peaked features. "How are you feeling, minx?" His voice dropped to that quiet, seductive tone that sent a herd of goose bumps stampeding across her flesh.

"Horrible, if you want to know," she replied with a feeble smile. "And shame on you for getting me drunk. I had sworn off liquor after Aunt Martha's house-warming party. And you made me break my promise to avoid liquor."

"Now if only I could get you to break your promise of leaving me," he whispered as he traced her lips, just as he had seen Jace do a few minutes earlier. Lucas hadn't appreciated the attention Jace had been giving Catlin. It had awakened the jealous green dragon.

Her eyes dropped, avoiding his penetrating gaze. "Nothing has changed. Last night only confirmed—"

"What has last night got to do with it?" His hand dropped away as he released a wordless scowl. "Some love-starved traveler probably saw his chance to steal you for his pleasures. Just because some renegade wanted you is no excuse."

"Lucas, you just don't understand," Catlin sighed disparagingly.

"You're damned right I don't and you refuse to enlighten me!" he burst out and then caught himself before his sharp voice prompted his men to turn and stare at them. "Hell's bells, I might as well argue with a wall."

Grumbling, Lucas dragged himself to his feet. He didn't feel a damned bit better than Catlin after his bout with whiskey. His head throbbed and his leg was killing him. "Excuse me, Miss Quinn, I have work to do."

Catlin glared at Luke when he pulled himself up on his tender leg. "You should ride in the chuckwagon with Flapjack and give yourself a rest," she advised.

"And you should tell me what the hell is troubling you," Lucas countered with a disdainful glance.

"I can't," she murmured deflatedly.

"Then neither can I," he shot back. "I have fifteen hundred head of beeves to deliver to Fort Sumner and that is exactly what I intend to do, wounded leg and all."

As Lucas hobbled off to fetch a horse from the *caviada*, Catlin rolled her eyes skyward. That billy goat of a man was going to kill himself just to spite her. He badgered her because she wouldn't confide in him and now he was punishing her by making her watch him suffer with his injury—one that she was probably responsible for, one way or another.

Talk about arguing with walls! Cat thought huffily. If she was a wall, Luke was a rock mountain!

Just as Lucas predicted, the herd reached Fort Sumner late in the afternoon. The men cut off fifteen hundred head and drove them into the waiting pens. While Lucas

319

transacted business with the commander of the post, half the cowboys drove the remainder of the herd north, pushing them through the night. Lucas had no intention of allowing the longhorns to drift back toward the fort where part of the herd lingered in pens. They had been conditioned to traveling as a group and now they had been split. In order for the cattle to adjust, Lucas ordered Bo to keep them moving, just as they had done when they left their native stomping grounds in Texas.

In defiance, Catlin had climbed into the saddle to ride herd over the contrary longhorns that tried to reverse direction to rejoin the other half of the herd. Since the herd's numbers were no longer as great, Lucas had sent half of his men back to Texas to begin another roundup of wild *cimarrones* that he intended to collect for his new herd. With only half the manpower available, Catlin felt she was needed beside the fidgety herd, at least until they grew accustomed to walking without those they had left behind.

When Lucas caught up with them the following evening, he was elated that he had made a sizable profit at Fort Sumner. At least he was in a good mood until Bo tattled on Catlin for riding herd over the cattle. Making a beeline for the rebellious sprite, Lucas informed her in no uncertain terms that she would be riding with Flapjack and that was that.

But that wasn't that, not to Catlin. She had a mind of her own and she knew how to use it. She quickly assured the scowling Lucas that she was going to carry her share of the responsibility since he was short-handed. And if he didn't like it then that was just too bad!

An argument ensued and Lucas trotted back to camp, cursing Catlin's infuriating stubbornness. "Damned fool she-male," he growled as he swung from the saddle and hobbled over to swallow his evening meal in three bites.

A wry smile hovered on Bo's lips. "Does this mean the engagement is off again?"

"No," Lucas snapped crabbily. "I ought to marry that misfit the minute I locate a preacher. Then I would have a legal right to throttle her when she disobeys orders."

"You ought to marry her alright," Bo agreed with a chuckle. "But a license isn't going to convince Catlin to snap to attention each time you bark a command. She's got more spunk and determination than any woman I know."

Lucas expelled a frustrated sigh. The closer they came to Denver the more exasperated he became. He could see the end of the trail and the end of his stormy affair with that saucy firebrand. Cat wasn't going to change her mind about leaving. Lucas kept imagining what his world was going to be like without Catlin in it and he cursed a blue streak. He kept wondering if they had created a child—a child he may never get to meet—and that made him swear two blue streaks.

Dammit, for the second time in his life he had found himself in love. History was repeating itself. He had walked away from Elise because he loved her enough to leave before he put himself at odds with Andrew. Now Catlin was leaving him because only God knew why! That violet-eyed sorceress had bewitched him and she kept her mysterious secret to herself.

And for the next few days, Lucas tried to accept his second bitter disappointment of love. He wasn't exactly sure what love should be, but he knew exactly what it shouldn't be. Wanting Cat frustrated him to no end. Trying to convince himself to let her go when she had no intention of staying was tearing him to pieces. To distract himself, he pushed his body to its limits so that he collapsed in exhaustion the instant he stretched out on his bedroll.

Lucas knew a lost cause when he saw one. And Catlin Quinn was out of his reach forever. Well, he hoped she was happy because she was making him miserable. And the day Catlin's mount had suddenly started bucking and snorting, Lucas had forced himself not to go to her rescue. Fighting for hard-won composure, he had allowed Jace Osborn to pull Catlin from the steed that had somehow managed to get hold of loco weed. But Jace didn't seem to mind. The past few days he had stuck to Catlin like glue.

Lucas had purposely kept his distance, trying to adjust to living in a world without that sassy blond. When she really was gone for good, he wouldn't have to cope with such a drastic change. But the experiment didn't work worth a damn, Lucas soon found out. He was left to wonder how many years it would take to get over Cat. Five years? Ten? Twenty?

"How long are you going to avoid Catlin as if she contracted the bubonic plague?" Bo questioned as he rode up to take Luke's place as nighthawk.

"When are you going to quit meddling in my love life?" Lucas growled.

"When you finally get it squared away, that's when," Bo replied before spitting tobacco juice out the side of his mouth. "And don't think the other men haven't noticed the way you've avoided Catlin. When you backed off, you may as well have waved a matador's cape in front of a herd of bulls. Catlin has more male attention than she knows what to do with. I think even Jace Osborn is sweet on her and I didn't figure a man like that could be sweet on anybody. He hangs around her all the time, fetching her horses and her meals."

Lucas didn't say a word. He simply disappeared into the darkness to let Bo take his two-hour shift and sing his lullabies to the cattle.

After skirting the majestic mountains to the west, the herd was split again. One-third of the longhorns were driven to Fort Lyon to feed hungry soldiers and one

322

hundred head were sold at Fountain City where disgruntled miners had turned to farming to support themselves.

Denver was only ninety miles away and Catlin constantly reminded herself that she would soon be on her own again. The past two weeks had been heartbreaking for Catlin. She had watched Lucas turn away from her, barely acknowledging her presence in camp. They had become strangers sharing the same space. Lucas was so remote and distant these days that Catlin wondered if she had ever really known him at all.

Jace Osborn had taken advantage of Lucas's lack of interest in Catlin. Although he was polite and attentive, Catlin refused to let him believe she had any romantic interest in him. Each time she looked into his dark, weathered features she remembered. . . .

A flash of memory shot across Catlin's mind, as it had so often lately. The hazy image of a face hovering above hers through splatters of water kept hounding her. A muddled frown clouded her brow as she trailed the dwindling herd through the stream they had encountered. As the water splashed up in her face, Catlin was reminded of her near brush with disaster in the Pecos.

Suddenly, Catlin felt as if she had been stabbed with a knife. Her eyes swung over her shoulder to see the harsh, tanned features of the man who was riding behind her, the same man who had flanked her that day she fell, or rather was pushed into the water amid the frantic longhorns. Jace Osborn! It was his face she had seen through the wall of water, she realized with a start. He had been there and he had—

Catlin's heart hammered wildly in her chest. Jace's mount had collided with hers. That's why she had been catapulted from the saddle. He had known he had caused her to fall, but it had been Lucas who had pulled her to safety and revived her.

Why? Her mind screamed in confusion. Why had Jace purposely tried to harm her? And if he hadn't rammed her steed on purpose, why hadn't he tried to retrieve her from the river? And if he had pushed her on purpose, why was he being nice to her now? Was he trying to compensate for what he had done? And if he was, why hadn't he apologized for nearly getting her killed?

That thought led Catlin back through time, back to the first moment she had been plagued with this monotonous string of bad luck. It had all begun when they forded the Concho River to trek across the waterless stretch of plains to Horsehead Crossing.

Catlin glanced at Jace who tossed her a lopsided smile. And come to think of it, she hadn't suffered one catastrophe until Jace joined the drive at the Concho. Was that a coincidence or . . . ?

An eerie shiver slithered down her spine when she recalled the girth strap that had snapped loose, plunging her to the ground beside the cattle she had been chasing. And then she remembered the rattlesnake that had turned up in her bedroll. It wasn't Jace's lightning-quick draw that had disposed of the snake. Jace could have grabbed his pistol and fired as quicky as Lucas had. The man was handy with his Colts. She had seen him in action once or twice. Although Jace had been standing beside Lucas, it was Lucas who had saved the day, not Jace.

The grim speculation hung over Catlin like a black cloud throughout the afternoon. Even the awe-inspiring mountains with their snow-capped peaks didn't lift her gloomy mood. She had waited months to gaze at the jagged precipices and now that she was granted a breathtaking view, her mind was fogged with doubt and suspicion. Over and over again, the scene at the Pecos River darted through her thoughts. Catlin knew she hadn't imagined seeing Jace when she fell. But for the life of her, she couldn't understand why a man who always seemed to be around when she met with an accident would suddenly become her constant shadow. It just didn't make sense.

To satisfy her curiosity, Catlin ambled over to the pouch in the chuckwagon where Flapjack kept strips of rawhide in case of emergency. Knowing how frugal cowboys were about throwing anything away that might come in handy later, she searched the pouch for the broken strap Bo had replaced for her.

And sure enough the broken cinch was there. Carefully, Catlin examined the strap. Her eyes narrowed pensively as she rubbed her finger over the smooth slice that extended halfway across both sides of the broken girth strap. It looked suspiciously as if the leather band had been cut and allowed to give way under pressure.

Poking her head around the wagon, Catlin's wary gaze focused on Jace Osborn. While Jace was conversing with one of the other men, Catlin wandered inconspicuously toward his saddle. She fished into his saddlebag to retrieve one of the cartridges of bullets from his rifle. Catlin knew she was probably leaping to ridiculous conclusions, but she wanted to compare the slug she had dug from Luke's leg to the one's Jace used in his rifle.

Catlin ambled away from camp to make her comparisons, chiding herself for being so suspicious in the first place. When she inspected the cartridges her breath stuck in her throat. She couldn't be certain that the bullet came from Jace's rifle. Winchester repeating rifles were popular among cowboys. Lucas himself owned one and so did several of the other vaqueros. The Henry Repeating rifle also used the same .44 caliber rim-fire cartridges as the Winchester. But if the bullet had come from Jace's cartridge, how had he managed to slip away from camp and why had he ambushed her and Lucas? And if he had bushwhacked them, what was his motive?

Catlin felt sick all over when she answered that

question. Emmet Blake! He must have sent the gunslinger (or whatever Jace really was) to dispose of her. That must be it, she concluded. That would certainly explain her rash of mishaps, wouldn't it? Jace was trying to dispose of her by making her the victim of accidents. Ah, how shrewd Jace Osborn was, how devious! She wondered how much Emmet had paid Jace to ensure Catlin never returned to point an accusing finger—

"Is something wrong, Catlin?"

Cat very nearly leaped out of her skin when she heard Jace's deep voice so close behind her. "No, of course not," she assured him, staring at the velvet shadows that were draped on the eastern slopes of the mountains. "I was just admiring the view."

Jace's blue eyes flowed unhindered over Catlin's shapely backside, not missing one minute detail. "You've been acting strange this afternoon. Why are you avoiding me?"

Mustering her composure, she turned to face the tall lean man whose severe features were puckered in a bemused frown. "Have I? I hadn't meant to," she murmured awkwardly.

Jace moved a step closer, his hungry gaze roaming over her exquisite features with undisguised desire. Impulsively, he reached out a callused hand to trace the delicate line of her jaw. "Such a waste. . . ." he sighed forlornly.

Catlin stood her ground, but she was trembling with apprehensive speculation. All the evidence she had uncovered led her to believe Jace had been hired to kill her. And yet, he was trying to be gentle with her. What game was he playing? Was he trying to lure her in, attempting to gain her trust? Was it a ploy he used before he pounced at an opportune moment? Or had she dashed to a cliff and leaped to the wrong conclusion about him? Just because the bullets matched didn't mean he was the only one in the territory with a Winchester rifle, for crying out loud!

It was at that moment when Luke stepped from the grove of pines to see Jace touching Catlin. It rankled him to see any man standing so close to that curvaceous sprite. But the fact that Catlin hadn't refused Jace's display of affection put Luke in a genuine huff! She had declared she didn't like Jace Osborn the instant he rode into camp. Apparently that fickle female had changed her mind. That was a first. Damn her.

Cursing fluently, Lucas stalked back to camp without making his presence known. Women! They were nothing but trouble and he didn't need that blond-haired she-male's brand of trouble. If Cat wanted Jace Osborn she was welcome to him. Lucas didn't give a flying fig what she did. Let her break Jace's heart before she flitted away. What did Lucas care?

Bo frowned at the mutinous scowl that was stamped on Luke's face. "What's the matter with you?"

"I'll be glad when this damned drive is over," he muttered grumpily. "I'm ready to go back to the Flying Spur and begin my new life."

Bo didn't believe him for a minute. "Where is she and who is she with this time?"

"Jace," Lucas growled. He poured himself a drink, then downed it in one swallow.

"I told you so," Bo gloated. "You backed off and Jace moved in. The rest of us want to keep our jobs and we know better than to get too close to that pretty pixie. But you have no hold over Jace Osborn. He strikes me as the kind of man who usually takes what he wants."

"Well, what the hell am I supposed to do about it?" Lucas fumed. "This isn't exactly the Stone Age where a man can club a stubborn female over the head and then drag her off to his cave. In case you haven't noticed, Cat is very much her own woman."

"And you are very much your own man . . . or at least

327

you used to be," Bo taunted, casting his friend a meaningful glance. "If you let Catlin go, you're going to be hell to live with and I will damned sure quit."

"At least I'll still have my pride," Lucas grumbled resentfully. "I draw the line at crawling to her on my knees."

Bo's broad shoulders lifted in a shrug as he pivoted on his heels. "Fine. Keep your pride, Doc. I'm sure it will be immensely comforting to you in the long lonely years ahead."

Lucas let loose with several colorful expletives. He felt like a man strung out on a torture rack. Part of him wanted to salvage what was left of his pride and pretend he didn't care what Cat was doing or with whom. And another part of him wanted to cling to the one woman who had broken Elise's spell after five tormenting years. Damn Catlin. Damn her for burrowing her way into his heart and then waltzing off, even after she admitted she loved him. Honest to goodness, he was going to be a raving lunatic by the time that woman got through with him!

Chapter 22

While Lucas was cursing Catlin for accepting the attention of Jace Osborn, Catlin stood her ground, speculating on Jace's motive. She searched the hard, leathery face that was poised above her, wrestling with her irrational suspicions. Jace's head came toward hers, his glistening blue eyes focused on her lips. When Catlin turned away, his mouth tightened in annoyance and he retreated a respectable distance.

"I suppose I can't match up to pretty boy Murdock," Jace snorted resentfully.

Catlin's chin came up, meeting those frosty blue eyes that had become as icy as a mountain stream. "What a man is on the inside is what matters most to me," Catlin told him frankly.

Jace seemed to have regained a smidgen of his self-control. The icy disdain faded and he graced her with a smile. "I'm beginning to see that for myself, Cat. As breathtakingly lovely as you are, it is your spunk and fierce determination that fascinates me most."

Slowly, Catlin drew the hand she held behind her around to unfold her palm. She carefully monitored Jace's reaction to the sliced girth strap and the two bullets she revealed to him. But there was no shocked expression in his gaze, only a long steady stare.

"Is that supposed to mean something to me?" Jace questioned somberly.

"Suppose you tell me, Jace," she retorted.

Steel blue eyes locked with probing violet. The silence was as thick as pudding.

"All I can tell you is that you arouse me in ways no other woman ever has," he murmured. "I want you to come away with me, Cat."

"Jace! You and Jesse Lane are on the first night shift," Lucas announced, his sharp voice rolling toward them like a booming cannon.

Jace didn't move, not even a muscle.

"Jace! Now will be soon enough," Lucas demanded impatiently.

Without a word, Jace pivoted on his heels and strided away. Catlin tucked the bullets and strap in her pocket, but her gaze was still riveted on Jace's departing back. She had been confused before she confronted the cool calm . . . whatever or whoever he was. Jace never mentioned his profession to anyone. He could have been a barber or a mortician and no one would have known for certain. And now that Catlin knew this mysterious man was attracted to her, she was more confused than ever.

The thought dissipated when Luke and Jace passed shoulder to shoulder. Catlin longed to rush into Lucas's arms, but he had barely spoken to her the past few weeks. He had closed the door on the past and Catlin couldn't reopen it. It was better this way, Catlin convinced herself. This torment was almost over. It had to be over. But just once more before they parted company she longed to . . . No, she had to be sensible. Sharing Luke's passion just once more would only cause her further anguish. She couldn't bare to leave him with their loving so fresh on her mind.

A muddled frown plowed Luke's brow as he stalked toward Catlin. There was a mist of tears in her eyes.

Bitterly, Lucas glanced over his shoulder at Jace, certain he was the one who had caused this willful beauty to cry. God, how he hated Catlin's tears. They tore him up on the inside and left him feeling helpless and frustrated. Danger he could face unafraid, but this one woman's tears always managed to get to him.

In those few seconds while Lucas was towering over her, peering down at her with eyes like melting chocolate, Cat made her decision. Ordinarily, she sat herself down, sorted through her emotions and thoughts and then arrived at her conclusions. But she had learned the importance of split-second decisions these past three months. Life-threatening encounters had a way of making a person quickly decide what to do and then see it done. And Catlin had made up her mind. She knew what was best for her and Lucas.

Reverently, she uplifted her hand to trace the craggy features of his face. Ah, it was a handsome face that God had lingered over to obtain just the right effect. There was a wild nobility about him. There was no refinement, but plenty of character in those rugged features. Wind and sun had carved the distinct lines that lit up his face when he smiled and cut deep into his tanned features when he frowned. His thick black brows could elevate in amusement in that special endearing way of his. And sometimes his brows flattened out when he was displeased. His full sensuous lips were the most kissable pair she had ever felt playing upon her mouth.

And then of course there was this magnificent body of his, she mused as her appreciative gaze wandered over his muscular torso. Lucas Murdock was scarred by his vindictive enemies, but beneath that bronzed flesh was whipcord muscle. He was a package of well-controlled vitality and potential strength. When he moved he was poetry in motion, a sleek panther who could stalk and pounce with swift efficiency. And more importantly, his strength of character made him a natural born leader who earned other men's respect without demanding it. He was a man among men and he could be both fierce and tender, depending upon his mood.

Catlin would never forget even one detail about this unique man—not the way he moved, the way he smiled, and especially not the incredible way he touched her. Through the tears that swam in her eyes, Catlin managed a smile. She reached up on tiptoe to press trembling lips to that warm full mouth. As her palm lay upon his massive chest, feeling the thud of his heart, she died a little on the inside with each steady beat.

This was good-bye—a parting kiss that spoke volumes without voicing one word. Catlin was giving her heart and her love away, knowing when she left that she would be leaving the very essence of herself behind. But with her, she would carry a satchel of precious memories that could never be replaced. *I love you* was whispered in the soft breath of the kiss she shared with this raven-haired cowboy who had come to mean all things to her. He would be with her always, lingering in the moonshadows and in warm, enticing dreams. . . .

"Doc! Come quick." Bo's voice was brimming with urgency. "Samuel got tangled up in a horse fight."

Lucas growled in torment. He didn't want to leave Catlin, not after she had made him the recipient of such a tantalizing kiss. There was something in the way she was peering up at him through that veil of long moist lashes that worried him.

But turn about was fair play, he supposed. Lucas had cursed Cat up one side and down the other when he found her with Jace. And even though he swore not to spare her another thought, he had returned to send Jace on his way to guard the herd. Now Lucas yearned for a few more minutes of privacy with this violet-eyed enchantress.

"Doc, Sam is hurt pretty bad," Bo called after a moment.

Expelling an exasperated breath, Lucas spun around and jogged away. When he disappeared in the deepening shadows flung by the last rays of sunshine that slipped down the jagged peaks, Catlin wiped away the tears. Resolutely, she ambled back to camp, composing herself along the way.

Since the herd was less than seventy miles from Denver, Catlin had decided it best for her to make the last leg of the journey alone. She wasn't sure what to make of Jace Osborn and she had just said her last good-bye to the man she loved. Emmet Blake would never know what had become of her. Even if he tried to pry information from Lucas he would learn nothing because Lucas wouldn't know where she had gone.

In the cloak of darkness she would gather her belongings and spirit away. And if Jace had been hired to kill her, he would never find her either. And if he wasn't Emmet's henchman, her absence would be the answer he had wanted from her earlier. Again she would resort to disguising herself as a man, using an alias when she stepped on the stage in Denver.

When Catlin returned to camp, the entire group of vaqueros were congregated around Sam Anderson. Although Catlin wanted to know the seriousness of Sam's condition, she was forced to take advantage of the darkness and the distraction. Discreetly, she drew her bedroll from the chuckwagon and laid it behind her saddle. She tied the jeweled ring Lucas had given her on a leather strap and draped it over the hook beside the pots and pans. Taking one of the horses that had been hobbled near the chuckwagon, Catlin slipped away undetected.

A rueful smile rippled across her lips as she glanced back through the stately pines and bushy cedars to view the campfire that flickered in the distance. It seemed as if she had been running away forever. First, she had run from the torment of losing her family and all her worldly possessions in Louisiana. Then she ran from the snarling maniac in San Antonio who had vowed vengeance on anyone she held near and dear to her. Now she was running away from a love that could never be and from Jace Osborn. Catlin still wasn't sure if he was her friend or enemy. But it was for certain that the long trail drive from Texas to Colorado was a closed chapter in her life. She was on her own again and she had profited from her experiences in this man's world. This time perhaps she would make a place for herself in some quiet little corner of the continent and live out her life in peace. Could a woman who had been through so much the past two years dare to hope for more than that? Catlin didn't think so.

Lucas stayed with Samuel Anderson for nearly two hours. From the reports he received, Sam had been helping Jesse Lane check the remuda for stone bruises and chipped hooves that resulted from trekking through rocky terrain. Sam had been doubled over, holding one of the horse's legs up while he trimmed a damaged hoof. Another steed had nipped the brown gelding on the rump. The gelding reacted instinctively by kicking at the mahogany bay with his hind legs. When the gelding dropped his foreleg (the one Sam had been holding) to brace himself for kicking, Sam had been thrown off balance. Before he could gain his feet, the horses scattered and a full-fledged battle between the two mounts broke out. Sam had been trampled by the warring steeds that had inadvertently stepped all over him while they attempted to establish the pecking order of the *caviada*. By the time Jesse and the other vaqueros separated the fighting horses, Sam had been beat all to hell.

Lucas had bandaged Sam's ribs but he was still in severe pain. Every time Lucas tried to leave his side, Sam begged him to stay. Finally, the laudanum took effect and Sam drifted off to sleep. Lucas rose to work the kinks out of his back. When he trudged over to retrieve a cup of coffee he spied the ring dangling on its string.

The agony of realizing why Catlin's violet eyes had been

misted with tears earlier that evening struck him like a physical blow. He hadn't been able to decipher the look on her elegant features at the time and he had been too damned frustrated to try. But Cat had been telling him good-bye in her own quiet way, without inciting an argument. Lucas would have refused to let her strike out on her own if she had stated her intentions. And so she had said nothing. Catlin had kissed him so tenderly that his legs had very nearly folded up beneath him. And while he was distracted, she had left the ring he had given her and she had sneaked away.

An emptiness swelled in the pit of his belly, an emptiness he had endured five years earlier. But this time it was even worse. Lucas had never been intimate with Elise. He had kissed her a few times, touched her briefly. But even the aching of forbidden love didn't hold a candle to the torch of emotions Catlin set off when she rode out of his life without telling him why she had to go. He had come to know that feisty blond-haired imp inside and out. They had been to hell and back together. And she had taken him to paradise each time he enfolded her in his arms. She had been through him like a fire in his blood, and he in hers. He had learned to be sensitive and aware of her needs and her moods and she understood him better than any woman he'd ever known. They had become like two pieces of a living puzzle. And without that daring wildcat, Lucas felt as if he were only half a man.

Damn her! She had made him vulnerable all over again. But this time was ten times worse. The right woman had come along at the right time in his life, but obviously not the right time in *her* life.

Lucas clutched the ring in his fist and cursed under his breath. Hell's bells, Cat may as well have cut out his heart. He couldn't be hurting worse than he was now. . . .

The sound of hooves trotting toward him, jostled Luke from his tormented musings. She had come back! Lucas jerked his head up, but it wasn't the violet-eyed minx who

335

stared down at him. It was one of his vaqueros of Spanish descent.

"Jace Osborn asked me to tell you he was pulling out," the cowboy reported in his thick accent.

"When?" Luke growled. The picture of Jace hovering over Catlin cut him to the quick and even deeper.

"About an hour ago. I took his place on the night watch and then he came by before he rode north."

Something inside Lucas snapped. He didn't have to be clairvoyant to know why Jace had suddenly decided to ride out. He had gone after Catlin! Lucas wasn't blind, after all. He had seen the hostility in Jace's eyes when they had brushed shoulders earlier. Jace wanted Catlin. He couldn't disguise his desire. And now that Catlin had spirited away, Jace was going to make his play for her.

Lucas was prepared to let her go when she was so deadset on it. He had convinced himself that he could learn to accept her wishes. But knowing there was another man waiting to take his place tore Luke to shreds. She was never between men. The moment she cast one man aside there was always another to take his place. Had she requested Jace to follow her? Is that what they were discussing when Lucas interrupted them?

Well, Jace was going to be sorry, Lucas thought bitterly. He would take Luke's place until Cat had no more use for him. Jace would find himself in the same cussed predicament Lucas was in now. Catlin would eventually demand her freedom. Next time it would be Jace who was left behind, just as Lucas had been.

Good riddance to both of them, Lucas muttered acrimoniously. And this time he really wasn't going to spare that wicked witch another thought. If she wanted Jace Osborn she was welcome to him. Luke didn't give a whit what they did. Damn them!

Moonlight shimmered down from the heavens, casting

its silver light on the bare white shoulders of the mountains that reached toward the sky. Below the towering precipice that carried Zebulon Pike's name lay the most remarkable towers of stone Catlin had ever seen. Gigantic slabs of rock rose from the grassy slopes, as if Hercules himself had hurled the huge boulders and stone spikes down from the sky and plunged them into the earth. Catlin was instinctively drawn toward the Garden of the Gods, awed by the towering rock formations that were bathed in the beams of light and skipping moonshadows. She swore she could see various profiles of animals and objects in the rocks. The rugged grandeur and huge size of the scupltured formations that were carved by nature left a warm feeling inside. The beauty of her surroundings helped to ease the sting of closing the door on the past and walking out of Lucas's life forever.

Lost in thought, Catlin walked her weary steed around the towers of stone, inspecting them at close range. There was something pacifying about the looming walls of rock that rose four stories above her. It was here that Catlin chose to make camp.

Employing the technique Lucas had used to start a fire when he was without a tinderbox, Catlin squeezed the trigger of her Colt and watched the flames dance on the kindling. The smell of cedar wood teased Catlin's senses as she propped herself on the ground, using her saddle for her pillow.

For the first time in months, Catlin was alone and had time to sort through her emotions. She missed Lucas terribly and she had only been gone five hours. She had heard it said that time eased the pain of love, but Catlin wondered how much time the authorities on pain and agony were discussing. A week? A year? A lifetime?

The crackling twigs tore Catlin away from her pensive deliberations. Automatically, she reached for her pistol, but the click of another trigger left her hand suspended in midair. Catlin remained paralyzed as a dark figure emerged from the underbrush. Her apprehensive gaze ran the length of the tall lean form and then focused on the barrel of the revolver that was aimed at her chest.

"You are an intelligent woman, Cat. A little too intelligent, I fear," Jace Osborn murmured in a low voice.

Catlin's eyes dropped to the pistol that was only a few inches away from her fingertips. But the Colt may as well have been a mile away for all the good it would do her now.

"Don't try it," Jace advised as he stepped from the shadows, allowing Catlin to see his craggy features.

His expression was grim. "Your suspicions about me were correct," he confirmed.

Catlin gulped hard. Her wide violet eyes were fixed on the pistol that lay in Jace's experienced hand.

"You were right. The girth strap was cut with a bowie knife and left to split apart while you were riding. The rattlesnake in your bedroll was no accident either," he admitted. "I planted it there to make your death appear to be a hazard of the trail drive. And it wasn't another stroke of bad luck that sent you plunging into the Pecos. I purposely collided my horse against yours and I didn't try to save you."

Although Jace's well-disciplined expression gave none of his thoughts away, Catlin was transparent. She didn't appear shocked by his incriminating testimony. Nor was there fear on her delicate features. Her expression was purely inquisitive while she waited for him to continue.

"But if you also assumed the bullet you dug from Murdock's leg was intended for you, then you were wrong," he added in a strange tone that provoked Catlin to frown bemusedly. "I sneaked away from camp during the night to locate you, to do the job Emmet Blake paid me to do. I'm a bounty hunter, Catlin, a gun for hire."

The words dropped like stones in the silence and Catlin's heart ceased beating to hang in her chest like a ton of lead. She had been right after all. Emmet had placed a death wish on her.

"When I found you and Murdock together, lying in each other's arms . . ." His voice trailed off into a wordless scowl and it took him a moment to compose himself. "I trained my rifle on the dirt beside Murdock's leg. If I would have wanted to kill either one of you I could have."

A growl that sounded far too ferocious to be human erupted from the clump of cedars. When Jace instinctively wheeled toward the sound, Catlin took her opportunity to dash to safety. And Catlin didn't look back. She didn't know what kind of beast had sprung from the bushes and she didn't care. That was Jace Osborn's problem. Catlin hoped he was ripped to shreds by the snarling mountain lion, grizzly bear, or whatever it was that had been lying in wait.

Catlin sprang onto her steed and thundered bareback around the gigantic pillars of stone. The sound of the discharging pistol provoked her to gouge her horse in the flanks, forcing him into a faster pace. Catlin rode as if she were pursued by demons, praying she could outrun the bounty hunter Emmet Blake had sent to kill her.

There was no consolation in knowing her darkest suspicions about Jace Osborn were correct. It only drove home the point that Emmet Blake would go to any length to protect himself and to dispose of her. The feud wouldn't end until she or Jace Osborn was wiped from the face of the earth. And if she managed to survive, she wondered if Emmet would send someone else to finish the task Jace had undertaken in his shrewd, inconspicuous way.

Tears streamed down Catlin's cheeks as she raced down the grassy slopes, past the huge pinnacles of stone that rose like specters in the night. Catlin circled southwest, hoping to elude Jace after he finished battling the creature that had attacked him. She didn't care if she ever saw that bounty hunter again. As long as he was alive, her days were numbered!

Catlin blazed down the slopes and then raced her

laboring steed up the gradual incline that was dotted with white fir, Ponderosa pines, and spruces. The trees provided precious cover and Catlin veered through the maze of branches and underbrush. In the dense tree-choked foothills she would find refuge from the hired henchman Emmet Blake had sent to murder her. She would be safe—

Catlin's shocked yelp sent the birds fluttering from their perches in the trees. Steely arms clamped around her, stripping her from her horse. Her breath came out in a "whoosh" when she and her captor crashed to the ground.

It was her good fortune that her fall was cushioned by the body that was plastered against hers. Limp arms fell away and Catlin bounded to her feet like a mountain goat, leaving her unconscious captor where he lay. But Catlin's relief was short-termed. Before she could dash to her horse, another Indian brave pounced from the shadows.

Instinctively, Catlin reached for her pistol and then erupted in a spew of inarticulate curses. Her Colt still lay beside her bedroll. She had been in too much of a rush to escape Jace.

Another shriek burst free when the warrior in buckskins launched himself at her, shoving her to the ground. Catlin emitted an agonized grunt when the Indian brave plunked down on her belly to hold her in place.

Now what would it be? she wondered morosely. Torture? Rape? Both? Catlin wished she hadn't been so hasty in outrunning Jace. He had probably planned to finish her off with a couple of well-aimed bullets. It might have been a quick painless death. But she doubted this renegade Indian would be merciful. She had heard too many horror stories about the savagery of the Indians that had refused to confine themselves to their reservations in Indian Territory. Catlin had the inescapable feeling she was about to discover, first-hand, how Indians violated and dismembered unwelcomed intruders in their domain.

Chapter 23

Jace's harsh features twisted in a sneer when his pistol was knocked from his hand. The Colt flipped end over end before slamming into the redrock wall. Since he had already cocked the trigger, the pistol discharged the instant it collided with the slab of stone. The bullet ricocheted through the clump of cedars from whence the attack had come.

Although the growl that had caught Jace's attention sounded more like a ferocious beast, he found himself attacked by a man whose menacing snarl denoted the full extent of his fury. Jace would have preferred to battle a grizzly bear than the man who had leaped on him. Lucas Murdock's killer instincts were in full force when he threw himself on his intended victim. He thirsted for blood and it was blood he intended to get—Jace's!

Lucas had puffed on his cigarillo and stomped around camp for all of ten minutes, telling himself that Jace was welcome to Catlin Quinn. But ten minutes was as long as his wounded pride could overpower his obsessive need for Catlin. Luke had bounded into the saddle, leaving instructions for Bo to drive the remainder of the herd to Denver. Like a flying carpet, Lucas had sailed across the rolling hills in fast pursuit of the man who was tracking Catlin.

When he spied the campfire, Lucas had folded himself into the underbrush, waiting to hear what Jace had to say. When he learned Jace was the one who had caused Catlin's rash of accidents his temper had snapped and he pounced like a tiger.

The fact that Emmet Blake had sent this bounty hunter after Catlin shocked Lucas to no end. He didn't have the foggiest notion what Catlin had done to provoke Emmet Blake to such drastic measures. But Luke was beginning to understand why Catlin refused to return to Texas. Whatever had transpired between her and Emmet had instilled a rare kind of fear in her. And it must have been something horrifying because Catlin Quinn was not the kind of woman who bounded off like a frightened jack-rabbit at the first sign of trouble. She fought her own battles until defeat was imminent or victory was secured.

Lucas had listened to Jace's condemning testimony as long as he dared before he pounced. Knowing how bold Catlin was, Luke feared she would make an attempt to retrieve her pistol and Jace would kill her where she sat. The thought of watching Catlin being shot down in cold blood provoked Luke to murdering fury. He had thrown himself at Jace, knocking the Colt from his hand and then he proceeded to pelt the bounty hunter with one meaty fist and then another.

But Jace Osborn hadn't survived thirty-five years in his dangerous profession without learning to protect himself with his fists as well as his weapons. He was a formidable challenger who gave as good as he got. When Luke's fist smashed against his jaw, Jace answered with a punishing blow to the midsection.

Like two rabid beasts, snarling and growling, Luke and Jace rolled in the grass. They punched each other with enough force to fell a mountain lion. Flesh cracked against flesh, forcing Jace's breath from his lungs in a pained grunt. The harder Lucas hit him, the more furious

Jace became. For more than a month Jace had harbored the insatiable desire to break every bone in Murdock's handsome face. Then Catlin Quinn wouldn't have found this cussed cowboy so damned attractive. Jace had had no personal vendetta against Luke until the previous month when he backtracked to find Catlin and Lucas lying together beside the Pecos. He found himself ruled by unreasonable jealousy and yet he begrudgingly admired Luke for his resourcefulness and his abilities. They may have even become friends if not for Luke's involvement with that violet-eyed spitfire whom Jace had been sent to kill.

When Lucas delivered a blow that straightened the break in Jace's crooked nose, he swore vehemently. Like a wild man, Jace doubled his fist and sent a stinging "right cross" plowing into Luke's jaw. The fierce blow knocked Lucas from his advantageous position on Jace's belly. Spitting blood, Luke rolled to his feet and lunged at Jace before the bounty hunter could scrape himself off the ground.

Again they rolled down the slope until they slammed into another huge slab of stone that jutted from the hill. They were both a mass of scrapes and bruises—some caused by raking against the jagged rocks and some caused by beefy fists that jarred bone and split flesh.

Hisses and grunts erupted from bloodied lips. Jace and Lucas expended every ounce of strength to counter each brain-scrambling blow and bruising kick. Their spurs were as deadly as their fists and both men employed every tactic of fighting in hand-to-hand combat they had ever learned. They were equally matched and both men were equally determined to walk away the victor. Each time they fell, they staggered back to their feet to level another punishing blow.

Lucas cursed mutinously when Jace managed to drag his wobbly legs beneath him and rise for the umpteenth time. His knuckles were swollen twice their normal size after ramming them into various parts of Jace's anatomy. And even though Jace's arms felt like rubber, he swung wildly to counter the blow that had knocked him to his knees.

Although Lucas tried to remove his sluggish body from the path of the oncoming fist, his reactions were slow and his strength depleted. His head snapped backward when Jace caught him in the chin. Growling, Lucas punched Jace squarely in the nose. The blow caused Jace to pitch forward, but it took the last of Lucas's strength to deliver that final blow from which Jace could not rise. Exhausted, Lucas dropped to his knees to glower poisonously at the bruised and battered bounty hunter.

"You miserable son of a bitch," Lucas hissed into Jace's swollen face. "What kind of a coward is it who hunts down defenseless women?"

"You bastard," Jace spat into Luke's bloody face. By God, this brown-eyed rake wasn't a pretty boy anymore. They both looked like human punching bags. "You didn't let me finish what I was saying to Cat."

"I didn't let you finish Catlin off, once and for all, you mean," Lucas corrected with a volcanic snort.

"No, goddammit, I mean I had no intention of killing her and you didn't let me tell her why," Jace snarled out the side of his mouth that wasn't quite as swollen as the other.

Jace hadn't been allowed to play out his hand. He had it all planned. He intended to throw down his pistol and confess his affection for Catlin. It would have been dramatic and effective and Catlin would have . . . Damn that Lucas Murdock. He had spoiled what would have been a long-awaited moment of privacy with Catlin.

"Now Catlin is gone and she still thinks I want to kill her when, in fact, that's the very last thing I want to do to her."

A muddled frown puckered Luke's brow. "But you said Emmet Blake paid you to dispose of her."

"He did," Jace admitted. "Blake gave me a thousand dollars and a detailed description of the malicious and wily bitch who had shot him in the arm and then, in a fit of jealous rage, set fire to her female rival's home, murdering the father and the young woman who carried her lover's child."

Hell's bells, Lucas swore under his breath. No wonder Catlin had been suffering from horrifying nightmares. No wonder she had lit out of Texas, vowing never to go back. But murder? That didn't sound like something Catlin would do. Ginger Hanley was her friend and Ginger had nothing but kind words about Catlin. Cat was many things—stubborn, willful, headstrong, deliberate, sensible—to name only a few. But she was not a vengeful, fiendish lunatic! Why would she set a torch to her friend's home after she had purchased paint and insisted on helping Ginger redecorate? Why would she deliver supplies and staples to Robert Hanley and then burn him and his daughter to a crisp?

Sweet mercy! What had really happened that night and why had Emmet Blake told this bounty hunter such a vicious lie? It had to be a lie, Lucas assured himself. Catlin wasn't capable of murder.

Jace watched the turmoil of emotions chase each other across Luke's puffy face. "In the beginning I believed Emmet and I tried to take Catlin's life by arranging her accidents. I thought she had played up to you to gain protection. But the more I was around her, the less I believed Blake's story. Something didn't ring true. Instead of devising ways to dispose of her, I began to observe her from a distance."

His steel blue eyes bore into Lucas's unblinking stare. "Catlin Quinn is one helluva woman, more woman than I've ever known. She is capable and daring and gorgeous and I was unwillingly drawn to her. I wanted her alright, but not in a casket. I wanted her in my bed," he added meaningfully. "If she is a murderer, she is the most convincingly deceptive vixen I've ever encountered. But I'd stake my bounty money on the fact that Emmet Blake lied to me and that he had another motive for wanting Catlin dead."

Luke's shoulders slumped in relief. "I can't imagine what his motive could be, but he obviously jumped to the wrong conclusions. Catlin wouldn't kill the woman she called her friend, even if Ginger was carrying my baby."

The comment confirmed Jace's suspicions. "You're the son of a bitch, Murdock," he snarled hatefully. "You're the lover Blake said Catlin had, aren't you? If Cat was my woman, I wouldn't have been dallying with another chit. She deserves better, damn your soul."

Lucas wasn't expecting to be on the receiving end of a lecture on integrity from a ruthless bounty hunter. Obviously, Jace had more scruples than most men in his profession. "Dammit, I knew Ginger long before Cat came to Texas," he defended hotly. "And I can't swear the child Ginger Hanley carried was even mine. I was only intimate with her once."

"For crying out loud, man, how many times do you think it takes to make a baby?" Jace scowled in question.

"That's exactly what Catlin said," Lucas snapped sourly.

"Good for her," Jace snorted. "Maybe you were the one who set fire to the Hanley house to avoid taking responsibility for the girl and her baby."

"I was on the trail by then," Lucas declared in an indignant tone.

"What a convenient alibi," he sniffed, his expression testifying to his lack of faith in Lucas."

"It's the God's truth." Lucas glared flaming arrows at the infuriating bounty hunter. "And speaking of trying to dispose of someone, why the hell did you shoot me?"

"You're a reasonably intelligent man. You figure it out," Jace growled.

"You jealous bastard," Lucas snarled when he put two and two together.

"It was obvious Cat cared for you. When I found the two of you together, doing what I wanted to do with that shapely minx, I wanted to kill you. The fact is I only intended to scare you off, but the bullet ricocheted into your leg. And the truth is I wasn't all that sorry I didn't miss you as I had originally planned."

Jace raked Lucas with blatant disgust. "When you were ambling around camp, you avoided Catlin like the plague. And then at night you stole off to pleasure yourself with her. You treated her like a whore, Murdock. I was damned sick of it!" he roared. "You're lucky it wasn't my intention to blow your cussed head off!"

The vision of Catlin and Lucas together provoked Jace to throw another punch—one that Lucas deflected with his forearm.

"You curse me for touching her, but you would have been doing the same thing right now if you had had the chance," Lucas harshly accused.

"But I would have married her and I would have taken her anywhere she wanted to go—as far away from Emmet Blake as possible. I wouldn't have treated her like my convenient concubine, brushing her aside until lust overcame me. You seemed to be either hot or cold, never in between with Cat. She deserves more respect than she has been receiving from a womanizer like you!"

Hot and cold? Lucas would have laughed out loud if his lips and ribs weren't killing him. It may have seemed hot and cold to Jace. But on the inside, Lucas had always been on fire for that minx, even if he refused to expose his feelings to the rest of the men.

"I wanted to marry that she-cat," Lucas informed him

curtly. "But she refused. She wouldn't tell me why she left Texas, but she swore she wasn't going back. What the hell was I supposed to do?"

"That's your problem, not mine, Murdock," Jace scowled, his voice nowhere near sympathetic. "You lost her and now it's my turn to win her. And if you hadn't jumped me when you did, I might have been able to make her understand that I had been deceived and that I would never hurt her again."

Lucas's thick brows formed a line across his forehead. "You aren't taking her away from me," he growled threateningly.

"Just hide and watch me," Jace scoffed. "You had your chance."

"I'd kill myself before I would lose Cat to someone like you," Lucas sniffed distastefully.

"Would you like to borrow my pistol?" Jace offered sarcastically.

Lucas speared him with a glance that was meant to maim.

"When I catch up with Cat, I'll treat her the way a lady ought to be treated." With considerable effort, Jace dragged himself to his knees.

Lucas did likewise. "What the hell do you know about treating a lady like a lady, Osborn? Cat is probably the first one who ever let you near her."

"That isn't my fault," Jace defended huffily. "I've had a hard life. I've been on my own since I was ten years old, living by my wits and my guns. And I can't help it that I wasn't born with your pretty face and your ability to charm women with the wink of an eye!"

"My life hasn't exactly been a bowl of cherries either," Lucas muttered as he staggered to his feet. After he ripped open what was left of his shirt, he gestured to the unsightly scars that crisscrossed his chest and back.

"What the hell happened to you?" Jace chirped, his astonished gaze riveted on Lucas's marred chest.

"I survived the lashes and cuts given by a pack of Yankee guerrillas who tried to torture information out of me. When I wouldn't tell them what they wanted to know they left me for dead. A pretty boy?" Luke laughed bitterly. "I have more seams than a waistcoat. It was two years before I found the nerve to go near a woman for fear she would be offended by my hideous scars."

"Well at least you didn't get stuck with this face," Jace countered resentfully. "Not many decent women can get past my looks to determine if I have any saving graces. I shouldn't have to be the one to tell you that Catlin Quinn looks deeper than exterior beauty. She may even come to love me if you would back off and give me half a chance with her."

"I'm not sure I like you well enough to do you any favors, Osborn," Lucas sneered as he weaved over to retrieve Catlin's abandoned pistol.

Lucas was silent for a long moment. Pensively, he brushed his finger over her discarded revolver and stared at the satchels she had left behind in her haste to elude Jace. Finally, he raised dark eyes to meet the icy pools of blue. "If it was anyone but Cat I might be more lenient in letting you make a play for her," he admitted in a less hostile tone.

Jace bent down to scoop his hat and Colt off the ground. The semblance of a smile touched his blood-caked lip. "Face it, Murdock, you've already lost her. Catlin isn't going back to Texas. I don't know for certain what happened in San Antonio, but if she refused to marry you because of it, she isn't likely to change her mind at this late date. I can offer her a haven from the nightmares, but you intend to tote her back to them. Go back to your herd, Murdock," Jace advised. "I'll track Catlin. That's what I do best."

If Lucas could have mustered the strength he would have knocked Jace flat. As it was, he barely had the energy to hold himself upright. Every bone and muscle screamed in pain after his knock-down-drag-out fight with his equal match.

"I'm not letting Catlin go," Lucas informed him in no uncertain terms.

"Neither am I," Jace declared with great conviction.

"She won't let you near her," Lucas mocked. "She still thinks you want to kill her."

"She wants nothing more to do with you either," Jace predicted. "If she did, she wouldn't have left camp and struck out on her own."

"I'm still going after her," Lucas grumbled, stamping toward the horse he had left tethered in the brush.

"So am I," Jace proclaimed as he propelled himself toward his steed.

"Just don't get in my way," Lucas advised.

"And you stay the hell out of my way," Jace snapped.

With their warnings issued, both men swung into their saddles to follow Catlin's tracks. Jace was a master at finding people who didn't wish to be found. And Lucas was an expert at trailing human or beast. Naturally, they both wound up like two bloodhounds sniffing the same scent. Like it or not (and neither of them did), they wound up riding side by side, trailing the hoof prints left by Catlin's steed.

A grim frown clouded Lucas's brow when he held up his improvised torch to detect the evidence of a scuffle in the clump of pines. Broken limbs dangled from the trees. The nest of pine cones and needles beneath the trees had been scattered hither and yon. Two sets of moccasin tracks were imprinted in the soft grass beside Catlin's boot prints.

"Cheyenne Indians," Lucas breathed in frustration.

"Brilliant deduction," Jace said flippantly. He reached down to scoop up the feather that lay among the cones. The Cheyenne always used turkey feathers for the quills of their arrows. Everybody knew that. "I'm sure those redskins just stopped Catlin to ask directions."

Lucas flung Jace a withering glance. "Your concern for her welfare is touching."

"I'm worried as hell," Jace retaliated. "I'm only mocking your statement of the obvious. And if you hadn't blundered into camp when you did, Cat would be safe with me. It's your fault she ran headlong into the Cheyenne."

"You'll never convince Catlin that you have her best interest at heart, even if she lives long enough for you to explain yourself. After all, why should she believe a man who tried to kill her thrice?"

"Don't press your luck, Murdock," Jace warned, casting his companion the evil eye. "I've had just about enough of your taunts."

"Don't badger me and I won't hassle you, Osborn," Lucas muttered in an ominous tone. "I'm not the least bit pleased to be sharing the same space with you."

"The feeling is mutual, Murdock. I have yet to figure out what Catlin saw in you in the first place."

"I happen to love her," Lucas bit off.

"So do I," Jace snapped in the same defensive tone. "And I was all set to tell her so when you jumped me."

Cautiously, both men picked their way through the pines, unsure what gruesome sight awaited them. After finding the broken limb with blood caked on it, Lucas's imagination was running wild. He could envision Catlin suffering through every torture devised by Indians. After the massacre of Black Kettle's clan at Sand Creek, the Cheyenne band was extremely hostile toward whites.

The harassment of settlers in this area had decreased after the government relocated the tribe in Indian Territory. But there were many bands of Cheyenne who resisted the move from their hunting grounds. A man never knew if the braves he happened onto were still harboring vendettas or if they were simply hunting game on their familiar stomping ground. If Catlin had been captured she was probably scared to death or mad as hell. She never did take kindly to anyone deterring her when she was bent on her purpose. God, he just hoped Cat lived long enough to have a purpose left! If he found her tortured to death, he might as well throw himself off a mountain. Living without her would be nothing short of hell.

Would he ever learn what had really happened in San Antonio? he asked himself as he trailed southwest, unable to find tracks on the hard ground of the mountain meadow. From the look of things, Catlin wouldn't be around to tell him her side of the story. Damn her! She had better not get herself killed. He wasn't ready to give her up. All the love he had kept bottled up inside him sought release and he would go mad if that violet-eyed vixen met with disaster.

Cat had expended one too many of her nine lives after courting one catastrophe after another. He could only pray that she-cat had one life left. And if she didn't . . .

His glaze flickered over Jace's lean frame and then Lucas growled to himself. When two men wanted the same woman, one of them had to lose. Lucas had lost once and he had no intention of doing so again. Jace Osborn was obviously man enough to protect a feisty misfit like Catlin but—

"Don't look at me like that," Jace commanded crankily.

"Like what?" Lucas questioned in a grouchy tone.

"Like you wish I'd drop out of sight and leave Catlin all to you."

"Hell's bells, wouldn't you know I'd get stuck with a clairvoyant bounty hunter," Lucas snorted sarcastically.

"I'm not backing off when we catch up with her," Jace assured him in an unrelenting tone.

"Neither am I, Osborn."

Casting each other venomous glances, Lucas and Jace trekked across the meadow, searching for signs that would lead them to the Cheyenne braves who had attacked Catlin.

Chapter 24

Catlin swore she was about to lose her scalp when the second Indian plopped down on her midsection. While he sat there snarling down at her like a starved cougar, Catlin groped for an improvised weapon and had found it in the form of a broken limb—one big enough to crack the man's skull if need be. And there definitely was a need!

With the quickness of a striking snake, Catlin clubbed her assailant and watched in relief as he toppled sideways. Sending a prayer of thanks to heaven, Catlin wriggled free from the limp legs that lay across her hips. Rounding up all three horses, she picked her way through the rocky terrain, searching for refuge from the two Cheyenne warriors. Her gaze focused on the thick clump of trees and the two huge mounds of rocks that glowed in the moonlight. When the winding path that led up the granite mountain became too narrow for the horses, Catlin grabbed the blankets off the Indian ponies and scurried along the perilous ledge that was skirted by scraggly cedars.

Locating a high vantage point, Catlin tucked herself in the blankets in a crevice in the rocks. The spot she had selected left very little room for lying down so she propped herself against the granite wall to catch a few moments of sleep. The sound of rushing water in the distance lulled her into dreams and finally Catlin gave way to her exhaustion.

When the sun peaked over the stone walls that towered around her, Catlin pried open her eyes and gasped in dismay. Her gaze dropped down a thousand feet to the canyon floor beneath her. The darkness had hidden the precariousness of her position the previous night. But in broad daylight, Catlin could see that one false move on crumbling rock could send her plummeting to her death. That gruesome thought caused her stomach to flip-flop and she instinctively shrank away from the perpendicular wall. Her wide-eyed gaze followed the narrow chasm which was concealed by the jagged rocks and jutting trees that towered another five hundred feet above her. Enthralled by the panorama of the canyon, Catlin drew her feet beneath her to explore the chasm she had accidentally wandered into. The incessant murmur of water lured her to follow the treacherous path that eventually wound down to the floor of the gorge.

Catlin walked the mile's length of the chasm, her head lifted in wonderment. She marveled at the ominous stone walls and the splattering of trees that rose more than fifteen hundred feet on either side of her. The canyon offered the most panoramic scenery Catlin had ever seen. Mother Nature had outdone herself when she carved this magnificent chasm of granite and dotted it with a smattering of fir, cedar and pines that grew from the floor of the narrow valley and from the crevice in the rocks.

Spellbound, Catlin wound her way through the V-shaped dell to locate the source of the murmuring water that had called to her. And there at the head of the picturesque canyon wasn't just one magnificent waterfall, but rather a series of seven beautiful cascades that bubbled and tumbled their way down the jutting rocks to the base of the chasm, forming a sparkling blue pool. The melting snow and springs from higher elevations poured from the upper rim of the chasm like a pitcher of stars streaming down from the heavens. Catlin was awestruck by the roaring cascades that spilled over nature's ladder of rock to splash in the pool and flowing river below.

Enthralled by this haven she had discovered, Catlin weaved her way up the rocks and trees that lay beside the rumbling falls. Just as she eased onto a stone slab to enjoy a closer view of the seven falls, she spied the figure of a man poised beside the pool.

The sight of the swarthy form caused her heart to swell with pleasure. Lucas! He must have tracked her from camp. Catlin didn't have the foggiest notion how he had found her, but she was ever so glad to see him, to share the beauty of the surroundings with him. Reversing direction, Catlin scuttled down the rocky slope, clinging to the protruding tree limbs for support. A radiant smile hovered on her lips as she inched down the last boulder. Before she found solid footing a pair of arms enfolded her from behind and carefully set her to her feet.

Catlin twisted to fling her arms around his neck. "Lucas, how did you . . . ?"

Her smile transformed into a shocked gasp when she found herself face to face with Jace Osborn. Catlin came unglued, writhing and twisting for freedom. Her eyes had obviously deceived her! She had scurried down the rocks to throw herself into the arms of the man who had been sent to dispose of her.

"Cat, I'm not going to hurt you," Jace muttered, trying desperately to cling to the wiggling bundle of femininity.

"Catlin!" Lucas's sharp booming voice caused her to freeze in midstruggle.

"He was purposely sent here and he wants to kill me!" she shrieked when her frantic gaze landed on Lucas who stepped from the clump of trees and brush. Where the blazes had Jace come from? Had he deceived Lucas into thinking he wanted to help track Catlin down before she got into more trouble?

"No, he doesn't," Lucas contradicted.

"Oh, yes, he does!" Catlin squawked, struggling in earnest.

"No, I don't!" Jace blared as he clutched Catlin against his lean frame. "You didn't let me finish what I was trying to tell you."

"Lucas!" Catlin railed in exasperation. Blast it, why didn't he do something before Jace stabbed her in the back with his bowie knife?

"He's telling you the truth," Lucas assured her solemnly. His gaze darted to Jace. "Let her go."

Reluctantly, Jace released her and she flew into Lucas's outstretched arms like a homing pigeon returning to roost. Lucas had no idea how she had eluded the Cheyenne, but he reminded himself that this resourceful minx usually managed to escape disaster, somehow or another. Tenderly, Lucas cradled her against him, thankful she was still in one piece—however she had managed the feat.

The look Catlin flung Jace when she peeked up from Lucas's shoulder, cut him to shreds. "I don't want to hurt you," Jace assured her softly. "It's true that Emmet Blake sent me to dispose of you for crimes he told me you had committed. He said you were wily and treacherous and that you had shot him and then set the Hanley house on fire in a jealous rage."

"That isn't true," Catlin protested hotly.

A gentle smile softened Jace's hard features. "I figured that out after I got to know you, Catlin. It was then that I stopped inventing accidents to befall you and started protecting you. I was trying to explain that to you when Murdock pounced on me like a crazed leopard."

Catlin's owlish gaze bounced back and forth between Jace's bruised face and Lucas's battered one. They both looked as if they had gone several rounds with a grizzly bear and lost. Confusion etched her brow as she regarded first one man and then the other.

"When I realized you couldn't have done the horrible things Blake said you had done, I discovered something else . . ." Jace murmured with a smile.

Before Jace could woo her with his confession, Lucas grabbed her by the elbows and peered into those lavender eyes that reminded him of the delicate columbine flowers that grew wild in the mountain meadows. "Jace has told me everything he knows about the incident that sent you fleeing from Texas. Now I want the truth, Cat—all of it."

Catlin was as closemouthed as ever. She had made a vow she had to keep—for Luke and Martha's sake. The fact that Emmet had hired Jace and plied him with lies was proof enough that she couldn't win against that maniac who knew how to throw his weight around.

Lucas was becoming more frustrated by the second. He gave Cat a firm shake, snapping her head backwards, sending the tangled mane of sandy blond hair rippling over her shoulders. "Dammit, I want the truth, Cat," he all but yelled at her. His stormy brown eyes drilled into her. "Start at the beginning and don't leave anything out!"

"She doesn't have to tell you anything if she doesn't want to, " Jace cut in, stamping forward to rip Lucas's hands from Catlin's forearms.

Jace's affectinate gaze dropped to Catlin's exquisite face. "I'll take you anywhere you want to go, Cat. You and I can begin a new life. I'll wire Blake and tell him I succeeded in my mission. We'll take the bounty money he paid me and make a fresh start anywhere you say."

Catlin blinked bewilderedly. He really meant it!

"I want you with me," Jace insisted, his voice raspy with emotion. "I've never met a woman like you. I love you."

"Don't listen to him," Lucas blared in exasperation as he pushed Jace out of the way. "Don't throw away what we have together. Tell me what happened in San Antonio and I'll make it right again."

Her anguished gaze lanced off Jace and then Lucas who were busy trying to shove each other out of the way. Jace was offering her protection and a new life. She was flattered by his admission. She could never love Jace the way she loved Lucas, but he—

"Cat, for God's sake, when are you going to stop running?" Lucas growled as he elbowed Jace in the midsection and then yanked Catlin to him to breathe down her neck. "You pulled up roots in Louisiana when your land was sold out from under you. And then you pulled up stakes in Texas to go west when you found yourself in another battle you couldn't win. What happens if you clash with another impossible situation that you refuse to let Jace handle for you? Will you run again?"

"I can't tell you what you want to know. If I do, he'll have you killed, too!" Catlin blurted out, her eyes full of anguish. "I can't go back and I refuse to jeopardize your life as well as Aunt Martha's."

"Then it's resolved," Jace declared, dragging Catlin away from Luke. "Catlin goes with me. Emmet will be none the wiser."

"She's not running away again," Lucas snapped, prying her loose from Jace's grasp.

Catlin felt like a yo-yo and her temper finally got the best of her. "I'm not going anywhere with anyone!" she announced in a stern tone.

"You are going to let your aunt live with the humiliation that her niece is a murderess?" Lucas growled in question.

"At least she will live," Catlin muttered.

"You keep saying that, but you're making no sense." Lucas threw up his hands in a gesture of futility. "What exactly do you think you are saving me and Martha from?"

"From Emmet Blake—" Catlin could have bit off her tongue. Desperate, she shot toward Jace to curl her arm around his elbow. "I've decided to go with you."

Jace beamed like a lantern on a long wick.

"No, you aren't," Lucas bellowed at her as if she were deaf.

"She made her decision. Now leave her be," Jace gloated.

"If you don't tell me what Emmet Blake has to do with this, I'll ask him myself and if I don't get a satisfactory answer I won't let up on him until I do," Luke vowed fiercely.

"If you dare cross him you won't live to enjoy owning the Flying Spur," Catlin flared.

With tremendous effort, Lucas tugged on the trailing reins of his temper and expelled a deep sigh. His dark eyes riveted on Jace. "Give me a few minutes alone with Cat," he requested. "If she is still certain that running is the only answer, I will make no more attempts to intervene."

For a long moment, Jace and Lucas stared each other down. Jace would have preferred to rip off an arm than to leave this charismatic rake alone with Catlin. Murdock held some strange power over her and Jace didn't want to lose this violet-eyed beauty.

"Please, Jace," Lucas murmured beseechingly.

Heaving a deflated sigh, Jace pressed a kiss to Catlin's brow. Casting Lucas a fleeting glance, Jace reluctantly pivoted on his heels to stride along the narrow trail that led up the towering granite walls of the chasm. It took every ounce of will power to walk away, leaving Catlin with Lucas. Pretty boy Murdock could be very persuasive when he turned on his charm. Damn him. He had better not change Cat's mind!

When Lucas did as Jace predicted, Catlin very nearly melted on the spot. The look he gave her sparked the intimate memories that lay buried in shallow graves. He didn't touch her but he might as well have. Those potent brown eyes roved over her in a possessive caress that threatened to shatter her self-control. Being alone with Lucas in such a place as this made gashes in her firm resolve. The canyon with its seven spectacular falls, complimented by the one man who could ignite fires in her blood, was a combination that was impossible to resist.

Deliberately, Lucas closed the space between them, holding her hostage with his penetrating gaze. Catlin anticipated the feel of his arms enfolding her, the warm intense pressure of his lips rolling upon hers. But suddenly his expression changed to a cold accusing stare that knocked her sideways.

"I will never be able to understand why you killed the only friend you had in San Antonio," he growled in a hateful tone. "And I'm not sure I could ever forgive you for it. Maybe it is best that you trot off with Jace."

His drastic tactic proved effective. Catlin was already rattled by his devastating presence and the fact that he knew more about the incident in San Antonio than she wanted him to. And of all the things she had expected him to say, that wasn't even on the list! He couldn't have hurt her more if he had pounded her flat with a sledgehammer. While she was totally vulnerable, Lucas had slashed her legs out from under her with his cruel, condemning remark.

"I didn't kill Ginger," she protested, wounded by his accusation. Although Catlin fought the vision, the horrible nightmare flared up to torment her. Her body shook like an earthquake. "I didn't kill her. I tried to save her, to save myself."

The dam of self-control broke and tears came pouring out like a cloudburst. Even the deep breath Catlin inhaled didn't help, not when Lucas glowered disgustedly at her.

"Spare me the sobs, Cat," he scoffed, forcing himself not

to buckle to the stream of tears. Lucas didn't care what he had to do to pry the truth from her. This time he wasn't letting up on her until he knew what happened. "Is that why you shot Emmet? Because he tried to stop you from murdering the Hanleys?"

"No!" Catlin wailed in denial.

Lucas knew he was being cruel by forcing her to confront the specters that haunted her. And even as condemning as he had been, Catlin still hadn't spilled her confession. God, he hated doing this to her, but there seemed no other way. Whatever had happened had struck incredible fear in this courageous woman. She was frightened by the memories. Lucas could see that emotion reflected in those animated violet eyes that shimmered with tears.

"Emmet discovered what you intended to do and so you tried to dispose of him," Lucas sneered at her.

"I didn't shoot him," Catlin vehemently contested. "I tried to stop him from slashing Ginger with his scalpel, but he did anyway. Ginger was overwrought with grief. She had accused Emmet of poisoning her father and she—"

Catlin's knees buckled and so did the last bulwark of self-control. The nightmare came at her in full force. Through wrenching sobs that threatened to tear out Luke's heart, Catlin watched the terrible incident explode before her very eyes.

Lord, he wanted to hold her to him, to console her. But he couldn't yet, not until she told him everything he wanted to know.

"Was it because Ginger carried my child that you wanted her dead?" Lucas prodded when she didn't continue. "Was that what put you in a jealous rage?"

Catlin was so frustrated that she wanted to shake Lucas until his teeth rattled. He was making her more furious and upset by the minute and all she could do was blubber through the unrestrained tears that scalded her cheeks.

"I wasn't in a rage," she sobbed hysterically. "When Emmet told me Ginger was carrying your baby, I went to inform her that you had written to me denouncing our engagement."

Lucas inwardly cringed. Even though his well-disciplined mask remained in place while Catlin fell apart at the seams, he bled for her. She had lied for Ginger's sake and she had probably intended to leave town when she learned Ginger was pregnant. In her own self-sacrificing way she would have seen to it that he assumed his responsibility.

"I was in town when Ginger stormed into Emmet's office. She . . . she . . . confronted him with a gun," Catlin explained through soul-racking tears. "I tried to stop her, but . . . but she and Emmet were both crazed with anger. Ginger grazed Emmet's arm with a bullet and . . . he slashed her with his scalpel and then shot her in the leg. I tried to get her away from him, but he followed us to the house. I . . . I . . . tried to reason with him. . . ."

The nightmare flashed before her like a lightning bolt and Catlin shuddered. "Emmet forced me to accompany him into the house, leaving Ginger unconscious in the carriage. Then he struck me with his pistol."

Lucas caught himself the split-second before he rushed over to scoop Catlin's quaking body into his arms. Crestfallen, she sank down to her knees. Tears boiled down her cheeks and her doubled fists clenched so tightly together that her knuckles turned white. Never in all his dealings with this proud, stubborn beauty had he seen her so shaken and vulnerable. It killed him to watch her crumple before his eyes. But Lucas willed himself to stand his ground until the last of her carefully guarded secret poured out.

"While I was unconscious, Emmet must have carried Ginger inside and then set the house ablaze." Her shoulders quivered as her haunted gaze lifted, spilling another river of tears. "When I awoke the house was fogged with smoke and flames billowed like the fires of hell. I could do nothing but crawl out the door before the blazing rafters collapsed. When Emmet saw me outside he took a shot at me, but I managed to escape in the buggy. He pursued me, screaming murderous curses, promising to destroy you and Martha if I dared to show my face in town."

The utter helplessness in her wild-eyed gaze slit Luke's heart in two.

"I . . . I couldn't fight him, Lucas," she sobbed as she sank back on her heels and covered her tear-stained face with her hands. "It was his word against mine. What chance would I have had against the doctor who owns half the town? Twice he has tried to kill me—once in the fire and then by plying Jace with lies. He'll turn his bizarre brand of vengeance against me upon you and Martha. He swore he would. . . ."

Catlin could no longer speak. With a blood-curdling scream she watched the raging fire engulf the home, just as it had so often in her nightmares. Trembling uncontrollably, she doubled over to wail in hysterical sobs, releasing all the pent-up emotion that had tormented her for three months.

Lucas couldn't stand another second of watching Catlin succumb to the horror of reliving her nightmare. He dropped to his knees, drawing her shuddering body against his. Enfolding her, he rocked her, cradling her while she cried. He could feel the emotion undulating through her as she clung to him, spilling even more tears of grief and frustration.

When a long shadow fell over him, Lucas glanced up with tormented eyes to meet Jace's grim expression. Jace had heared Cat's emotional rendition of the incident and he cursed himself a dozen times over for his attempts on

363

her life. God, how he wished he was the one who was consoling Catlin while she grieved. But she was where she wanted to be. Even if Jace convinced her to ride off into the sunset with him, he knew he could never take Luke's place in her heart. She loved Lucas enough to sacrifice her affection for him by running away. She had been trying to protect him from the madman who had come dangerously close to taking her life by his own hand, as well as Jace's.

The look the two men exchanged needed no translation. A rueful smile bordered Jace's lips as his blue eyes drank in Catlin's curvaceous figure. When Lucas stared at Jace, he could see himself turn and walk away as he had done five years ago. He knew what was running through Jace's mind when he silently relinquished his claim on Catlin. Luke coud feel Jace's loss and he knew, full well, the sacrifice this gunslinger had just made when he silently reversed direction and strided through Cheyenne Canyon to retrieve his horse.

As Lucas soothed Catlin, he found himself wondering how long Jace would carry his torch for this feisty beauty. Lucas sympathized with Jace. He had endured what Jace was enduring now.

Oh, Jace would list all the consoling platitudes the next few months, Luke predicted. Jace would congratulate himself for being noble. But deep down inside, beneath that calloused exterior, Jace would bleed. His dreams would center around a pair of enchanting violet eyes that rivaled the beauty of the columbine—that wild, windswept flower with its white and lavender petals that swayed on the Colorado hillside. Jace would see that lustrous mane of blond hair waving in the breeze. He would close his eyes and inhale the subtle feminine fragrance that clung to him and then he would lament his loss. And when the memories swelled out of proportion and loneliness got the best of him, Jace would sit himself down with a bottle of whiskey and drink until he couldn't think or feel or see. . . .

"Lucas, what am I to do?" Catlin sobbed against his already damp shirt. "By telling you, I have condemned you. Emmet was right. I have poisoned every life I have touched."

Adoringly, Lucas cupped her tear-stained face in his hands, lifting her agonized gaze to his comforting smile. "The blame lays with me, violet eyes, not with you. You tried to right my wrong, to protect Ginger and me and your aunt. But you should have let me bear your burden instead of concealing it from me." Ever so slowly, he bent his ruffled raven head to take her trembling lips under his. "This is one battle you and I are going to fight together," he insisted huskily.

"But it's still Emmet's word against mine," she choked out.

"He'll pay for the torment he put you through," Luke promised.

Catlin gave her head a denying shake, sending the wild tendrils rippling around her. "I'll go on paying," she faltered. "You weren't there, Lucas. You didn't see the demented look in his eyes. You didn't hear him screeching at me like a madman. Emmet has convinced himself that I am to blame for the horrendous disaster. The moment I set foot in town he will have me arrested and hanged by a lynch mob. He will stand on his reputation and twist the truth so convincingly that you won't recognize it."

"Sh . . ." He pressed his index finger to her quivering lips. "I'll make sure he comes to us—on our terms. Just trust me . . . for once. We'll see this matter through."

For the moment, Catlin let herself believe him because she had run out of arguments. Lucas countered her every protest in that quiet, comforting voice that could chase her fears away, at least for a time. She had been through the gamut of emotions for more than three months. She had harbored her love for Luke, mustering her courage in the face of one unexpected pitfall after another. But now that all the walls had come tumbling down, Catlin had no strength left to fight. She had revealed her carefully guarded secret. And once she freed her fears and feelings there was nothing more to hide. She needed Luke to hold her until she regained her composure. The upheaval had turned her wrong side out.

"Stay with me, violet eyes," he whispered against her petal-soft lips. "We will get through this together."

Catlin gave herself up to the magic of his tender kisses and soul-shattering caresses. She was vulnerable and receptive and she needed to feel whole and alive again. The turmoil of divulging the tormenting incident that had caused her such fear, grief and heartache was still too fresh on her mind.

When Lucas drew her down beside him in the plush grass, Catlin couldn't have found the will to resist, even if her life depended on it. The feel of his skillful hands gliding beneath her shirt to make scintillating contact with her bare flesh took her breath away. The soft whisper of his kisses was like an incantation of magic. The nightmares evaporated in the fog of pleasure. This mystical wizard could chase the world away with his masterful lovemaking.

As Lucas greeted every inch of exposed flesh with worshipping kisses and deliberate caresses, Catlin cried in the sheer joy of recapturing the splendor she thought she had lost forever. He made her body sing out with rapture, made her pulse beat in the rhythm of a melody that had become ingrained on her mind, body, and soul. Over and over again, his wandering hands floated over her quivering skin. The roar of Seven Falls faded into oblivion and the blue sky turned as black as pitch. The gigantic granite walls of Cheyenne Canyon shrank to be replaced by the bruised but undeniably handsome face that hovered so close to hers.

It was a reverent coming together, a precious moment in time. Flesh became flesh and one heart beat only for another. When his muscular body covered hers, Catlin experienced the most exquisite ecstasy imaginable. She was gently lifted from one cloud to another, allowed to revel in each wondrous sensation before she drifted to a higher pinnacle. She could feel the sweet rhapsody of love burgeoning inside her. The crescendo swelled, beating louder and louder until every fiber of her being vibrated like harp strings.

And then, like flower petals opening to the warmth of the sun, Catlin basked in the glorious pleasure of loving and being loved. And like weightless feathers fluttering back to earth, Catlin sank back into the grass.

Lucas thought he had experienced it all, but there was something in the way Catlin had responded to him that left him spellbound. At times, the passion between them flared like a wildfire, engulfing all within its path. But this time it had taken on the most remarkable quality of tenderness. The love he felt for her had tempered his savage passions and he had discovered sublime satisfaction by reveling in each sweet, tender moment.

It was as if he had grasped that one special instant that pursued and captured perfection. No one could stir him the way this amethyst-eyed beauty could. They were one beating, breathing essence. She was a part of him and he was a part of her. They were harmony in its purest form. Lucas had never been as content as he was now, never so satisfied to be anywhere as he was in this magnificent canyon with this irreplaceable woman.

The Flying Spur and his dreams of success didn't matter quite so much as they once had because he had employed his aspirations to prove he could find happiness without Elise in his life. But all he really needed was this spirited nymph in his arms.

Emmet Blake wasn't taking Catlin away from him, he

promised himself fiercely. Emmet had made Cat's life a living hell. He had laden her with guilt and fear, the likes she had never known. He had been cruel and unreasonable and Lucas vowed, then and there, that Catlin would never again suffer because of Emmet Blake.

Lucas was the one to blame for Catlin's torment. His recklessness had affected too many lives. Catlin had been caught in the middle, fighting his battle for him. But she wasn't running from Emmet ever again, not because of or in spite of Lucas. It would take a month to trek back to Texas. In that amount of time he would figure out a way to handle Emmet Blake, to counter his vicious lies.

When Lucas peered down into Catlin's delicate face he forgot all except the powers of passion embroidered with love. He had but to look at this feisty elf and it drove him over the edge. He could feel her pliant body imprinted on his and he went hot all over. Like an eternal spring, passion bubbled forth and Lucas allowed himself to be swept away in the emotions this stunning blond so easily aroused in him.

"I feel like loving you again . . ." he rasped as he drank the intoxicating nectar of her lips. "And again . . ."

Catlin swore she was tumbling down the succession of cascades that toppled from the rim of the canyon when Luke's caresses swirled around the crests of her breasts. His moist lips whispered over her cheeks and eyelids before gliding over the column of her throat. His touch was as light and gentle as a butterfly's wing. But the sensations triggered by his tantalizing touch sent out a fleet of tidal waves. Catlin barely had time to recover from the titillating currents of passion before she was buffeted by another frothy wave.

And this time their lovemaking was explosive. First they had savored each other and now they devoured. It was different and yet always the same when passion left them spinning in a whirlpool of all-consuming emotion. No words could describe the splendorous release of pleasure, the incredible sensations that accompanied their lovemaking.

Catlin pitied anyone who had never fully enjoyed the sublime revelation of love. One just had to be there to understand. And even then, the experience defied words. How did one describe holding a sun beam in one's hand, watching it sparkle with its own mystique? How did one explain the glorious beauty of this panoramic chasm and its sparkling waterfalls without doing such grandeur an injustice? It was simply a feeling way down deep inside that had to be experienced before it could be comprehended.

But Lucas understood perfectly well and that's why the kiss Cat bestowed on him in the aftermath of love knocked the props out from under him. He swore he had died and gone to heaven. There were no more secrets between them now. They would face Emmet Blake together and he would answer for his villainous crimes. But until that time, Lucas was going to enjoy the beauty of Seven Falls and Cheyenne Canyon with this one very special woman.

Much later, after Lucas had dozed in the warm sunshine and then dived into the cold pool that lay below the bubbling falls, he led Catlin up the rocky slope to enjoy a bird's eye view of the canyon floor, the waterfalls were even more spectacular. To the southwest, the sprawling valleys reached toward the deep purple shadows cast by the ridge of mountains. And to the northeast lay the magnificent canyon where they had loved the afternoon away.

"It's beautiful," Catlin breathed in appreciation. Her wide eyes swept from the canyon to the graceful flood of grasses and wild flowers that stretched out before them. A radiant smile captured her features as she looped her arms over Luke's broad shoulders. Reaching up on tiptoe, she pressed a steamy kiss to his lips. "Let's stay here forever and ever."

Lucas darted her a grin and then returned her kiss. "We'll come back next year." He felt her body tense beneath his wandering caresses. "There will be a next year, Cat," he assured her. "Don't let your apprehension spoil our time together." A teasing smile quirked his lips as he made a wide sweeping gesture with his arm. "How can you have a care in the world with this spectacular view to greet you?"

He was absolutely right, Catlin decided. It was important to live each moment to the fullest. She had Lucas and the most magnificent mile of scenery in the world. Who could ask for anything more?

"There is something inspiring about this point of rock," Lucas was saying as he drank in the plummeting falls, enchanting canyon, and unhindered view of the rolling meadows.

"Mmm . . . there certainly is," Cat purred as her fingers tunneled beneath his chambray shirt to trace the scars on his belly.

Although Lucas had no intention of resisting, he lost all control when he glanced down into those expressive violet eyes that dominated her elfin face. There was a unique sparkle in those pools, something he had never noticed before. Yes, there had always been a living fire in her eyes, but now there was a hint of deviltry. She looked as if she meant to gobble him alive and she didn't care if he knew her intentions.

"Brazen woman," he teased playfully. "How dare you take advantage of a poor defenseless man like me."

Unabashed, Catlin peeled off his shirt and recklessly cast it aside. "Defenseless?" she repeated in a throaty purr. "That, my handsome devil, is one thing you will never be." Her exploring hands spread over his scarred chest, marveling at the hard contours of his body.

"I am defenseless with you," he admitted hoarsely. His voice rattled with the devastating effect she had on him. Her answering smile was so full of impish delight that it blew all thought from his mind.

And when Catlin settled down to the serious business of mapping each inch of his masculine physique, Lucas went down like a drowning swimmer. The feel of her soft fingertips wandering to and fro left Lucas moaning in unholy torment. Cat had become a skillful seductress who gave so freely of herself that he shuddered in response to her adventurous caresses. She had undressed him with magical inventiveness, creating a thousand fires that burned out of control. She not only accepted his ungovernable hunger, but she returned it with each devouring kiss. Her questing fingers measured the expanse of his chest and counted his ribs. Her lips explored his masculine contours, wooing him with her teeth, her hands, her body. And there, upon the inspirational point that overlooked the grandeur of the canyon, she came to him, whispering her need and her love.

If this intimate journey across the horizons was any indication of what Lucas could expect for the rest of his life, he had been granted his dreams. Ah, life couldn't be better than this! And he and Catlin were going to make wild sweet love every day for an eternity.

When she matched his fierce ardor and sent him gliding like an eagle in motionless flight, Lucas relinquished his last thought. He wasn't going to spend time planning tomorrow or fretting over the turmoil and trouble that awaited him in San Antonio. He was going to enjoy each new dawning day with this saucy tigress by his side.

And if anything did go wrong, he was going to reach back through time to grasp these wondrous days and nights. This exhilarating feeling of loving and being loved was what forever was all about. It made each torment and heartache worth the long agonizing wait. Nothing worth having came easily. Lucas only hoped the trouble he had encountered on the way to getting the woman he wanted was over. But knowing that Emmet Blake possessed a dark foreboding side of his personality left Luke doubting that he had seen the last of trouble.

But he wasn't going to think about that right now, he reminded himself. He was going to look past the black cloud that hung over Texas, brewing trouble for him and Catlin. And he wasn't going to wonder how Jace Osborn was coping with the loss of the light and love of his life. For once Lucas had the world in the palm of his hand and he was going to revel in the pleasure of loving this lively vixen with his body, his mind, and his soul. After all, she already had his heart even if she was too cynical to believe it.

Chapter 25

When Catlin and Lucas rejoined the herd, a round of cheers went up among the weary cowboys. Although Lucas hadn't expected to be greeted by Jace Osborn, he was there waiting their return. And while the procession progressed toward its final destination of Denver, Lucas eased his mount up beside Jace who was riding flank.

"I see you have allowed the lady to ride wherever she pleases," Jace smirked, his gaze sliding back to the shapely blond who was presently explaining to Bo Huxley how she had managed to elude the two Cheyenne braves who had attacked her.

"I have a difficult time saying no to Cat," Lucas admitted, watching the flicker of lambent desire in Jace's blue eyes.

"I can see your problem," Jace replied with a wistful sigh.

Silence stretched between them. Awkwardly, Lucas shifted in the saddle and stared straight ahead. "I couldn't let her go, Jace," he said quietly. "I knew she would have been safe with you. And if it had been any other woman besides Cat . . ."

Rumbling laughter echoed in Jace's chest. His harsh features softened in a melancholy smile. "You said that once before, Murdock. But if it wasn't for the love of that sexy blond, I wouldn't have challenged your right to her."

Odd, Lucas remembered saying something like that to Andrew five years ago. He had thought the world revolved around Elise. She had given him back his pride and self-respect after he had been sliced to shreds and she had earned his love. His gratitude had involved into such a deep emotional attachment that Luke had one helluva time letting go of the memories.

"But you're mistaken if you think I'm walking out of Catlin's life," Jace added, flinging Lucas a pointed glance.

Dark, penetrating eyes riveted on Jace's determined stare. After a full minute, Jace cracked a wry smile. "I'm going back to Texas with you, Murdock," he announced. "I don't appreciate the fact that Emmet Blake deliberately lied to me, that I almost killed an innocent woman." His gaze never wavered from Lucas's ruggedly handsome face. "And then, of course, there is always the outside chance that Cat will come to her senses and decide to ride off with me."

"You're making it impossible for us to be friends, Osborn," he grumbled sourly.

Jace's shoulder lifted in a careless shrug. "I'm saving that as my last resort. For Cat's love, I'd risk having you as an enemy."

Lucas's lips compressed in a stern frown. "I'm going to be honest with you, Jace. . . ."

"When haven't you been?" he smirked.

"I've never wanted a woman as much as I want Cat," Lucas declared. "After the hell she has been through I intend to grant her every whim. But I draw the line at being generous with her where other men are concerned."

A devilish grin claimed Jace's tarnished features. "Then you better make damned sure you're man enough to keep her, Murdock. If this romance crumbles you can expect me to be there to pick up the pieces."

"It won't," Lucas assured him gruffly.

"Time will be the judge of that," Jace murmured as he nudged his steed into a trot.

Lucas sat there glaring daggers at Jace's broad back. Damn that man. He wasn't letting up for a minute. God, why did he have to fall in love with a woman every man wanted as his own? Lucas asked himself. Why couldn't Catlin have been a plain-faced, docile female who was built like a blockhouse?

Hell's bells! What was he saying? Her mystical combination of beauty and spunk was what had attracted him in the first place. What man wouldn't want this sassy minx? She was, after all, the stuff masculine dreams were made of and Lucas was certain Jace Osborn was hallucinating about Catlin at this very moment.

Pensively, Lucas glanced back at the curvaceous blond who was poised on a buckskin gelding beside Bo Huxley. God, she was a sight to behold. Every time he glanced at that lively nymph he went hot all over. Would this newness ever wear off? Lucas wondered. After three and a half months he had no more control over his passion than he had in the beginning. No wonder Jace was so bewitched by Catlin. The feelings simply refused to fade. If anything, the craving grew more intense with each passing day. Jace was thriving on his fantasies, envying the intimacy she and Lucas had shared. Lucas knew what Jace was going through and he couldn't honestly blame the man for refusing to give up his pursuit. If their roles had been reversed, Lucas knew he wouldn't have backed off either, not this time, not with this rambunctious firebrand who had fulfilled his every fantasy.

Well, he was going to ensure that he kept the magic alive in their romance, Lucas promised himself faithfully. Cat would want for nothing, especially not another man! She deserved a little happiness and pampering after the hell she had been through, Lucas vowed she would have it!

*　　　*　　　*

A faint smile tripped across Catlin's lips when she peered at the crude fort that lay on the bank of the San Saba River. For the past month Catlin had set aside her apprehension of facing Emmet Blake while Lucas swept her off her feet. Although they had not discussed their future, they had made the most of every available moment. Lucas had become the epitome of good humor and teasing camaraderie. Her days were filled with joy and her nights with splendor.

The moment Lucas had sold the last of his herd in Denver, he had splurged to purchase her several sets of new clothes at Stewart's department store. The owner had imported the costliest silks and copies of Parisian fashions. There were dainty bonnets, silk and lace gowns, patent leather gaiters—several of which were now a part of Catlin's extended wardrobe.

Cat and Lucas had wined and dined at Apollo Hall in the Apollo Hotel. They had attended a performance given by a show troupe who offered their rendition of *Richard III* on the candle-illuminated stage in the Hall. While the cowboys celebrated the trail's end at Edward Jump's gambling hall and paid fifty cents for a five-minute dance with the Hurdy Gurdy girls, Lucas was taking Catlin on treks through the mountains and showing her the sights around Denver.

Ah, they had done a lot of living those four days before they began their journey back to Texas. What they had shared was almost too good to be true. But the closer they came to Texas, the more Catlin wondered if her bubble would burst. Lucas had never clashed with Emmet Blake the way she and Ginger had. He didn't know the man was violent and relentless when he was provoked. Catlin hadn't expected such a furious display of temper from the illustrious physician. If she hadn't seen his demented rampage with her own eyes, she wouldn't have believed it. There was no telling what Emmet would do when he was confronted.

Having Jace Osborn return with them to Texas was comforting. He had assured Catlin that he would testify to the lies Emmet had told him when he was hired to dispose of her. During the past month, Catlin had come to respect the rough-edged gunslinger. Jace had a certain sense of integrity that appealed to her. He treated her like a queen, fetching her food and drink each afternoon and evening when the procession paused to rest. Although Lucas seemed to resent Jace's gentlemanly attention, Catlin was honestly flattered by it. Here was a man who had been fed a crock of lies and had been paid to dispose of her. When less honorable men might have taken the money and made quick work of her, Jace questioned what he had been told about her. And he had tried to compensate for the injustice he had come dangerously close to committing.

When Lucas was scouting their path through perilous country, Jace rode beside her like a cautious sentinel. Even though he wasn't particularly handsome, he possessed many good qualities and Catlin had grown to like him quite a lot—which was exactly what Jace had counted on during his never ending quest for her love.

When she dared to suggest that he find another profession to support himself, he smiled rakishly and replied, "The right woman could make me put down roots. Until she agrees to ride away with me, I'm doomed to earn my wages by apprehending offenders of the law."

Jace had peered at her with those intense blue eyes that held decipherable messages. "In my profession, I have learned the importance of patience and perseverance, Cat. I know exactly what I want. And until I can have it, I'll wait."

And that was the way it was with Jace Osborn. He was the picture of manly devotion in a reserved sort of way. He was always there—like her shadow, standing as posted lookout. Catlin rather imagined that Jace's behavior toward her was his way of making amends for the first two months of "accidents" that had befallen her. She knew how he felt about her but she was careful to offer friendship without leading him into thinking there could be more between them.

Catlin had become less cynical of men in general after the many different relationships she had experienced with Lucas, Jace, Bo, and the other vaqueros. To one man she was a lover, to another a friend. To Bo she was a student in the ways of the West. And she had become like a sister to the men Lucas had warned to treat her with polite respect and nothing more if they valued their lives. . . .

Her pensive musings scattered when they neared Fort McKavett. The last few days of traveling through the long waterless stretches had been tedious. Catlin was anxious for a bath in the private quarters Lucas had promised her. It had been more than two weeks since she and Lucas had shared quarters at Fort Sumner and had slept with a roof over their heads instead of a dome of stars. During the one night they spent at the fort, she could don one of the expensive dresses Lucas had purchased for her in Denver and shed her tattered buckskins.

A dreamy smile pursed her lips. This would be her last chance at privacy with Lucas until they reached San Antonio. Catlin intended to make the most of the evening. She would comb the rattails from her wild mass of hair and lace herself into something feminine.

That tantalizing thought lingered on her features as Lucas trotted his steed up beside her. And as always when Lucas approached, Jace backed away. Catlin missed the silent exchange between the two men because her gaze was fixed on Luke's craggy features. Oh, how she adored this strong capable rake. And tonight she would express her affection all over again.

A curious frown knitted Luke's brow when he focused on the impish face that was shaded by the wide-brimmed sombrero. There was a flare-up of mischief in her eyes. "Why are you looking like the cat who swallowed the canary?" he demanded suspiciously.

"You'll find out soon enough," Catlin replied in a saucy tone.

His dark brows jackknifed. "I don't think I can tolerate the suspense," he growled in a low, provocative voice.

Catlin reached over to clutch his gaping shirt, drawing him and his steed nearer. Without preamble, Catlin planted a swift, but passionate kiss to his lips before resettling in her saddle.

Lucas instinctively glanced at Jace to determine if his rival had witnessed the exchange. Jace had noticed alright. His mouth tightened in an envious scowl. And just to antagonize Jace, Lucas hooked his arm around Catlin and deposited her in his lap. The answering kiss was hot enough to evaporate the water in the San Saba River.

"Just wait until I get you alone, woman," he murmured in that husky voice that could melt a woman into puddles. "That kiss was mere child's play in comparison to what I have in mind for you tonight. . . ."

"Devil," she teased saucily.

"Witch," he flung back. "You make my blood boil. I'm tired of keeping my distance because of our constant audience and your relentless watch dog."

Catlin shared his eagerness for privacy. It had been more than a week since they had found an excuse to wander away from camp to frolic in the spring Lucas had located.

Gathering her composure—something that always scattered when she came within ten feet of this devastating rogue with sexy brown eyes—Catlin slid back to her own mount.

"I will expect you to be on time after you speak with the commander," she said in a businesslike tone.

"My report of sighting renegade Comanches will be brief," Lucas assured her and then broke into a rakish grin. "But with you I intend to be very thorough and long-winded." His voice dropped to a scintillating tone, sending a flock of goose bumps fluttering across her flesh. "Very thorough indeed . . ."

"I'll be waiting," Catlin purred in eager anticipation. "I'll be counting the minutes."

When the procession halted on the grassy slope where Spur and the horses could graze and drink their fill, Lucas accompanied Catlin to the fort. Leaving her in their crude quarters with a long-awaited tub of water, Lucas strided toward the commander's office. As was his custom at each fort on the trail, Lucas reported the whereabouts of roving bands of Comanches. Since it was the soldier's duty to protect the frontier, the army was anxious to know the location of raiders and outlaws who harassed the trail herds, settlers, and travelers.

After Lucas and Commander Brown shared a drink, Lucas cited the locations of the three bands of Indians he had cautiously detoured around during their return trip. He also reported their confrontation with the marauders who had stolen twenty-five head of cattle.

"Consider yourself fortunate," Commander Brown commented between sips of brandy. "The last trail boss who passed through here last month lost almost a thousand head. And more than three months ago one of our scouting parties came across a massacre of settlers. We also picked up a young woman who had been seriously wounded. I can't say for certain if Indians molested her because she refuses to speak of the incident or her past. She begged to stay here, serving as camp laundress and physician's assistant until her child is born."

Lucas's face fell like a rockslide. It couldn't be? Could it? "Describe the woman to me," he requested urgently.

"She's a pretty little thing," Brown informed Lucas who sat on the edge of his seat. "Dazzling green eyes and chestnut brown hair. But she has the saddest little smile I've ever seen. I don't know what haunts her, but I swear she is afraid of her own shadow."

Lucas gulped down his thundering heart. "Where is she?"

"Do you know her?" Brown inquired curiously.

"Seeing her will determine that," Lucas murmured as he climbed to his feet.

"She says her name is Margo Foster. She occupies the small cabin at the west end of the compound. But she could be anywhere—the commissary or dining hall or the infirmary."

Lucas made a beeline for the small cottage. His heart was racing a hundred miles a minute as he rapped on the door. If Margo Foster was in actuality Ginger Hanley, both she and Catlin could present their case against Emmet Blake. Ginger's presence might complicate his future with Catlin, but the possibility of Ginger surviving the fire would certainly ease Catlin's torment.

But first and foremost on his mind was clearing Catlin's name from the crimes Emmet accused her of committing. Lucas wasn't sure what he was going to do about Ginger and his child, but for certain, Catlin would expect him to accept his responsibility. And Lucas felt the obligation after what Ginger had been through. Ginger had suffered. But God, if he had to give Catlin up it was going to kill him, especially with Jace Osborn hovering around, waiting to take his place!

A muttered curse erupted from Lucas's lips when his rap on the cottage door was greeted with silence. Wheeling about, he marched toward the commissary to inquire as to the whereabouts of Margo Foster. From there Lucas was directed to the infirmary.

Inhaling a steadying breath, Lucas eased open the door to see a young woman garbed in a green calico gown, shawl, and bonnet. She sat beside a wounded soldier. Her fingertips were clasped around his hand. The same melancholy smile Commander Brown so aptly described hovered on her lips. Quietly, she conversed with the lieutenant who had been wounded during a confrontation with renegade Comanches.

With his nerves taut and his body rigid, Lucas waited until the young woman noticed him lingering in the doorway. When she recognized him, her features shed the expression of unhappiness and controlled reserve.

"Lucas," Ginger whispered tremulously as she rose from her chair. Tears instantly flooded her eyes and spilled down her cheeks. With a cry of relief, she rushed to him with outstretched arms.

Catlin circumnavigated the room, wondering what had become of Lucas. Every few seconds her anxious gaze darted toward the door, expecting him to appear. He had promised to return in thirty minutes and Catlin had hurried through her bath to make herself presentable before he arrived. An hour had passed and still there was no sign of Lucas. Vaguely annoyed with the wasted minutes in their one night of privacy, Catlin wandered outside to peer at the light that splintered from the window of the commander's headquarters.

A muddled frown clouded Catlin's brow when she spied Lucas standing in the open doorway of the infirmary. From a distance, Catlin caught only a brief glimpse of the woman who darted past the window and into Lucas's waiting arms. And when he cuddled her against him so tenderly, Catlin's heart ceased beating and hung in her chest like a stone. When the woman entwined her arms around his neck and clung to him, Catlin debated about what she should do.

Was this one of Lucas's lovers? One he had dallied with while he came and went from trail drives? Had he shared her bed when they passed this way bound for Colorado? Would it always be like this when he ran across some woman from his past? The entire state was probably brimming with women who had been intimate with Lucas at one time or another. Chances were this wouldn't be the last time some sentimental female threw herself at him.

Crestfallen, Catlin turned her back on the tormenting

scene and strided back to her quarters in stiff precise steps. She had been plagued with the feeling her bubble would burst and it certainly had—even sooner than she anticipated. Seeing another woman in Luke's arms cut Catlin's pride to shreds. For a month she had heard Lucas whisper his need for her. It hadn't occurred to her until now that he might have been in the habit of murmuring I-love-yous when he finally had a woman where he wanted her—in his bed, at his beck and call. How could she and Lucas make a new life together when he snuggled up to every female that crossed his path? Damn him, he had said their affection for each other could be the lasting kind. And just exactly what did that mean? That he still expected to gallivant all over the country, rekindling old flames and then returning to her after stoking a few fires?

Come to think of it, Lucas had never even mentioned marriage since that night at the Flying Spur. Catlin was frustrated to no end. Seeing another woman in Lucas's arms had her questioning the strength of the bond between her and that brown-eyed rake who attracted women the same way sugar drew flies.

Muttering under her breath, Catlin peeled off her expensive gown and climbed back into her buckskins. With her satchel in hand, she stamped out the door. Her eyes swung to the empty doorway of the building where Lucas had stood and she cursed him soundly. Whatever he and the wench were doing, they weren't doing it in full view of the doorway and that made Catlin all the madder.

Catlin stomped off to retrieve her horse, cursing Lucas every step of the way. What did Lucas take her for? A blind fool? He said he would be gone a few minutes. A few minutes indeed! He had probably sought out his lover, knowing full well Catlin was bathing and wouldn't be around to see him hugging another woman. Well, so much for Lucas being faithful and true-blue, Catlin mused as she nudged her steed and galloped away from the fort.

Men. She should have known better than to believe Lucas would devote himself to one woman. No matter what he said to the contrary, Catlin knew he still carried a torch for his sister-in-law and he obviously suffered from a severe case of roving eye. Luke would never love Catlin the way he loved the memory of Elise. First loves left a certain amount of vulnerability. She was a shining example of it herself!

By damned, Lucas could rekindle as many old flames and cling to his memories of Elise if he wanted to, but she wasn't going to be the sensible, practical female who waited at home while he sowed his wild oats. That was the bottom line, Catlin realized as she trotted across the moonlit countryside. To Lucas, she had become a rock to lean on when there was no one else around—the sensible, practical stick of furniture who would adorn his home. If anything, she might become the wife he thought he needed to enhance his position of landowner. But who knew for certain since Lucas had said nothing about a wedding ceremony. He had mentioned being engaged a few times but he really hadn't proposed. In fact, when he asked her to wait for him at the Flying Spur, she was the one who demanded to know if he was proposing. And what had he said? "It certainly sounds like it." What kind of answer was that? For a man who was usually blunt and to the point, Lucas hadn't been quite so definite when it came to an outright proposal of marriage.

Catlin thought back to her female friends in Louisiana before the war. Marriages had taken place right and left. Looking for stability and security, soldiers had very often proposed, just to have a woman waiting for them when they returned. And influential men took wives to indemnify their dignified positions. And those same men, as well as soldiers, swaggered off to enjoy fleeting affairs and mistresses while they were away from home. Perhaps Lucas was like so many of his gender. If what she had seen the previous hour was any indication, he was *exactly* like the other men she had known!

Despite all Luke's endearing qualities there was one pitfall he could never overcome, Catlin reminded herself bleakly. Lucas Murdock was one hundred per cent male. And men, curse their damnable souls, had certain inborn flaws when it came to relationships with women. They possessed voracious appetites and they clung to the theory that variety was the spice of life.

Women naturally flocked to men like Lucas—men whose vitality and virility was the devil's own temptation. Lucas had shown his true colors at Fort McKavett. He was the personification of the theory which stated that a man's character was best exemplified by what he did when he didn't think he would get caught. Once a womanizer, always a womanizer, Catlin mused cynically. As long as Lucas still harbored love for Elise he would never be completely satisfied, Catlin reckoned. His affection for Elise would constantly prompt him to search in hopes of finding his ideal match.

Catlin reflected on the conversation she and Luke had about his brief but complex affair with Ginger Hanley (God rest her soul). Ginger had come to him for comfort, he had said. He wasn't even sure why she had sought him out, he had said. But being a man, Lucas had accepted what she offered and he had given far more than consolation, that was for sure!

And now, when an unidentified female flew into his arms, his male instincts came back to life. Catlin hadn't waited around to confront him in a compromising situation with his latest clinging vine. It would have crushed her to watch him betray her with another woman. If he hadn't wanted that female in his arms, if he feared it would threaten his relations with Catlin, he would have sent her away from him. Honest to goodness, it wasn't as if that woman had wrestled him to the ground and forced herself on him! But Lucas had been waiting for her with open arms. Now did that sound like a man who was emotionally involved with only one woman? No, dammit, it did not!

Lucas's old habits were resurfacing when he confronted temptation. He had failed the test of fidelity. Catlin was not the kind of woman who marched up to throw an indignant tantrum while he was trifling with another female. That simply wasn't her style. She confronted trouble head-on, but not her lover's indiscretions. In that instance she ran the other way. It was lucky for her that she had been reminded of the flaw in Lucas's character before she began believing they enjoyed a match made in heaven. Ha! What a joke that was. Well, if Lucas thought he needed a practical, sensible wife to keep the home fires burning while he chased skirts, then he could damned well search elsewhere. Catlin wasn't going to let herself in for more heartache. There would always be obstacles between her and Luke and the biggest one of all was Emmet Blake. . . .

Emmet's face rose above her like a specter in the night. Flashbacks of disaster assaulted her. Catlin braced her courage. She was going to find a way to expose that maniac for what he was. Lucas was right about one thing. She couldn't run from Emmet forever. It was time she dealt with that lunatic and his lies—on her terms. Catlin wasn't sure what she intended to do, but she had time to devise a plan before she reached San Antonio. She should never have run from him in the first place, she supposed. But fighting him had seemed impossible. By now Emmet had spread his lies and had swung public opinion against her.

But what did she have to lose by confronting him now? she asked herself. She knew she could never truly have Lucas's love. He had been and he would always be as wild and free as the wind. Each time he struck off on a trail drive, she would be left to wonder if his roving eye had led him astray.

A rueful smile pursed Catlin's lips as she allowed her

mount to pick his way through the darkness. What she had shared with Lucas had been the impossible dream. It had been rare and special but it simply wasn't meant to be a way of life. In retrospect, Catlin realized that those qualities that lured her to him against her will were the very things that had constantly torn them apart. If Luke had really tried to be faithful to her, if he had tried to relinquish his preoccupation with other women and they with him, he would have come to resent Catlin's insistence that it had to be all or nothing.

What they had together was the result of complex complications that had thrown them together. Aunt Martha had taken her turn at matchmaking. Emmet Blake had tried to pull them apart. Ginger and her impossible situation had also been an external influence on this . . . this "thing" betwen Cat and Lucas. It had been love on Catlin's part. But she wasn't sure Lucas knew what love was. His disappointing relationship with Elise had caused him to go through women like a man thumbing through a file cabinet in search of something he couldn't possibly hope to find. When Cat came along and then wound up accompanying him on the drive, he found her convenient and he decided to settle for second best. He saw her as a dependable, sensible woman who might suffice for the position of wife at the Flying Spur.

But the truth was, Lucas had realized he could never find what he really wanted. He had allowed his expectations of what life might have been with Elise to form the dimensions of his dreams. But every woman he had encountered for more than five years had fallen short of the mark. He had taken what women could give without experiencing those same elusive sensations he had felt for Elise. He had decided five years was long enough to carry a torch and he planned to settle down on his new ranch with a dependable female to tend to his household chores—whether she be wife, lover, or maid.

Catlin's shoulders, slumped. She could analyze Lucas

Murdock until she worked up a ferocious headache, but it wouldn't change anything. She knew what she had seen at Fort McKavett—a man accepting the affection of a woman because it was second nature to him. Lucas wasn't the man of her dreams. True, he had come closer than most, but he could never be what she expected him to be. And if he tried to change her, then he would no longer be the Lucas she had come to love.

Lord, was she making any sense? She was! And that's what really worried Catlin. In a way, she had become like Lucas—pining for a love that could never be. Any future relationship with men would form the guidelines set by the hopes and dreams she had conjured up during this tempestuous affair with Lucas. She was doomed, just as Lucas was. Neither of them could enjoy their heart's desire because what they wanted simply did not exist. It had become an elusive fantasy that could never collide with reality.

From this day forward, Catlin would look back on her love for that brown-eyed rake as a fleeting dream. And if she ever decided to marry, she would seek the sensible and practical. When she was ready to put down roots she would seek a sound, uncomplicated relationship—one totally unlike the one she experienced with Lucas. It would be a comfortable marriage that provided security and a deterrent from loneliness in the golden years to come. It would have more to do with stability than uncontrollable passion—the kind she had experienced with Lucas.

Lucas . . . Dark, compelling eyes and a roguish smile that could melt a woman's heart when she wasn't guarding it closely. Lucas . . . Hot explosive kisses and heart-stopping caresses. Lucas . . . Volatile arguments, wild, death-defying adventure. After listing all the exciting qualities that had magnetically drawn her to him, Catlin neatly folded the memories and tucked them in the shadowed corners of her heart, just as Lucas must have done five years ago with Elise.

Time and time again Catlin had tried to lock the door on the past. But she would sever all ties this time. Catlin promised herself fiercely. What she and Lucas had was really over. Watching Lucas open his arms to the woman who ran to him at Fort McKavett had forced Cat to accept the fact that he could never settle down, even if she nailed his boots to the floor. It would be like caging a wild free bird, refusing to let it fly as it had been born to do. Lucas was unable to accept the limitations and expectations of Catlin's love for him. She loved him enough to let him go—for his sake as well as her own. And maybe she would take Jace Osborn's offer if she survived her confrontation with Emmet. Jace knew her heart belonged to Lucas, but he was willing to accept whatever she could give. And like Lucas, she would settle for second best because that was her only alternative. Jace Osborn may not have been the man she wanted, but he just might be the man she needed at this point in her life.

On that sensible thought, Catlin set aside her pensive musings to contemplate her upcoming encounter with Emmet Blake. The satisfaction of repaying him for the hell he had put her through would compensate for giving Lucas up. It had to. Her crusade was all that kept her spirits from nose-diving to rock bottom! Either Catlin or Emmet would walk away from this showdown. Catlin reminded herself grimly. Neither of them would be satisfied as long as the other one lived. And if Catlin were to die, her only consolation was that she had a fifty-fifty chance of being removed to a higher sphere. It had to be better than this torment on earth! And at least she was reasonably certain she wouldn't meet Emmet Blake in heaven. That demon was surely meant to spend eternity in hell! But, considering the way her luck had been running, she would probably find herself frying over Lucifer's fire—with Emmet roasting beside her forever more. Now that would be hell!

Chapter 26

While Ginger sobbed in Lucas's arms, he soothed and comforted her. Lucas was vividly reminded of the afternoon when Catlin had finally broken down and told him what had tormented her so. But Ginger wasn't as strong as Catlin, and she fell completely apart. It was fifteen minutes before she managed to speak at all. Lucas led her to a chair and gently eased her down to face him. Through heart-wrenching sobs, Ginger offered her jumbled rendition of the nightmare. She swore Emmet had purposely poisoned her father and she was totally unaware that Catlin had survived the blaze.

"How did you escape the fire?" Lucas questioned, taking her trembling hands in his own.

Ginger muffled a sniff and struggled for composure which was still slow in coming. "When . . . I . . . came to, I was lying on the couch in the parlor." She bit her quivering lips, trying to present a precise account of the incident without breaking into another round of sobs. "I was so terrified by the flames that I was oblivious to my injuries and crawled out the closest window to hide in the smokehouse and tend my wounds. I didn't dare show my face in San Antonio for fear Emmet would try to kill me again."

Tortured eyes peered up into Lucas's grim frown. "Emmet is a madman when he is provoked. I could think of no way to defeat him so I took our mule and fled. I didn't know where I was going and I didn't really care, so long as I put miles between me and Emmet." Her gaze slid back to the young man who lay abed, nursing his injured leg. "I located a farm house where I hoped to take refuge. But it had been attacked by Comanches shortly before I arrived. When the cavalry patrol happened along, Lieutenant Simms found me and brought me here."

More tears boiled down her cheeks as she clutched Lucas's hand. "I'm so sorry to have to tell you this, Lucas, but Emmet killed Catlin in the fire, just as he intended to cremate me. I stopped at your ranch on my way out of town, hoping Catlin had miraculously managed to escape." Ginger inhaled a tremulous breath. "But she—"

Lucas gave his raven head a contradicting shake. "Catlin did escape and she is alive," he informed her. "Catlin also managed to crawl out of the house before she succumbed to the smoke and flames. Emmet caught sight of her and tried to shoot her, but she climbed in her buggy and outran him. I think it is correct to assume that, if not for the distraction Cat provided, you may not have been fortunate enough to elude Emmet. She may very well have saved your life twice in the same night."

"She's alive?" Ginger's misty green eyes flew wide open.

"Yes. In fact, she is here at the fort and she is probably wondering why it's taking me so long to return." A gentle smile pursed Lucas's lips as he watched relief spread over Ginger's features. "I think Cat is going to be just as delighted to discover that you survived, too."

The prospect of seeing Catlin again was dampened by the unsettling thought of rehashing the hellish nightmare all over again. Tentatively, Ginger glanced at the young lieutenant who was watching her like a hawk.

Ginger's hand slid to her swollen abdomen—a gesture

391

that stabbed through Lucas's soul like a knife. It was going to be an awkward reunion between the mother of his child and the saucy sprite whom he had wanted to remain by his side always.

"Lucas. I'm so sorry about . . . everything. . . ." Ginger faltered. Another round of tears trickled down her cheeks.

He held up his hand to silence her. "First things first," he insisted. "Catlin has lived far too long with the torment of thinking you died in the fire."

Assisting Ginger to her feet, Lucas shepherded her toward the door. But Ginger refused to stir a step. Her gaze flew back to the wounded lieutenant. "I'll be back to sit with you in a few minutes, Allen," she promised him.

Curiously, Allen Simms studied the swarthy man who kept a steadying hand around Ginger's waist. His gaze bounced back and forth between Ginger and Lucas, speculating on the fierce hug she had given the stranger when he appeared at the infirmary door. It left him wondering at the connection between them. Reluctantly, Allen nodded in compliance and then settled back on his pillow.

With mounting anticipation, Lucas propelled Ginger toward the crudely furnished quarters where he had left Catlin. She was going to be in for the surprise of her life, he thought to himself. But when Lucas opened the door he was the one who was in for a surprise. He could find hide nor hair of the feisty blond.

Luke's brow furrowed. Catlin's satchel of clothes had disappeared along with her. What the devil was she up to? Had she become aggravated with him for being detained and decided to return to camp? Or did Jace Osborn have something to do with her disappearance? Lucas wouldn't have been the least bit surprised.

"She was here an hour and a half ago," Lucas mumbled when Ginger cast him a questioning frown. "Maybe she gave up on me and rode out to rejoin my men."

Promising to bring Catlin back to the fort, Lucas left Ginger with the injured lieutenant and thundered off to camp. Dammit, what had gotten into that woman? Had Jace showed up to steal Cat away while he was occupied? he wondered. Luke wouldn't put it past that rascal. Jace wanted Catlin any way he could get her.

Chomping on that infuriating thought, Lucas galloped into camp and yanked his steed to a skidding halt. In a single bound, Lucas dismounted and stamped toward Bo. But there was no reason to interrogate Bo when he practically stepped on Jace who was stretched out on his pallet beside the campfire—all by himself.

"Where's Cat?" Lucas growled in question.

Jace propped himself up on an elbow. "I haven't seen her since the two of you trotted off to the fort. I thought she was with you." His harsh features puckered in a disdainful scowl. "You better not have lost her, Murdock."

"If she isn't at the fort and she isn't here, where the hell could she be?" Lucas questioned Jace in an accusing tone. "Now what game are you playing, Osborn?"

"Dammit, I told you I haven't seen her," Jace muttered crossly.

Lucas emitted an aggravated snort. "Good God, you don't suppose she decided to sneak off to confront Emmet Blake all by herself . . . ?"

The words were no sooner out of Lucas's mouth before Jace snatched up his saddle and charged toward his horse. The unsettling thought provoked Lucas to dash back to his mount. Hell's bells, Lucas had been certain he had convinced Catlin to let him handle Emmet. But it seemed old habits were hard to break. Catlin had been fighting her own battles for so long that she must have decided to satisfy her vengeance by herself. Damn that little daredevil! She had purposely sneaked away, just as she had that night in Colorado! Just once he wished that she-male would announce her departures instead of spiriting off without a word to anyone.

Still grumbling, Lucas wheeled his mount toward Bo. "Ginger Hanley is at the fort infirmary. Fetch her and bring her back to San Antonio."

"But what about . . . ?" Bo tried to ask.

"Just do it!" Lucas blared impatiently. "I'll expect you to travel as fast as Ginger can tolerate without tiring her."

Bo didn't have the foggiest notion what Lucas meant by the remark, but the urgent tone prevented Bo from posing too many questions. It was obvious Lucas was anxious to overtake his misplaced fiancée before she got herself in trouble.

While Lucas and Jace rode at a breakneck speed, Bo saddled his horse and trotted off to retrieve Ginger. But he was in for a shock when he found the young lady. Her delicate condition knocked Bo for a loop. He sat down before he fell down. He didn't have to be a genius to figure out whose child Ginger carried. Bo groaned miserably to himself. He wasn't sure what had happened but he thought he knew why Catlin had ridden away without informing anyone of her intentions. He reckoned it had everything to do with Ginger and her condition. Bleakly, Bo assisted Ginger into the only available carriage to be found at the fort and rumbled off in swift pursuit.

Lucas cast the shadowed figure beside him a hasty glance. He knew Jace recognized Ginger's name and had made the connection. Jace annoyed Luke to no end at times, but there was nothing wrong with the gunslinger's mathematics. Jace had put two and two together. And as Lucas predicted, Jace was overjoyed with the implication of Ginger returning to complicate matters between Cat and Lucas.

"You're going to lose her," Jace chortled victoriously. "But I guess you already know that, don't you, Murdock?"

"Nothing has changed," Lucas gritted out.

A mocking smile quirked Jace's lips. "Maybe not for you, pretty boy, but Catlin won't stay with you when you have obligations to Ginger Hanley," he speculated. "Maybe she already saw you two together. Perhaps she decided three was a crowd . . . or maybe she was reminded of the adage about baby making three."

Lucas grimaced at Jace's well-aimed taunts. "I don't know how she could possibly have seen Ginger. And even if she had, Catlin would have rushed over to ensure her eyes hadn't deceived her," Lucas insisted.

"Would she?" Jace smirked. "Maybe she thought it wiser for the two of you to be alone to discuss your future. And as I recall, Cat isn't big on theatrical exits. If she decides to go, then she leaves without ado."

"I'd give anything to know what possessed her to pack up and leave without a word," Lucas muttered sourly.

"Maybe she doesn't care about you as much as you thought she did," Jace antagonized him.

Luke's fingers clenched on the reins, wishing he had a stranglehold on Jace's throat. The man constantly needled him. He was like a damned vulture hovering around, waiting to swoop down and carry Catlin off.

"I don't blame you for wanting her," Lucas muttered irritably. "But I hate it when you gloat. You do it too damned well, Osborn."

"Wouldn't you be gloating if you were me?" Jace questioned point-blank.

Lucas stared him squarely in the eye. "You and I are a helluva lot alike, Osborn. You're as plainspoken and straightforward as I am. When I look at you, it's like looking at my reflection in the mirror."

"Yeah, we're a helluva lot alike except that you're the one with the pretty face," Jace grumbled resentfully. "But it won't matter anymore because I'm going to be the one who walks away with the prize, pretty face or no."

"Promise me something, Osborn," Lucas murmured

deflatedly. "Promise me you'll love her enough for both of us."

Jace's head swiveled on his shoulders to gape at the ruggedly handsome rogue whom he had envied for two long months. Lucas wore the expression of a man who knew his complex situation had bested him. He had begun to accept what he couldn't change—Catlin's mind. She would never remain with Lucas while Ginger needed a father for her child. Lucas knew that just as surely as he knew his own name and so did Jace.

A long sigh escaped Jace's lips as he focused on the imaginary point in the distance—the same point that seemed to demand Lucas's attention. "I will," he assured Luke. "If she'll have me . . ." He darted Lucas a fleeting glance. "And for what it's worth, Murdock, I admire you, even though we have been at cross-purposes most of the time."

"If that's supposed to make me feel better, it doesn't," Lucas grumbled.

"I just wanted you to know," Jace added in a sincere tone.

"Coming from you, I accept the compliment, Osborn." His dark eyes slid to the lean gunslinger before he stared straight ahead. "And the feeling is mutual, even if I'm going to hate you for taking something I want as my own."

In silence, both men rode toward their destination, hoping to overtake Catlin during the night. But tormented frustration was riding a swift horse. Catlin pushed herself and her steed to their limits in order to put great distance between her and Lucas for reasons that neither Bo, Jace, nor Luke could guess. But she was still just as gone and no one was going to catch up with Catlin when she was determined not to be caught!

Chapter 27

By the time Catlin reached San Antonio she had decided how she would approach the treacherous Emmet Blake. Knowing exactly how dangerous he could be when he was angry, Catlin armed herself with her pistol and the knife Lucas had purchased for her before their return trip to Texas.

Still disguised in her baggy buckskins and sombrero, Catlin proceeded to the sheriff's office to determine whether or not Emmet had posted a warrant for her arrest. Sure enough, he had, damn him!

It was midafternoon when Catlin emerged from the sheriff's office to confront Emmet. But instead of encountering the physician, Catlin was greeted by Emmet's new assistant. As fate would have it, Emmet was making his rounds to attend his bedridden patients.

While Catlin awaited Emmet's return, she mentally rehearsed what she intended to say to him. And it wasn't going to be easy or pleasant, she mused grimly. Catlin dreaded the confrontation, knowing if she made one false move she would wind up dead. She had to provoke Emmet to the same frenzied state to which he had reduced himself that harrowing night four months ago. Otherwise, he would stand before her, denying her allegations, just as he had done when Ginger approached him with her accusations. It was only when Emmet's temper got the best of him that Catlin could deal with the lunatic who had tried to kill her. But by doing so, she would be taking a perilous risk.

And yet, what did she have to lose? Cat asked herself dismally. She had no future with Lucas. He had proven he could never be loyal to her, not while there was another female under the age of eighty on the planet. If he really wanted a wife at all, it was because he thought he needed one to suite his position as landowner and upstanding citizen of San Antonio. But quite honestly, Catlin doubted Lucas would ever get around to marriage, not while he coveted his memories of Elise as if they were twenty-four karat gold.

If Catlin managed to walk away unscathed after her clash with Emmet, she had no alternative but to leave Texas with Jace. She would always be vulnerable where Luke was concerned. That handsome rake would always be a temptation she couldn't resist. The only practical method of preventing herself from buckling to his roguish charms was to let Jace accompany her west.

Catlin's heart leaped into triple time when the door creaked open and Emmet Blake entered his office. All the anger, fear, and frustration mushroomed inside her when she came face to face with the man who destroyed lives as easily as he saved them. With her pulse pounding in her ears and her hands quivering, Catlin unfolded herself from her chair.

"What can I do for you, young man?" Emmet questioned pleasantly.

Catlin handed a note to the young redhead who now served as Emmet's assistant. The girl unfolded the paper and read the message. After casting Catlin a puzzled glance she exited from the office. Catlin had no intention of allowing an innocent bystander to be caught in the middle of this feud. She had found herself in just such a situation the night Ginger stormed the physician's office to voice her accusations.

A muddled frown clouded Emmet's face as he watched his new assistant scuttle away without explanation. When his buckskin-clad patient strode purposefully into the examining room, Emmet followed in "his" wake.

"Would you mind telling me what is going on?" Emmet requested as he set his medical bag aside.

Catlin positioned herself behind the chair for safe measure. Removing the oversized sombrero, she allowed the tangled mass of blond hair to cascade over her shoulder. When Emmet recognized his unexpected visitor, his attitude immediately changed and his eyes popped.

"You . . ." he growled poisonously.

A goading smile bordered Catlin's lips as she watched Emmet coil like a snake. Her body was taut—expecting anything to happen and everything to go wrong. She knew she was flirting with disaster, but it had become a habit with her. Cat was very careful not to take Emmet for granted. He could be ruthless and she had to be prepared to deal with the madman who lurked just beneath that sophisticated veneer.

"The bounty hunter you sent to dispose of me failed in his mission," Catlin declared, struggling to maintain a steady voice.

"I sent no one after you, bitch," Emmet hissed furiously.

Taunting laughter erupted from her lips, "Jace Osborn tells a different story."

"What did you do, turn your wicked charms on the man, just as you did on Lucas?" he sneered insultingly. "I should have known an evil witch like you would spread yourself beneath any man if you thought you could gain from it."

Catlin got a tight grip on herself. She couldn't afford to lose her temper. She had to remain cool and calm. "You sent Osborn to dispose of me because you were afraid I would return to point an accusing finger at you. And being guilty of both murder and attempted murder, you

399

were frantic, weren't you, Emmet? And you did poison Ginger's father, just as she suspected. Then you killed Ginger because she was a threat to your reputation, just as I am."

"You're mad," Emmet spluttered in outrage. "I have dedicated myself to lengthening life, not cutting it short. You'll find yourself hanging from a rope if you dare to accuse me of wrongdoing. You are the one who is wanted for murder."

Her gaze dropped to Emmet's right hand—the one that was indiscreetly inching its way toward his medical bag while he spoke.

"Were you tired of offering medication to Robert Hanely—your terminal patient? Or did you dispose of him to get your revenge on Ginger for something she did to annoy you?" Catlin was grasping at straws—anything to pry the truth from this two-faced doctor who had proved himself to be both devil and saint.

"I did no such thing!" Emmet exploded as he reached into his leather bag. "You are as mad as Ginger was."

Catlin was poised and waiting for the attack. When Emmet lunged with scalpel in hand, Catlin whipped up the chair to protect herself from the fire-breathing dragon. "You tried to kill me and the Hanleys to protect yourself from your crimes," she growled accusingly. "You're a murderer, Emmet, a bloodthirsty murderer!"

The harsh allegation caused Emmet's temper to snap. Angry sparks leaped from his eyes as he wrestled the chair away from his daring challenger. "Curse your soul," he snarled, flinging her a malicious glower.

Like a canonball, Catlin shot sideways to dodge the swishing blade. But Emmet was intent on his purpose. Profanity spewed from his curled lips as he wildly slashed at Catlin, anxious to carve her into bite-sized pieces. With a frightened yelp, Catlin darted behind the examining table to retrieve her pistol. Oh, how she wished she possessed Jace or Lucas's lightning-quick draw! It seemed to take forever to worm her pistol from her belt.

She had hoped to drag an explanation and a confession of guilt from Emmet but he was already too crazed with fury to admit to anything. He simply spouted epithets to her name and attempted to slash her with his scalpel.

"You're the one who put ideas in Ginger's head," Emmet muttered as he kicked the pistol from Catlin's hand before she could train it on him. "I had her convinced to do as I ordered . . . until you came along." His arm whipped through the air, missing Catlin's shoulder by inches. "She would have accepted my orders and complied to them, if not for your meddling."

Catlin didn't have the foggiest notion what he was ranting about and she didn't have time to question the lunatic when he launched himself at her again.

A horrified shriek burst from her lips when the blade slashed across the back of her hand. Things weren't going as she had anticipated. And where the devil was the sheriff? The note Catlin handed to Emmet's assistant requested that she summon the sheriff to eavesdrop on this conversation. Hell's bells, why couldn't the sheriff have arrived on time? How long would she be forced to ward off Emmet's attack before help arrived?

Catlin groaned when Emmet purposely tripped her. The floor came flying up at incredible speed. Frantically, she twisted to grab his wrist before he plunged the scalpel into her belly.

"Emmet!" Lucas's voice rumbled across the room like foreboding thunder.

Moving with the quickness of a frightened rabbit, Emmet sank down on his haunches. He pulled Catlin in front of him like a shield. The scalpel lay at Catlin's throat, daring Lucas to pull the trigger on the Colt that was clutched in his hand.

A shocked gasp erupted from Emmet's lips when Jace Osborn, who also pointed a revolver in his direction, Bo Huxley, and Ginger Hanley appeared in the doorway.

401

"Ginger?" Catlin squeaked in disbelief.

It was beyond Lucas that Catlin could sit sprawled in front of Emmet with a blade at her throat, looking absolutely elated to see Ginger Hanley alive and well. He expected her to be relieved to learn Ginger had survived, but considering the circumstances, she should have been a helluva lot more concerned about her own predicament.

And indeed Catlin was thrilled to see Ginger. She instantly recognized the green calico gown, shawl, and bonnet Ginger was wearing. The saints be praised! Ginger was the woman Lucas had embraced at the fort.

Catlin could go to her grave knowing Lucas did care for her in his own way, despite his preoccupation with Elise. They could never enjoy a life together because Lucas had obligations to Ginger anyway, Catlin reminded herself. Even if she survived this clash with Emmet, she and Lucas were through.

"Put those pistols down or I'll kill her!" Emmet threatened. His wild eyes jumped from one stormy face to the other.

"I want to know the truth before I die," Catlin demanded, her gaze fixed on Ginger who was as white as flour. "What was Emmet trying to force you to do against your will?"

"He—" Ginger began.

"Shut up!" Emmet blared, glowering mutinously at Ginger.

"I have allowed you to browbeat me for the last time, Emmet," Ginger gritted out. Her chin tilted to a defiant angle that closely resembled one of Catlin's rebellious gestures. "Some of us may not walk out of here alive, Emmet. But the survivors are going to know the truth about you."

"I said shut up!" Emmet squawked like a disturbed owl. His hand clamped tighter around Catlin's shoulders—like a child tugging a security blanket about him for protection.

Ginger raised the bottle that was clasped in her hand. "You thought the medicine you gave my father lay with the other charred ruins, didn't you, Emmet?" Bitter laughter tripped from Ginger's lips. "I hid this bottle in the smokehouse before I confronted you that night—just in case you tried to get your hands on it. I didn't want you to dispose of the poisoned medicine as easily as you did when you fed arsenic to Ann Livingston—the young medical assistant who preceded me. When she became a threat to your reputation, you disposed of her and placed the blame elsewhere. Last time the other doctor in town was your scapegoat. This time it was Catlin."

A puzzled frown knitted Catlin's brow. She didn't know what Ginger was driving at, but obviously Emmet did. His body went as rigid as a flagpole.

"That's a lie!" Emmet protested in a shrill voice.

"Is it?" Lucas retrieved the bottle from Ginger's hand. "If there is nothing wrong with the medication, why don't you prove it to us by taking a few teaspoons," Lucas challenged. "If you don't become violently ill, we will believe you instead of Ginger."

Deliberately, Lucas approached Emmet who was huddled in the corner with his back to the wall. Lucas's dark eyes darted hastily to Cat who looked suspiciously as if she were reaching for the dagger she kept stashed in her boot. Damn that daring little imp. She was going to get herself killed, sure as hell!

When Emmet shrank away from the bottle Luke thrust at him, Catlin could no longer inch her hand toward her knife. Thank the Lord! Lucas thought to himself. Emmet would have slit Cat's throat before she could wrap her fingers around the stiletto and turn it on him.

Emmet's refusal to take a swig of the medication he had given to Robert Hanley was silent testimony that the bottle had been tampered with.

"There, you see? Emmet is afraid to take his own medicine." Ginger expelled a disdainful sniff and glared flaming arrows at Emmet. "You couldn't convince me to do as you demanded and you retaliated by poisoning my father. You couldn't convince Ann Livingston to leave town either, so you conveniently prescribed a medication laced with arsenic for her. Then you trotted off with your wife to visit relatives. When Ann died during your carefully planned absence, you accused the other physician in town of malpractice and ran him off," Ginger said harshly. "All this to save your precious reputation and drive away the physician who was becoming as well-respected as you were. Only God knows how many other victims have suffered because you wanted them out of the way for one reason or another."

"And then I came along to request a job to support my ailing father. You agreed to hire me and provided Papa with the expensive medication. I thought you were being generous, but too late I realized that you wanted to manipulate and use me the same way you used Ann. She and I had a lot in common, didn't we, Emmet?"

"You are leaping to ridiculous conclusions," Emmet growled furiously. "I am innocent!"

Tears clouded Ginger's eyes as the haunting flashbacks from the past converged on her. "You are guilty as sin, Emmet, and you damned well know it. I was at your mercy. Without my job and the expensive medicine you provided, my father would die. I had to take orders from you and do your bidding or I would lose my father."

Her tortured gaze darted to Lucas who was as taut as a freshly strung fence wire. "Emmet gave you the loan for your cattle drive, just so you would feel obligated to him. He intended to manipulate you the same way he man-uevered me. He wanted to pressure us into a marriage so we would be his puppets—indebted by his supposed generosity." She spat the last word like a curse.

"I did what I had to do because I was afraid Emmet would get back at me through my ailing father if I didn't obey him." Contempt swallowed Ginger's delicate fea-

404

tures as her misty eyes shifted back to the scowling physician. "Emmet delights in owning everyone, in exerting his power and influence over them. He surrounds himself with people who feel an obligation to him. It makes him feel like a demigod."

"Damn your soul!" Emmet growled, his face purple. Panicky, he clutched Catlin even more tightly against him for security. "That is a crock of lies! You are trying to discredit me. I have done nothing wrong."

"No, damn *your* soul," Ginger hissed at Emmet. "You have done everything wrong. You saw Catlin as a threat to your carefully laid scheme and you tried to drive her away from Lucas because you already had plans for him. She became your scapegoat more than once and you tried to make her feel cheap and selfish. You admitted that you had purposely confronted her when I interrogated you on the matter. It was your conversation with Catlin that prompted her to inform me that Lucas had broken their engagement. But he hadn't. Catlin lied to me because you had her convinced that I needed Lucas more than she did. When I decided to behave as bravely as Catlin, to assert myself in my dealings with you by threatening to expose you for what you are, you were outraged. You poisoned my father to frighten me away, to prove to me that I was no match for a man of your power and influence."

Ginger's attention shifted to Lucas once again, her lips trembling, her body quaking. "Emmet did kill my father. I know that as surely as I know my own name. When I confronted him with a pistol, things got out of hand and Catlin tried to save me from Emmet. That was when Emmet decided to murder Catlin and me so we couldn't accuse him of his dastardly crimes."

Frantically, Emmet struggled to his feet, keeping Catlin in front of him like a suit of armor. No one could touch him as long as Catlin was his captive. And Emmet played to his only advantage.

"Move aside," Emmet growled, pressing the scalpel to

Catlin's throat, drawing blood.

When Catlin winced, Lucas died a thousand deaths. Never in his life had he been possessed by such murdering fury, not even when he faced his Yankee butchers. Lucas had wanted to tear Jace Osborn limb from limb when he thought the bounty hunter was about to dispose of Catlin. But watching Emmet use Cat as his shield of armor, watching him spill her blood a second time brought out Luke's most violent killer instincts.

"I'll hunt you down, you bastard," Lucas threatened in a venomous tone. Begrudgingly, he was forced to step aside when Emmet approached with his hostage. To Luke's dismay, the physician wasn't foolish enough to present his back as a target. If he had, Luke would have dropped him in his tracks without batting an eyelash.

"If you try to follow me, you can watch me cut this meddling bitch to pieces," Emmet cackled dementedly. "Even when you all ganged up against me, you still couldn't win! You never will!"

Catlin's eyes darted about her, biding her time until Emmet herded her into the outer office—away from the congregation of people who crowded the doorway. Catlin knew she was risking life and limb, but she wasn't going anywhere with this lunatic! If she did, she would only prolong the inevitable. If she were to die, she would choose the time and place. But for certain, she was taking Emmet with her, not the other way around!

While Emmet was verbally sparring with Luke, Catlin took advantage of the distraction. With the quickness of an uncoiling spring, Catlin dropped toward the floor, purposely entangling her legs with Emmet's. As he stumbled forward to gain his balance, the heel of her hand shot upward, forcing the scalpel away from her neck, but not without drawing another drop of blood.

With a furious roar, Emmet launched himself at Catlin, intent on plunging the scalpel into her back. The force of his momentum caused Catlin to ram her head against the edge of the desk. A dull groan tumbled from her lips when pain plowed through her skull. The world turned black as pitch. . . .

As Catlin collapsed, two pistols barked. Emmet didn't have a prayer. There wasn't a doctor in the world who could have patched him up. Lucas and Jace were deadly accurate. The scalpel that hovered only two inches away from Catlin's back toppled from Emmet's fingertips as he pitched forward in a lifeless heap beside Catlin's unconscious form.

The office door banged against the wall, heralding the arrival of the sheriff. Emmet's medical commendations and certificates crashed to the floor as the bewildered sheriff glanced from Emmet and Catlin to Jace and Lucas's smoking Colts. Stunned, he stared at Ginger whom Emmet had named as one of the victims of the fire that demolished the Hanley home three months earlier.

"I thought you were dead," the sheriff croaked, dumbfounded.

"The report of Ginger's death and Catlin's vicious crimes were grossly exaggerated," Lucas declared. "All that Catlin is guilty of is attempting to save Ginger from a raving lunatic." He indicated the crumpled form of the physician. "Here lies your murderer who attempted to take another life this afternoon."

While Ginger and Bo offered a jumbled rendition of what had transpired in the office, Jace and Lucas shoved each other out of the way to reach Catlin first. It was a fight to the finish.

A muffled roar escaped Luke's lips when Jace tripped him up. While Lucas was bouncing off the wall, Jace scooped Catlin in his arms. Like two angry children playing tug-of-war over a toy, Luke and Jace battled to drag Catlin onto their laps. The abrupt jostling brought Catlin awake, but the blow to the back of her head had blurred her vision. All she could see was two fuzzy gray heads hovering over her. One sluggish arm reached up to curl itself around Lucas's neck—except it was really Jace she cuddled against.

To Luke's outrage, Jace soundly kissed Cat and she automatically responded. "Give her to me," Lucas growled menacingly.

Jace was too busy enjoying his long-awaited kiss to comply. He simply drank the sweet nectar of Catlin's lips until he was forced to come up for air.

"Marry me, Cat," Jace wispered raggedly. "I love you. We'll make a new life together."

It took a moment to recognize Jace's voice and for the hushed words to filter into her foggy brain. When they did, Catlin nodded agreeably. Why shouldn't she accept? she asked herself dazedly. Jace was offering her an escape from San Antonio and Lucas had obligations to Ginger. Her throbbing head, neck and hand, compounded by her blurred vision, prevented her from thinking or seeing much of anything except the end of her stormy affair with Lucas. Catlin hurt all over. She was dizzy and wounded and thankful to be alive. That was about all Catlin could hope for after what she had been through.

Lucas glared furiously at Jace who was grinning like a baked possum. Then he glowered at Catlin who had difficulty seeing him at all. Curse that minx. She had spirited away from Fort McKavett without a word and he had suffered all the torments of the damned while trying to reach San Antonio before Cat got herself killed. He had survived nine kinds of hell while Emmet held her hostage. And this was the thanks he got!

Hell's bells, if he lived a century he would never figure this firebrand out. She had impulsively agreed to marry Jace. Was that why she had dashed off from the fort without a word? Was that her way of saying good-bye? Obviously, Lucas mused in annoyance. Catlin had set a precedence of leaving him without a word. Dammit, if she really didn't want to marry him why couldn't she have just said so?

Two months earlier, Catlin had proclaimed Lucas was her first and only love. And since that time, this fickle chit had abandoned him twice. Did that sound like proper behavior for a woman who insisted she was hopelessly and completely in love? Lucas didn't think so! Now she had consented to marry the very man who had tried to kill her three times. How fickle and unpredictable could one woman be? This one was driving him nuts! Maybe he did have an obligation to Ginger, but dammit, how was he going to get through the rest of his life without Cat? The sun rose and set in those lively violet eyes. She had become every step he took, his reason for being. But Jace was taking Lucas's place and that thought cut through him like a sword.

Scowling mutinously, Lucas stormed into the examining room to retrieve bandages and antiseptic to tend the slashes on Catlin's head, hand, and neck. Still sulking, he returned to thrust the supplies at Ginger who gladly accepted the task, leaving Lucas to field the rest of the sheriff's questions.

Catlin was still in a blurred daze. Her head pounded like a bass drum and the antiseptic that Ginger dabbed on her burned like fire. Catlin squeezed her eyes shut and cuddled against Jace's sturdy frame.

After adding his two cents worth to Ginger and Bo's testimony, Lucas elbowed his way through the crowd that had congregated outside the office and propelled himself toward Martha Lewis's home. No doubt, Martha was beside herself, wondering what had happened to Catlin the past four months. She had been plied with lies and it was time she knew the truth.

When Lucas rapped on the door, a much thinner Martha greeted him. From all indication, the mental anguish caused by Emmet's vicious lies and Cat's disappearance had taken their toll on her. Deep circles clung to her eyes and her welcoming smile lacked its usual enthusiasm.

"Oh, Lucas, I'm so glad you're back. The most horrible things have happened. I know the malicious rumors about my niece can't possibly be true, but—" Martha burst into tears as she half-collapsed against Luke's broad chest.

"Everything is alright," Lucas consoled her. "Catlin is back and she has been exonerated of the charges Emmet filed against her. He was the one who committed the crimes and blamed them on Catlin."

Astonished hazel eyes blinked up at Lucas from behind wire-rimmed glasses. "What?" she croaked. "Where is she?"

"Ginger will accompany her home in a few minutes."

"Ginger?" Martha clung to Lucas when her legs threatened to fold up like an accordion. "But I thought . . ."

"She's alive, thank God," Lucas sighed. "And if you can get yourself in hand, I could use a drink . . . or three."

"Oh my goodness, I almost forgot!" Martha gasped as she pushed herself into an upright position. "You have guests. They arrived two days ago. Since I had extra room I invited them to stay with me until you returned from the drive."

Luke's brow furrowed as Martha clutched his hand and led him down the hall to the dining room where her guests were enjoying a slice of Martha's famous apple pie.

Lucas very nearly stumbled over his own feet when he spied the two visitors who were seated at the table. He stood as still as a pillar of stone while memories swamped him like a tidal wave. He wasn't prepared to excavate emotions that belonged in another lifetime while his present and future were in such chaos. But he was left with no choice as he came face to face with what his life was like before Catlin Quinn barged into it. Hell's bells, he needed a whole damned bottle of brandy, not just a few drinks!

Chapter 28

"Do you feel well enough to stand up?" Ginger murmured, peering into Catlin's blank expression.

Catlin stared at the hazy vision that was swarming with gray and black cobwebs. She felt as if she were looking at a silhouette in the darkness. When Jace set her to her feet, the hazy world whirled about her and Catlin swayed dizzily.

"You had better carry her," Ginger advised Jace.

Catlin felt herself being lifted into Jace's strong, capable arms and she instinctively snuggled closer, needing consolation after her unnerving ordeal. When he brushed his lips over her forehead, she found herself wishing it had been Lucas who offered affection. But at the moment, Catlin was desperate for compassion. She took what she could get, reminding herself she could accept nothing from Lucas ever again—not sympathy or passion.

While Catlin was being carried through a crowd of faces that were no more than indistinguishable shadows, she sighed in relief. She still couldn't see a damned thing and her hand, neck, and head were killing her. But at least Emmet had received his just desserts. For that she was thankful. She may never be able to see straight again but being blind was ten times better than coping with nightmares of Emmet and the grief of thinking Ginger had perished.

Poor Ginger, Catlin mused compassionately. Her life had been nothing short of hell. Well, it was going to be a damned sight better from this day forward! Lucas was free to assume his responsibility and to provide for their child. Ginger would never want for anything. Catlin would see to that . . . somehow!

When the front door opened Catlin vaguely recognized Martha's thin face. She managed a semblance of a smile for her aunt.

"My poor darling! I can't begin to tell you how relieved I am to see you," Martha bubbled. "And Ginger! Thank God you're alive. I thought the entire world had come tumbling down."

Like a busy bumblebee, Martha buzzed down the hall, indicating the sofa in the parlor where Jace was to place Catlin. While Jace carefully eased Catlin to her back, Martha scurried off to fetch another bottle of peach brandy for her injured niece (Lucas having polished off the other one).

Groping in the fuzzy shadows, Catlin clutched Ginger's hand. The ferocious headache that rumbled through her skull was a hindrance, but Catlin mustered an encouraging smile. "Now that we have dealt with Emmet, we are free of the tragic nightmares. I will see to it that you are properly cared for," Catlin promised Ginger. "You and your baby will be settled at the Flying Spur and Lucas . . ."

Soft laughter bubbled from Ginger's lips. Catlin was the only true friend Ginger ever remembered having—the one person who had been there for her during the worst of times. They had known each other for only a month before the tragedy, but Catlin had offered more than compassion and friendship. She had very nearly sacrificed her own life to spare Ginger.

"You don't have to fret about me, my friend." Ginger

gave Cat's hand an affectionate squeeze. "After I climbed from the burning house and took refuge in the smoke-house, I rode off into the night, certain you had been killed. A very nice young Lieutenant from Fort McKavett by the name of Allen Simms found me after I had collapsed. He has been kind and understanding. In fact, we would have been married last week, if he hadn't been wounded in a skirmish with the Comanches. But as soon as he is back on his feet and you are feeling better, I would be pleased if you would consent to be my maid of honor."

With each passing minute, Catlin's vision was clearing. She began to recognize colors and shapes. At last she could see Ginger's smiling face poised above hers. There was no longer that underlying hint of sadness in Ginger's round green eyes. It was as if a heavy burden had been lifted from Ginger's shoulders.

Solemnly, Catlin squinted up at Ginger. "Does Allen know what happened to you?"

Ginger gave her dark head a negative shake. "I couldn't bring myself to talk about it," she admitted, dodging Cat's probing stare. "I was afraid Allen might decide to avenge my torment by confronting Emmet and I didn't dare let him clash with that demented murderer."

Catlin had experienced the same reluctance to speak of the incident, hoping to protect those she held dear. It was understandable that Ginger had been secretive about her past.

"But Allen has been very patient and he hasn't forced me to discuss the nightmare. He is willing to accept my child as his own, no questions asked. Allen is thoughtful and considerate and I am very much in love with him. Now that this ordeal with Emmet is finally over, I can divulge the truth to him and pray his feelings for me won't change."

Catlin glanced back at Jace, casting him a pleading smile. "Would you mind leaving us alone for a few

413

minutes," she requested.

Jace shifted Catlin's head to a pillow and agilely climbed to his feet. With a hesitant stare in Catlin's direction, Jace strided out the door. When he was gone, Catlin soothingly patted Ginger's hand.

"I want you to be happy, Ginger. You deserve to be." There was a long pause while Catlin attempted to formulate a tactful way to convey her feelings. "If you are marrying Allen because of my engagement to Lucas, you needn't. I have consented to marry Jace. You can count on Lucas to accept his responsibility where you are concerned."

A befuddled frown knitted Ginger's brow. "Lucas's responsibility?" she repeated dubiously.

Catlin awarded Ginger with a compassionate smile. "You needn't pretend, my friend. I know the secret you have been hiding for the past five months. Emmet told me it was Luke's baby you were carrying and I took the liberty of informing him of his—"

"Is that what Emmet told you?" Ginger chirped. "He swore all he said to you was that I was in need of a husband to help me care for my father. That miserable . . ." Her voice trailed off in a wordless growl.

Now it was all beginning to make sense. That was the real reason Catlin had denounced her engagement to Lucas and concocted the story to spare Ginger's feelings. Emmet had Catlin believing it was Lucas's child that Ginger carried.

"Emmet lied to you, Catlin. I didn't want to have to admit this in front of everyone in the office, but the baby is Emmet's," Ginger confessed though reluctantly. "Emmet wanted me to take a husband, and quickly. That was why he tried to shove me at Lucas every chance he got." She paused, unable to meet Catlin's startled stare. "That was why he demanded that I go to Lucas's cottage the night I informed Emmet I was carrying his child. If Emmet was successful in his matchmaking, I suppose Lucas would have assumed the child was his and I would have been afraid to tell him otherwise. But even if I had married Lucas, I knew Emmet would still expect me to provide him with sexual favors because he was providing my father with much-needed medication."

Catlin cringed, disturbed by the thought of what Ginger had endured. She had become Emmet's unwilling pawn, his object of pleasure. Cat couldn't help but wonder if Emmet's wife knew her husband had taken advantage of women while he was pretending to be the devoted husband.

Ginger knotted her hands in the folds of her gown, forcing herself to continue the unpleasant explanation. "When you announced your engagement, Emmet became desperate and attempted to discourage you from marrying Lucas. I was fond of Lucas, it's true. I would have been content if he had asked me to marry him. But when I realized Luke was interested in you, I gave up any hope of a relationship with him."

She inhaled a deep breath, her voice still on the unsteady side. "You once encouraged me to slay my own dragons and handle my own problems. I mustered my courage and I went to Emmet, demanding that he accept full responsibility for the child. I threatened to soil his precious reputation if he didn't acknowledge his dalliances with me and provide for my child."

Catlin held herself accountable for the unfortunate confrontation between Ginger and Emmet. Damn her and her free advice! "I should have kept my mouth shut," Cat grumbled, self-critically.

"No, you were right," Ginger hastily insisted. "A woman should stand up for herself and I should have stood up to Emmet a long time ago. It was the first time in two years that Emmet felt threatened. I had not even dared to tell what I knew about his affair with Ann Livingston because I was indebted to Emmet. I knew what he wanted from me and I was trapped into submitting to his amorous attentions. He was keeping my father alive and I was afraid to jeopardize my father's life by exposing Emmet for what he was—a manipulator, a philanderer who preyed on destitute women like me who did not have the strength, power, or position to fight him." Her green eyes darkened with bitterness. "But Emmet certainly had it coming and it was high time I defied him. You only encouraged me to do what I knew I should have done in the beginning."

Grimly, Ginger stared into Catlin's anguished face. "The real reason Emmet disposed of Ann Livingston was because she was also pregnant with his child. But she went so far as to demand that Emmet leave his wife and marry her. Ann was a friend of mine. She had confided her problems to me, as well as her fears about what Emmet would do to her. That was why I didn't dare take you into my confidence. I feared Emmet would turn on you as well. And even when you didn't know the truth, you were still caught in the middle of our conflict. Emmet was accustomed to using shrewd methods that were at his disposal. He poisoned Ann and blamed the other physician for her death. Then he poisoned my father to put the fear of God in me so I wouldn't dare discredit him. But I went after Emmet with a pistol instead of cowering."

Catlin's jaw hung on its hinges while she digested Ginger's words. Lord, all this time she believed Lucas had fathered Ginger's child and Ginger had no idea that Emmet had given the lie to Catlin to protect his position and reputation. They both had been deceived by Emmet's manipulative lies.

"While you are recuperating, I think I will lie down a bit," Ginger said tiredly. "My journey from the fort was exhausting and the confrontation with Emmet has sapped the last of my strength."

As Ginger turned away, Catlin called after her. "I'm so

sorry about all you have been through," she said with genuine emotion.

Ginger returned the sympathetic smile. "And I'm sorry I brought Emmet's wrath down on you. I hadn't meant to. Indeed, I tried to prevent it."

When Ginger exited the parlor, Jace entered. Catlin levered up to stare at the man she had consented to marry. My, what a complicated tangle her life was. She had been influenced by so many misconceptions that it made her head ache worse than it already did!

Jace broke into a rueful smile. He knew what Catlin was thinking because he had eavesdropped on her private conversation with Ginger. When Jace begged for Catlin's hand in marriage she had been laboring under the erroneous belief that Ginger carried Lucas's child. Catlin had intended to step aside for Ginger's sake. But now everything had changed. Lucas was free of any obligation. Yet, Jace had no intention of giving up easily. This was his last chance to persuade Catlin to ride away with him and he intended to take advantage of their privacy.

Like a prowling cougar, he paced from wall to wall, organizing his thoughts. "I left the room as you requested, but I purposely listened in on your conversation," he admitted unrepentantly.

Jace inhaled a breath and stared down into those enthralling violet eyes that were usually so full of spark and spirit. Now they were dull from a nagging headache and a severe blow to the head.

"Perhaps Ginger's confession makes a difference to you, but it doesn't matter to me. You thought Lucas was obliged to care for her. But what I feel for you is strong, Catlin—too strong to brush aside as if you don't matter to me."

Slowly, he folded himself, squatting in front of the daring beauty who threw herself into danger with incredible panache. She had very nearly gotten herself killed the previous hour and Jace was still unnerved by what he had seen.

"I meant what I said, Cat," Jace declared. "I love you and I want to spend the rest of my life with you. I'll take you anywhere you want to go. I'll show you places as spectacular as Cheyenne Canyon. We can travel to California or Oregon or anywhere that meets your whim. I want you with me and I crave whatever you can give. I won't expect your complete devotion if you are not prepared to offer it to me. I can only hope that in time you might even come to love me as much as I love you."

Tenderly, Catlin reached up to trace his chisled features. "You must know I have grown fond of you, Jace, but . . ."

"But I can't take pretty boy Murdock's place in your heart," he finished for her in a deflated tone.

The hint of a smile touched Catlin's lips as she smoothed away Jace's resentful frown. "Do you know, in the beginning I refused to allow myself to like Lucas. I didn't want to. I was cynical of all men. I have gotten over hating him, but I can't seem to make myself stop loving him, even if we can never completely settle things between us. I believe he cares for me, but I'm not sure he can give me all of himself when the memories of another woman weigh heavily on his mind. And I could not be a good wife to you when I harbor thoughts of—"

"I can live with that," Jace insisted, cutting her short. "I'll give you time to get over Murdock without pressuring you. I hope I can make you forget him, but if I can't, I'll still be willing to settle for something in between all and nothing. I don't care what I have to do to have you with me."

Her soft laughter tickled his senses. "You are a most persistent man, Jace Osborn," she teased softly.

"Maybe so," he contended with a hollow laugh. "It comes with the job, I suppose. The offer is still open, Cat. I'll be riding out tomorrow morning and I want very much

418

for you to come with me."

Martha whizzed into the parlor to check on her long lost niece and to await introductions to Catlin's attentive guest. Although the man wasn't particularly handsome it was obvious that he was hopelessly enamored with Catlin. Jace could barely take his eyes off her.

Declining Martha's invitation for a slice of apple pie, Jace ambled toward the door. There he paused to glance back at the shapely blond who had become the siren in his elusive dreams.

Although Jace spoke not a word, Catlin could decode the message in those probing blue eyes. He was willing to settle for the scraps of her affection, knowing she loved another man. But Catlin, unlike Jace, refused to be satisfied with less than a perfect relationship of mutual affection. She had to know if Lucas wanted her for better, for worse, and all phases in between. If Lucas needed no more than a warm body in his bed, a hostess and a companion, she had no choice but to ask Jace to take her to another state to begin a new life—alone.

Lucas apparently didn't want her with him all that much, she mused dispiritedly. He had walked off after her ordeal with Emmet without so much as a good-bye. If he hadn't wanted her to accept Jace's proposal of marriage he could have said so! It wasn't as if Lucas Murdock ever refrained from saying exactly what he was thinking and feeling, after all. Dammit, he hadn't voiced one word of protest when she accepted Jace's proposal. And he hadn't even waited around to determine if she was going to be addled and blind for the rest of her life either! Lucas had sauntered off to do only God knew what, leaving her in Jace's care.

And even if she and Lucas did resolve most of the conflicts and misconceptions between them there was still one obstacle that Catlin doubted she could ever overcome. She had the inescapable feeling that the memory of Elise would always stand between them. Catlin couldn't bear to play second fiddle to Luke's first true love. She needed more than security and passion, more than a home and a ranch. She had to feel wanted and needed, to believe she truly belonged in Lucas's life. Without that assurance Catlin was prepared to turn her back on the only love she had ever known.

Although it hurt deeply, she understood why Lucas had felt compelled to put a world between him and his brother's wife. She comprehended his need to break free of the emotional attachment that spanned miles and years. If she remained in San Antonio without marrying Lucas it would be torment. Not seeing him at all would be easier than being assaulted by the bittersweet memories each time they crossed paths. Now that Catlin knew Lucas had not fathered Ginger's child, she didn't have to fret about those complications. But nothing was going to erase her major conflict in obtaining Lucas's love—Elise. It boiled down to the simple fact that Catlin had to mean more to Lucas than Elise did.

When Martha thrust a brandy at her and rattled on about what had transpired during her absence, Catlin was still distracted by a vision of dancing brown eyes and a rakish smile. It was only when she heard Martha mention Luke's name that Cat perked up her ears and paid close attention.

"Lucas has been here?" Catlin squeaked in surprise. "When?"

"Indeed he was," Martha confirmed between sips of brandy. "He came to tell me you were back in town and that Ginger was tending your wounds. He had also come by to pick up the money his brother was supposed to wire to him from Georgia. But the money Luke asked me to keep for him until he returned from the trail drive never came. Instead, Luke's brother and his sister-in-law delivered the inheritance money in person. Lucas has taken them to the ranch to show them around.

"Elise is here? In Texas?" Catlin chirped like a sick cricket.

"In the flesh," Martha affirmed with a smile. "And what a lovely lady she is, too. I so enjoyed her company. She managed to lift my spirits with her charm and wit. In some ways she reminds me of you. Elise is so full of vim and vigor. Why, a room fairly lights up when she walks into it. And you should see Andrew Murdock." Martha tittered delightedly. "He is every bit as handsome as Lucas is."

Catlin felt the sofa drop out from under her. "I've got to go to the ranch," she murmured absently.

"No, you've got to lie down!" Martha contradicted. "You have had a rough day, young lady. You may have a concussion after you bumped your head. You yourself admitted you still weren't seeing clearly."

Despite Martha's protests, Catlin climbed to her feet, swaying slightly in her attempt to maintain her balance. "I have to talk to Lucas. It can't wait."

Martha flung up her hands in exasperation when Catlin weaved toward the door and clambered down the steps. Catlin had made up her mind to go and nothing was going to stop her . . . as usual. She wanted to inform Lucas that he was not the father of Ginger's child. But more importantly, Catlin wanted to get a good look at Elise, to see her and Lucas together. Catlin had to know if those long-harbored feelings Lucas felt for Elise were still there, to determine if she had a chance of winning Lucas.

Lord, she faced another critical encounter today, Catlin thought as she retrieved her horse. It wasn't enough that she had confronted Emmet and very nearly got herself stabbed to death. Now she had to view Lucas's reaction to being reunited with his first true love. Catlin wasn't sure which was worse—facing Emmet or the sultry brunette Martha had described. Damn, if she knew what was good for her, she would locate Jace and request that they depart from San Antonio within the hour!

That thought caused Catlin to pause in the street and glance toward the hotel. Jace could take her away from her torment once and for all. He had accepted the limitations of her affection for him and he was prepared to take whatever she offered. What sensible woman would dare ask for more than that?

Indecision etched Catlin's brow when Jace ambled from the hotel to lean negligently against the supporting post. When he glanced in Catlin's direction he didn't bother to disguise the hunger in his eyes. And Catlin wished with all her heart that she felt the same way about Jace as she did about Lucas.

Why shouldn't she take the easy way out? Catlin asked herself. She was tired of these uphill battles and lost causes. California was probably lovely this time of year. Maybe she ought to see it for herself. . . .

Part 3

The Cat and the Love you give away
always come back to you

Chapter 29

Darkness had spread its cloak over the rolling hills. Catlin had been sorely tempted to approach Jace, but instead she had reined her horse southwest, cursing herself for wanting to appease her curiosity about Elise Murdock. By the time Catlin reached the Flying Spur, the bunkhouse was ablaze with lanterns and the vaqueros were celebrating their return to Texas.

Clinging to the moonshadows, Catlin tethered her horse a good distance away and crept toward the ranch house. Even though she was taller than average height and she pushed up on tiptoe, she couldn't see over the window ledge to spy on Lucas and his guests. She could hear the sound of voices in the dining room and the ripples of laughter, but she required a ladder to peep at Andrew and Elise Murdock.

Spur's low bawl caught Catlin's attention and an idea instantly hatched in her mind. Quick as a wink, she trotted down the hill to the cottage which Bo Huxley now called home. Catlin snatched up the grain bucket for Spur and lured him beneath the dining room window. After setting the pail of feed under Spur's nose, Cat climbed on his back to gain a better view. Spur didn't complain that he had become an improvised ladder, not when he was allowed to enjoy his nightly treat. He merely gobbled up the grain while Catlin window peeked.

Catlin's spirits nose-dived when she spied the curvaceous brunette who sat across the table from Lucas. To her chagrin Cat couldn't see Lucas's expression because he had his back to her. Elise was another matter though. Catlin could appraise the woman's enchanting features, dancing eyes, and spellbinding smile. Although Catlin tried to be objective, jealousy and resentment plagued her while she surveyed Lucas's one and only true love.

And sure enough, Elise was everything Martha said she was—charming, elegant, yet teeming with vitality. But to make matters worse, Elise was stunning. In fact, to say that Elise was a raving beauty was nearer the mark. No wonder Lucas couldn't exorcise Elise's memory from his mind. Elise had it all—delicate bone structure, a face God had labored over with tender loving care, hair as thick and rich as velvet, dark hypnotic eyes that were fringed with long sooty lashes. And honest to goodness, the room did seem to light up when Elise burst into a smile! Her radiance could have led a lost traveler through a blizzard. Damn!

And if the memories weren't enough to torment Lucas, Elise had reentered his life to stir up his emotions all over again. Confound it, if only Catlin could have seen Luke's face so she could determine his reaction to the blinding smiles Elise was bestowing on him. The poor man was probably melting in his boots, turning envy green and wishing he was his brother. Double damn.

If Lucas was peering at Elise the same way Andrew was, Catlin didn't have a prayer. The elder Murdock was indeed as attractive as Lucas was and the infatuated look on his face attested to his affection for his wife. Ah, the irony of it all, Catlin mused glumly. Here were two handsome brothers who were hopelessly in love with the same woman.

How could Catlin ever hope to compete with this

bewitching goddess? Lucas still carried a torch for Elise and he always would. Elise would not be easily forgotten, not with a face that could launch a few thousand ships and a shapely body that could halt a stampede. Hell's bells, her female rival was—

A shocked squawk flew from Catlin's lips when her four-legged ladder finished his treat and decided to trot down to the cottage to sip a few gallons of water. Spur kicked up his heels and shot off, leaving Catlin clinging to the window sill by her injured hand and fingernails.

"What the hell . . . ?" Lucas vaulted from his chair to wheel toward the window. All he could see was a bandaged hand and a tangled mass of blond hair in the splintering light that sprayed through the window. Hurriedly, he lifted the pane to meet Catlin's sheepish smile.

Lucas, who had been in a sour mood all evening, glared down at the peeping Cat. "If you have come to invite me to your wedding or ask me to give the bride away, I'll be busy that day," he growled in a most unpleasant tone.

Jealousy, mortification, and bitterness all fought to gain control of Catlin's emotions. "I haven't even told you which day," she snapped back at him.

"It doesn't matter which day," he snorted as he pried her fingers from the window ledge and watched with wicked glee as Catlin kerplopped in the grass. This was one Cat who hadn't landed on her feet. He hoped she sprained her shapely derriere, damn her. "I plan to be busy every day. But even if I don't attend the ceremony, I hope you and Jace will be deliriously happy together." His tone implied he hoped nothing of the kind, which of course he didn't.

After scraping herself off the ground Catlin massaged her bruised backside and nursed her wounded pride. Two more heads poked through the window to peer down at the ragamuffin in her oversized buckskins. Catlin stared up at Andrew Murdock who bore such a striking resemblance to his younger brother that they could have been mistaken

427

for twins. Obviously, Elise had found it necessary to flip a coin to decide which of these two attractive rakes she should marry.

Catlin didn't spend overly long sizing up Andrew Murdock. Instead, her gaze drifted back to the dazzling brunette who was standing a little too close to Lucas to suit Catlin. Again Cat found herself comparing Elise to the rising sun. When Elise smiled in amusement, her dark eyes sparkled with an inner radiance that was impossible to ignore.

"Aren't you going to introduce us to your friend, Lucas?" Elise prompted, her soft voice bubbling with barely restrained laughter.

Lucas muttered irritably before making the brief introductions. "Elise and Andrew Murdock, meet my ex-fiancée. She threw me over for a bounty hunter who tried to kill her a couple of times. Too bad for him that he was unsuccessful."

"Lucas!" Elise reprimanded her brother-in-law by gouging him in the ribs.

"I'm glad to meet you, Miss . . ." Andrew patiently waited for their wild-haired guest to fill in the blank. Although Lucas had been ranting and raving about this delightful misfit all evening long, he referred to the young lady only as "Cat." Andrew thought it more polite to request a formal introduction, just in case "Cat" was an intimate nickname that only Lucas had been allowed to use when addressing her.

"Quinn. Catlin Stewart Quinn." Mustering as much dignity as the situation permitted, Cat drew herself up to proud stature. "It is nice to meet you, although I wish it could have been under better circumstances," she tacked on with a sheepish smile.

"Why don't you come around to the front door and join us, Miss Catlin Stewart Quinn," Andrew suggested with a cordial grin. "Lucas can fetch you a cup of coffee."

428

"I'm all out of coffee," he grunted.

Well aware that she was as welcome at the Flying Spur as a gang of rustlers, Catlin demured. "Thank you but no. I have to be going."

"Do run along, Cat. I'm sure your fiancé will be beside himself, wondering what sort of nocturnal prowling has detained you this time," Lucas smirked sarcastically.

It was lucky for Lucas that Spur trotted off and that her horse was grazing a good distance away from the house. If she had some sort of improvised step ladder at her disposal she would have pulled herself up to window level to deliver that infuriating varmint a punch in the nose.

"I can come and go as I please without answering to any man," she spewed, her temper dangerously close to the end of its fuse.

It was bad enough that Lucas was ridiculing her in front of his family. But the fact that she looked like a windblown weed in comparison to Elise was putting sizable dents in Catlin's already crushed pride.

"Ah, yes," Lucas mocked dryly. "How could I have forgotten that the fickle butterfly flits hither and yon, flirting with disaster and anything in breeches that she happens onto while she's out doing her prowling." Briefly, he glanced at his older brother. "If you happen to have a crusade that needs to be fought, Andrew, just call on Cat. She thrives on thrills that put her life on the line."

"Lucas, you are being frightfully rude," Elise admonished.

"It's alright," Cat purred pretentiously. "It's only one of his zillion faults. The man is rife with them . . . or didn't you know?"

That did it! Lucas was already in a snit. He had tried to be the perfect host for Elise and Drew. But by being the picture of cheerful politeness, he had curtailed his anger and frustration with this sassy minx. Now his irritation was simmering and Catlin's taunt caused his temper to boil like a tea kettle. With a wordless scowl, Lucas shoved a leg over the window sill and hopped to the ground to thrust his face into Catlin's.

Catlin was certain Lucas had a full set of teeth when he began chewing her up one side and down the other. She could count them one and all!

"Okay, you've had your fun," he bit off. "If you came to flaunt your engagement, you've accomplished your purpose. Now why don't you sashay back to Jace and leave me to entertain my guests whom I haven't seen in over five years."

When Catlin pivoted to stamp away, Lucas grabbed her arm to blare a few more of the insults that had been whirling through his mind the past few hours. Quietly, Andrew eased the window shut and escorted his wife into the hall. From all indications, the lawn had become a battlefield.

"Well, what do you think of Miss Quinn?" Drew questioned his wife.

"I do believe Lucas has finally met his match," Elise declared with great conviction. "He hasn't stopped talking about Catlin all afternoon, even though he said some terrible things about her. I think his degrading remarks were meant to convince himself that he doesn't care as much as he truly does. He protested a bit too much to convince me. And Catlin appears to give as good as she gets. Lucas needs that in a woman."

A wry smile pursed Drew's lips as he gave Elise a loving squeeze. "Are you disappointed, sweetheart?" he murmured, peering into the dark, expressive eyes that formed the dimensions of his dreams.

Elise graced her husband with an adoring smile. "I never meant to hurt Lucas. I only wanted to reassure him after he had his pride and his body cut to shreds by those Yankee guerrillas. But I know I made the right choice almost six years ago, Drew. I pray Lucas will make Catlin as happy as you have made me."

Her full lips parted in invitation, one Drew eagerly accepted. But it was difficult to concentrate on kissing while Lucas was having a cat fight on the lawn. Since the skirmish looked to be the kind that would last all night, Andrew detoured toward the steps. He could think of far better ways of spending the evening than engaging in verbal warfare. It seemed his younger brother still had a lot to learn about women. Andrew had discovered that arguing wasn't half the fun that loving was. The sooner Lucas settled his differences with that sassy little blond, the happier he was going to be. Unfortunately, Lucas was too tormented to figure that out just yet. He was still blowing off steam!

"I do not appreciate having you spy on us," Lucas snapped brusquely.

"And I do not appreciate having you ridicule me in front of your family," came her blistering reply. "If you had said good-bye properly this afternoon, I wouldn't have had to seek you out!"

"Just how stupid do you think I am?" Lucas sneered derisively. "I know damned well why you came here—to have a look at Elise. You wanted to assure yourself, as you have so often, that I'm still carrying a torch for her."

"You are, aren't you?" Catlin muttered, her voice laced with a bitterness she couldn't disguise. "Not that I blame you, mind you. But I was right all along."

"You were wrong all along," he contested. "But, being the stubborn, muleheaded she-male you are, it would take an act of God to convince you."

"And being the fool you are, you aren't smart enough to figure out that I knew the only reason you asked me to marry you in the first place was simply because you wanted to say you had a wife. You don't need me. You

431

never did. I have never been anything more than a substitute for Elise."

Catlin matched his booming voice and let him have it with both barrels. "All you want is a warm body when your lusts overcome you. You want a cook and a housekeeper, a Jill-of-all-trades to tend your new ranch and your voracious male desires. But I would have demanded all of your love and I would have expected nothing less if we had married. I wouldn't have shared you, Lucas, not with another woman or Elise's memories. But you couldn't have accepted being confined to one woman for the rest of your life because you cannot forget what Elise means to you. You live in a dream world and you don't know beans about what love really is," she spouted.

"But you do, of course," he scoffed sarcastically. "Well, let me tell you something Miss God Almighty Quinn. Love isn't something you can plan out with your practical, sensible methods. You can't make out an alphabetical check list and go around grading a man, trying to fit him into your specific qualifications." Lucas inhaled an agitated breath and roared on. "And for once, I wish you would stop trying to tell me what you think I want and need in a wife . . . if I decided to acquire one. If I were being sensible and practical I certainly wouldn't choose you. Not only do you attract trouble, but you go out of your way to find it!"

"Look who's talking," Catlin inserted with an intimidating smirk. "I was doing just fine by myself with Emmet and here you came again, poking your nose in places where it didn't belong."

"Doing just fine?" Lucas crowed incredulously. "You nearly got yourself killed again!" He brandished his finger in her flaming face. "Sometimes, woman, I swear you are hellbent on self-destruction."

"One is often reckless when one thinks one has nothing

432

to lose." Her tone softened and her wide eyes locked with those stormy dark pools.

"You were simply throwing our love away because you didn't think it was worth fighting for," he harshly accused, still frustrated as hell. "You have constantly run away from me and I'm constantly chasing after you. I wish I was doing the running and you were doing the chasing for a change. Maybe then you would understand why I died a little each time I thought I was going to lose you. I swear to God, Cat, you have done everything within your power to send me to an early grave."

Lucas couldn't tolerate peering at her for another minute. Swiftly, he spun about, preferring to give his soliloquy to the darkness at large. "And now I have lost you because of my obligations to Ginger. You intend to trot off with Jace and forget I ever existed. Well, fine. Go! I hope you're happy knowing I'm miserable."

"You have no responsibility to Ginger," Catlin informed him, staring at the wide expanse of his back. "Emmet lied to me. Ginger confessed to me privately that the child was Emmet's. He forced her to submit to him in exchange for the expensive medication he prescribed for Robert. And Ginger has asked me to be the maid of honor at her wedding. It seems she and a young lieutenant from Fort McKavett have fallen in love. It's a shame it couldn't have been that easy for us."

Lucas wheeled around to gape at her in astonishment. His mouth opened and closed like a damper on a chimney for several seconds before emitting a chirped question. "Are you sure?"

"Very sure," Catlin confirmed. "Ginger didn't want to blurt out the name of the father of her child with an audience surrounding her. She didn't know Emmet had given me the lie until I mentioned it this afternoon. So you see, Lucas, you are as free as you ever were. No woman has any ties on you. You are bound only by

Elise's memory."

Her last remark put him in a huff all over again. "Now that you have reassured yourself that I have never gotten over Elise, then you can go back to Jace and leave me be," he muttered sourly.

"I'm not marrying Jace," Catlin told him matter-of-factly. "I only consented because I thought Ginger needed you and I wasn't going to stand in her way."

"And I knew the minute I laid eyes on Elise that she wasn't what I needed to make my life complete anymore. I need someone who will stick by me through thick and thin, someone who shares the same dreams and aspirations. You could have been that woman, but I have given up trying to convince you that I love you. It's a hopeless battle."

"Are you trying to propose again?" Catlin wanted to know that very instant.

"No, I am not," Lucas declared in a terse tone. "I knew what I wanted and needed that night four months ago when I asked you to marry me. It felt good and right. I proposed three times in the same night. And the third time I said it was the last time I was going to ask. Since the night you said you would consider marrying me and wait my return, you have run away from me thrice and accepted the proposal from another man. I have had it with you, woman. I don't need all this torment."

His voice rose to a roar. "Either get out of my life once and for all or stay for better or worse. And if there is any proposing to be done around here, you are going to have to do it!" His chest swelled with so much frustration that he nearly popped the buttons on his shirt. "You are driving me nuts and I'm not asking you to marry me again *ever!*"

With that, Lucas spun around and stalked toward the front door.

Catlin stamped her foot and emitted a string of inarticulate curses. "Tell me here and now, Lucas

Murdock, do you honestly love me, and only me, or don't you?"

"Yes, dammit," he threw over his shoulder without breaking stride. "But I meant what I said. I'm never going to chase you down and tell you again. If you want me, this time you'll have to come and get me."

Come and get him? Why should she? He sounded too militant to convince her that he really and truly loved her. Catlin pulled a face at his departing back. Come and get him? That was how she got tangled up with that infuriating man in the first place. He had lured her into wanting him and she had sneaked from this very house, asking him to teach her the ways of passion. And just look where it got her! Because of her tempestuous affair she had almost gotten herself killed more times than she cared to count.

When the front door slammed shut with such force that the entire house rattled, Catlin winced. Why should she go after that ill-tempered rascal? She ought to ride off with Jace. He would make no demands on her and he wouldn't make her propose to him to satisfy his colossal male pride. And Jace wouldn't make mincemeat of her emotions the way Lucas did, that was for sure. But then, Jace couldn't set fires in her blood the way Lucas did either, she reminded herself. Only one man ignited sparks inside her. Only one man held the key to her heart. Now the question was—did she want to be happy for the rest of her life or did she merely wish to go through the paces of living?

Lucas Murdock had more than his rightful share of peccadilloes, but living without him would be nothing short of hell. Cat had lived through enough hell the last two years. Enough was enough! Lucas wanted a proposal, did he? Well, by damned she would swallow her pride and give him one. And if he turned her down she would kill him. That rat. He was probably sitting in his room, just waiting for her to propose so he could tell her he wouldn't marry her if she was the last woman on earth.

Squaring her shoulders, Catlin propelled herself around the corner of the house and marched up the front steps. Inhaling a courageous breath, she let herself in and quietly ascended the stairs.

Damn that varmint! she silently fumed. Who ever heard of a woman proposing marriage to a man? Honest to goodness, Lucas was the one who was driving her crazy, not the other way around.

When a woman proposed was she supposed to get down on her knees or pop the question standing up? Hell's bells, she shouldn't have to be doing this at all. Lucas was loving this, curse him. And he had better not refuse her because she was only going to ask him once—which was once more than she should have had to ask him in the first place! Women proposing to men? Indeed!

Chapter 30

Catlin eased open Lucas's bedroom door to find him peeling off his shirt. Her all-consuming gaze wandered over the scars that marred his chest, watching his whipcord muscles ripple as he carelessly flung his shirt aside.

The lantern light flickered over his craggy features and Catlin fell in love with him all over again. Sometimes Lucas made her so furious she wanted to pound him into the ground. Sometimes he intimidated her to the point that she wanted to slap him silly, but through it all, through the torment and the misconceptions that played havoc with her emotions, there was this slow burning fire that nothing could extinguish. There would always be conflicts between them, she knew. They were both too stubborn and headstrong to be dominated. But the bond between them had always kept them together, even while they were pulling in opposite directions.

One thick brow elevated as Lucas raked her ill-fitting garb. "Well? Did you come to propose or did you come to say your last good-bye?" he questioned point-blank.

Her long lashes fluttered up to meet those dark, entrancing eyes. "Yes," she murmured awkwardly.

"Yes what?" he demanded in an impatient tone. "Yes,

437

you are going to propose to me or yes, this is your final farewell?"

Blast it, he was spoiling the moment with his snide third-degree. Catlin was already feeling self-conscious and unsure of herself and Lucas wasn't helping matters one whit.

"Well, which is it?" he snorted derisively. "I haven't got all evening. Cats may prowl all the live-long night, but the rest of us need our sleep. If you've got something to say, then spit it out!"

After flashing Lucas an agitated glare, Catlin pirouetted on her toes and marched down the hall. Without announcing herself, Catlin barreled into Andrew's room to interrupt the couple midkiss.

"What on earth . . . ?" Andrew croaked as he clutched the sheet around him and his wife.

"I would greatly appreciate it if you would tell that impossible brother of yours that I want him to marry me because I am very much in love with him . . . although why I'm not certain. It isn't because of his rosy disposition or because he is warm and receptive to my affection for him. I'm not sure I can live with that infuriating man, but I don't think I can live without him either. I would be miserable. But he won't shut up long enough for me to propose as he demanded."

Catlin threw up her hands in a gesture of frustration. "Can you imagine that? He wants *me* to propose to *him!*" Her breath came out in an exasperated rush. "Why should I have to propose to him anyway? He should have been smart enough to know I loved him enough to marry him a long time ago if there hadn't been other people and other considerations standing in our way. Lucas said I was driving him crazy, but the truth is he has turned me wrong side out. That's why I'm behaving like an idiot—window peeking, barging in on you without announcing myself.

And for that I apologize."

A becoming blush stained her cheeks when she realized how foolish she must look to the couple who was staring frog-eyed at her. "The fact is I considered myself to be very sensible and practical until Lucas came along. Now I'm not sure which way is up, thanks to him! And to make matters worse, I have been clubbed over the head three times in four months. If I'm addle-witted I have every reason to be!"

Andrew and Elise bit back grins when they glanced past the feisty, wild-haired hellion who stood at the foot of their bed to see Lucas propped negligently against the door jamb.

"Did you hear all that, little brother, or must I repeat it to you?" Andrew inquired, muffling a chuckle.

"I heard," Lucas grunted. "I'm just not sure I believe it. Cat and I have been through this before. Dealing with this minx is like riding a runaway carousel. She was all set to accept David Krause's marriage proposal when I proposed. Then she broke our engagement, accepted another proposal from Jace Osborn before she decided to go back on her word to him. She has run away from me without explanation so often that I wake up each morning wondering if she'll still be where I left her the night before. Now I ask you, does that sound like a sensible, practical woman to you, big brother?"

"You ignoramus!" Catlin exploded, wheeling on him. "You know perfectly well why I felt I had to leave each time I left. And when I regained consciousness this afternoon I thought we were through for good. I was trying to do both of us a favor by accepting Jace's marriage proposal. Every blessed time I try to do someone a favor it backfires in my face. I'm finished playing the good Samaritan. All it gets me is—"

"Would the two of you mind continuing your argument

439

somewhere else," Andrew requested. "It's bad enough that we have two toddlers barging in on us while we're at home. We had hoped to make this trip to Texas a second honeymoon. But still we find ourselves interrupted by squabbling children."

Catlin blushed up to her eyebrows. Lord, she wouldn't be surprised if Andrew and Elise did believe she was a raving lunatic. Well, maybe she had lost her mind. But if she had, Lucas was the one who had driven her over the edge.

Wearing an amused grin, Lucas ambled over to grab Catlin's arm. "You can go back to what you were doing, big brother," Lucas murmured as he shuffled Catlin out of the room. "Cat won't disturb you for the duration of the night." Twinkling brown eyes focused on the enchanting face that was enhanced by flickering candlelight. "I'll see to it that she is distracted."

"You are going to marry her, aren't you?" Elise wanted to know.

Lucas glanced back at the sultry brunette who was barely covered by the sheet Andrew kept protectively about her. There had been a time when Lucas envisioned Elise in his bed and it made him ache with unbearable wanting. But seeing her with Andrew assured Lucas that Elise was where she belonged. The old flame had finally burned itself out. Catlin had barreled into his life and exorcised the haunting memories of the past. Now it was Cat's vision that tormented him. If he lost Cat now he wasn't going to get over her in five years or fifty years.

"I have to marry her," Lucas murmured as his eyes slid down Catlin's concealed figure in total possession. "Trying to get along without her hasn't worked worth a damn."

The feel of Lucas's hand absently gliding around her waist sent tantalizing tremors rippling across her skin.

440

Without protest, Cat allowed Lucas to lead her to his room. But she did object when his nimble fingers tugged at the lacings of her skirt.

"You said if I wanted you I had to come and get you," she reminded him in a throaty voice. "And I know exactly what I want, Lucas."

"Do you?" he queried in a hoarsely disturbed whisper.

When her straying hands slid down his hair-matted chest to loosen his breeches, Lucas swore his blood pressure was about to spring a leak. Catlin knew how and where to touch to instill a ravenous hunger in him that only she could appease.

"All I have ever wanted was for you to love me as much as I have come to love you," she murmured as her kisses mapped his masculine contours. He not only heard the quietly uttered words, but he felt them whispering over his sensitized flesh. "It's because I love you too much. And that all-consuming kind of affection cries out for a total commitment—the kind that accepts no stipulations, the kind that will endure forever."

Tenderly, Lucas cupped her exquisite face in his hands, holding her unblinking gaze. "I do love you, Cat," he said with sincere affection. "Nothing frightened me until I risked losing you. Each time you were hurt or tormented, I bled. And when I saw Elise again, I fully understood why I had to be the one who left Georgia while my brother stayed behind."

His lips grazed hers in the slightest breath of a kiss—a reverent kiss that communicated his devotion to her. "I have come to realize there is a time and a season for all things. You are my time, violet eyes. I didn't realize until just now that, as much as I thought I wanted Elise, she wasn't right for me. But you have stirred each and every one of my emotions. You were my reason for restlessly roaming, my reason for searching for a love that was my

441

very own. You aren't just what I thought I wanted, Catlin, you are what I need to make my life full and rich and promising."

"Do you honestly mean that, Lucas?" she queried, her jewel-like eyes misty with sentiment.

Even though the answer was in his adoring smile, he offered her the words she needed to hear, words that erased the last sediment of doubt. "I mean it with all my heart, Cat," he whispered softly. "I can look into your violet eyes and see a new dimension in time—*our* time, *our* future. And I have only just begun to show you all the wild, wondrous ways I love you. . . ."

Catlin swore she would melt all over his bronzed chest when he took her lips under his in a most incredible kind of kiss. He had kissed her before, but never quite like this. He had touched her before, but not as reverently and patiently as he did this night. Each caress was embroidered with love—the kind that held intimate promises of a splendorous life together. And Catlin expressed her heart-felt affection by returning each touch for worshipping touch, each kiss for tender kiss.

It was as it had been in the beginning—a rare, special kind of magic. They rediscovered each other—giving and sharing the pleasure of passion that was tempered with unselfish love. Their bodies sang out in glorious harmony as they made the most intimate of journeys across the star-spangled sky.

Catlin swore she had been catapulted into the heavens where the stars symbolized each wondrous sensation she experienced when she was in Luke's arms. Comets blazed across the darkness and shooting stars left trails of white-hot light. One delicious sensation after another piled upon her as Lucas took her on a magical flight through space. They were one, lying flesh to flesh, touching soul to soul. She could feel his heart thudding in frantic rhythm with hers, feel the mystical powers of love consuming her spirit, her mind, and her body.

When Lucas shuddered above her, Catlin clung to him, unable to draw a breath that wasn't thick with the intoxicating scent of him. She was left suspended in time, engulfed in wild ineffable emotions that matched nothing else in all the universe. It was love that cradled her in ecstasy. It was love that carried her down from the dizzying pinnacle of passion and left her content in the never-ending circle of Lucas's arms.

"No more doubts?" Lucas breathed in question as he nibbled at the swanlike column of her throat.

An elfish grin lit up her face and Lucas caught his breath when he peered down at the bewitching features that were caressed by lantern light and moonshadows.

"If I say yes, will you convince me of your love all over again?" she teased playfully.

A roguish smile quirked his lips. Absently, he combed his fingers through the wild spray of sandy blond hair that cascaded over his pillow. "How many more doubts, minx?"

"A dozen, give or take one or two," she replied saucily.

"A dozen?" Lucas chirped. "Good Lord, woman, I am not a love machine!"

Her brazen caress glided down the muscular planes of his back. "Perhaps not, but you are a magical wizard. You brought love into my life when I was too cynical of its existence and its powers. You chased my fears and doubts away. When I'm with you, Lucas, nothing is impossible. . . ."

The erotic fondling that accompanied her softly uttered words convinced him that he was every bit the man she believed him to be. His body roused by leaps and bounds, stirred by her titillating caresses and soul-shattering kisses.

Lucas didn't get much sleep that night. But he didn't complain. At long last he had found his dream come true. Catlin was not only everything he wanted, but she was everything he needed. He wanted for no more than this saucy pixie could give.

This night was a new beginning that teemed with hopes and fantasies. When he had this violet-eyed Cat in his arms, his world was filled to overflowing. His thoughts trailed off when Catlin came to him again, leading him down the sensual corridor to paradise. . . .

As the first light of dawn spilled through the window, the whinny of a horse brought Lucas slowly awake. There had been times the past few years that Lucas felt nine years older than God when he roused in the morning, but today he felt sixteen and hopelessly in love.

The quiet chirp of a bird that sounded a little too human to be fowl prompted Lucas to inch away from Catlin. He glanced out the window to see the silhouette of a man poised on the rolling hill. Quietly, Lucas slipped into his breeches and tiptoed down the hall. He wasn't surprised to see Jace Osborn standing like a posted lookout, staring pensively at the second story window.

"She's here with you." Jace didn't pose a question. He muttered the statement as fact.

Lucas watched Jace's keen gaze travel over the scars that marred his chest, waiting for the gunslinger to raise his piercing blue eyes. "She's here and she's staying," Lucas told him plainspokenly.

A long sigh escaped Jace's lips. "I concede," he grumbled in a resentful tone. "I guess you win after all, Murdock."

Thick black lashes swept up to stare at Jace. "I'm sorry, Lucas murmured.

The semblance of a smile hovered on Jace's lips as he pulled his hat down on his forehead, shading his eyes from the rising sun. "Like hell you are," he snorted in contradiction. "You are no more sorry than I would have been if I had convinced Cat to go away with me." He inhaled a defeated breath and slowly exhaled it. "Tell her good-bye for me, Murdock. And you damned well better love her enough for both of us or I might come back to test your quick-draw. Next time, winner takes all."

Lucas watched Jace nudge his steed toward the west. When Jace disappeared over the hill, Lucas ambled back into the house. This time he was the one to remain behind instead of riding off into parts unknown. His wandering days were finally over and Jace's had just begun. It was going to take Jace an eternity to forget Cat, Lucas predicted.

A quiet smile rippled across Lucas's lips as he eased a shoulder against the door jamb and peered at the enchanting nymph who lay in his bed. A cape of blond hair spilled over Cat's bare shoulder and one silky arm lay upon the spot Lucas had vacated. God, she was so lovely, so full of vitality. Just thinking of the hours of ecstasy they had shared caused a wider, more rakish smile to dangle on one corner of his mouth.

Lucas jerked upright when a hand touched his shoulder. He swiveled his head around to see his brother peering back at him.

"Almost six years ago, I felt selfish for marrying Elise when I knew how much you wanted her. . . ." Andrew's voice trailed off when Lucas's eyes swung back to Catlin, watching her stir beneath the sheet.

"Cat is what I wanted and needed," Lucas whispered. "It just took me half a decade to find her."

The last feelings of guilt and regret faded from Andrew's face while he surveyed his younger brother who was visually devouring the bewitching sprite. The look on Lucas's face lent testimony to the fact that he no longer cared that Andrew had married Elise. The memories of the past were a dim flame compared to the fire of love that burned in Lucas's brown eyes. Andrew had never seen a more tender, adoring expression on his younger brother's face. Catlin had healed the wounds of first love's disappointment. Andrew and Lucas were no longer rivals for Elise's affection. Lucas and Andrew shared an understanding—each man knew the contentment of finding his own unique brand of love.

"Be as happy as I am, Lucas," Andrew murmured earnestly.

A wide grin split Lucas's lips as he closed the door in his brother's face. "You can't be happier than I am. I've got Cat."

Andrew's brows elevated to a challenging angle as he wedged a bare foot in the doorway. "Don't you think what Elise and I have can compare to what you found with that sassy hellion?"

Lucas's eyes twinkled with arrogant amusement. "Love can't ever be better than this," he informed his older brother.

As the door eased shut, Andrew frowned pensively. Did Lucas know something Andrew didn't? Naw," Andrew assured himself. He knew all there was about love-making . . . didn't he?

For a long moment Andrew stared at the closed door. Well, just in case there was something he had overlooked the previous night . . .

While Andrew tiptoed back to his room, Lucas shucked his breeches and eased down beside Catlin's warm, shapely body. Cat was the best there was, Lucas assured himself. This violet-eyed nymph was the one special love of a lifetime. It was inconceivable to him that what Andrew and Elise shared could be anything remotely close to what he felt for Catlin. Lucas was certain of that. No matter how good Andrew thought he had it, Lucas had it better!

Each time Cat had spun her tantalizing web of pleasure over him she had made him more than a man. She had made him immortal. She took him higher than he had ever been. Andrew didn't know what flying was! Lucas mused as his hands skied over Catlin's curvaceous body, rousing her from the depths of sleep. With Cat in his arms, Lucas could catch the wind and soar over rainbows. And when the sun dipped low on the horizon he could find his way through the moonshadows, following the beacon of light that sparkled in this siren's violet eyes.

Catlin drifted from one fantastic dream into another when Lucas invented new ways of communicating his love. "I love you" was in his kiss and his caress. She had stopped running at long last. This ruggedly handsome rake formed the perimeters of her whimsical dreams. Her senses were filled with his masculine scent. She was addicted to the taste of him, mesmerized by his masterful touch.

"I love you madly," Lucas whispered as he braced himself above her.

"I'll never tire of hearing you say that," she assured him as she looped her arms around his muscled shoulders and drew his sensuous lips to hers.

"I'll never grow tired of saying it because I'm going to love you for ever and ever. . . ."

And that was the last thought to whiz through his mind. He could feel this vivacious beauty absorbing his strength, stealing his breath and siphoning his energy. She drew upon each and every emotion and she made living and loving seem infinitely more gratifying than they had ever been before.

447

Jace Osborn was right. Lucas wasn't one bit sorry that Jace had to ride away. After almost six years of searching Lucas had found everything he had ever wanted all wrapped up in one high-spirited package of femininity. Lucas had Cat. Nothing else mattered quite as much to him as this saucy minx did. And he was going to spend the next century reassuring her that she was all he would ever need. Because when Lucas said he loved her beyond all else, that was exactly what he meant!

And before they rose from bed, Lucas had made a believer of Cat . . . and she of him!